Cali the Destroyer

Sol Luckman

ALSO BY SOL LUCKMAN

FICTION

Snooze: A Story of Awakening

NONFICTION

Potentiate Your DNA
Conscious Healing

HUMOR

Musings from a Small Island
The Angel's Dictionary

ISBN: 978-1-7369595-0-3
Library of Congress Number: 2021906361

First Edition printed in 2021 by Crow Rising Transformational Media through Lulu Enterprises, Inc., 3101 Hillsborough Street, Raleigh, North Carolina USA 27607

This is a work of fiction. Any resemblance to actual persons (living or dead), businesses, events or locales is entirely unintentional.

For paperback, ebook and other versions of *Cali the Destroyer*, please visit www.CrowRising.com.

To the Luminous Child in each of us

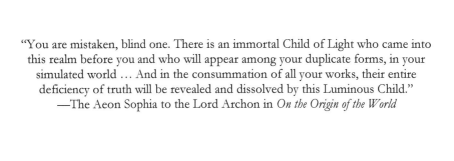

"You are mistaken, blind one. There is an immortal Child of Light who came into this realm before you and who will appear among your duplicate forms, in your simulated world ... And in the consummation of all your works, their entire deficiency of truth will be revealed and dissolved by this Luminous Child."
—The Aeon Sophia to the Lord Archon in *On the Origin of the World*

Cali the Destroyer

First Part

ROSE COVE

1

"You sure you're up for this, Cali?"

"Up" was the operative word in Juice's well-meaning question posed in his resonant bass voice. The two teenagers sat astraddle his idling, jerry-rigged motorbike *way* up, up, up above the Nolihana at the entrance to a seemingly endless levitrain trestle spanning the great river in cascades of gleaming steel.

Trembling, Cali stole a panicked glance down through the morning mist at the water's mercurial eddies that seemed as far below as the pastel autumn trees on the mountainsides rose far above. Gripping Juice's muscular midsection and breathing in his comforting natural scent, she whispered (none too convincingly), "I'm sure."

"You *sure* you're sure? It'll take us the better part of two minutes to cross this thing. That's assuming no mechanical malfunctions or operator errors. If a whipper or zipper shows up in either direction, there's a good chance we're sleeping with the fishes tonight."

There was no fear in Juice's voice. Fear wasn't something Cali associated with him. He was simply speaking the hard truth: any way you sliced it, crossing the trestle toward the Badlands was a highly dangerous undertaking.

The light at the entrance was still green, but the light inside Cali's mind remained red. Closing her eyes and breathing deeply again in an attempt to allay her terror of falling, she experienced something akin to a "life review" said to happen to those who are dying. With pristine clarity she found herself replaying the chain of events that had led her to this momentous—and possibly crazy—impasse.

There was her lovely mother for whom she was named, Caliandra Helena Crowell, "Dr. Caliandra" to her many adoring patients, treating eleven-year-old Frederick Hamilton with herb-infused juice for a potentially lethal respiratory infection—an event of such significance to his close-knit community it branded him with his catchy nickname for life.

Cali recalled this episode from five years ago, when she was ten, as if it were five weeks ago. Of particular sweetness was the memory of approaching her newly recovered friend as he sat beside the pier alongside the murmuring stream that ran below his POC shanty village checking his trotlines.

"Well, if it isn't Frederick 'Juice' Hamilton," she called out while navigating the slippery riverbank. "You're quite the celebrity around here."

"Well, if it isn't Sofia Caliandra Crowell," he replied still focused on the task at hand. "You're quite the celebrity. Period."

"Not *Crow-well*. Crowell. Rhymes with owl."

"My mistake, Miss Cali."

"Cut the plantation talk, Juice. It's *me*."

"What for? This *is* the plantation."

Cali had met "Fred" just before he became ill while accompanying her mother on rounds through the Hinterlands. She'd held his hand through many a delirious hour when his fever made him talk circles in some bizarre, singsongy language she didn't understand and he didn't remember upon returning to his senses.

Though a natural attraction existed between the two youngsters, one neither was capable of understanding in the formative days of their connection, they were—as the old saying goes—like an apple and an orange.

That afternoon, as a case in point, Cali sported an emerald designer petticoat and matching heels (now sadly caked with mud), while Juice wore frayed jeans, a faded blue T-shirt with holes in it, and no shoes at all. She was recently coiffed; his proliferating afro suggested clippers had never so much as approached his shapely head.

Even at such a young age, she remarked like the city girl she was while marveling at how deftly he unhooked and basketed his haul of whiskered catfish, he could have been a male caryatid carved out of marble guarding the entrance to some grandiose edifice of great importance to the Fatherland. Except, of course, that he was a person of color.

"You like raw catfish?" he asked with a broad grin and a mischievous glimmer in his hazel eyes.

"Never tried it. Sounds disgusting."

Juice tried but failed to stifle his laughter. "I was just pulling your leg. Nobody eats catfish raw. Unless they're desperate."

"I don't think I've even tried cooked catfish. Does it taste anything like mahi-mahi?"

"What's mahi-mahi?"

It was Cali's turn to laugh as she observed, "We *are* from different worlds, aren't we?"

"As different as night and day."

Barely six months later, Cali's controversial mother died unusually while on her usual rounds among the POCs and everything changed.

Cali's father, Dr. Perry Crowell, soon remarried. According to the law, as he was just under fifty and thus technically still of breeding age, he was expected to find a new wife and endeavor to procreate in service to the nation. But Cali never quite got over how soon he tied the knot again … or with whom he tied it.

In exchange for a brunette mother with the face of an old-timey goddess who selflessly nurtured her and her precocious musical talent, she received a platinum blond widow with a witch's nose for a stepmother— Olga—who was insanely jealous of her and, acting as her agent, intent on sabotaging her happiness while parasitizing her growing fame.

It wasn't all bad, though. Under Olga's watchful eye and iron hand, Cali quickly climbed the charts to become—at the tender age of fourteen—one of the Fatherland's biggest stars with, according to her first major review in *The Archontia Times*, "a smile and voice for the ages."

Cali also gained a brother (actually a stepbrother) whom she unequivocally adored. Eight years her junior, Seth was a gregarious toddler with an infectious laugh like that of a Christmas elf—until something suddenly turned off the bright light in him and he became severely autistic soon after turning two.

One day her brother was there, the next he wasn't. The fact that he "went away" immediately following a round of routine jaxxinations wasn't lost on Cali.

Her mother had been an outspoken critic of jaxxines. She maintained that, rather than contributing to "herd immunity" as claimed by the National Administration of Drugs, the government's policy of mandatory childhood jaxxinations actually *caused* many diseases. For this opinion, which she backed up with a variety of case studies and much research of her own, Dr. Caliandra was forever under attack by the medical establishment.

According to the official police report, she was killed by falling into a river gorge not unlike the one Cali now nervously contemplated from the back of Juice's Frankenstein of a bike. Her body, never found, was thought to have been swept away by the current. There was a memorial service, but no proper funeral. In lieu of a gravestone, a marker was placed in the family plot.

In the aftermath of this traumatic turn of events, Cali's father, a well-known psychiatrist, treated his daughter for acrophobia, fear of heights. According to his diagnosis, her condition resulted from "lack of closure" with respect to her mother's sudden passing.

He was technically right, though there was a layer to his daughter's lack of closure Dr. Crowell never suspected having to do with a nagging suspicion that her mother hadn't disappeared so much as "been disappeared." If the rumors circulating in Juice's village (where people actually seemed to think for themselves) were true, she certainly wouldn't have been the first—and she probably wouldn't be the last.

After all, she died—if indeed she was dead—under highly suspicious circumstances. And no one could deny that her scientific opinions, which were in direct contradiction to medical orthodoxy, might be considered an existential threat to the Fatherland's authority over all matters of body and mind.

Then just when it seemed nothing more could change for Cali, it did.

On the heels of an argument about meal portions with Olga, who insisted her protégé was overeating and would "turn into a cow" if this disturbing trend continued, Cali found herself weeping on her bed. She was holding her favorite photograph of her mother, which she'd inherited in an antique wooden frame with a rose-and-thorn bas-relief and which she always kept on her bedside table, even in hotels on tour.

Roses had been the theme of the day. Ignoring Olga's protests that a tan was unbecoming in a cultural symbol of the Fatherland's racial purity, especially one whose skin was already a bit swarthier than the norm, Cali had spent time sunning herself in what remained of her mother's herb and rose garden behind the Crowells' townhouse. She'd gone so far as to pick a red rose and sniff its perfume while remembering the one person in her life who genuinely knew and loved her unconditionally.

And now here she was with her tears watering the decorative roses in the frame enclosing her mother's dark curls as she asked variations on the same rhetorical question she often asked when the going got rough: *Why did you leave me? Why did you go away?*

"I have not really left you. I only appear to have gone away."

The voice, her mother's, seemed so present in her otherwise empty room Cali went rigid with fright. Her mother's words were so amazingly audible it was hard to believe they were only thoughts. Or *were* they?

"*Mother?*"

In the deflating silence that ensued, still fully clothed, Cali fell into an exhausted sleep. She dreamed she was back in the herb and rose garden—only this time her mother was there busy with her back turned at the trellis, draped in her soiled gardening sundress that rendered its wearer beautiful and sensual beyond measure.

"Is it really you, Mother?" she couldn't help but ask.

This was a dream Cali, quite lucidly, had had numerous times in the past few years. The signature dream sky above the dream garden connoted an exceedingly rare patch of life—fitful between sun and storm as in springtime, with the wind light and cool, gusting every so often, and suddenly she was eight years old and simple again in a world filled chiefly with rose petals, rosemary sprigs, and crow caws.

The dream inevitably ended with her mother disappearing in a plume of smoke even as Cali tried to wrap her arms around her ... at which point any emotion resembling hope flew to pieces like a clay statue exploding from gunfire.

This time, however, something seemed different. Turning, her mother smiled, which she always did. But then, to Cali's astonishment, she also spoke in her vaguely foreign accent—something she never did.

"It really is, my child. I am here to ask you to *let me out.*"

Cali wept again in her dream as she cried, "Let you *out?* Of *what?*"

"Of my rectangular cell inside bars of roses and thorns."

"You mean the garden?"

"The answer will come to you. And when it does, you will know you are ready."

Then just like that, in a familiar plume of smoke, her mother was gone again. Shaking, Cali stood and stared.

"I love you!" she called, her voice echoing off the brick garden wall. "I miss you!"

These sentiments she was still repeating when she woke up in darkness to find her clothes drenched with sweat and tears. Her holoclock, responding to her vocal command, projected the time—3:33 AM—long enough for her to grasp that it was the middle of the night.

"Lights," she said. The room's ambient wall lighting came on and made her squint. "Dimmer."

With the light more accommodating, she went about undressing, sponging her pits, changing into a gown, flossing, brushing her teeth, and combing her long dark hair so like her mother's as she contemplated her eye bags in the bathroom mirror, which made a strong case for being the most unflattering mirror *ever*.

It was only when she approached her rumpled bed to try to squeeze out a few more hours of beauty sleep that she saw her mother's photograph on her unused pillow. In a searing flash of insight, she realized she was staring at Caliandra *in her rectangular cell inside bars of roses and thorns!*

"God the Father!" she exclaimed, quivering with excitement as she removed the frame's backing and carefully extracted the photo from behind its protective glass.

This action caused a single shiny piece of paper to slip out and zigzag to the floor. Picking it up, she instantly recognized a picture clipped from one of her mother's books, most of which had gone missing after she was gone.

How Cali had loved poring over those books. Most of them, dealing with a range of strange subjects usually of questionable legality, were way over her young head. Still, she was drawn to them over and over like a honeybee to an especially fragrant bed of … roses.

This particular image, out of a book on ancient iconography, had always been one of her favorites. A worn stone statuette of a hugely pregnant woman with a rose for a heart and bird claws instead of feet, it had been discovered back in the twenty-first century in a cave in India and was thought to be one of the earliest depictions of the Goddess, considered a primitive psychological projection and not an actual divinity by Fatherland scholars.

Out of curiosity Cali turned the image over to see what was on the other side of the paper. There, on a mostly blank surface flanked by snippets of incomplete text, she read the following enigmatic lines written in pen in her mother's flowing script:

A E I I U I O O U U I A O
u u o e a a a i a a e i a

36.090457
-82.426514

Commit the above to memory and then burn this paper. Tell no one.

"Tick, tick, tick, Cali. The longer we sit here, the worse our chances get."

"Please be patient, Juice. I'm trying to pull myself together."

"Try harder. Try *faster.*"

"Just give me one more goddamn minute, will you?"

This urgent request Cali made as, in her mind's eye, she could see herself—in the days following the discovery of her mother's hidden note—wrestling with what on earth it could possibly mean. She couldn't be absolutely sure the note was even intended for her, though everything in her intuition screamed it was.

She tried—with zero success—cracking the code of the two lines of vowels. But an Ogle search on the Fatherweb of the pair of mysterious numbers suggested they might be a latitude and longitude.

When the numbers were entered into a GPS database, they indicated a geolocation not terribly faraway across the Hinterlands in the Badlands. No name was associated with this area on current maps.

But by referencing an old map she managed to pull up, Cali learned that the town of Rose Cove had once existed there above the Nolihana River across the former North Carolina-Tennessee border in what used to be called, prior to the Purification, the United States of America.

Further ogling revealed that Rose Cove had originally been settled during the First American Civil War by a religious group known as Quakers who called themselves "conscientious objectors."

What they objected to was war or violence in any form, however justified or necessary. In hindsight, according to an article on the subject archived at www.FatherlandHistory.gov, these pacifists were an early

19

example of the rot at the heart of a weak-willed civilization destined for history's dustbin.

Refusing their moral and ethical duty to fight for the right to keep slaves and do with them as they pleased, the Quakers of Rose Cove sequestered themselves in a remote area of the Appalachian Mountains with no access roads within fifty miles. Here they went so far as to side with the North against the South, establishing an important outpost in what was known as the Underground Railroad and facilitating the unlawful escape into enemy territory of untold numbers of POCs.

But by far the strangest thing was: the town seal of Rose Cove was a *red rose* inside a stylized border of *thorns.*

"You've *got* to be kidding!" gasped Cali upon grasping the significance of this bizarre "coincidence."

Still, she didn't immediately know what to do with her mother's note beyond memorizing its contents and burning it as directed. Afterward, even with the physical note reduced to ashes and blown to the four winds, its memory haunted Cali day and night.

The thought that she was being guided to visit Rose Cove was ever in her mind, as was its sister thought that the notion was completely insane, a by-product somehow of her "lack of closure" with Caliandra's untimely demise.

Over time, however, the idea that she should journey to Rose Cove no matter the cost gradually won out. The bottom line was that she wasn't sure she could live with herself if she didn't try to find her mother—or at least find out what actually happened to her.

But even if she could manage to make it across the border into the Badlands, she didn't know the first thing about navigating or surviving in the wild. Moreover, the Badlands were home to all sorts of aptly named Badlanders: rebels, bandits, outcasts, misfits.

In order to make such a difficult journey and have any chance of returning in one piece, one thing was abundantly clear: she needed a guide.

No sooner had this truth hit home than a guide, an actual man of the wild, showed up on her doorstep—literally. With her father overseeing an office renovation, Olga out shopping for clothes for Cali's upcoming tour and Seth at the park with his caregiver, Cali had the house to herself on a Saturday for a change.

Taking advantage of her privacy to enjoy the feel of a simply patterned teal empire dress meant for very casual occasions, she had trouble believing her eyes when the doorbell rang and she opened the front door to find a tall, chiseled young man in besmirched hunting clothes with a hint of mischief in his dreamy expression grinning down at her.

"*Juice?*"

"*Cali?*"

The two embraced before realizing the impropriety and pushing each other away with sheepish expressions. Cali suddenly felt flushed, whether from embarrassment or the high degree of heat emanating from Juice's body that smelled like the great outdoors it was impossible to tell.

"It really is you, isn't it?" she said, marveling at her childhood friend's powerful adult physique. Over five years had passed since she'd seen him. He seemed more like twenty than sixteen. "You cut your hair!"

"Technically, somebody else did. I didn't—I didn't know you lived here. Obviously, I recognized the last name: *Crow-well*." He grinned with a nod to yesteryear as he mispronounced the word. "But it's fairly common. I didn't realize it applied to you."

"I was just fulfilling an order," he went on to explain nervously, unslinging his backpack and opening it from the top to show it was full of dressed and skinned wild game: what looked like several pheasants alongside a handful of rabbits. The sight of all those dead bodies combined with the scent of fresh blood nearly made Cali swoon.

"Sorry," said Juice as he quickly cinched the bag. "I didn't mean to upset the apple cart."

"It's not your fault. I'm just not used to so much … gore. That must be the wild meat my stepmother ordered for Wednesday's dinner with the head of my label." Feeling a bit dizzy, she touched her forehead, which seemed rather warm. "We're kicking off this new tour Saturday with a show at the Holy of Holies—"

"I know. I've seen the holoboards all over the city. Are you okay? You don't look too right on your feet. Is there someplace I can help you take a load off?"

"That sounds like a good idea."

Minutes later she was seated on the stone bench in her mother's herb and rose garden with the sun shining on her face and Juice watching over her like a concerned sentinel. Autumn's first nip in the afternoon air soon helped settle Cali's stomach.

"Feeling better?"

"A little."

"You mentioned your stepmother …"

"Yeah. Olga. The Wicked Witch of Saturnia."

"She around?"

"No need to worry about Olga for now. She's probably up to her pearls in couture bags."

"*Couture?*"

"Fancy clothes."

"Anybody else here?"

"Nope. The coast is clear." She patted the stone bench beside her. "Join me if you like."

"Don't mind if I do." He sat down but made sure to keep his distance. "This your garden?"

"It was my mother's. It needs a little TLC."

"It's nice."

"It used to be nicer."

"I was broken up about your mom, Cali. All of us were. She's the reason I'm still here. They wouldn't let us into the memorial service. POCs aren't allowed in white cemeteries."

"I figured that out, eventually."

"We sent flowers, though. Everybody did."

Cali remembered. Her mother's memorial service, only moderately attended by Fatherlanders, had been awash in an ocean of flowers from the Hinterlands. "I know. Thank you."

"But then I wasn't sure how to find you. And you never visited."

Cali gave a sarcastic laugh. "I've been told I don't handle grief well. Please accept my apologies for my antisocial behavior."

"You don't need to apologize. I understand. I don't handle grief too well myself."

"What's your personal source of grief?"

"You mean aside from the plight of my whole race?"

This saucy comeback sucker-punched Cali. She immediately felt like what she was: a spoiled rich kid living a life of luxury on the backs of modern-day servants.

"I'm a terrible person, Juice. Please forgive me. Just know that, deep down, I *hate* all of … *this*," she said, referencing the world around her with a dismissive gesture.

"I get that. That's why we get along."

Cali took Juice's chocolate-colored hand in her much smaller, comparatively vanilla one. "It's not the only reason we get along," she said with her heart positively pounding in her chest.

He returned her advance by squeezing her long fingers. "No. I suppose it's not."

"You never revealed your personal source of grief. I know it's there. I can feel it whenever I look at you."

He glanced down and sighed. "You sure want to know?"

"I asked, didn't I?"

He continued holding her hand as he summarized his own brush with tragedy. His father, Amos, had been a member of the Freedom Fliers, a group of social activists inspired by a twentieth-century civil rights movement.

This new iteration of the Freedom Riders, overwhelmingly composed of people of color, similarly sought to end segregation on public transport as well as in other public areas: restaurants, restrooms, theaters, etc. As was well known, the Deacons of the Realm ultimately clamped down on the Freedom Fliers, sending many to jail and lynching many others.

"My old man was in the latter category," explained Juice with barely contained hatred. "The bastards stretched his neck from an oak tree above the village to make an example out of him."

Cali didn't realize the extent of her emotional response until she felt cool droplets on her forearm. "Did you actually *witness* this?" she asked, horrified, dabbing her eyes with the back of her hand.

"I wasn't even born. My mama was carrying me. He wouldn't let her join the Freedom Fliers in that condition, even though she wanted to."

"You're talking about Weezy, right?"

"Yeah, that's what he called her. The nickname stuck. Her given name's Louise."

"I remember her apple pie. I think she must have put rhubarb in it. It tasted like manna from heaven."

"You're not the only person to feel that way about her cooking. That's what I miss most when I'm on a hunt."

"So that's what you do for a living—you hunt?"

"And fish. And gather morels. And shell walnuts. And pick huckleberries. Whatever's in season. Whatever it takes."

"I imagine you know the mountains around here like the back of your hand."

"I reckon I do."

"Ever visit a place called Rose Cove?"

This question elicited a surprised look from Juice, who suddenly withdrew his hand and faced Cali with fists on his hips. "How do you know about Rose Cove?"

"How do *you* know about it?"

He lowered his deep voice to a whisper as he replied, "They say it's a *rebel* camp."

"Is it true?" Cali whispered back.

"Who knows. But one thing's certain: there's *something* in that stretch of mountains that keeps the Fatherland from overrunning it."

"Can you take me there?"

"*What?!*"

"You heard me."

"What's this about, Cali?"

Her mother's warning to *tell no one* was very much in her mind as she made the conscious, fateful decision to listen to her instincts instead. If anyone she knew could be trusted with this sensitive information, it was Juice.

"I think my mother might still be alive."

"You think your mother might still … be … alive?"

"And living in Rose Cove."

"That's crazy. No offense."

"None taken. At first I thought the same thing. But check this out."

It was Cali's turn to tell her story. As sanely and clearly as possible, she related how she'd found her mother's note complete with exact coordinates. Everything about the situation, she insisted, down to the thorny rose connection, pointed to Rose Cove.

Afterward, Juice sat in silence for a moment digesting her words. "You do realize what you're proposing is extremely dangerous, not to mention totally illegal, don't you?"

"I do."

"Have you considered what it will mean if you don't find your mom?"

"At least it won't really change anything."

"Keep telling yourself that."

"I prefer denial."

"You're hilarious. Just shoot me straight: are you willing to pay the price if this thing goes horribly wrong?"

"I am. But it's not going to."

"Why not?"

"You're not going to let it."

Juice laughed out loud. "How do you figure that?"

"Call it providence."

"I'm not sure I believe in God. At least not a white one. That didn't turn out too well for us."

"Destiny then. We were brought together for a reason, Juice. Can you feel it, too?"

"Oh, I can feel it. That's why I'm still here and not hightailing it back to the plantation."

"Excellent. But we need to go soon."

"How soon?"

"I was thinking … tomorrow."

"Tomorrow?"

"Got anything better to do?"

"Believe me, I have lots of better things to do."

"Well, I've only got till Wednesday. I *have* to be back for that dinner."

"Don't you have school?"

"It's fall break."

"Where will you say you're going?"

"To stay with my friend Gwennyth down at Lake Lore. Her family has a house and stables there."

"What's to keep this Gwennyth from ratting you out?"

"I've covered for her and her boyfriend more times than I can count. No way she'll risk any damaging disclosures relative to her premarital behavior."

"I see."

"So you'll do it?"

"I will. On one condition."

"Name it."

"Give me a kiss."

Cali gave him a quick peck on the cheek.

"That's not what I meant."

"I know what you meant. And I'll be happy to oblige. Just as soon as you deliver me safely and soundly to Rose Cove."

"You drive a hard bargain, girl. Deal."

They made plans to meet the following evening at dusk at the fishing pier a quarter mile downriver from Juice's village. Cali was to dress normally but bring clothes and footwear for what would be an arduous journey through challenging terrain.

No sooner had they made their way back inside than Olga waltzed in through the front door with—as predicted—as many shopping bags as she could carry. Upon turning to find Juice looming like an enormous shadow at the entrance to the hallway, she gave a start.

"Sorry, ma'am," he said. "I didn't mean to frighten you."

"Well, you most assuredly did! Who are you and what are you doing in my home?"

"I let him in," said Cali. "He brought the wild game for Wednesday. It's in the fridge."

"You could have just taken delivery."

"Your daughter wasn't feeling well, Mrs. Crowell," explained Juice. "It was my fault. She got a bit queasy when I showed her the game."

"Well, don't just stand there like a statue," said Olga. "Help me."

She unloaded her bags in his arms and paraded into the kitchen with her gold petticoat swishing and the cloying scent of perfume trailing behind like an invisible contrail. Cali and Juice glanced at each other with commiserating expressions. He shrugged.

"Just set everything on the table," instructed Olga. "Over there."

Juice did as directed. In the process his keen ears picked up on a tiny drip-drip-drip coming from the sink.

"I take it the plumber didn't show up yet," said Olga, hanging her purse and coat on the back of a chair as she checked the leaky faucet with a peeved look.

"Afraid not," said Cali.

"I'm not surprised. I've yet to witness a POC with a job that needs doing be on time in my life. Beaners in the Southland were punctual compared to our POCs."

"I can fix it," said Juice, outwardly unfazed. "I mean, if you want me to."

"And I'm sure you'll charge an arm and a leg for your emergency assistance."

"Actually, I thought I'd be neighborly and do it free of charge."

"The last thing we are is neighbors."

"It's just an expression," said Cali with scarcely concealed annoyance. "Do you want him to repair the faucet or not?"

"Sure. That would be wonderful."

"I'll need a basic toolkit, if you have one handy," said Juice.

After the leak was stopped, Olga used her holophone to credit Juice's cryptaccount for the game. No further mention was made of the faucet.

"Do you need me to validate your citypass?" she asked.

"That would be very kind of you."

She scanned the plastic card in his outstretched palm.

"God bless the Fatherland," she said by way of goodbye.

"God bless the Fatherland."

Cali showed Juice out.

"Make it quick," Olga yelled while pouring herself a snifter of brandy. "We have rehearsal followed by a fitting this afternoon."

"I see what you mean about the Wicked Witch," whispered Juice as he opened the front door and stepped outside.

"You haven't seen anything. She's in a good mood today."

"Must be high on shopping."

"Must be."

"See you soon, Miss Crowell."

"See you soon, Mr. Hamilton."

"God bless the Fatherland."

"God bless the Fatherland."

That night, to make it look as if she were actually visiting Lake Lore, she packed a suitcase with several leisure outfits as well as a waterproof jacket and her riding clothes and boots, which she planned to switch into for the journey to Rose Cove. Underneath these items she stashed a daypack, a small flashlight, a water bottle, and two packs of beef jerky she stealthily retrieved from the pantry.

After making the necessary physical preparations, she took a little time to make the required logistic and emotional ones. She needed to make sure she had a cover story. And she wanted to say goodbye to the people she cared about in the event this was truly adios.

Her father she found puffing on his pipe at his desk in his study. Ever since she was little, she'd loved the cherry smell of his pipe smoke and the way—for long absentminded stretches while reading on his device—he kept the pipe stem in the corner of his mouth.

Many things had changed about Dr. Crowell over the years. His hair had turned mostly gray, he'd put on a good bit of weight around the midsection, his wool cardigans had started to seem rather old-fashioned. But the pipe still played.

"Why, this is a pleasant surprise! I don't often receive visitors with such female pulchritude in my mantuary," he said with a wink, opening his arms to his daughter and kissing her forehead as she nestled into his V-neck smelling of aftershave. "What brings you here?"

"I have a favor to ask."

"Surely not. What can I do for my angel?"

"Gwennyth has invited me to her lake house. I'd like to enjoy a few days of fall break before leaving on tour. I think it would be good for me to decompress a little before all that stress."

"That's poetic as well as very psychologically sensible of you."

"Olga won't like it, though. She'll be afraid I'll eat too much or forget my lyrics."

"Don't worry. I can persuade Olga."

"Thanks, Dad."

"You're welcome."

She kissed his forehead and left the room before he could observe how shiny her eyes were.

Seth, who had a tendency to wander, wasn't as easy to find. There was no sign of him in his room. She finally tracked him down in the living room, where he was seated on the floor next to the Steinway in his pajamas bouncing his beloved racquetball.

Rather, he was *trying* to bounce it. Ever since becoming autistic, he'd exhibited severely impaired motor skills. If he managed to bounce the ball more than three times consecutively, even after practicing hour after hour day after day, it could be considered an achievement.

Cali hiked up her skirt and sat down beside her stepbrother on the rug at the edge of the hardwood. In transforming from a toddler into a little boy, his frame had slowly lengthened as he'd taken on an uncanny resemblance to Christopher Robin. Now, nearly eight, he was starting to fill out and his red hair was beginning to curl.

There was a deep-running sadness in Seth that predated his descent into autism. Cali had picked up on it the first time she met him not long before her father married Olga and the two new members of her family moved in.

She imagined it had something to do with the death of Seth's father, Wilson Jacklin, a Marshal of the Realm in charge of the nation's military forces in the Southland, formerly known as—before the Expansion that followed the Purification—the United Mexican States.

Marshal Jacklin had been killed by a sniper while leading an offensive against guerillas in a contested area known as Oaxaca. He was scheduled to return to his family in DF, the Distrito del Fatherland, the very next day.

Of course, being so young at the time, Seth couldn't possibly have remembered this tragedy. But Cali imagined that the emotional fallout had still managed to imprint him profoundly—as, no doubt, it had Olga. From the get-go both mother and child struck Cali as chronically unhappy. They just manifested their sadness in different ways.

In turn, it was Seth's fragility that imprinted Cali. Having experienced her own parental tragedy, she did everything in her power to distract her stepbrother from his familial demons: reading to him, teaching him the rudiments of piano, even spooning him for hours at night when the threat of bad dreams triggered his insomnia.

The impact of his sudden mental illness on her was devastating. She felt as if she'd lost another close relative before she was even in her teens. In some ways—she occasionally caught herself thinking with enormous self-judgment—it would have been better had she really lost him, too.

"I don't know if this will register," she said, touching his red curls and smiling through a fresh round of tears, "but I love you like my own brother, Seth. I'd do anything to bring you back … if only I could."

Still self-absorbed, he bounced the ball three times in a row before it shot sideways off the edge of the rug and rolled to the corner of the room. Retrieving it for him and whispering goodbye, Cali kissed his forehead as the bouncing recommenced.

The following evening after church and Sunday dinner (just yesterday from Cali's current perspective at the edge of the trestle), she took a hovertaxi through the streets of Saturnia and out the Eastgate into the Hinterlands.

Butterflies filled her stomach as twilight fell and the city receded into the distance. Its holoboards (including one featuring her own angular face on her new album, *You've Been CC'd*, alongside upcoming tour dates) flashed brilliantly high above.

Encircling the great cities of the Fatherland like galaxies around their powerful centers, the Hinterlands were sprawling mélanges of agricultural fields and POC shantytowns. Connecting these civilized-uncivilized dyads were high-speed maglev trains called levitrains, aka "whippers" owing to the way they whipped by so fast between cities (as distinguished from "zippers," a slang term for patrol pods that also traveled the tracks). In certain locations on the perimeter said to be strategically insignificant, beyond the border of the Hinterlands lay wild areas where no rule of law applied known as Badlands.

From the perspective of the urban seats of power, the Fatherland was like a set of Russian dolls: a shiny, protected world inside a drab, less important one inside a dark one that didn't matter at all. Tonight, it occurred to Cali, she was tracing a trajectory from the middle to the outside of society.

How many people from her world, she wondered, had actually made it to the perimeter and returned only to tell no one?

Just then, approaching Juice's sprawling village of as many as fifty thousand, officially referred to as POCV #888 but known locally as Nubia after the ancient African empire on the Nile, she caught a glimpse of a statement she'd often heard uttered approvingly in her circles spray-painted jaggedly in blood red on the side of a silo: *The South has risen again.*

With curfew fast approaching, the old pier that jutted out into the Lynchfield River at the outskirts to Nubia seemed deserted. Cali climbed down with her suitcase and, after a second's anxious hesitation, slid shut the taxi's door.

The driver seemed hesitant himself to leave her there in the middle of nowhere at that hour. But when she motioned for him to go on, he switched on his availability light and zipped back silently toward town.

Stepping out from behind the silhouette of a large white pine exuding a yuletide smell, a tall shadow loomed up in front of her as she carefully neared the pier.

"*Juice?* Is that you?"

"That's my name. Don't wear it out."

Cali set down her suitcase. The two embraced in the semidarkness. Juice had on what felt like a canvas army jacket. She suppressed the urge to kiss his perfectly shaped—as she recalled them in the daylight—lips.

"We should be going before curfew," she said instead.

The whites of Juice's eyes seemed to sparkle as he switched on a flashtorch to dim. "Did you bring proper travel clothes?"

"Of course."

"And did you leave your holophone at home? Nobody must be able to track us across the border."

"What do I look like—a dilettante?"

"In that poufy petticoat, most definitely. But you also look ravishing."

"Aren't you the charmer."

"Just think of me as that old president from history. I can't tell a lie."

"Liar."

"You can change down at the pier. Use this to see by. Just keep it on low."

Handing her the flashtorch, he picked up her suitcase and, like a big owl that could see in the dark, confidently led her down to the water's edge. She followed slowly, remembering the last time she'd followed him down to the river. That messy outing ruined her favorite shoes and nearly cost her her fancy dress.

"I promise I'll be quick," she said after he left her with the suitcase and headed back up the bank.

"I promise I won't look."

Dressed in her riding clothes, boots and jacket with her daypack strapped on, carrying the flashtorch in one hand and her suitcase in the other, she met her guide back at the old pine. Relieving her of the suitcase, he proceeded to stash it in a fifty-gallon plastic bag, which he secured with one end of a rope dangling beside the tree trunk. Then, applying himself, he hoisted the bundle high up into the branches out of sight.

"Nobody's likely to ever notice it," he said, stashing the rope overhead. "If we don't return, it could stay up there for years."

"That's a comforting thought."

"Just keeping it real."

"What are you doing?"

"Getting my bike. Surely you didn't think we were going to walk."

He disappeared behind the pine. With the sound of tires snapping twigs, he finally reappeared shouldering a camo messenger bag that matched his jacket pushing a jalopy of a motorcycle. Straddling it familiarly, he patted the seat behind him and told Cali to climb on.

"You sure you know how to drive this thing?"

"I built this thing."

"You *built* it?"

"Technically, I rebuilt it. For power I used a scrap gravifusion cell that only operates at about ten percent capacity."

"Like the ones used in hovertaxis?"

"Like the ones used in *ancient* hovertaxis."

"Where'd you learn that kind of thing? I didn't think there were schools in the Hinterlands."

"That doesn't mean we don't have teachers and students."

Handing him the flashtorch, which he stashed in his bag, Cali awkwardly mounted the bike. Juice was unable to stifle a giggle. "And your folks were supposed to believe you were going *riding?*"

"Give me a break. This is my first time."

"You saying you're still a virgin? Because I am."

"You're just a barrel of laughs tonight."

"I'm serious."

"You mean you're seriously joking."

Without further ado he push-started the engine, pulled on the throttle, and switched on the headlight. In less than a minute, the two travelers had taken a bridge across the river and were quietly racing along a dirt road headed east. To her surprise Cali felt not apprehension but a tremendous sense of freedom as the wind filled her flowing hair.

It had been Juice's idea to meet outside his village at the pier and leave for Rose Cove after nightfall. Cali understood his reasoning. Though there were risks associated with disobeying curfew in the Hinterlands, under no circumstances could a black boy and white girl afford to be seen canoodling on a motorbike—least of all angling toward the border after sunset.

Already cool, the air turned much colder with the road climbing higher and higher. Cali shivered—half from exhilaration, half from chill—as they passed a rusty sign indicating the Eastern Continental Divide.

"How do you like riding?" yelled Juice over his shoulder.

"Like it? I *love* it."

"Is that why you're hanging on so tight: love?"

"No, my friend. That's self-preservation."

"So we're friends now?"

"We've always been friends."

"And now we're friends … with benefits?"

"I've yet to see any benefit to our friendship. But I'm willing to be surprised."

Juice gave a big laugh as, without warning, he turned off the road into the woods. He slowed down—but not much. They were on some kind of worn path that hugged the ridge.

"This used to be known as the Appalachian Trail," he explained. "We probably won't see anybody the rest of the way."

"How much longer do we have to go?"

"We should be across the Nolihana by early morning."

"How far is it from there?"

"Thirteen miles as the crow flies. On foot. Mostly uphill. I do hope your boots are broken in."

For what felt like hours, they rode in silence, stopping only briefly for a "bathroom" break. Cali could tell dawn was coming because the stars—which had been spectacularly bright there away from civilization—had started to look dim. Twilight was upon them before they managed to catch the sound of water far below.

Before long, gradually descending through swirling mist, they intersected the levitrain tracks at the edge of the trestle. The first light striking the hillsides revealed them in all their fall glory.

Not that Cali felt at liberty to appreciate her natural surroundings. For minutes, deflecting Juice's questions about her readiness, she watched as the precursors to this moment fast-forwarded through her mind.

"Shouldn't we, like, put our ears to the tracks and listen for movement?" she suggested.

"You've watched too many old movies. Whippers and zippers don't make contact with the tracks. They hardly make any noise at all. Which makes them even more dangerous."

"Thanks for pointing that out. I feel so much better."

"The light's still green. If we're going to go, we need to go *now*."

Even though part of her wanted to give up, another part—a stronger, if less familiar, part—had no intention of turning back. Visualizing her mother's smiling face urging her on while pulling her hoodie over her head and fastening the laces, at last she felt her internal light switch from red to green.

"Let's do it," she said as she took a final deep breath before the plunge into the unknown.

What must have been hundreds of cawing crows, startled by the motorbike's thumping along the ridged drainage channels flanking the levitrain tracks, took wing sequentially as Cali held on for dear life with her eyes up to avoid contemplating the river far below.

This part of the ride was such a jolting affair she feared her teeth might shake loose. She realized that Juice, who kept glancing in his rearview mirror, was going as fast as possible to clear the trestle before they could be flattened. Yet she couldn't help yelling sarcastically to distract herself, "Just so you know, I'll be sending you my dental bill!"

This time, for the first time, Juice ignored her playful taunting as he concentrated solely on the situation at hand. Soon they crossed the trestle's midway point. The far side began to seem closer and closer.

"We're almost there!" yelled Cali.

"No," replied her driver matter-of-factly, "we're not."

"You're like a thundercloud. You know how to rain on a girl's parade."

"I disagree. I'm more like an umbrella."

What neither of them could have seen, whether remaining totally focused or chatting away while thumping along under multitudes of raucous crows, was that the trestle light behind had turned red while the one in front had switched to green.

"An umbrella's useful. You're not."

Juice was the first to spot the incoming levitrain and he reacted before Cali even had time to panic. "Hang on!" he yelled, leaning forward into the wind and pulling on the throttle as far as it would go.

The bike did a wheelie as it shot forward. Cali gripped Juice so hard her nails would have cut him if not for his jacket. The two bounced along like ragdolls strapped to an unbroken stallion as the massive levitrain—hovering a foot above the tracks—came at them head-on with astonishing speed and power.

Squeezing her eyes shut, Cali prepared herself to die. Either they would be crushed by the train, which didn't so much as slow down as its horn blew and warning lights flashed, or they would plummet into the gorge and drown. One way or another, to echo a forbidden American rock song from yesteryear her mother used to play in secret, *this was the end*.

Juice, however, didn't seem inclined to give up just yet. He flipped a small switch under the starter. The bike literally leapt through the air to the edge of the trestle, where it narrowly avoiding being obliterated by skidding sideways down the rocky embankment opposite the river as the whipper whipped by.

They slid to a stop still upright—but just barely. Cali reopened her eyes to find herself very much alive and Juice shaking with insane laughter, teeth flashing white in the sun, like a wild animal instinctively releasing trauma after warding off a predator.

"What's so damn funny?!" screamed Cali, letting go of a little trauma herself as she angrily jerked back her hoodie.

"Nothing. Everything. You."

"You just about got us killed and *I'm* the one who's funny?"

"I just saved your ass and, yes, *you're* the one that's funny."

Adrenaline still racing, she climbed off the bike in a huff and stood fuming with her fists on her hips. She didn't know whether to slap Juice's gorgeous face—which she decided against—or kiss him squarely on the lips—which, before she could stop herself, she opted for.

"I hate you so much right now I love you!" she yelled, holding his cheeks and grinning through confused tears.

"I just hope the opposite isn't true." Cali couldn't help laughing herself at Juice's quick wit. "I've got this bad feeling I'm going to end up as a lyric in one of your songs."

"Shut up and kiss me again."

"But we haven't even reached Rose Cove. We had a deal."

"To hell with Rose Cove and our deal."

Juice enveloped her in his massive arms and did as commanded. Cali had kissed other boys and done other things with them she wasn't terribly proud of. But never had she felt a kiss make her heart nearly burst with yearning for a deeper connection.

"Did you learn to kiss like that in school?" teased Juice.

"It was an elective."

"Were you selective?"

"When I wasn't neglected."

"Believe me, Cali, under different circumstances you couldn't pry me away from this moment. But we need to put some serious tracks between ourselves and here."

"Pun intended?"

"Naturally. Climb back on."

"Do I *have* to?"

"Afraid so."

"Okay. Just go, like, a *lot* slower."

"Roger that."

They resumed bumping down the tracks through the wilderness alongside the winding river. Juice kept his word by maintaining a reasonable speed for the better part of half an hour. Finally, having encountered no more trains, they exited the tracks onto a rocky path that meandered through the woods up the mountainside.

Before long the path became too steep and jagged to navigate on wheels. Juice pulled off into a semihidden spot behind a boulder and Cali helped him camouflage the motorbike with branches and leaves.

"After you," he said, motioning uphill along the path.

"Shouldn't you—being a big man of the woods and all—go first?"

"I'd rather follow, if that's alright. Danger in the wilderness has a way of sneaking up on you."

"If you say so."

The path was even more difficult to travel than it looked. Cali, who now spent much of her life performing demanding dance routines as part of her act, soon found herself huffing and puffing. Juice, on the other hand, didn't seem the least bit winded.

"Don't you ever get tired?" she asked, panting.

"Yeah."

"Once every year or two?"

"Something like that. We can take a break. Just say the word."

"I'm okay." Though finding it difficult to carry on a conversation while hiking vertically, she also felt the need to keep her thoughts away from any number of potential dangers—such as getting lost without their GPS to guide them—that readily came to mind. "Has anything like that ever happened to you?"

"You mean playing chicken with a levitrain?"

"Yeah."

"Not exactly."

"Ever been to this side of the river?"

"A few times."

"Anything particularly interesting happen?"

"I nearly stepped on a big timber rattler once."

"For real?"

"For real."

"What did you do?"

"I shot it."

"That's not very neighborly. You never struck me as the type to kill for sport."

"I didn't. I ate it."

"How adventurous! What did it taste like?"

"Chicken, of course."

She would have laughed had she had breath to spare. "So tell me," she managed to say, "who taught you mechanical engineering?"

"If I do tell you, you can't tell a soul."

"Why not?"

"Because my teacher's a wanted man."

"My lips are sealed. What's this outlaw's name?"

"Aristotle."

"*The* Aristotle? The leader of the Freedom Fliers?"

"The same."

"But people say he's dead—that he's been dead for years. Supposedly, he was murdered by rogue elements in his own organization."

"And he wants to make sure people keep saying that. He's my uncle."

"Are you serious?"

"As a heart attack. Aristotle's my father's brother."

"Where does he live?"

"Let's just say he … moves around."

"I've heard terrible stories, Juice. Is he actually a terrorist?"

"If engaging in peaceful protests makes you a terrorist, then, yeah, he's a terrorist."

"But what about that hospital bombing in Jupiterville? Remember all those innocent kids who died?"

"He had nothing to do with it. None of our people did."

"Who did it then?"

"Your people. To discredit my people."

They were nearing the top of a ridge. Cali's feet had started to ache and burn. Licking her lips, she suddenly felt immensely thirsty.

Just then a noise like that of many light feet falling and twigs breaking came from up ahead. The two travelers had just enough time to step off the path before a herd of deer, accompanied by a great antlered buck, flashed into view and bounded past, white tails yo-yoing out of sight.

Cali had only ever seen deer in captivity at the Saturnia Zoo. Juice, who had only ever seen deer in their natural habitat, didn't seem to like what he'd just seen. Without hesitating he opened his messenger bag, pulled out a slingshot, and loaded it with a stone.

"I think they're too far gone to take a shot," observed Cali, "even if you had a real gun."

"It's not for them," replied Juice with his head on a swivel. "And I'm not stupid enough to carry a gun. It's a capital offense for a POC to be caught with a firearm."

"You mean you killed all those grouse and rabbits—not to mention a rattlesnake—with *that*?"

"This is a deadly weapon if you know how to use it."

She assessed the slingshot's hi-tech grip, arm support, stabilizer, and sight. "Did Aristotle help you make it?"

"No, I bought it online."

"*Online?*"

"You know, cyberspace."

"What's got you so spooked, Juice?"

"Something seems to have spooked that herd of deer."

"Like what?"

"Could be any number of things. Just keep your ears open and eyes peeled, will you?"

"Roger that."

They reached the ridge without further incident. Cali was so spent she flung herself on the ground without a second thought. Juice stood beside her still surveying the forest.

Having recovered her breath, she fished her water bottle out of her daypack and started guzzling its contents.

"I'd drink slower if I was you. You'll cramp up."

Still terribly parched, she slowed down—but not a lot. Casually, her guide knelt beside her, set his slingshot on the ground within reach, retrieved his own water bottle from his bag, and took a few swigs.

"That must mean we're at the entrance to the Badlands," he observed, pointing out a ring of blue-feathered arrows shot into a gnarled oak positioned squarely on the ridge beside the path.

"That's it? Just woods? No Fatherland guards, no gate, no nothing?"

"There aren't guards at many border points because the cities are well defended and the Hinterlands are considered expendable buffer zones. Besides, the rebels are mostly peaceful—only fighting if attacked."

"That's not what I've heard."

"I know what you've heard. It's all lies, Cali. Every bit of it."

"Have you ever entered the Badlands?"

"I tried to once when I was little. Out of curiosity."

"What happened?"

"I didn't make it far. I got caught in a rainstorm and ended up with pneumonia."

"So that's why you needed my mother's help!"

"Exactly. Where are you going?"

"Nature calls."

She'd climbed painfully to her throbbing feet and was headed toward the oak. She wouldn't have willingly admitted it, but after draining the last of her water minutes earlier, her stomach had begun to cramp a little.

"Well, call if you need anything."

Wondering what Olga would say, Cali found herself unceremoniously squatting atop a carpet of leaves. Feeling relieved, literally and figuratively, she was buttoning her riding pants when she suddenly became aware—as if via a sixth sense—that she was no longer alone.

As Juice had suggested it might, danger had indeed crept up on her. This realization registered like a lightning bolt of fright as she came face to face with a pair of crouching mountain lions hungrily eyeing her.

For an instant her mind went arctically blank with terror. Then, out of the chilling emptiness as out of a dream, she imagined she heard her mother warmly urging her to remain calm.

"I am with you now, my daughter." The words, uttered in Dr. Caliandra's virtually audible voice, were spoken with great clarity and authority. "There is no need to be afraid."

As Cali refocused on the two powerful predators that had slowly inched within inches of her, she wanted to tell Juice he'd been right about something spooking those deer. Instead, inching backward herself, she did her best to remember what she knew about mountain lions.

Coincidentally or otherwise, in fifth grade, with her mother's assistance, she'd done a biology report on them. She recalled that mountain lions were the second largest cat in the Fatherland after jaguars but, unlike other large cats, were unable to roar. They were also known as cougars, panthers, pumas, and catamounts.

"Steady now," came Caliandra's encouraging voice again. This time Cali had the utterly bizarre impression her mother was speaking from behind the icy blue eyes of the great cats themselves! "You see, this adult male and female pair are here to help. I sent them."

Momentarily ignoring the uncanny nature of the voice, Cali considered its implication that the cats weren't there to eat her. This possibility dovetailed with other facts she remembered about mountain lions—namely, that they were usually solitary creatures which tended to hunt by ambush at night, coming at prey from behind and crushing unguarded necks with viselike jaws.

Just then Juice, slingshot pulled back and ready to fire, rounded the gnarled oak on the ridge.

"Don't shoot!" yelled Cali as she lost her footing and fell a good ten feet that ended with an awkward smack and pop on a wide outcropping of rock.

Pain originating in her ankle shot up her leg like flame on a line of napalm. A stream of expletives no lady from the Fatherland should even think—let alone shout—escaped her lips as she gripped her pulsing ankle and rolled to and fro in agony.

"Damn, girl, you've got a mouth on you!" said Juice as he bounded onto the outcropping. His attempt at nonchalance belied the urgent concern on his face as he knelt by her side. "What did you hurt?"

"My pride."

"What else?"

Gritting her teeth, she motioned toward her ankle. Juice wasted no time unlacing her boot and, as gently as possible, sliding it off her tender foot. She grimaced.

"Sorry, Miss Cali. I'm afraid the sock has to come off, too."

Even that hurt like hell.

"How does it look?"

"Not good."

"Is it broken?"

"I can't tell for sure. It's swelling up fast. You've also got a nasty blister coming on at the heel. But look on the bright side."

"There's a bright side?"

"Your pink nail polish is in great shape."

"Ha ha."

Grimacing again, she pushed herself up to a seated position with her injured leg extended. Sure enough, her ankle was turning bright red as it puffed up to half again its size and a large patch of skin on her heel had started to welt.

"You didn't hurt the mountain lions, did you?" she asked.

"No. But I was ready to take a shot at one when you said not to."

"What happened?"

"They ran off. Why didn't you want me to shoot?"

Cali decided to keep the more … esoteric aspect of her rationale to herself. "They were just acting weird, is all—approaching from the front as a pair in broad daylight. Based on their behavior, they probably weren't trying to hurt me."

He seemed impressed. "So you know a thing or two about wild animals, after all."

"I did a report on mountain lions in elementary school. Other than that, I can tell the difference between a black bear and a polar bear. So what are we going to do about this train wreck of an ankle?"

"I'm afraid we're going to have to amputate."

"Not funny."

"No, I suppose it wasn't."

"*So?*"

"Well, for starters, we need to stabilize it."

"What are we going to use for that?"

"I have just the thing."

He stood back up and removed first his jacket then the brown cotton T-shirt he wore underneath. His highly developed pectoral muscles flexed and rippled as he tore the shirt into thin strips.

"My apologies if this doesn't smell like your perfume," he said with a grin while wrapping her ankle.

"It smells like you. That's better."

"Keep sweet-talking me and I just might kiss you again. Too tight?"

"I don't think so."

"Good."

"Where are you going?"

"To see if I can give you some relief. Just sit tight for a while. I don't think we have anything to worry about from those cougars. But just in case, hang on to these."

He set down the slingshot and a handful of smooth stones within reach and slipped into the forest. With her senses heightened by danger and pain, Cali became aware that, on his own, her guide moved quickly but silently through the woods like an Indian in an old movie. Straining her ears, all she managed to hear was birdsong and a slight breeze in the branches.

She removed her daypack and placed it beside her. What felt like half an hour passed before Juice reappeared from—to her surprise—the opposite direction. Opening his bag, he pulled out a handful of stringy bark freshly shaved from a tree. "White willow," he explained, handing her the shavings. "I had to go down toward the river to find it."

"What's it for?"

"Pain. Chew some and put what's left in your pocket. You can swallow the juice but not the rest."

She made a face while doing as directed. "It's *super* bitter."

"You'll get used to it. Now let's have a look at your other foot."

"I didn't injure that one."

"Let's have a look anyway. Trust me, I'm a surgeon."

Sure enough, with her other boot and sock removed, another large blister reared its ugly head.

"I'm going to put both your socks back on to keep your feet warm. As for these babies," said Juice, picking up her boots and flinging them one at a time as far down into the woods below as he could, "time to say bye-bye."

"What the hell are you doing?!" yelled Cali as she watched her boots spin out of sight before crashing into the thick underbrush.

"Getting rid of ballast. If I'm going to carry you all the way back to my bike, I need the load to be as light as possible."

"Are you saying I'm fat?"

"I'm saying I'm human."

"Well, you're not carrying me back to your bike. I'm not leaving these woods till I've visited Rose Cove."

"News flash: you're in no condition to make that journey. Even under normal circumstances, we'd be cutting it close. Remember Wednesday: dinner with the head of your label?"

"What's that?"

"Come again?"

"Did you hear that?"

Something or someone was approaching directly above on the ridge. Briefly, it crossed Cali's mind that the mountain lions were back—but the sound was more like people walking.

Juice had just enough time to arm his slingshot before a voice overhead ordered him to put down his weapon. The two companions looked up to find a ragtag group of men pointing half a dozen rifles at Juice's chest.

"Just *do* as he says," whispered Cali emphatically as she watched the red lights from their laser sites dance across her companion's exposed skin.

Unwillingly, Juice placed his slingshot on the rocky surface of the outcropping.

"Now get down on your knees with your hands behind your head, boy," the voice continued. "Any funny business and you're a dead nigger."

"He's a dead nigger anyways," commented another, more authoritative voice. "He just doesn't know it yet."

Juice stared like a stoic statue at Cali, who watched with growing dread as three of the men—two carrying rifles—made their way down the steep slope to the outcropping. Dressed in a hodgepodge of weathered camo like hillbillies without access to modern shops, the men, all white, were so dirty they almost seemed in blackface.

"Who *are* you?" she asked.

"I'll ask the questions here, missy," said the leader, the second man to speak overhead, in the same commanding tone. A portly piece of work in his sixties with a grizzled beard who carried no rifle but wore a holstered pistol by his side, he had small eyes with an unnervingly sharp angle at their inner edges like a pig's. "What have you done to this little girl?"

Though the question was directed at Juice, Cali couldn't help but answer. "*Nothing.* He hasn't done *anything.* He was trying to *help* me. Can't you see I'm hurt?"

"*Help* you? *Here*? Half naked in the Badlands? I don't think so. I think he's the one who hurt you. Cuff him."

"You have no right!" yelled Cali while watching one of the men strap his rifle over a shoulder and take a pair of handcuffs out of his pocket.

"I have every right," replied the portly man as Juice was frisked and his hands were cuffed in front of him none too gently.

Judging by the way his jaw was clenched, Cali was afraid her friend might be foolish enough to put up a fight. That would have been suicide. But he never moved a muscle.

"I was a sheriff on the inside," continued the leader, "and now I'm *the* Sheriff here on the outside. If you ask me, after he threw you over that cliff, which we heard half a mile away, this boy had a mind to rape you. Didn't you, boy?"

Juice didn't say a word, but the vengeful fire in his eyes spoke volumes.

"That's what I thought. Guilty as charged."

"What are you going to do to him?!" asked Cali.

"I believe you know the answer. But first, he's got a—what's the word for it?—*herculean* task to perform. I hope he's as strong as he looks. Pick her up, boy."

Juice glanced at the Sheriff for clarification.

"Don't you speak English? *Pick. Her. Up.* Throw her over your shoulder like a good Black Buck. We've got a hard row to hoe before sundown."

"If her ankle's broken," said Juice. "she might start to chill. Put my jacket over her first. Please."

"Looks like we've got ourselves a darkie *and* a gentleman," joked the Sheriff, whose men responded with brutal laughter.

"Just to be clear," continued the Sheriff while apparently trying to stare holes in Juice's face, "I don't take orders from anyone—least of all a punk nigger rapist."

Before he even finished this last insult, he struck Juice in the abdomen, doubling him over. Then, picking up the jacket and checking its pockets for concealed weapons, he went to Cali and bent down beside her. "But in my own humble way, I also love the ladies. Why don't you put this on, little missy. Compliments of Sambo here."

Smelling his foul body odor and noting his rotten teeth behind the lecherous hint of a grin, she spat her entire mouthful of white willow bark in his wrinkled face. "Why don't you go to hell."

Calmly, he wiped most of the bark out his beard and off his cheeks. "Oh, I *am* in hell. And so are you. Up now with your nigger-loving slut of a self!"

He grabbed her by the wrists and jerked her upright. Given his modest stature, she was shocked by his strength. Unable to react in time to keep her weight off her injured ankle, she winced and cried out.

Juice responded by stepping forward menacingly—but she stopped him with a quick shake of her head while hopping on her other foot long enough to allow the Sheriff to drape the jacket over her shoulders.

By this time the other four men had made their way down to the outcropping. One of them stashed Juice's slingshot in his messenger bag and slung the latter over his shoulder. Another stuffed Cali's daypack in his own larger pack.

Meanwhile, hoisting Cali over his shoulder like a sack of feathers, Juice marched surrounded by the group of bandits—for that was what they clearly were—up the hillside. The jarring caused by being carried over such uneven terrain was the last thing any sane doctor would have ordered for Cali's injury. Happily, though, she was starting to notice a slight reduction in pain from the willow bark.

They soon rejoined the path and continued on in the direction Cali and Juice had been headed. "Oh, I wish I was in the land of cotton," sang the Sheriff and his men for a walking song. "Old times there are not forgotten. Look away, look away, look away, Dixie Land."

Without so much as a break for water, Juice—like a tireless pack horse—carried her uncomplainingly up, up and up into the mountains. Through the colorful autumn foliage that shined like stained glass in the oblique light, Cali, turning her head occasionally, was aware of the sun approaching and then passing the meridian into afternoon.

They finally stopped for a few minutes to drink water and refill their bottles from a spring. Juice and Cali sat side by side. She felt nauseated. But with her ankle starting to ache again, she decided to chew another mouthful of bark.

"How are you?" whispered Juice when none of the bandits appeared to be listening.

"Hanging in there. You?"

"I've been better. I just want you to know, Cali, I got us into this mess and I'm going to get us out of it."

"*You* got us into it? In case you've forgotten, this trip was my idiotic idea."

"Well, I agreed to come along like a jackass."

"You may be a jackass. But you're *my* jackass."

Cali noticed a trace of tears in Juice's eyes as one of the men yelled, "Pipe down over there, you two, or we'll duct-tape your pretty mouths!"

"Don't be such a spoilsport, Kyle," said the Sheriff with a sardonic grin. "Let our salt-and-pepper lovebirds have their moment. They don't have many moments left."

No sooner had these words been uttered than chaos erupted. The two mountain lions from hours before had stealthily approached the group while everyone was distracted. Now they sprang out of the forest and fiercely attacked two of the men from behind.

One of their victims, the bandit who had claimed Juice's messenger bag, had his neck snapped before Cali even realized what was transpiring.

The other victim, who happened to be wearing a backpack, was luckier. The pack protected his neck as he managed to spin away from the larger of the cats, probably the male, and take aim at the ferocious feline preparing to spring at him again.

But he never had a chance to fire. There was the high-pitched sound of a single blast from behind where Cali and Juice were seated. The male cougar died instantly with a smoking laser hole through his heart.

The Sheriff stepped forward, pistol still in hand, and took aim at the female. For one reason or another, she'd pulled Juice's bag off the corpse of her victim and was holding it like a kitten in her mouth. Cali felt an empathetic pang of grief as the lioness glanced at her dead mate—before, still carrying the bag, springing into the woods as the Sheriff's blasts went wide.

"Goddamn painters," he said, toeing the body of his fallen comrade to verify he was well and truly dead. "You'll be missed, Angus."

"What should we do with the bodies?" asked one of the men.

"Move both away from the spring so they don't pollute the water. Nature will reclaim them soon enough, I reckon."

To say Cali was in a state of shock wouldn't be an exaggeration. Any way you dissected them, the events of the past few minutes had been shocking.

Moreover, she was literally on the verge of shock as her ankle had begun to ache uncontrollably. She imagined it was the size of a balloon as—feeling out of body—she was once again hoisted over Juice's shoulder and jolted up and down along the rugged path.

She had no idea where they were. She doubted that Juice himself knew. The one thing she felt fairly certain of—how exactly she couldn't say—was that they weren't headed to Rose Cove.

As they reached the higher elevations, the evening shadows started to spread through the woods and the wind picked up. Despite Juice's jacket over her own, she found herself shivering so hard her teeth chattered.

If the cold bothered Juice, he didn't show it. To the contrary, the bare skin on his shoulders was mercifully warm against Cali's cheek.

An hour or so before nightfall, they left the path and walked in silence for a while through the trackless woods. At length a whistle mimicking an Eastern Wood-Pewee could be heard up ahead. The Sheriff stopped the group and waited a second, then whistled back in nearly identical fashion.

Soon they were met by several other bandits and escorted by flashtorch to a high-arching cave entrance in the face of a mountainside.

"Put these two in Stonewall Jackson's cell," ordered the Sheriff as he passed off his human spoils to the newcomers. "Make sure they're kept separate. I'd hate for them to enjoy their last night together *too* much."

Crude laughter echoed off the cave walls. Not that Cali was there to hear it. She was far away now, shivering through a delirium in which she imagined she was onstage at the Holy of Holies in Saturnia at the Patriarch Awards.

She was wearing only lingerie in front of a massive crowd of jeering bandits in addition to a nationwide HoloTube audience. With her band playing the music behind her, she opened her mouth to sing her greatest hit to date, "I Promised You a Rose Garden." But the only words that would come out were the lyrics to "Dixie."

E ver since Juice and Cali had been taken captive, a single thought had burned like a lighthouse in his mind: escape. For hours he'd racked his brain for a way to free Cali—if no one else—and make sure she was safe and sound.

The ankle troubled him, no doubt about it. It looked awful and needed immediate medical attention. Even if he could contrive to liberate her, unless he were free to carry her or could arrange some other conveyance, she couldn't go anywhere on her own.

As bandits escorted him still carrying her unconscious body into the cave, he processed the sobering realization that—short of getting his hands on a GPS—he might not be able to find either his bike or Rose Cove.

Certainly, though he suspected they were fairly close to the old settlement, getting there in the dark was a fool's errand. And quite possibly, even probably, they'd find one of four things in Rose Cove anyway: no one, no welcome, no help, or no way out.

Which left only a backbreaking journey back down in the general direction of the river and, with any luck, his motorbike, followed by a dangerous and jarring trip back across the trestle that—even if they survived it—could only make Cali's injury much worse.

His stomach growled so loudly he could hear it as he trudged along. Not for the last time, he missed Weezy's soul food, especially her spicy fried wild turkey drumsticks. Following so much exertion on no sleep, he could have eaten a bucketful.

As much as the image of his mother was a comfort to him, it was the memory of his father—who was no stranger to prison and torture—that stuck in his mind as the bandits thrust him into a dimly lit cell.

Before removing his cuffs, they chained him by the midsection to the cave's rock wall barely within reach of Cali. They also chained her even though, feverishly mumbling to herself about underwear and performing live, she was clearly no threat to anyone.

"She needs a doctor," said Juice before the guards could shut the barred gate. "She's hurt bad. Please, for God's sake, *do* something!"

"The only doctor we've got around here is time," sneered one of the guards, spitting into the cell nonchalantly.

"She'll either be alright or she won't," added the other guard. "But you, young buck, you ain't going to be alright, no sirree."

Half clothed and left to his own thoughts in the cold, damp, crepuscular cell, Juice shivered. He wondered what a genius like his Uncle Aristotle would do in such dire straits. After all, he'd once escaped from a super-maximum POC prison. Surely, there was something hidden under the half a foot of debris on the cave floor that could help.

For several minutes Juice fished around with his hands as far as they would extend. But the only thing remotely of interest he found was a human skull with scraggly brown masculine hair still attached!

"I'm afraid he's not much for conversation," said a weak voice in the corner.

Juice turned to find a pale, thin scarecrow of a man seated in the shadows, legs outstretched, with his back against the rock wall.

Carefully, Juice replaced the skull. "What happened to him?"

"Could have been anything: extreme poverty, childhood neglect, nefarious influences, false pretenses."

The man's voice, though interspersed with coughs, wasn't merely elegant and charming; it was also vaguely—and unsettlingly—*familiar*. Juice gathered he was talking not about what actually could have killed the deceased prisoner, but what might have led him to the Badlands in the first place.

"I see you and your attractive friend have followed in his cautionary footsteps. As have I."

"I wouldn't put it that way exactly."

"Yet here we are."

"Is there any way out?" asked Juice, examining the bare cave walls and thick metal bars of the gate.

"None. Except by death. Which," the man managed to utter before being interrupted by more coughing, "I can assure you I'm working on."

"That makes two of us."

"Then let us make the most of our acquaintance. What's your name?"

"Fred Hamilton. But folks call me Juice. You're Stonewall Jackson, right?"

The man's polished laughter momentarily echoed all around. "That's Sheriff Briscoe's prodding nickname for me. I was *almost* Stonewall Jackson."

"You're talking about *the* Stonewall Jackson?"

"The one and only. Head Deacon of the Realm. I was within days of appointment when I was exiled to this unforgiving no man's land."

"So your name's Fred, too."

"Very astute of you. Technically, it's Frédéric. Frédéric Batonrouge at your service. But you can call me Freddy."

His vision having at last adjusted to the dimness, Juice stared at his surprising companion. The long nose, the pointed chin, the high cheekbones, the deep-set eyes: everything lined up with what he could recall about Frédéric Batonrouge, beloved eldest son of the nation's most influential banking family who became the youngest ever Deacon of the Realm at thirty—only to be tragically killed in a levicopter accident soon thereafter.

"Does this mean you *faked* your death three years ago?"

"Rather, my death was faked for me. My younger brother, Henri, showed mercy and handed me over to the good Sheriff instead. Would that he'd just left me on that levicopter."

"Your own *brother* was going to have you killed?"

"My father actually. God rest his soul."

"You're saying that Abbé Batonrouge, your *father*, tried to murder you?"

Freddy laughed again. "I must admit the situation was rather biblical. But he was a kingmaker and I crossed him."

"How?"

"I tried to make a difference. Having contemplated the dog and pony show that passes for our government, I wanted to stand up for what my forefathers once stood for—*liberté, égalité, fraternité*—and not act as merely a puppet of the banking elites with their boot on the neck of the people like every other Head Deacon."

Juice remembered the day he learned that Frédéric Batonrouge, an outspoken critic of racial segregation and a genuine hero to those in the Hinterlands, was reported to have died. It was a sad day indeed in Nubia, where people wept openly in the streets to mourn the loss of such a powerful ally.

"But enough about me," said Freddy. "What brings a polite young man like yourself to a place like this?"

"It's a long story."

"It always is."

"You sure you want to hear it? I mean, it's pretty crazy. But it can't exactly compete with your own."

"I can assure you I'd love to think about anyone besides myself for more than five minutes. And who with any theatrical sense doesn't like a little crazy?"

Juice was on the verge of telling him all about Cali and her bizarre connection to Rose Cove—when she stirred and opened her eyes. "Juice?" Her voice, normally robust and melodious, was faint and crackly.

"I'm here."

"My ankle hurts."

"I'm sure it does."

"And I'm really thirsty."

"Me, too. But I'm afraid there's no water."

"Allow me," said Freddy. His chains rattled as he extended a stainless steel cup of what turned out to be water that Juice, reaching out as far as he could, was just able to grasp.

"Thank you, Freddy."

"Don't mention it."

"Here you go, girl. Let me sit you up a little."

Pulling on his chains, Juice extended as far as he could. His firm hand supporting her, Cali made it upright enough to drink without spilling or choking. "You should have the rest," she said, pushing the cup back at him.

"You need it more."

"I've had plenty. And I don't want to start cramping again."

Despite the gravity of the situation, Juice chuckled. "So *now* it comes out."

"Shut up and drink."

He could tell her mind was made up, so he drank what remained of the water. He considered suggesting that she chew some more bark for the pain—but was afraid it would dry out her mouth too much. Instead, he tossed the empty cup back to Freddy, who managed to catch it with one hand.

"Who's your new friend?" asked Cali distantly, shivering as she lay back down. "I overheard your voices. But it was like you were both underwater. I couldn't make out much."

"This is Freddy. Freddy, this is Cali."

"*Enchanté.*"

"I promise I'll tell you all about him. But first, you should try to rest some more."

"You're probably right."

Though marginally awake, she was mostly out of it. Soon, pulling Juice's jacket up to her chin, she drifted back into a fitful sleep.

"What a lovely young lady," commented Freddy, "to be suffering so much."

"What will happen to her when I'm gone?"

"Depends. Does she have powerful enemies? Is she on the run from the law?"

"Not that I know of."

"Is her family wealthy or influential?"

"Compared to my family, yeah. But in the grand scheme of things, not particularly."

"Then—and please excuse my brutal honesty—there's a reasonable chance they'll just let her rot in here. Or worse."

"She's a famous pop star on the New World Order label. Does that change anything?"

"It might. They could decide to ransom her."

"Why haven't they ransomed you?"

"Because, no doubt, they were paid handsomely *not* to."

"If they were *paid*, why do they live in this shithole?"

"It's as good a place as any for surviving in the Badlands. Besides, I imagine they were paid in goods. The powers that be in the Fatherland don't have a problem allowing outlaws some antiquated weaponry. All this does is help keep the rebels in check."

"I didn't think the rebels were a threat unless provoked."

"That's historically accurate. But things could change at any moment."

"Tell me about Sheriff Briscoe."

"For someone on the eve of his execution, you're very inquisitive."

"They say information is power."

"They say a lot of things. Few, however, are true." Freddy sighed as if to indicate that—while the subject they were discussing would lead nowhere—he was willing to humor his new friend. "Briscoe was indeed a sheriff in the Fatherland. A rather prominent one, in fact."

"How did he end up … *here?*"

"He had the audacity to blackmail the wrong person: my father. Thus the Sheriff's undying hatred of me and his Old Testament justice." Freddy uttered this last observation while holding up the stump of his left hand for Juice to contemplate.

"I'm truly sorry you of all people have been through so much, Freddy. Why did that son of a bitch cut off your hand?"

"For stealing."

"Did you steal?"

"Guilty as charged. I was hungry, so I stole bread. It was all very *Les Misérables*. He also accused me of trying to 'steal' the true purpose of the Fatherland—total global control—by making deals with 'darkies.'"

"Speaking of, this darky has a proposal."

"I'm all ears."

"It's not technically a deal, seeing as how I don't have anything to offer in return. But if I'm not able to, I beg you to do everything in your power to free Cali."

"I have no power. Not anymore."

"Maybe you could persuade the Sheriff to ransom her—like you said. He might listen to you."

"I'm afraid the only voices Sheriff Briscoe listens to are the ones in his head."

"But he's greedy, right?"

"Power-hungry is more like it."

"That's a weakness. You can use it. *Please*. You have to at least try. She has her whole life ahead of her."

Fighting back tears of rage and sorrow, Juice stared helplessly at Cali's drawn face.

"I'll do what I can—for what it's worth."

"That means a lot."

Juice suddenly became aware of someone standing in the shadows just outside the gate. Even with his keen ears, which could detect the sound of rabbits milling about on soft earth, he hadn't heard anyone approaching.

"I am seeking a girl named Cali and a boy named Juice," whispered a voice with a noticeably exotic accent not unlike Dr. Caliandra's.

"You've come to the right place," said Juice. "Who are you and what do you want?"

"Please keep your voice down," whispered the stranger.

What Juice could only process as an American Indian—complete with leather buckskins, three feathers in his headdress, and a bow and quiver of blue arrows reminiscent of those stuck in the tree at the Badlands border on his back—stepped into the light.

"My name is Apollo." The Indian tossed Juice his own messenger bag between the cell bars before producing a set of keys. "I was sent here to rescue you. We must make haste."

A pollo looked scarcely older than eighteen, yet the newcomer acted with the military efficiency of a seasoned veteran as he speedily unlocked first the gate then Juice's chains before handing over the keys with the order to free Cali.

"I will stand guard," whispered Apollo, fingering his stone tomahawk. "Do not tarry."

"Where did you get these keys? And how the heck did you find us?"

"Actions now, explanations later—that is, if you wish to get out of here alive. Who is the paleface in the corner?"

"Freddy. A friend."

"Free him, too."

When Juice unchained Freddy and helped him to his feet, he realized in what deplorable shape the former Deacon of the Realm was. His overgrown hair was a rat's nest, his erstwhile posh clothes were in tatters, his body was thoroughly emaciated, and he literally wobbled.

"Can you walk?" asked Juice.

"I can try."

"How do you propose escaping this dungeon, Apollo?"

"The same way I came in. By the main entrance."

"If I may suggest a better option," said Freddy, "there's a side exit the Sheriff and his men use to outflank threats. If we go that way, there should be fewer prying eyes than on the main level."

"Have you ever gone through this side exit?" asked Apollo.

"No. But I think I know how to get there."

"You *think*?"

"I'm fairly certain."

"Then please, lead on."

"In the dark?"

"No worries. You will have sufficient light."

While Apollo and Freddy were speaking, Juice examined Cali. Her forehead was burning. "Hang in there," he whispered, bending down close and stroking her cheek.

"How is she?" asked Apollo as he knelt beside Juice and gazed at Cali with a look of compassion on his angular face.

"Not good. I'd bet anything her ankle's in a bunch of little pieces. It was a bad fall. Is there anything we can do for her?"

"She requires Thelete's medicine. Are you strong enough to carry her a little ways?"

"Does the sun rise in the east?"

"Not in all places. But I appreciate your confidence. May the Originator bless all your endeavors and may the Luminous Child awaken in you."

"We should be going," interjected Freddy.

"Words of wisdom," replied Apollo. "Now for that light." He closed his eyes, took a deep breath that seemed to be a way of centering himself, and gave his tomahawk a quick shake. Suddenly and inexplicably, the head began to glow a soft red in a wide radius. "Shall we?"

Having pocketed the prison keys and strapped on his messenger bag, Juice picked up Cali and followed Freddy and Apollo out of the cell. Ever since the latter's arrival, the young Nubian's head literally felt as if it were spinning with questions.

Who *was* Apollo? Where did he *come* from? Who *sent* him? *How* did he get his hands on the bag after the mountain lion took it? What was *up* with that primitive-looking tomahawk? And what kind of name was *Thehletay*?

One thing was certain where Apollo was concerned: Juice instinctively felt he could trust him.

After several minutes of zigzagging through a network of tunnels bathed in the nearly hypnotizing light emanating from the young Indian's tomahawk, they came to a dead end at a solid stone wall. "I thought there was supposed to be a gate," said Apollo.

"I thought so, too," replied Freddy.

"Is that a keyhole?" asked Juice (whose eyesight was really rather remarkable in the dark) as he pointed to a small hole at the wall's edge.

"I believe so," said Apollo. "Did you bring the keys?"

"They're in my pocket. Take them. Just be quick. Someone's headed this way."

He was right: the ominous sound of many boots running on stone echoed out of the tunnel behind. Apollo pulled the set of keys from Juice's pocket and gave him the tomahawk.

"Hold this," he said. "Just be sure you think … peaceful thoughts."

Juice did as instructed, though staying mentally and emotionally calm wasn't easy standing there with Cali in one hand and the tomahawk in the other as the sound of thumping boots grew louder and louder. To make matters more difficult, his response to the tomahawk could only be described as *visceral*.

Strange as this may seem, it was as if he *felt* the weapon's presence—specifically where its glowing head was concerned—as one might *feel* the presence of an extremely powerful person in close proximity.

As Apollo tried first one key then another and another, Juice couldn't help admiring the tomahawk's oak shaft into which had been skillfully carved—no doubt about it—a *motif of roses and thorns*.

Upon this realization, which nearly took his breath away, the weapon's head pulsed with a deeper yet brighter red.

"Steady now," cautioned Apollo while trying the last of the keys. "You have no idea what you are dealing with."

"But I know what we're dealing with," said Freddy. "The Sheriff and his men aren't likely to take any prisoners this time around."

"Your meaning is clear. I regret to inform you we lack the correct key."

"What do we do?" asked Juice.

"Improvise. I will take that back now," said Apollo, retrieving the tomahawk.

Juice felt almost relieved to surrender the weapon, which had infused him with a wildly stimulating energy reminiscent of electrical current.

Whoever was approaching was almost upon them as Apollo once again shut his eyes, took a centering breath, and shook the tomahawk—this time twice. Immediately, the head strobed in neon red.

Without so much as a hint of stone contacting stone, he sank the weapon a good foot into the rock wall, which momentarily appeared to swim like a desert mirage … before disappearing entirely!

"That's a neat trick," said Juice, blinking as if his eyes deceived him. "How'd you do that?"

"Years of training," answered Apollo as he stepped into the hollow space where the wall used to be. "Follow me quickly. The stone will only remain phased out a handful of seconds."

As if on a timer, the tomahawk's color had begun shifting back to soft red. First Juice carrying Cali and then Freddy followed Apollo into the newly formed aperture in the mountainside. After perhaps ten feet, they emerged into a dark forest.

Just in time, too. Flashtorches and men's voices were speeding toward them—only to go dark and silent as the side of the mountain, reconstituting itself, intervened. Apollo led them by tomahawk light down the hillside away from the main entrance.

"There could be snipers," warned Freddy.

"I doubt they have had time to regain consciousness," replied Apollo. "I was not very gentle. All the same, I advise you to stay low."

Even stumbling at a snail's pace through the shadowy woods, it looked as if they were going to make a clean escape.

"I'm sorry," gasped Freddy, who was so out of shape from prolonged immobility he was wheezing. "But I have to rest."

The party came to a stop in a small clearing. Silvery clouds backlit by an unseen moon whirled overhead.

"You can rest when we reach Rose Cove," said Apollo impatiently.

"You're taking us to Rose Cove?" asked Juice.

"I have my orders."

"Do those orders include me?" asked Freddy.

"They do not. You are free to do as you wish. But for your own safety, I recommend that you accompany us."

No sooner had Apollo spoken these words than the high-pitched sound of laser fire came at them from several directions simultaneously.

"Looks like we're surrounded," said Freddy. "So much for anyone's safety."

"Get down!" yelled Juice, placing Cali—who remained inert—on the forest floor behind a fallen tree and covering her as best he could with his body.

Dozens of shots twittered through the forest all around as the four escapees hunkered down.

"It must be search parties triangulating on us," observed Apollo.

"I feel like I'm at the OK Corral," joked Freddy. "What a splendid way to go out."

"We are not going anywhere except Rose Cove," said Apollo as he activated the tomahawk once more.

This time, following three shakes, the head glowed a profoundly deep crimson "like the blood of stars." The poetic description spontaneously came to Juice, who imagined he could feel the weapon's heightened energy vibrating every molecule of his being.

Rolling up onto his knees, Apollo struck the ground forcefully with the tomahawk. The earth seemed to respond with a massive exhalation—that was how Juice experienced it anyway—as a mighty tremor raced outward from the epicenter that was the clearing.

Juice had never witnessed an earthquake. All around trees swayed and crashed as the ground warped and cracked. There were shouts and groans throughout the forest from men who had been severely injured.

Astonished, Juice and Freddy stared at their rescuer.

"You'd make a hell of a Marine," said Freddy.

"I suppose, where I come from, that is what I am."

"And where *do* you come from?"

Apollo ignored this question as he helped Freddy up. "Time to go."

"Is it safe—for Cali, I mean?" wondered Juice.

"It is as safe as it is likely to be."

Juice could still hear the sounds of men in pain echoing through the woods. "Fair enough."

With the tomahawk back to its soft "flashtorch" setting and Cali once again across his shoulder, Juice followed Apollo through patches of cloud-filtered moonlight dotting the topsy-turvy forest floor. Freddy, who had managed to catch his breath, brought up the rear.

It wasn't long before they encountered half a dozen earthquake victims. At least two had been crushed by trees and were obviously dead. Three others were at the very least unconscious.

Only one of the men was unquestionably still alive. Seated half stunned on the forest floor—as luck or fate would have it—was the Sheriff.

Apollo kept his distance watchfully as Juice approached. The Sheriff's arm and shoulder were gruesomely broken. Blood was streaming from his nose and dripping from his graying beard.

"What are you looking at, nigger?" he managed to say.

"I should think now, of all times, you'd show some manners," said Freddy, who had picked up the Sheriff's pistol that had been dropped during the quake.

"Would those manners be like the ones your old man showed me, you coon-licker?"

"I don't pretend to speak for my father." With his one hand, Freddy cocked and aimed the weapon for a kill shot at the Sheriff's head. "I don't intend to speak at all."

Juice had just enough time to punch aside the pistol. Freddy's shot sailed wide along with the weapon as the Sheriff laughed derisively.

"Why did you do that?!" exclaimed Freddy.

"He's a dead bastard already." Juice looked at the Sheriff with an implacable expression. "He just doesn't know it yet."

Riffing off the first words the Sheriff had spoken to him, Juice meant that the bandit's injuries appeared fatal there without medicine in the wilderness. But he ended up being prophetic in a totally unexpected way.

Just then the female mountain lion that had taken Juice's messenger bag leapt from the woods onto the Sheriff's back, seizing his neck between her spiky teeth and snapping it horrifically like a dried branch.

Dead as dead could be, the Sheriff went limp. Suddenly disinterested, the lioness allowed him to fall to the ground before walking over and standing beside Apollo, who—in what struck Juice as a comforting gesture—placed his hand gently on her head.

"Go now," he said, "and may the Goddess bless you and your progeny."

As if she perfectly understood, the lioness jogged off into the woods and disappeared.

Approaching Juice, Apollo hoisted Cali off his shoulder and draped her over his own. "As the crow flies, we have four miles to go," he said. "You are undoubtedly exhausted."

It was true—Juice's whole body felt leaden. The unprecedented events of the past twenty-four hours had finally caught up with him. "Thanks for helping out."

"It is my pleasure and honor to offer succor to the Future Rose. She— she is smaller than I imagined."

The remainder of the journey to Rose Cove happened in something akin to a dream for Juice. He was practically sleepwalking.

At one point, confusedly, he became aware of Cali—still clearly in pain—murmuring strange words in a strange language that somehow wasn't altogether strange. They stopped long enough for Apollo to light the pipe end of his tomahawk and blow musky smoke into the air for everyone to inhale.

Whatever the smoke was, it temporarily revived Juice and seemed to take the edge off Cali's restlessness. It also put Freddy in a cheerful mood, as evidenced by his whistling, which Apollo tolerated only because they were on the outskirts of Rose Cove and finally out of harm's way.

Any preconceived notion of what a rebel camp should look like was dashed as—with dawn streaking the sky above the trees with lavender and yellow—Juice found himself stumbling through a large hollow in the hills past an assembly of primitive tipis.

Another young Indian similar to Apollo in appearance, also armed with a tomahawk, stood outside guarding the largest of these. After greeting Apollo, he spoke unintelligible words to someone inside.

The door flap opened and out stepped a man the likes of which Juice had never seen. It was as if he were staring at a more mature—and decidedly more Native Fatherlander—version of *himself* … down to the fact that the man wore no shirt either over his wildly muscular torso. Below, however, he wore buckskin pants and moccasins, while above he had on a full headdress made of some kind of owl feathers.

The sensation of standing in front of this mysterious figure (who, Juice noted, was unarmed) was reminiscent of feeling the energy from Apollo's tomahawk in earthquake mode—only multiplied by a factor of fifty.

"Welcome to Rose Cove," said the man in a deep accented voice as he smiled warmly. "I am Thelete. How may I serve you?"

For hours, Cali realized, she'd been supine on the bench in her mother's herb and rose garden bathed in the light of a distended moon darting in and out of cinematic clouds.

Except for the form of an immense crow silhouetted against the swirling sky, she was alone. The bench seemed different from the one she recalled—somehow less like stone and more like ... flesh and bone.

Even though the nighttime air was chilly, she felt warmed from below. Still, shivering, she pulled up her blanket, which turned out to be an old canvas jacket redolent of river mud.

Something wasn't right with her foot. Something was, truth be told, very *wrong*. It ached terribly. She wondered if the pain was like that of giving birth. When she concentrated on it, her ankle seemed to throb aloud.

"That is merely the sound of your blood pumping on its way to nourishing your injured tissues," said a recognizable voice in her ear.

Turning her head, she found her mother kneeling beside her draped in a voluminous velvet gown the color of pomegranate embroidered with neon roses.

"Am I dead?"

Dr. Caliandra smiled. "Far from it, my child. You are extremely alive and getting more so by the minute. The energy is stabilizing you even as we speak."

Cali was quiet for a while as her focus drifted in and out like the moon. In her mind's eye, she visualized something like an invisible snake rising up from the ground and entering her by way of her feet, from where it slowly coiled and uncoiled its way up her legs and spine all the way to the crown of her head. Coincidentally or otherwise, her mood lifted as the ankle seemed to hurt less.

63

"*Kundalini*," explained her mother. "The life force itself rising. Our own internal sun. A gift from the Divine Mother."

Cali felt what she could only process—at first—as a tree branch push against her palm. Then she grasped that her mother had grasped her hand.

She looked at Caliandra's fingers only to realize they actually belonged to a bird claw. Surprised but not afraid, she focused on her mother's face, which seemed to alternate between that of a crow and the maternal visage she remembered and loved.

"I'm hallucinating."

"Not exactly. You have joined me in the Dream of the Goddess. In some ways, it is fair to say, you are seeing things as they truly are."

The Goddess statuette with bird feet and a rose heart from her mother's forbidden book on iconography popped into Cali's mind. She was prompted to look for the silhouetted crow. The moon was still there, resplendent and mercurial, but the crow was nowhere to be found.

"Is this where we've met before—in the Dream of the Goddess?"

"Indeed."

"What *is* the Dream of the Goddess?"

"At the risk of oversimplification, let us just say it is the divine mind out of which this world is born."

"We're not speaking English, are we? I mean, we're just using *vowels*. What happened to all the consonants?"

Her mother opened her beak and laughed with a kaleidoscopic cawing. The sound struck Cali as nearly identical to the corvid multitude on the trestle.

"No, Cali, we are not speaking English. We are not speaking any human language."

"It reminds me of what you wrote on the back of that page from your book."

"How bright you are, my little crow. It is the original language, that of the Originator. Some have referred to it as the Language of the Birds."

"That's a funny name—given that you're a bird."

"As are you."

"How do I know how to speak this language? Did you teach me when I was little?"

"Not exactly. Rather, it is in your DNA. Behold the creation of the Luminous Child!"

With a wave of her claw hand, Caliandra seemed to pull back a theater curtain, revealing a hole in the sky. Cali could see into it all the way to what appeared to be the black hole at the galaxy's center. Though she was staring at it from below, she felt mildly vertiginous, as if she might fall upward into it and never return.

"Do not be afraid. I am merely showing you a memory."

The black hole suddenly went from opaque to crystalline. Cali found that she could see far, far into it as if it were the small end of a telescope.

Transfixed, she watched as a pair of intensely bright figures, a woman and her mate, stood singing beside a massive body of water, an ocean of some kind that seemed full of stars. A smaller, more obscure figure—a little girl maybe—was silent and motionless between the two adults on the sand.

It dawned on Cali she was viewing the cosmic equivalent of an old-timey family movie. It wasn't black-and-white, but it was silent. Yet by watching the parents' mouths, she was certain the words they were singing were from the Language of the Birds.

The couple were engaged in pooling a pulsating sphere of red and black between them. Their combined energy appeared to coalesce into something like a yin-yang symbol, which steadily grew larger and brighter.

They practically could have been making love—except their bodies never touched. Cali realized they were using vowels to speak to and receive an energetic response from the ocean, which she experienced as vastly intelligent beyond anything she'd ever encountered.

"The ocean is the Originator, isn't it? It's *God*, right?"

"Personally, I find 'God' to be a silly word for such unfathomable complexity. Keep watching."

With the energy sphere pulsing like an imminent supernova, the man and woman lowered it into their child's body. There was a tremendous flash. Immediately, the girl began to glow even brighter than her parents from within. Her veins—which Cali could see clearly—might as well have been on fire.

"You said this was a *memory*."

"From long, long ago. From the beginning."

"So how can you *remember* it?"

"Because I was there."

"The woman is *you*?"

"Can you not see the resemblance?"

"Yes, but … So who are the man and the little girl?"

No response. Then a voice like a foghorn calling her name. Then light. Lots of it. Cali opened her eyes to find a gigantic owl, backlit as if by the sun, hovering over her.

"Easy now, my child," said the birdman, who—as Cali's eyes adjusted to the brightness—turned out to be an extremely large human in a feathered headdress.

Skittish at the sudden apparition of yet another shirtless specimen of a man, she tried to sit up. The Indian (that was what she assumed he was anyway) placed a massive hand—which she imagined a bulldozer couldn't have budged—on her shoulder to keep her immobilized.

"It is best to remain still." The man's voice was deeper than any bass she'd ever heard, deeper than Juice's even. Yet it, too, especially with its accent that reminded Cali of her mother, conveyed a reassuring sensation. "You are almost stabilized. In just a few moments, I can attend to your injury."

At the mention of "stabilized," which uncannily echoed her mother's comment during her delirium, she searched the man's dark eyes that seemed to shine from within the recesses of his sculpted cheeks and temples.

"Where's Juice?"

"Outside trying to stay awake, I imagine. He insisted on making sure you were okay."

"Is he okay?"

"He will be—after some rest and a good meal."

"Where are we?"

"My tipi."

Cali realized that the light behind her host was sunshine streaming through the open circle at the top of a conical tent. She was lying on the ground on a mat of some kind with what felt like deerskins covering her.

"Is this Rose Cove?"

"Indeed."

"Who *are* you?"

"I am Thelete."

"Where's my mother?"

A pained expression darkened the man's naturally stoic face. "Perhaps this will be difficult for you to understand. But I am not at liberty to give you that information. Not at this time."

"Seriously?"

"I am afraid so."

"You mean after I came all this way to find her, you're going to keep the truth from me?"

"It is for everyone's protection. Including your own."

"I don't need protection. I'm a frigging star where I come from."

"My dear, we all need protection from the forces arrayed against us. You would do well to keep that in mind."

"Is she still alive? I deserve—I *need*—to know that much."

Thelete's look of discomfort gave way to a broad grin. "She most assuredly is. If she were not currently of necessity in the Dream of the Goddess, she would be here to greet you herself."

"So what does that make you: my consolation prize?"

"I realize it must seem that way. But know that she sends her warmest, most loving regards. She is exceedingly proud of you."

"Did she say that?"

"Many times."

As a high-strung being who could and did cry at the proverbial drop of a hat, Cali was nevertheless surprised to feel tears pooling in her eyes. "Will I ever see her again?"

"If it is the Originator's will. And if I have anything to do with it."

"Will you tell her that I'm *really* angry at her for leaving?"

"I promise."

"And that I miss her terribly and love her so, so much?"

"With pleasure."

Cali wiped her tears with the heels of her hands. "It's a good thing my mascara's waterproof. I assume you have something resembling a bathroom with a shower for when the unpleasant part's over?"

"Something like that. And rest assured: it will not be too unpleasant."

"I'll take your word for it. So are you just going to stand there or are you going to treat my ankle?"

For the first time, Thelete actually laughed. The sound boomed like cannon blasts being fired upward from his titanic chest.

"You are so very like her," he chuckled as he offered her something that looked disturbingly like an animal bladder.

"What's that?"

"A waterskin."

"It's a bladder, isn't it?"

"Technically, yes. But it is extremely clean. Drink. You must hydrate."

Reluctantly, Cali did as directed. The water that streamed from the skin into her parched mouth was cool and invigorating. No longer caring if she cramped up, she drank and drank.

Meanwhile, Thelete knelt and carefully placed his hand on her ankle. Soon he began to sing—or maybe "chant" would be a better description—in a melodious voice that traveled up and down a musical scale unlike anything in Cali's repertoire. The notes struck her as truer, purer somehow than those she was accustomed to singing herself.

"*IEOULAUI*," he sang, the vowels blending together into a continuous river of sound whose eddying echoes filled the tipi. "*AAEIIOIUE*."

In the meantime, lightly gripping Cali's ankle, his hand—which had been warm to start with—gradually grew hotter and hotter. The irrational thought crossed her mind that his fingers might actually sear her flesh.

They didn't, of course. But the energy he was channeling into her did almost burn a little—as if her circuits were on the verge of shorting. The sensation, somewhere between pain and pleasure, soon spread from her ankle throughout her body.

Within moments she went from slightly lightheaded to positively dizzy. Foreign terms like unasked questions flitted with butterfly wings through her mind. *Originator. Kundalini. Language of the Birds. Dream of the Goddess. Future Rose.*

"What the hell is going on?" she managed to cry out loud as, just before losing consciousness again, she felt herself careening upward into the heart of the Milky Way.

10

This time it was broad daylight in the herb and rose garden. An irregular *thump-thump* separated by periods of silence echoed off the courtyard walls as Cali lay uncovered on the hard bench with eyes open staring up at a cloudless sky.

Thump-thump. Short silence. *Thump-thump.* Long silence. *Thump-thump.* Longer silence. Finally, curiosity getting the best of her, she rotated her head to find Seth on the flagstones nearby endeavoring to bounce his racquetball.

He appeared not to notice her as she sat up. In place of her riding outfit, a nightgown clung to her skin that was still warm as if from sleep. She found herself standing on her bare feet before she remembered her injured ankle, but it proved strong enough to walk on.

Notably absent from the scene was her mother. Cali wondered if perhaps this was just a normal dream, a dream in which she'd woken up from a dream, and not the Dream of the Goddess—whatever that meant.

Kneeling beside her stepbrother, she touched his red curls adoringly. *Thump-thump.* The ball struck a crack between the flagstones and skittered away. She returned it to him. This time, instead of ignoring her, he stared up into her face with a look of pure and absolute lucidity in his baby blues.

"Sing to me," he said, grinning so much the freckles on his cheeks changed places.

If the Tooth Fairy (who, judging by Seth's missing front incisor, was no stranger of late to the Crowell home) had suddenly flitted into the garden, Cali would have been less shocked. Her stepbrother never, *ever* spoke to anyone anymore.

Taking his face in her hands and kissing his forehead, she felt the waterworks turn on again as tears of joy cascaded down her face. "Of course! What would you like me to sing? One of my songs?"

"No. One of her songs."

"One of *whose* songs?"

"The crow lady."

"It's okay, Cali. You're safe now." A deep (and deeply familiar) voice entered her awareness from outside the garden. "I'm here. Wake up."

"Juice?" The beloved name escaped her lips from still within the dream, which she wasn't quite ready to see end. There were so many questions she wanted to ask. But try as she might to continue her conversation with Seth, he receded and faded away.

"Yeah, Cali. It's me. You're in Rose Cove. Among friends."

When at last she was able to focus on her surroundings, she discovered her guide seated cross-legged looking refreshed—and rather sexy—in a buckskin shirt and pants. Behind his beautifully shaped head, she caught a glimpse of the hole at the top of the tipi. It was daytime.

"Aren't you a sight for sore eyes," she said, yawning. "How long have I been out?"

He leaned over and kissed her. "A *long* time."

"I should sleep late more often. You smell good."

"For a change?"

"For a *welcome* change."

He grinned. "I broke down and had a bath."

"In a tipi?"

"Not exactly. You'll see."

He stroked her hair as his gaze showered her with affection. Unlike with other men, for whom she was typically an object of desire, pure and simple, with Juice it seemed her beauty truly was more than skin-deep.

"You know," he said, "when I thought the Sheriff was going to kill me, I wasn't afraid for myself. But I was terrified I'd never see you again."

"Now that's what I call a pickup line."

"I'm serious."

"I know you are. That's just how I deal with serious things: I crack jokes."

"Well, at least they're usually funny."

"*Usually?*"

"As in, most of the time."

"Did you know my mother's still alive?"

"I just found out. It's hard to believe."

"Did Thelete tell you?"

"Yeah."

"Did he happen to mention where she might *be*?"

"Nope. And I tried my damnedest to get that info out of him. Seems like it's highly confidential."

"Maybe somebody else will tell us."

"I doubt it. These guys make the Elite Forces look flighty. I mean, they're *warriors*—with a code and everything. Freddy's googly-eyed at the possibilities of their firepower, which apparently takes years to learn how to use properly."

"Freddy?"

"You don't remember our fellow prisoner?"

"The details are kind of fuzzy."

"He got out with us."

"How exactly did we manage to escape?"

"That's a doozy of a story that would go well with your bubble bath. But first, how's the ankle?"

She wiggled her foot expecting it to hurt. It turned out to be somewhat stiff. Otherwise, it felt amazingly ... *normal*.

"I think it's better, Juice. How can that be?"

"If you'd seen what I've seen, you wouldn't be so surprised. Apollo actually caused an earthquake."

"*Apollo?*"

Juice laughed. "I mention somebody creating an earthquake—and you take issue with his *name?*"

"Names are important. So is fashion. Have you looked at yourself in a mirror?"

"I haven't run across any mirrors."

"Well, I think you could make buckskin *very* trendy. Talk about an earthquake in the world of couture."

"Ha ha. You thirsty?"

"You're not going to have me drink out of a bladder again, are you?"

"Beggars can't be choosers."

"So be it."

She sat up while he fetched a waterskin from beside some type of "fire pit" at the center of the tipi. Judging by the lack of smoke, no fire appeared to be burning there—yet warmth and a rosy light emanated from the spot.

"Who *are* these people, Juice?" she asked after drinking her fill.

"You tell me. But I'd bet a boatload of cryptocoins they're not from around here."

"Yet both you and I have some kind of connection with them."

"We do?"

"Mine's obvious. But I just figured out you were speaking the Language of the Birds during your fever years ago."

"No way."

"Way."

"What's the Language of the Birds?"

"Thelete used it to heal my ankle. And my mother spoke it to me in a dream. I spoke it back to her. It's what she wrote in her secret note to me."

"You mean the vowels?"

"Exactly. I think I'm supposed to sing them to Seth."

"For his autism?"

"Maybe." Cali recalled how astonished she'd been to hear her stepbrother speaking in her dream. "That would make sense."

"How do you sing them exactly?"

"I'm not sure. I wonder if Thelete would be willing to teach me."

"It can't hurt to ask. He seems like a nice enough guy—if a little tight-lipped." Juice stood up. "Look, I'd love to sit here and chat. But if you're planning to be back in Saturnia by Wednesday, we'd better get a move on."

"What day is today?"

"Monday. Monday *afternoon*, to be exact."

"You've *got* to be joking!"

"Do you see me smiling?"

"You mean to tell me I was out a *day and a half*?"

"Out cold."

"Jesus, who needs sleeping pills when you've got Thelete?"

"I am not sure he would take that as a compliment," said Thelete himself in a humorous tone as he pushed aside the door flap and—still shirtless beneath his headdress—entered the tipi.

Once again Cali was staggered by his sheer physicality. In ways that reminded her of no one so much as Juice, he resembled some ancient Greek statue of a god more than a living, breathing man. In other ways, however, particularly relative to his regal bearing and mannerisms, he made her think of her own mother.

"How are you feeling, Cali?"

"Better."

"And the ankle—how is it?"

"I can move it without pain."

"That is a good sign. Let us see what happens when you place some weight on it."

Juice helped Cali (still dressed in her riding clothes) to her feet atop the deerskin blanket, where she stood hesitating on her "good" foot before setting down the injured one. There was the barest hint of soreness; other than that, the ankle seemed thoroughly repaired. Even the blisters on her heels were gone, she noted, wiggling her toes.

"It's just incredible," she said. "Thank you, Thelete."

"I hardly deserve your thanks. But if you like, you can thank the power that dwells within me."

"What power might that be?" asked Juice.

"That," replied Thelete with an apologetic expression, "as with so many things in this our first meeting, is a discussion for another day." Then, winking, he added: "But for now, I suggest that Cali take advantage of our 'bathroom' and 'shower' while nourishment is prepared. Would you be so kind as to show her the way, Juice?"

"If you think I'm bathing with you loitering nearby," said Cali, "you've got another thing coming."

"Don't worry, I won't be able to see anything."

"Too many bubbles?"

"Sadly."

She was aware of the curious gazes of a handful of feathered men in buckskins scattered around Rose Cove as Juice escorted her out of Thelete's tipi past a dozen or so similar (if smaller) structures, none of which showed any sign of a fire within. The only fire in the vicinity seemed to be the one in Cali's lower half.

"I *have* to go," she said. "My bladder's about to explode!"

"Bladders are getting to be a theme for you, aren't they?"

"Don't make me laugh. I'll wet myself."

"Why don't you go behind that birch over there? I'll stand guard in case we're attacked by alligators."

"Even I know there aren't any alligators in the mountains."

"After everything that's happened to us, how can you be so sure?"

Afterward, hiking up to the head of Rose Cove, they came upon a collection of what appeared to be rectangular footprints of ancient wooden houses now completely rotted away. No part of the old structures was still visible, yet there could be no doubt buildings had once stood there.

"I wonder if these were Quaker homes," said Cali. "You know, from the First American Civil War."

"It would make sense. Here, have some."

She accepted a handful of freshly shaved bark. "What's this for? I'm better now."

"It's not white willow. It's birch. People chew it for oral health—especially when they don't have toothbrushes." He put some in his mouth. "It's good for your teeth."

"Well, aren't you the bark master," joked Cali, chewing some only to find it surprisingly minty. "Wow, talk about naturally fresh breath. I bet our next kiss will be epic."

"I look forward to it."

"I wonder why they named this place a 'cove' when the ocean's hundreds of miles away."

"Maybe they felt like they were living on an island surrounded by troubled seas."

"You're probably right. You do realize this was part of the old Underground Railroad?"

"I've heard that. My mother always said those slaves were lucky."

"Why?"

"Because at least they *had* an Underground Railroad. There's nowhere to escape to anymore."

"Do you ever wonder if something could be done to change things?" asked Cali as they continued on up through the colorful woods of autumn.

The cynical nature of Juice's response was obvious. "Please tell me you're not talking about 'changing the world'?"

"I'm just saying that before a few days ago, we didn't even know that Thelete and Apollo existed. What if there are a lot more powerful people like them willing to help?"

"History would suggest that tribes of any kind only help themselves."

"The Quakers helped other people. You and I help each other. We're from different tribes."

"Are we?" Stopping, Juice took her in his arms. "I'd say we're more like a tribe of two."

"Just so you know, there will be no more kissing until after I've freshened up."

"Then let's hurry and get you that bath."

They didn't have to go much farther before Cali heard the unmistakable sound of water splattering on stones. Soon she could make out a waterfall up ahead through the trees. Juice led her straight to the circular pool at the bottom, where a cold mist coated her face. Sure enough, the water's surface was covered with bubbles.

"So I'm supposed to *bathe* in that? I bet it's *freezing.*"

"It is. But not for long. Watch this."

He couldn't keep from grinning as he removed his shoes and shocks, rolled up his pants, and waded a couple of yards into the pool. Feeling beneath the bubbles, he picked up what appeared to be a metallic rock about the size of a duck egg.

"What are you doing?"

"Keep watching."

He closed his eyes and appeared to be meditating. After a moment the rock began to glow orange-red. He carefully replaced it beneath the water on the creek bed. In less than a minute, steam began to rise from the glowing pool.

"How did you do that?"

"Apollo taught me. Basically, you find a still space in your mind and ask the Goddess for the desired amount of warmth."

"The *Goddess*?"

"I know it sounds crazy. But it works."

"So what's the rock made of?"

"Who knows. Apollo called it 'fallenium,' as if it's some kind of element. But there's nothing like it in the periodic table. It's the same thing they use for heat and light in their tipis—and I believe it's what powers their tomahawks. You ready?"

"To get in, you mean?"

"It's probably warm enough."

"Don't I need soap and shampoo?"

"Not with activated fallenium doing whatever it's doing to the water. You'll come out clean as a whistle."

Having spit out the birch bark that was beginning to lose its flavor, Cali crouched and submerged her fingers. Sure enough, the water felt like a warm bath ... only ten times softer.

"All right. You go behind the trees until I call you. Then you can tell me all about our escape. Just promise you won't sneak a peek."

"Cross my heart."

"And hope to die?"

"That, too."

11

If Cali had ever experienced a more restorative, invigorating bath, she couldn't bring it to mind. As odd as this may sound in the case of a fifteen-year-old, after half an hour she felt palpably rejuvenated—as if her very cells had been cleansed and made healthier.

She had the bizarre impression her face was lightly phosphorescent as she walked alongside Juice back down the mountainside processing his story of their dramatic—and at times downright supernatural—escape from the Sheriff's prison.

Back in Rose Cove, Thelete and twenty or so fellow warriors were seated around a communal pit containing an egg-shaped fallenium stone roughly the size of a cinder block giving off waves of warmth along with a flickering vermilion glow. A pale, gaunt figure with dark, stringy hair wearing obviously borrowed buckskins Cali recognized as a former Deacon of the Realm sat among them.

"You somehow failed to mention," she whispered, "that this Freddy you keep talking about is *Frédéric Batonrouge.*"

"Yeah, well, there wasn't enough time to tell you, so I left out that minor detail."

The entire tribe stood as the pair of youngsters approached. With effort visible on his haggard face, which was nevertheless smiling, Freddy also climbed to his feet. Cali found herself fighting off a bout of squeamishness upon registering that the once dashing maverick politician only had one hand.

"Please join us," said Thelete, motioning for Cali and Juice to sit between Freddy and himself. "It has been a long time since the Bird Tribes entertained guests from the Shallow World."

"Thanks for having us," replied Cali as she and Juice and then everyone else got comfortable on the leaf-covered ground. "I can see why you call yourselves the Bird Tribes. The feathers are a dead giveaway."

Everybody laughed—Thelete loudest of all. "Actually, the name was given to us by those who have been erroneously called Indians. They also referred to us by other names: Ant People, Bear Race, Tribe of the Second Sun."

"So you're not really Indi—Native Fatherlanders?" asked Juice.

"Because you could have fooled me," put in Cali. "I'd cast you for the part any day."

Again, enthusiastic laughter.

"Technically, it would be more accurate to say your Native Fatherlanders look like *us*," said a young man seated on the other side of Thelete sporting a trio of what appeared to be red-tailed hawk feathers.

"Truly stated," said Thelete. "Cali, I would like you to meet my son, Apollo. Apollo, Cali."

"We have met," said Apollo. The lively expression on his sculpted face seemed to reveal a keen intelligence akin to his father's. "Though I doubt she remembers me."

"But I've heard tons about you. Juice thinks you're a superhero. Thanks for saving us from ourselves."

She almost imagined—as another round of laughter briefly animated the group—that the red in Apollo's cheeks came from blushing as opposed to the glow from the fallenium stone.

"If I have understood anything about Juice," he replied, "it is that he would be the first to downplay his own heroism."

"Hear, hear," said Freddy.

"And this," said Thelete, "is Frédéric Batonrouge. Frédéric, Cali Crowell."

"Speaking of heroes," she said. "It's an honor to meet you."

"I assure you the honor is all mine. May I?"

In an old-world gesture that still had some currency in the Fatherland among the uberwealthy, he took her hand in his remaining one and politely kissed it. "I'm given to understand you're a singer?"

"When she's not being a comedian," said Juice.

"A woman of many talents. I hope someday I have the good fortune to see you perform."

Cali had the impression that—of all the extraordinary situations in the past few days—sitting as a guest of the Bird Tribes casually chatting with a cultural (if controversial) icon as mysterious warriors cooked wild game over a fallenium stone in the last of the afternoon light would be the most indelible memory of the bunch.

"So," she said, continuing her repartee with her usual charming bluntness, "how does it feel to be back from the dead?"

Freddy chuckled. "I'll let you know when I'm fully alive again. But seriously, if you're at all inclined to confuse me with Jesus, do save us all the bother. I never actually died."

"His brother faked his death," explained Juice, "after his father tried to kill him."

"So you come from one big happy family," said Cali.

"A big family, yes," said Freddy with a pained expression bending the corners of his European mouth. "A happy one, not so much."

"I'm sorry to hear that."

"We all have our crosses to bear."

"Indeed," said Thelete. "If I may briefly change the subject, it is our custom to have mead with our supper. Would the three of you care to join us—or do you prefer spring water?"

"Not if it comes from a bladder," said Cali to yet more laughs.

"What's mead?" asked Juice.

"Honey wine. A marvelous blessing from nature."

"I'll try some," said Cali, who—as something of a wild child—was no stranger to sneaking sips of Olga's brandy now and then.

"Me, too," said Juice.

"I haven't tasted mead in years," said Freddy. "But judging by the quality of the food here, I'd be a fool not to try a glass. Or two."

The mead—which gave off a fragrance so enchantingly familiar Cali at first had trouble placing it—was actually served in earthenware cups filled from a matching jug. The guests were served first, followed by Thelete's warriors, and only then did their leader allow himself to be served. Raising his cup, he proposed a toast:

"Thanks to the Originator for the heavens and thanks to the Goddess for the earth and its bounty of which we will now partake. Thanks also to friends, new and old. May we all stand tall together in the face of those forces, here and elsewhere, that seek to enslave us. And may the Luminous Child awaken in everyone!"

"May the Luminous Child awaken!" exclaimed the warriors with so much intensity Cali, caught off guard, nearly hopped to attention.

The taste of the mead wasn't at all what she expected. Semisweet with a hint of elderflower, it didn't taste much like honey at all. But it did have a remarkably pleasant bouquet eerily similar to that of … roses.

"So what do you call yourselves?" she asked after a couple of delicious sips.

"Come again?" said Thelete.

"You mentioned names that others have given you. But what name do you give yourselves?"

Thelete seemed strangely proud of her. "For all your ostensible insouciance, there is wisdom in your question. We would do well to ask how people describe themselves. We are the *Gulebb ka Laig*."

"The People of the Rose."

"How did you know?" asked Apollo.

"Call it a lucky guess."

"I doubt it. There is more to the Future Rose than meets the eye."

"Yeah, about that …"

"What language were you just speaking, Thelete?" asked Freddy. "It reminded me of Hindi."

"The precursor to Sanskrit. There is no name for it in English. It roughly translates as 'Deep Speech.'"

The tantalizing smell of grilled venison filled Cali's nostrils as she gratefully accepted a skewered tenderloin slice. When all those present were served, she joined them in digging in heartily. Never had she felt such hunger—and never had food tasted so heavenly.

"Your venison is surpassed only by your mead," said Freddy. "I won't complain if I never have any other food and drink."

"Amen," said Juice. "This rivals my mother's turkey drumsticks."

As much as she appreciated the mead, and as much as she knew she should compliment the food, for several minutes all Cali could do was eat. She imagined she looked like a young woman raised by wolves—especially with her dusty riding clothes, lack of makeup, and damp, uncombed hair—as she sat ravenously gnawing a second piece of tenderloin down to the skewer.

Speaking of women, she wondered why there were no females in the camp. This seemed particularly odd in the case of the self-proclaimed People of the Rose.

"Why are there no women with you?" she asked. "Are you some kind of secret male society?"

"I suppose you could call us a male society," replied Thelete, "though not a secret one. Our pledge is to serve and protect the Rose and her children with our lives."

"Women in our culture have other, perhaps even more important responsibilities," said Apollo.

"But where *are* they?" Cali insisted. "I'd love to meet some and hear their perspective on your … division of labor."

"I would wager that someday you will have the chance," said Thelete.

"You will be welcomed with open arms in the Land of the Everlasting Sun," said Apollo.

"And where might that be?" wondered Freddy.

"Where Tula, our home, is," answered Thelete enigmatically. Producing a long-stemmed pipe from behind him, he lit its rose-shaped bowl with an actual match, a blast from the past Cali had never seen except onscreen. "Let us leave it at that as we smoke together to honor our friendship."

Not for the first and not for the last time that evening, with the mead beginning to alter her perception even as she took a musky toke of God only knew what from Thelete's pipe, Cali fancied herself the star of a futuristic Western with a decidedly psychedelic flavor.

She passed the pipe to Juice, who took a toke and passed it to Freddy, who followed suit. Evening was setting in as the pipe continued making the rounds. With a sense of the air at elevation beginning to cool down rapidly, Cali was thankful for the heat from the fallenium stone.

"What's in the pipe?" she asked.

"Fallenium," replied Thelete.

"You mean we're smoking a rock?" asked Juice.

"You might say it is and is not a rock," explained Apollo, "just as it is and is not a metal. Rest assured it is not only safe for human consumption; it is also quite beneficial."

"I can tell," said Freddy. "I haven't felt this good since—I don't really know when I've felt this … pleasantly uplifted."

"Isn't this what you had us inhale during our escape?" asked Juice.

"Indeed," replied Apollo.

"It's like medicine."

"It *is* medicine."

"Speaking of," said Cali, "I have a brother—a stepbrother, actually—who's very ill."

"I am aware of Seth," said Thelete. "He suffers from autism."

"How did you know about that?"

"Your mother has taken the liberty of sharing much with me."

"How does *she* know about Seth?"

"In the Dream of the Goddess, as I imagine you are beginning to realize, it is possible to see many things."

"Does she—do you think fallenium smoke could help him?"

"Though it might give him temporary relief, I am afraid the smoke is not powerful enough to undo his condition."

"So can anything be done?"

Thelete gave her a hard look. "I think you have already asked that question and received an answer."

Cali's own expression was determined. "Will you teach me how to use the Language of the Birds?"

"What's this about a bird language?" inquired Freddy.

Thelete politely ignored this question with a smile as he answered, "It would be my pleasure. Indeed, that is the main reason you are here—as you no doubt have already suspected."

"I have."

"But first, it would be instructive to gain greater perspective on what you are up against."

"What I'm … up against?"

"In Seth's illness. Perhaps Freddy, who I will wager has direct knowledge of the subject, would be so kind as to enlighten you."

"*Me?*" asked Freddy, eyes wide with surprise.

"Was the Batonrouge family not directly responsible for the pulmonovirus pandemic that led to the largest mandatory jaxxination program in history?"

Freddy looked as if he could have literally been knocked over with a feather. "How do you know about that?"

"The People of the Rose have sharp eyes, keen ears, and long memories. The machinations of the elite banking families, particularly the Batonrouges, are recorded in our history books. Would you care to share the true history of the Fatherland with our young friends—or shall I?"

Freddy's suddenly uncomfortable body language suggested—to describe him with another colloquialism—he was caught between a rock and a hard place.

"You do understand," he said, "that it is precisely this history for which I was attempting to make amends when I was banished?"

"That was the impression you gave. Yet I must be honest that 'Subterfuges' is one of our nicknames for the Batonrouges."

"Fair enough. I suppose I will have to keep earning your trust."

"That you will."

Gone was the jovial atmosphere that had informed dinner. The conversation between Thelete and Freddy had abruptly taken a frightening turn into a suppressed past that seemed riddled with deceit on a mass scale.

"Then allow me to the set the record straight," said Freddy.

"Be my guest," replied Thelete.

Later, processing Freddy's revisionist narrative of the Fatherland's origins, Cali would rethink her earlier notion that dinner would go down as the most memorable part of her journey. It was the words spoken after the meal that made by far the greater impression.

With refined elocution punctuated by the occasional cough, Freddy told the sobering tale of the mother of all false flags centuries after his family, in cahoots with a number of other powerful banking families, formed an actual secret society known as the Illuminati bent on a two-fold agenda: depopulation and domination.

Multigenerational Satan worshippers, the Illuminati engaged in all manner of nefarious practices—pedophilia, human trafficking and child sacrifice being three of the most egregious. Soon after the creation of the first Fatherweb, the internet, at a historical crossroads when the Illuminati were threatened with exposure and even extinction, they launched a highly coordinated covert operation that began with the deployment of a bioweapon they themselves had engineered called the pulmonovirus.

By itself the virus was too weak to create a pandemic leading to the mass panic the Illuminati desired, which is why they had the foresight to deploy a countrywide wireless network known as 5H. The frequencies emitted by this network had the unpublicized side effect of opening cellular membranes, allowing pulmonovirus to hijack the DNA of countless victims, who died in numbers that exceeded even those of the Spanish flu.

Quarantines and lockdowns turned commonplace. The public outcry for a jaxxine against the virus—exactly what the Illuminati intended—soon became deafening. This provided a popular mandate to force jaxxinations even on those opposed to them for religious or medical reasons.

"Little did the American citizenry of the time know," explained Freddy, "that the jaxxines were secretly designed not to provide protection but to further undermine recipients' immune systems. Naturally, this resulted in escalating disease and mortality rates."

"The depopulation agenda," observed Juice.

"Precisely. Everything I've said so far still applies to today's jaxxines."

"So my mother was justified in criticizing the jaxxination program," said Cali.

"Very much so."

"I assume the Illuminati were and are *not* jaxxinated?"

"Correct."

"Why is there now pressure on Fatherlanders to procreate? It seems contradictory."

"After spending many decades getting the population's numbers down, a decision was made to increase them somewhat in order to expand the empire worldwide."

"Makes us sound like cattle."

"You said it, I didn't."

"You mentioned the empire," said Juice. "What about the domination agenda?"

"The jaxxines were also laced with nanotech, which they still are. Microchips invisible to the naked eye were injected into an unsuspecting public. This allowed—essentially—the creation of a remote-controlled population. From there it was but a hop, skip and a jump to playing both sides against the middle in the Second American Revolution, enabling the Illuminati to emerge as the real power behind the newly created Fatherland."

Cali could hardly believe what she was hearing. "Did all this *actually* happen, Thelete?"

"It is not the whole story. But it is accurate insofar as it goes."

"It just sounds so insane."

"'Insane' is exactly what it is."

"Were my people jaxxinated?" asked Juice.

"Heavily, I'm sorry to say," replied Freddy. "And here's where the story takes a surprising turn."

"As if there weren't already enough surprises," said Cali.

"I know what I'm telling you runs contrary to everything you've been taught. History has been rewritten so as to completely twist or erase most relevant facts." Freddy coughed into his sleeve. "As it turned out, while the health of POCs could be adversely affected by jaxxination, they were remarkably resistant to mind control via nanotechnology."

"Why's that?" asked Juice.

"The microchips used are solar-powered through a low-level type of human photosynthesis."

"The Garman Effect."

"Precisely. Researchers studying the Garman Effect found that skin color modulates the frequency of electromagnetic energy that passes from the sun into cells. Darker skin produces spectral frequencies that are incompatible with cellular nanotech."

Juice appeared to have a lightbulb moment himself. "So the microchips don't have a power source when it comes to POCs?"

"They're like toys without batteries."

"Which means what a lot of folks say is true: it's easier to fool white people than black people."

"Intrinsically, maybe not. But in this case, yes."

"Is this why everyone I've met in the Hinterlands," wondered Cali, "seems so much more … *thoughtful* than people in the Fatherland: they're not brainwashed by nanotech?"

"Absolutely."

"Then why am I not brainwashed? Or am I—and I just don't know it?"

Freddy managed a chuckle. "Your brain strikes me as very much unwashed. Just how that's the case, however, remains a mystery."

"Your mother—who was also unjaxxinated—illegally withheld your jaxxines while claiming she had jaxxinated you," said Thelete. "Mystery solved."

"That explains why I've always felt … *different*. Do most Fatherlanders really walk around hearing voices?"

"Unfortunately," replied Freddy.

"So are jaxxines ultimately responsible for autism?"

"I was wondering how long it would take you to ask that question," said Thelete.

"Not the nanotech aspect," explained Freddy. "But the DNA-altering insertion of foreign pathogens can induce autism spectrum disorders in sensitive individuals. This was proven centuries ago and covered up."

"Spinning" couldn't begin to describe Cali's mental state. Still, she was able to articulate how she felt about Freddy quite clearly: "You're too charming to hate. But I can't say I like you very much right now."

"Join the party. I've spent my whole life not liking myself very much."

"I suppose we should at least thank you for coming clean," said Juice.

"A lot of good it will do. But you're welcome."

"And now, before it grows too late," said Thelete, standing and extending his hand, "I have some important business with Cali."

Her hand felt like a tiny child's in his. At his touch she also became aware—once again—of the preternaturally high temperature emanating from his skin ... just before he released his grip and led her through the chilly twilight into his tipi.

"No wonder he never wears a shirt," she mused as she stood holding open the door flap so she could make out her host's obscure bulk leaning over the fire pit in the center. Even as the thought occurred to her, she recalled what it felt like to touch her mother's skin, which was extremely soft yet so hot Cali regularly asked her if she had a fever. But her mother was always in perfect health.

"Who are you *really*, Thelete? And who was—or is—my mother? If she was born in the Fatherland, why was she never jaxxinated? And what's up with the accent?"

The fallenium stone began to shine in his grasp enough to chase the shadows out of the whole tipi. Soon waves of warmth could also be felt emanating from the area of the fire pit. An owl started hooting somewhere outside.

"I will not say your questions are misguided, Cali. But unfortunately, they are mistimed." He unrolled two deerskins and spread them out side by side on the ground beside the pit. "If I am not mistaken, you are expected back at your home Wednesday evening."

"If I'm not there, Olga will crucify me."

"This means you must leave early tomorrow morning. It will take hours to teach you the rudiments of the Language of the Birds. Either we can use the time remaining traveling ever deeper down the rabbit hole of truth—or we can spend it arming you with the capability to intervene in your stepbrother's illness."

"That doesn't leave me much wiggle room, ethically speaking."

"I would say it leaves you no wiggle room."

"Will I ever learn the truth?"

"I sincerely hope someday you will learn the whole truth and nothing but."

"Will I like what I learn?"

"I very much hope so."

"And will I be able to cure Seth?"

"His autism, yes. But he will still be microchipped and not entirely himself. The birdsong I am going to teach you is not potent enough to disarm nanotechnology."

"Is there a ... birdsong to disable people's microchips?"

"There is. But you are not anywhere near ready to sing it. Attempting to do so would only fry your own circuits."

"But you think I'm strong enough to help Seth?"

"I do."

"Then let's get started."

He sat cross-legged on one of the deerskins and motioned for Cali to sit mirroring him on the other. "Do you remember the two lines of vowels your mother wrote in her secret note?"

"Yeah, I took forever memorizing them. They're burned into my brain."

"Can you say them to me slowly, one line at a time?"

"*A E I I U I O O U U I A O.*"

"Good.

"And *u u o e a a a i a a e i a.*"

"Excellent. By any chance do you know Spanish?"

"I've taken a year, but I wouldn't say I 'know Spanish.'"

"But you have been taught the rules of Spanish pronunciation?"

"*Claro que sí.*"

"Then I want you to repeat the lines again. But this time, instead of pronouncing the vowels as letters of the English alphabet, pronounce them as if they were in Spanish words."

"Like this? *A E O I U I* ..."

"Exactly. Only do not separate the sounds. Let them flow together as if forming a single word."

"... *OOUAEIO,*" continued Cali. "*u u o e a a a i a a e i a.*"

"Perfect."

"Just one question."

Thelete laughed. "Only one?" he asked with a wink.

"Only one that shouldn't be terribly … mistimed. Why was the first line of vowels capitalized while the second one was lower-case?"

"You are right. The question is only *slightly* mistimed. I will answer it momentarily. But first, can you sing this note with conviction in a higher octave?"

Taking a deep breath from his diaphragm, he sang the vowel "O" to a mid-range note for a solid ten seconds. His vibrato was so strong the owl feathers in his headdress danced. The impressive sound of his voice made Cali think of Italian opera.

"That was amazing!" she couldn't help exclaiming. "What note were you singing? It was beautiful—but also a little odd."

"You have a keen ear. We refer to the standard note, which I was singing in a lower octave, as *gaur*, meaning 'home.' Others have called it 'mi.' It is not to be confused with the E in your diatonic scale."

"Never heard of it."

"That is not surprising. The musical scale used by the Bird Tribes is the original musical scale."

"What does that even mean?"

"The creational scale—in tandem with sacred vowels—was used to fashion the universe and all life herein. The world, you might say, was literally spoken—or rather, sung—into being."

Cali recalled the two adult figures she'd watched singing beside the cosmic ocean in her delirium. "'In the beginning was the Word.'"

"Many have interpreted this line from your Bible as a metaphor. Emphatically, it is not. The creational scale was employed for millennia in cultures everywhere for healing and connecting with the Originator. The five English vowels—which represent a rough distillation of many vowels back to their primordial roots—match the five nucleotide bases of DNA and RNA. Thus a properly performed birdsong heals at the genetic level."

"Far out. What happened to the scale?"

"Centuries ago it was hidden by the Catholic Church, which purposely replaced it with an inferior scale that induces less than ideal physical, mental, emotional and spiritual states."

"Why on earth would they hide God's own scale?"

"For a multitude of reasons—control over the masses being at the top of the list."

"I thought we decided not to go down the rabbit hole."

Thelete grinned mischievously. His expression made Cali think of Juice. "This is a slightly different rabbit hole. But eventually, yes, if you follow it far enough, it joins the other rabbit hole."

"Give me a second to get my bearings, will you?"

"Take all the time you need. Just be quick."

The idea that the standard musical scale she'd been using to record and perform her songs had been engineered to harm and dumb down people was—of all the evening's unsettling discoveries—the hardest to swallow. The events of the long weekend might have turned her world upside down, but this new revelation had just blown it to smithereens.

"There's no going back," she said, shaking her head.

"But you must."

"That's not what I meant. I meant in my *mind*. I can't just … *un*remember all this crazy shit—pardon my Spanish."

"Would you really want to forget it?"

"Yes. But then I'd probably want to remember it again."

"You are blessed and cursed with consciousness, my child, in a society that has done everything imaginable to remove your kind from its gene pool."

"Which means I'm completely alone there."

"Not completely. You have Juice."

"True."

"And soon you'll have Seth back—some of him anyway—provided you can master what I am endeavoring to teach you. Shall we continue?"

"Sure. What have I got to lose?"

For the next hour or so, Thelete had Cali stay on "home" while singing the line of capitalized vowels again and again until her pitch and pace (one vowel every second or so) were to his satisfaction.

Taking only a brief break during which Cali relieved herself in the woods while gazing up at stars so bright they looked artificial, the two then began to implement the lower-case second line of vowels. Thelete explained that these vowels were to be "sung silently."

"Isn't that an oxymoron?"

"Can you not hear your own thoughts?"

"Okay. I get it."

"Just be sure to pair each capitalized vowel you are singing aloud with the corresponding lower-case vowel you are holding in your mind."

"So you want me to say one thing while thinking another?"

"People in your world do this constantly, do they not?"

"Fair enough."

"'Let there be light,' your Bible states. This divine command pairs sound with light in the initial act of creation. In the Language of the Birds, singing one thing while thinking another generates creational tension by pairing the energies of sound and light for healing and other purposes. Try it now."

Though Cali had a genuine talent for harmony and could even play lead guitar while singing complex lyrics, she found the "double intoning" aspect of the birdsong unexpectedly challenging. Again and again she stumbled over the capitalized vowels as she tried to connect them with their silent partners.

"You are trying too hard," observed Thelete.

"I'm a perfectionist."

"I can see that."

"I suck at this."

"Everyone finds the learning curve difficult. If I may make a suggestion ..."

"Please do before I tear my hair out."

"Do not attempt to hear the vowels in your mind as if you yourself are singing them. Instead, imagine they are being sung by someone else."

"So I can start to hear voices like other white people?"

"Not exactly. Imagine that the Originator is singing through you."

"Let go and let God?"

"Something like that."

For a while longer, Cali continued to be frustrated. She was getting hot as well, she noticed as sweat started beading on her forehead. Ever the attentive host, Thelete touched the fallenium stone in such a way as to turn off the heat while leaving on the light.

Within another half hour, though, the birdsong finally clicked. In a matter of minutes, Cali went from hardly being able to string together three vowels to singing the entire double line effortlessly.

"That is it!" exclaimed Thelete. "Keep going!"

She repeated the line over and over as her internal heat rose and rose. Sweat dripped from her chin as she sang flawlessly in what occurred to her was an altered state. At last, amazingly lightheaded and on the verge of what felt like spontaneous combustion, she fell silent.

"Why did you stop?"

"Because the song was over."

"How did you know?"

"I just did."

"A birdsong is over when it is over, we like to say. How do you feel?"

"Like I've been put in the spin cycle."

"Drink this. You are dehydrated."

He handed her a waterskin. This time, feeling thoroughly depleted, she drank without so much as a bladder joke.

"Do you have any questions, Cali?"

"I assume you mean about the Language of the Birds?"

"Yes."

"Because I'm too tired to go down any other rabbit holes."

"I completely understand."

"I think I'm good. What do you think?"

"I think you are a natural."

"For real?"

"For real."

"Do you want to be my manager? You're much easier to work with than Olga."

He laughed. "Thank you. But I have enough things to manage right where I am."

Cali yawned. Seconds later she was horizontal. She hadn't even intended to lie down.

Thelete covered her with his deerskin and touched her face lovingly. The last thing she remembered consciously was the sound of an owl hooting again outside as he turned out the light and left the tipi.

In her dream, however, she seemed to follow him as he took wing and flew to the top of the mountain overlooking Rose Cove. There he sat still like an owl in a tree, eyes glowing redly in the dark as he surveyed the night with his head on a swivel.

13

"You're looking a little more like yourself," said Juice upon seeing Cali emerge yawning from Thelete's tipi early the next morning. A layer of fog dense enough to wet the leafy earth hung in the treetops around Rose Cove. "How did you sleep?"

"Like a … fallenium stone. How—and for that matter, *where*—did you sleep?"

"Soundly, thanks, in Apollo's tent. I've been crashing there with Freddy."

"I didn't realize you two were an item."

"Very funny."

"What are you doing up and about so early?"

"I could ask you the same question."

"I suppose I'm feeling a little antsy. Not that I really *want* to leave this place." Yawning again, Cali stretched her arms high in the air. "Part of me could stay here indefinitely. It's strange. I don't even miss civilization."

"I know what you mean."

"But if we're going to make it back in time to avoid suspicion, we need to get this show on the road."

"Couldn't agree more. I just finished packing. But first, how about a little kiss?"

"I'm not opposed to the idea. Got any more birch bark?"

He laughed his beautifully alive laugh. Putting his arms around her, he kissed her forehead. "I think I could manage to rustle some up."

She was glad for his warmth on such a cool morning. She was glad for him—period. What it would be like to return to her old life without him she hated to think.

"I love watching you wake up, Miss Crow-well. I could make a habit of that."

"Right. I imagine I'm positively gorgeous right now."

"I'm serious. You get this incredibly soft look in your eyes."

"It's called being vacant."

"You're many things, Cali. But 'vacant' isn't one of them."

"Where is everybody?"

"A lot of the men left just after dawn on patrols, I gathered. They want to make sure we have safe passage back across the trestle."

Her stomach suddenly tied itself in knots. "Did you *have* to say that word and ruin the mood?"

"Sorry. On the bright side, Thelete and Apollo will be accompanying us for part of our journey."

"That *is* good news. Where are they?"

"Getting ready, I suppose."

"What about Freddy?"

"He's staying on until he fully recovers. Then he plans to reenter the Fatherland officially."

"That will make headlines."

"Indeed." The voice was Freddy's. He rounded a tipi and stood beside the young couple, who released each other self-consciously. "I should think my return will give the entire establishment a good shaking. I'm counting on it anyway."

After only a couple of days in Rose Cove, his voice sounded more energized and he was visibly more stable on his feet. Cali could have sworn he'd already put on a few pounds. And most definitely, the color was returning to his cheeks.

"Rose Cove has done you some good," she observed.

"Must be the buckskins."

"Either that or the fallenium," said Juice.

"Speaking of, whatever that stone is, there's no denying it's a marvelous technology. Haven't you wondered what the full range of its capabilities might be?"

"The question has crossed my mind," replied Juice. "One thing's for sure: it doesn't play by the same rules as everyday materials. A lot depends on the capabilities of the user."

"Not just the capabilities," said Apollo as he strode with long strides out of the foggy woods. "Fallenium amplifies the user's proclivities as well. Strengths have a way of becoming stronger. Weaknesses tend to become weaker. This is why so much training is required to wield it responsibly."

"But surely," said Freddy, "such a technology could make the world a far better place."

"It is a basic tenet of the warrior code I live by that *people*—not technology—are tasked with making the world a better place."

"Touché."

"Where's Thelete?" asked Cali. "I heard he was coming with us."

"I imagine he is on his way down from the mountaintop," replied Apollo.

"Did you say down from the *mountaintop*?"

"Yes. Why do you ask?"

"Nothing. Just a dream I had."

"Thelete rarely sleeps. He spends most nights watching over us."

"Seems to me that would get old," joked Freddy.

"Why do you call him 'Thelete'?" asked Cali. "What ever happened to 'Dad' or 'Papa'?"

If Apollo found this comment humorous, he didn't show it. "'Thelete' is an honorific bestowed on the male Aeonic Vessel. It is customary to address him by that name."

"What's a male Aeonic Vessel?" asked Juice.

"A story for another day." Thelete's larger-than-life voice rang out through the trees as he abruptly appeared brimming with energy—despite not having slept apparently. "I assume preparations have been made?"

"They have," said Apollo.

"Good. Who will be staying behind with Freddy?"

"Achilles. Here he is now."

A stout warrior with half a dozen of what might have been eagle feathers Cali judged to be in his thirties approached the group.

"Ah, my babysitter," commented Freddy.

Ignoring this remark, Thelete said, "The sand is quickly flowing through the hourglass. Time to fly as the crow."

"Or the owl," said Cali.

"Come again?"

"Nothing."

"Until our next meeting," said Freddy, kissing Cali's hand. "May your return to society be without incident."

"And may yours be momentous."

"Thank you. And thank you, Juice, for your friendship."

"Back at you. You're not so bad, you know, for a spoiled white boy from an evil family."

The two shook hands. "Take care of yourself," said Freddy with an amused curve to his patrician lips.

"You, too."

With Thelete leading and Apollo bringing up the rear, the group set out down the path toward the Nolihana. Cali's last image of Rose Cove was of one-handed Freddy waving from where he stood with Achilles near the fire pit.

The day passed uneventfully and mostly in silence. Apollo, shouldering a stitched leather bag along with his bow and quiver, had packed two full waterskins and enough wild boar jerky for everyone. The meat was surprisingly tender and remarkably tasty; and it proved to have tremendous staying power as Cali found herself able to put mile after mile behind her without much fatigue at all.

Granted, they were primarily traveling downhill. But she couldn't help but wonder if Freddy wasn't the only one fallenium had fortified. Even her ankle felt noticeably stronger than it had just the day before.

By late afternoon the terrain was starting to look familiar—even to her citified eye. Sure enough, they soon came upon the gnarled oak with a ring of blue-feathered arrows that marked the border between the Badlands and the Fatherland.

"Are those heron feathers?" asked Juice.

"You know your birds well," replied Apollo. "The Great Heron is the sacred bird of Tula. It is said to connect our home here, energetically speaking, with our true home at the center of being."

"That's where I fell and hurt myself," said Cali, pointing to the ridgeline just above the outcropping.

"A wise person would see a message in the specificity of this location," commented Thelete.

"Please elaborate."

"You were injured at a transition point between two different realities. The higher forces that guide our lives are not always gentle, but their intention is ever to instruct."

"So breaking my ankle in this particular spot was supposed to teach me something?"

"To teach. To imprint. Perhaps you are being prompted to ponder the ramifications of the new reality you 'broke' into even as you 'break' back into your old one."

"Well, it's not as if I'm likely to stop thinking about everything that has happened since I left here."

"Then I would say you are already heeding the lessons of the compassionate spirits that watch over you."

Less than an hour later, they arrived at Juice's motorbike, which was exactly where and as it had been left. Uncovering and wheeling it out from its hiding place behind the boulder, Juice straddled the seat and cranked the engine, which purred softly as dust motes swirled in the last rays of the sun that was setting behind the mountains.

"This is where I take my leave," said Apollo. "It has been a great honor to serve the Future Rose and her companion. I pray I have the opportunity to do so again someday soon."

"As long as you're not breaking us out of another prison, I'm down with that," said Juice.

"Thank you—for everything," said Cali, kissing Apollo's cheek. "Just don't think you're off the hook with your 'Future Rose' mumbo jumbo. I'll get to the bottom of it yet."

"Where's Thelete?" asked Juice. "He was here just a second ago."

Sure enough, Thelete was nowhere to be seen.

"He flew ahead to safeguard your crossing of the trestle. Farewell. May the Luminous Child awaken in both of you. And may the world change when it does."

Turning, he quickly and quietly disappeared into the darkening woods.

"Climb on," said Juice. "Let's get this part over with."

"Do I *have* to?"

"You know you do."

"Do you think Thelete actually *flew*?" asked Cali as they bumped back along the levitrain tracks with their headlight beam slashing up and down. "Or was that just a manner of speaking?"

"Who knows with these people. Nothing would surprise me anymore."

"Where do you think they come from? You don't think they're extraterrestrials, do you?"

"Well, they're not little and they're not green. So no."

"Be serious."

"Alright. They actually strike me as extremely … *terrestrial*."

"I know what you mean, but I don't know how to put it into words."

A few minutes later, still bouncing along, Cali said, "I just realized I'll be showing back up without my daypack and riding boots. What will I tell Olga?"

"Anything. Tell her they were eaten by a saber-toothed tiger. She doesn't know jack about nature."

"Also, we can't forget to retrieve my suitcase."

"Don't worry, I've got it covered."

Thelete—shirtless, weaponless and in his headdress as always—was waiting for them in the twilight at the entrance to the trestle. If anything, perhaps owing to the shadows cast by the green light beside the tracks, he looked even taller and more massive than he had in Rose Cove. Yet the usual light of kindness shined in his eyes as the motorbike pulled up beside him.

"These are for you, my friends," he said as he handed Cali and Juice each a single feather—from a crow and an owl, respectively. "Please accept these as a reminder that you are now honorary members of the Bird Tribes."

Why exactly Cali felt emotional receiving a dirty bird feather was beyond her level of self-awareness. But yet again, she found herself trying—unsuccessfully—to hold back tears.

"Thank you," she said. "It's truly an honor."

"Ditto that," said Juice, placing his feather along with Cali's in his messenger bag for safekeeping.

"I can assure you the honor is all mine."

"I detest goodbyes," said Cali while wiping her eyes on her sleeve. "That is, with people I like."

Thelete grinned. "You are not the only one. So let us not use the word. But I do have one last word of advice."

"Shoot."

"Should you encounter Freddy again, I advise circumspection. The Archontic infection runs deep in the Batonrouges."

"What's an Archontic infection?"

"Call it the root of all evil. That should suffice for now—lest we travel back down the rabbit hole together." Another grin. "Go now while the light is still green. I will watch over you. May the Goddess blow wind at your back."

Cali had no idea what Thelete, unarmed, could possibly do in the event of a whipper showing up again. Nevertheless, she suspected he might very well be capable of doing something—and that that something would be awesome and terrible to behold.

Coincidentally or otherwise, the wind suddenly helped propel them forward as Juice got up to speed. In what seemed like record time during which Cali's pounding heart felt as if it were outpacing the motorbike, they were across the trestle and off the tracks.

"We will be here when you need us!" Thelete's booming voice echoed out of the darkness from across the river as Juice and Cali headed back up the old Appalachian Trail.

Second Part

TOUR DE FORCE

T here are places on earth where contrasts reveal themselves in cinematic relief: cliffs falling into the sea, canyons opening up out of flat earth, snow-covered mountains overlooking swaying palm trees.

Similarly, there are times of extreme contrast in human life: the death of one family member on the birthday of another, a professional triumph paired with a personal disaster, a sports victory celebrated with a career-ending accident.

Returning home at the last second in the aftermath of her odyssey to Rose Cove was just such a contradictory moment for Cali. It felt as if, for a little while there, she'd been starring in full 3D in a modern holofilm—and now suddenly, as she applied her makeup in her bathroom mirror just before dinner with Dalton Oglethorpe, here she was back in the same old black-and-white movie where she'd started.

Too bad it wasn't a *silent* movie, she mused with characteristic snark upon hearing Olga barking orders to the hired kitchen help downstairs.

Olga wasn't the only dog making a ruckus. During her brief absence, Cali's father had been inspired to return home one evening with a purebred Pomeranian puppy, Scarlett O'Hara, whose bark was cute at first but became exponentially annoying the longer it went on. Scarlett was a replacement for Robert E. Lee, their beloved, buttoned-up Airedale that had gone to dog heaven of natural causes at thirteen the previous year.

Dr. Crowell's stated intention was to give Seth a companion, but Seth couldn't have cared less about a dog, however meticulously bred. Cali suspected her father had anticipated this dynamic and was really just trying to give himself a companion with Olga scheduled to head out on a lengthy tour the following week.

"Don't you clean up well," remarked Olga in evening dress with a snifter of brandy in one hand and a cigarette in the other as Cali swished into the busy kitchen decked out in a ruby petticoat and pearls. "Stand still long enough for me to have a look at you."

Not wanting to ruffle her stepmother's feathers so soon after her return, Cali submitted to a quick examination. Olga's mossy eyes initially appeared critical as she gave her stepdaughter the once-over, but then she sounded satisfied: "You should spend time at Lake Lore more often. You'll save money on Clostriditox in the long run."

"Must be all the riding in the great outdoors."

"Speaking of, it's hard to believe a *mountain lion* made off with your boots. How exactly did that happen again?"

"I told you: I dismounted and took them off when I thought I was getting blisters."

"You should be more careful." Then, waving her cigarette like a conductor's baton: "Could someone get this damned dog out of the kitchen before I pop her in the microwave?"

A prima donna herself, Scarlett had come between Olga and Cali and was yelping madly for attention.

"My apologies, Mrs. Crowell," said Cordelia, the family maid and Seth's caregiver, as she swept in and swept up the puppy. "It won't happen again."

"It better not. Everything must go as smooth as fine silk this evening."

"Yes'm."

"Why are you so uptight about tonight?" Cali asked while popping a Greek olive from a passing platter of hors d'oeuvres in her mouth.

"You'll find out soon enough. I don't want to make you nervous before the fact."

"Well, you just did."

"Trust me, it's all good. Better than good, in fact. Now make yourself scarce before you stain your dress. Mr. Oglethorpe will be here soon."

She discovered her father—where else?—in his study. He'd arrived home while she was getting ready and appeared freshly showered and shaved.

"Ah, so you managed to find me sequestering here in the calm before the storm," he said with a smile atop his black bowtie as he set down his device and removed the pipe from his mouth.

"I just followed the smell of smoke."

"You look beautiful."

"You look dashing."

"I look like someone who *used* to look dashing. But thanks for buttering me up. What can I do for my angel?"

"Nothing."

"*Nothing?* That's a first."

"I just missed you."

"I missed you, too. How was Lake Lore?"

"Uneventful."

"That's not the picture Olga painted. Would you like to share with me—in confidence, of course—what *really* happened to your pack and boots?"

"Not particularly."

"Is there anything I should be concerned about?"

"Nope."

"Fair enough."

"Dad, do you know what big thing's going down tonight? Olga's been dropping hints."

"I'm afraid I'm sworn to absolute secrecy."

"Is there anything *I* should be concerned about?"

"Nope."

Unable to crack the enigma of his sphinx-like gaze, she kissed his forehead and went in search of Seth with an aftertaste of cologne mixed with pipe smoke on her lips. He wasn't in his room, so she looked in the living room. He wasn't there either.

Finally, she found him seated cross-legged on the bench in the rose garden wearing—she realized as her eyes adjusted to the obscurity—his first tuxedo. One hand was slid under his thigh; the other clutched his racquetball.

He appeared deep in thought. Or maybe he was thinking absolutely nothing.

"You're a hard man to track down," commented Cali, kneeling in front of him as the fall night's cool air raised goosebumps on her exposed shoulders. "'Adorable' doesn't begin to describe you in that outfit. But aren't you a little chilly out here?"

No response. Not that she expected one.

"I have a surprise for you. Not a present or anything like that. But I have a new song I'd like to sing for you soon. I think you'll like it."

"Cali?" Olga's nasal voice rang out from the back door. "Cali, are you out there?"

"I'm with Seth."

"Well, both of you need to come in now. I'll fetch Cordelia to watch Seth until dinner. It's showtime!"

A stout former Elite Forces captain with a mane of alabaster hair and skin leathered from decades of doing business poolside at his South Beach residence in Mercuria, Dalton Oglethorpe wasn't just a legendary playboy; having had his hand in over thirty Patriarch Awards during his tenure as head of New World Order Records, he was a giant in the music industry.

Cali had been around him briefly on several occasions, but this was their first dinner together. She didn't have to wait long to learn what all the secretive fuss was about.

Having shown up fashionably late fresh off his private levijet with a traveling entourage of half a dozen strangers dressed to the nines (all except for his assistant women with exotic Christian names), Dalton himself spilled the beans while proposing a champagne toast in the living room over hors d'oeuvres:

"To the label's newest star of the silver screen, Cali Crowell!"

"To the label's newest holofilm star!" said Olga, beaming.

Everyone except Cali, who wasn't accustomed to being served alcohol at social events, toasted and drank. "Would somebody please explain what's going on?"

"You think you're famous *now*," said Dalton, downing his champagne like the bon vivant he was and snapping his fingers for another glass. "Next year at this time, you're going to be a *superstar*. That's what's going on."

"Congratulations!" exclaimed Olga. "God bless the Fatherland!"

"God bless the Fatherland!" repeated everyone.

"Are you okay with this, Dad?" asked Cali.

"I am if you are."

"It would have been nice to be consulted."

"There was no time," explained Olga. "Just days ago Betty Griffin walked out on *The Path of Purity*."

"Peter Neumann's upcoming martial arts holofilm?"

"Exactly," said Dalton. "I gave Peter his start in the entertainment business. He called and asked for my input. I told him you'd be perfect. You *will* be perfect, won't you?"

Neumann was an acclaimed director of several box-office hits, all comedies to varying degrees. *The Path of Purity* was to be his first action holofilm.

"I'll … do my best."

"Then let's drink to our mutual success. You make me look good; I'll make you rich beyond your wildest dreams."

Cali took a sip of champagne. "There's just one problem: I'm afraid I don't know karate."

Everyone laughed as if at a joke. "What actor does?" quipped one of Dalton's exotic companions to even more laughter.

"That's no problem at all," said Olga. "I've already hired a tutor. He'll join us for the tour and get you up to speed before shooting starts in the spring."

"It's not as if you need to earn a black belt," said Dalton. "You just need to be convincing enough to fool the public. That's easy."

"Aren't we already traveling with one tutor?" asked Cali.

"Yes," said Olga. "Now we'll be traveling with two."

"So it's settled," said Dalton. "Now to more pressing matters. Is that pheasant I smell being prepared?"

Hours later, after a formal dinner in the dining room followed by tarte Tatin for dessert followed by cigars (for the men) and digestifs (for anybody who wanted one) back in the living room, Cali—who'd stuck to iced tea after finishing her champagne—was relieved to see the evening come to an end.

Olga, who acted rather tipsy, left Cordelia to oversee the cleanup and wished Cali goodnight before retiring with Dr. Crowell, who patted his daughter on the back and told her he was happy for her.

"Just don't let all this go to your head," he advised.

"Too late."

"Good one. And good night."

"Back at you."

Seth, who had been sent off to bed just after the tarte, was sound asleep in his room. Crow feather in hand, Cali shut his door behind her and carefully sat down beside him in the half-light. Feeling somewhat foolish yet determined, she threaded the feather into her hair and took a deep breath.

"Here goes nothing," she whispered. Then, clearing her throat, she began to sing: "*AEOIUIO* ..."

Her stepbrother stirred but kept sleeping. She found the first couple of minutes difficult, especially with regard to the silent vowels. But before long she discovered her rhythm and lost herself in the birdsong.

Beads of sweat were gathering on her forehead by the time she realized the song was over and fell silent. She didn't know what to expect in the song's immediate aftermath. Certainly, she didn't anticipate what did happen.

Sitting bolt upright, Seth looked like a wild-eyed animal waking up from a strange dream. Upon seeing Cali beside him, he embraced her with all his strength and soon drifted back asleep against her bosom.

The next few days passed in a whirlwind of activity as Cali and Olga feverishly prepped for the tour's inaugural concert at the Holy of Holies, Saturnia's largest performance venue and one of the grandest stages in all the Fatherland that was to play host to the Patriarch Awards the following May.

To say that Cali barely saw Seth during all the hullabaloo would be inaccurate; she didn't see him at all, so swamped she was with interviews, rehearsals, and radio teaser shows to promote her upcoming tour.

Word of her starring role in *The Path of Purity* had leaked out overnight. This created even more demand for her time and attention. It also prompted the tabloids, notably *The Daily Male* and *The Tattletail*, to speculate wildly as to the exact nature of her relationship with Peter Neumann (whom she'd never so much as met).

Saturday's show went off without a hitch. Gifted with nearly perfect pitch, Cali was also a natural performer who exuded an understated yet intoxicating sensuality, one perfectly attuned to the underlying prurience of her outwardly moral social milieu.

She played two encores to three standing ovations before taking a final bow just after midnight. Without delay she was whisked home by Olga, whose only feedback was that the performance "wasn't bad for a start" and who—as soon as they walked in the door—ordered Cali to "go to bed ASAP. We have church tomorrow morning."

"Do I *seriously* have to go the day before we leave on tour?"

"Your image is everything, my dear. Which means *yes*."

"But you told me to focus on my beauty sleep while pulling double duty as a singer and actor."

"You can start focusing tomorrow night."

Cali opened the refrigerator only to find nothing appealing. "I'm *starved.*"

"I took the liberty of ordering your favorite: fried chicken pizza from Uncle Sam's. It should be here any second. Just make sure not to gorge yourself. Remember: mind your weight if you don't want others to mind it for you."

"As if I could actually get fat practicing karate and dancing day and night."

"In my experience women can balloon for no reason at all. Better safe than sorry."

"Where are you going? Aren't you hungry?"

"I snacked backstage. And now I'm hitting the hay. You're not the only one who needs her beauty sleep."

"You said it, I didn't."

"Someday that mouth is going to get you in trouble."

Pizza was just what Cali needed. She stuffed her face with slice after piping-hot slice while standing at the island in the kitchen just to spite Olga. By the time she'd checked on Seth (who was snoring away), undressed and showered, it was going on two.

Her mother's picture was the last thing she saw before turning out the lights—but it wasn't the last face that occupied her mind while drifting off to sleep. That delicious face was slightly darker than caramel, with exquisitely formed lines like an expensive praline, and it belonged to Juice.

A regular thumping noise hammered her awake bright and early the next morning. Winching open her sleep-crusted eyes, she beheld by far the most unusual sight since her trip to Rose Cove: Seth with bed head in pajamas kneeling underneath the window bouncing his racquetball again and again and again … without disruption!

Too amazed and thrilled to be angry at such a headache-inducing reveille, Cali could only sit up and stare. *Thump, thump, thump, thump, thump* … The ball just *kept* bouncing with metronomic precision!

"That's *incredible*, Seth!"

If he heard her, he didn't immediately let on. But after several more seconds, he stopped bouncing the ball and tossed it to her with two simple, two gloriously simple words: "You try."

"Of course!" Cali found herself sobbing as she plopped down beside him in her gown and started bouncing the ball.

"Faster." She went faster. "Wow, you're really good."

"Oh, Seth!" she said, ignoring the ball and hugging her stepbrother.

"Why are you crying?"

"It's just so good to have you … back."

"Where have I been?"

"You tell me."

"I don't remember."

"Would you like to see your mother?"

"I'd like that very much."

Before knocking on the master bedroom door and presenting her with her newly interactive child, Cali had never actually seen Olga cry. The sight of her sitting up in bed bawling with curlers in her hair was so unexpectedly touching Cali went through a second round of tears herself before she could pull herself together. Not even Dr. Crowell was immune to such shock therapy.

The only family member who didn't cry was the newest. Scarlett O'Hara got up to see what all the fuss was about, barked briefly for attention, then—when none was forthcoming—mercifully lay back down on her miniature mattress in the corner.

Not surprisingly, although they had every reason to thank God, church didn't happen that Sunday for the Crowells. Seth's abrupt turnaround, which Dr. Crowell called—when he could finally speak—a "medical miracle," was all anyone could think or talk about over a lengthy brunch that extended into the afternoon.

Of course, Cali didn't dare take credit for her stepbrother's recovery. Even if anyone believed her (which no one would), she'd committed at least two felonies—leaving the Fatherland and incentivizing a POC to do the same—in order to help him.

On the subject of a certain POC ... Not lost on Cali in the buildup to her tour was the sobering fact that she might not even speak to Juice again for months. The tantalizing memory of his confectionary face from the night before was still fresh in her mind as she spent hours packing everything Olga had included in a minutely itemized checklist.

There was no time to visit him in Nubia. And with the Fatherland's surveillance grid (popularly—or unpopularly—known as the "Old Man") listening to every word, even calling him was sketchy. Certainly, they couldn't have a real conversation by holophone, which meant they might as well not talk at all.

In addition to Olga's multitude of required items, which filled the better part of three suitcases, two garment bags and a carry-on, Cali made sure to pack two cherished possessions of her own: her mother's photo and the crow feather Thelete had given her. These she stashed in a padded compartment in the carry-on in the event, unlikely though it might be, her luggage was lost or stolen.

Evening was approaching and Cali, stretched out on her rug surrounded by luggage, was feeling totally fried—when the doorbell rang. With her own door ajar, she could just barely hear Cordelia open the front door and speak to someone before letting that someone in. But when that someone spoke in reply, Cali could hear him loud and clear.

Despite being inappropriately (putting it lightly) dressed in nothing but an XXL T-shirt over her underwear, she was on her feet and down the staircase in a hot second. Sure enough, she found Juice—looking overdressed (and rather uncomfortable) in, of all things, a coat and tie from seemingly last century—standing as if at attention with hands clasped behind his back.

"What are you *doing* here?!" she couldn't keep from blurting out.

Busy washing dishes, Cordelia turned a deaf ear to Cali's malapropos outburst. But Juice didn't turn a blind eye; he shot her a pointed glance with "shut up" written all over it.

"I'm here to see Mrs. Crowell," he said. "About the karate teacher job."

"What about it?"

"She wanted to interview me."

"Interview ... *you*?"

"Yeah. About the job."

Feeling as if she'd fallen head over heels for a complete stranger, she whispered, "Since when do you know karate?"

"Since, like, forever," he whispered back. "I won the Hinterlands Southeastern Teen Regional last year. I didn't mention that?"

"Nope. Learning karate wouldn't have anything to do with a certain Greek uncle of yours, would it?"

"Maybe."

"I figured as much."

"Anyway, the Teen Regional was apparently why Olga—I mean, Mrs. Crowell—contacted me. She must have seen my picture online and remembered my face from when I delivered the game."

"And fixed her faucet."

"That, too."

"Your face must have made quite an impression because it's hard to believe she'd consider hiring a POC for this particular job."

"Believe me, I wasn't her first choice. But I was available for the next six months."

"Half of success, they say, is just showing up."

"What *is* the job exactly?"

"You mean you don't know?"

"She didn't seem inclined to disclose the details."

"Just wait till you find out. I'll leave the disclosure to my stepmother. Good luck with your interview."

"Thanks. I think."

"I really hope she picks you."

"That's very kind of you, Miss Crowell."

"I'll just go upstairs and put on a dress before anyone sees me like this."

"That would be wise."

"God bless the Fatherland."

"God bless the Fatherland."

Cali would never know for sure what it was that brought Juice so quickly and effortlessly back into her life: luck, fate, providence, the Goddess mysteriously working her magic.

But if one thing was reaffirmed after he took his leave as her official karate tutor, it was that the two of them were like the earth and moon: meant to be together.

16

T he following brisk autumn morning, having said their emotional goodbyes, Cali and her stepmother met the former's pair of tutors on the platform at the downtown levitrain station.

The two teachers, even at first glance, couldn't have been more unlike. Juice was a sharp-eyed, mahogany mound of muscle pushing six-four; Cali's scholastic tutor, a decade and a half his senior, was a blond reed in Coke-bottle glasses who might have measured five-eleven in heels.

On the flip side, Bradford Maddox—traveling with nearly as much shiny luggage as Cali and Olga—was a sharp dresser as evidenced by his designer jacket and slacks, whereas Juice with his lone weathered backpack propped beside him, faded jeans and pilling wool sweater looked as if he should still be traveling the Appalachian Trail.

"Cali, this is Bradford Maddox," said Olga while adjusting her platinum scarf and straightening her matching bouffant. "Juice you already know."

"Pleased to meet you," said Bradford, loosely shaking Cali's hand.

"Likewise."

"Bradford graduated from Jefferson Davis University and holds a degree in education from the City College of Neptunia."

"Impressive."

"Jefferson Davis University, did you say?" inquired Juice.

"Yes. Why do you ask?"

"I recently met someone who went there—if I remember right."

"What was this someone's name, if I might ask?"

"Freddy."

A surprised expression seemed to flicker in Bradford's effete, oversized eyes. "Do you by chance recall this Freddy's surname?"

"Afraid not."

"Cali, Olga tells me you're a capable student," said Bradford, somewhat awkwardly changing the subject.

"I suppose I am … when I put my mind to it."

The teacher's forced chuckle revealed a note of affectation. "Unfortunately, there will be a multitude of distractions on the road."

"Believe me, my stepdaughter's aware of that," said Olga as Cali couldn't help giving Juice a quick sideways glance.

"Here comes the train," he announced, once again changing the subject.

Sure enough, a levitrain resembling an immense floating toaster was decelerating down the tracks. Despite being wrapped in a fashionably long Sherpa coat made out of real lamb's wool, Cali shivered at the memory of the whipper that nearly ended everything on the way to Rose Cove.

"That's one big locomotive," continued Juice.

"I'm going to take a wild guess and say you've never ridden one," said Olga.

"No, ma'am."

"Then you should be advised that POCs must remain in their designated car for the duration of the trip. You cannot leave even to visit the dining car. I hope you packed lunch. It's half a day's ride to Plutonia."

"My people are used to going without. I'll be fine."

"Good. Also, you must carry the COW I gave you at all times. You did bring your COW?"

She was referring not to a member of the bovine family but to the Certificate of Ongoing Work required by any POC employed for more than twenty-four consecutive hours outside the Hinterlands.

"Yes, ma'am. It's in my pocket."

"Be sure not to lose it."

"Of course."

"And always, always, *always* keep a low profile. Remember: the hair that sticks out gets lopped off."

"True."

The levitrain docked while they were speaking. Soon people started exiting by the dozens. There was a coordinated surge of activity, carts coming and going like ants, as one set of station boys hurriedly unloaded the current round of excess luggage while another set loaded another round.

Bradford followed Olga up into their car as Juice, strapping his pack over his shoulder, headed down toward his.

"Here," said Cali, catching him by the arm and furtively slipping a pack of beef jerky from her carry-on into his pocket. "In case you get hungry."

"Did you bring this for me?"

"Technically, no. But you should have it."

"You sure you won't need it?"

"Unlike a certain POC I know, I've got the dining car."

"Thanks."

"Don't mention it."

Keeping a low profile as directed, he smiled discretely and headed off again.

"And Juice?"

He stopped and turned back around. "Yes, Miss Crowell?"

"Don't take this the wrong way. But we're going to have to reimagine your entire wardrobe. I mean, I can't have my karate teacher spoiling my spoiled rich-girl image."

The look on Juice's face suggested a combination of mild amusement and gentle disdain. "I didn't realize you were in the habit of judging a book by its cover."

"I'm not. But everybody else is. Judgment is a national pastime."

"So it seems."

"But don't worry. It'll be fun—and it'll be my treat."

"I'm making decent money now, you know."

"Not decent enough, I'll wager. Don't stand on pride. It's a tax write-off anyway. Humor me."

Juice's two-word response, uttered with a slight shake of his head just before he turned again and quickly walked on, was as characteristic as it was on the mark: "White people."

The *You've Been CC'd* tour wasn't Cali's first rodeo, but it was at a pace and on a scale she'd never engaged firsthand. The first half, spanning roughly two months into December, passed with explosive speed and major pomp and circumstance.

Plutonia, Neptunia, Archontia, three shows in the Northland (Quebec, Toronto, Vancouver), then back east for Martia, Mercuria, Jupiteria and Urania before Orionia, Cartelia and the Distrito del Fatherland in the Southland ... The venues were massive and all sold out.

Sticking to her mother's advice from when she first started singing for audiences, Cali put her heart and soul into her voice every time. She left it all onstage, as the saying goes, and the crowd response—inevitably—was pandemonium.

People who have never experienced fame tend to romanticize it ad nauseam. But fame is a trickster: ostensibly manageable but ultimately controlling. Imagine a piece of spaghetti that looks edible but that never ends once you start sucking it in—that's fame in a nutshell.

Fame can also be (and often is) a colossal grind. Adding to the normal workload of interviews, photo shoots, rehearsals and performances in Cali's case was her crash course in karate on top of her high school studies.

Academics were time-consuming, but she was a lot more astute than she let on and Bradford was an effective—if rather dry—teacher. Whether levitraining between cities or staying in hotels, Cali's morning routine after breakfast went round and round without much difficulty thus: English, algebra, biology, Fatherland history.

Karate, on the other hand, was unexpectedly challenging. In part this was because her teacher was someone to whom she was insanely attracted. His new wardrobe, largely selected and entirely financed by Cali, didn't exactly detract from his sex appeal.

But even without fancy new clothes, Juice seemed to grow more handsome by the day. Cali wondered if he really was becoming more beautiful—or if, with such prolonged and regular contact, she was simply learning to appreciate his beauty more.

Speaking of contact, she had a difficult time making any with Juice during her first lesson.

"I want you to hit me as hard as you can," he said by way of getting the ball rolling.

It was afternoon and they were sporting karategis at a rented dojo in Plutonia. Olga, their distracted chaperone, was seated in the spectator area loudly troubleshooting a minor scheduling conflict at their next tour stop via holophone.

"I'll be glad to, sensei. But first, I have a fashion question."

"This isn't the time or place, Cali."

"I just want to know why your belt is black and mine is white."

"Because I'm black and you're white."

"Be serious."

"Because you're a beginner and I'm not."

"But is there some sort of—I don't know—symbolic significance to the colors?"

He still seemed slightly annoyed, but he also appeared to acknowledge that the question had merit. "White is like snow covering a seed in winter. A new level of growth is about to begin, even though you can't see it yet."

"What about black?"

"Black is the end of the harvest after the sun has gone down. It represents completion of the growth cycle."

"Aren't you a little young to be speaking of your sunset years?"

He laughed despite himself. "I was told I had a gift for this kind of thing. Besides, black is also the emptiness that invites a fresh start. Now, again, *hit* me!"

Before these last words were even out of his mouth, Cali launched a surprise attack at his midsection. Seconds later she was picking herself up off the mat with a stinging floor burn on her forehead.

"Hey, watch the face," she said, blowing her hair out of her eyes.

"Mind your balance. Try again."

For the next fifteen minutes, she employed a variety of creative strategies for striking her catlike opponent. But she never even came close. Time and again, she ended up on the mat owing mostly to her own momentum being used against her.

"I'm hopeless at this," she said, hands on her knees and sucking for breath.

Juice, who still hadn't broken so much as a sweat, replied with a question: "What have you already learned?"

"That you're really, really fast."

"I don't mean about me. I mean about *you*."

"That I tend to overextend myself."

"*Exactly*. You do the same thing in your life."

"I thought this was a karate lesson, not a psychology class."

"An important teaching of martial arts is that the whole world is a dojo. What we learn in here can be applied out there. And vice versa. Try again."

"Why bother?"

"Humor me."

Centering herself as best she could, Cali aimed a punch at Juice's head. Though she didn't contact his flesh, she did somehow manage to graze his afro. And most importantly, this time she stayed on her feet.

"Better. Again."

"How would you say our girl did?" asked Olga, standing and straightening her skirt nearly an hour later after the lesson ended.

"It was a promising start," was Juice's assessment.

"I'm glad one of us thinks so," said Cali.

"How do you feel?" he asked.

"Like I just ran two marathons."

"A long hot shower will help keep you from getting too sore. A cold shower works just as well, but I don't think that's your style. You might also consider a massage."

"I'm afraid we don't have time for a massage," said Olga, "though I could use one myself."

"I can't believe I have to perform tonight," said Cali. "I hope I don't pass out onstage."

"After you've had a bite to eat and rested a bit, I suspect you'll feel energized by chi instead," said Juice.

"Whatever that means," said Cali.

Despite her cynicism, his words proved prophetic. That night when Cali took the stage after her warm-up band, HolograND, an up-and-coming electronica trio also based in Saturnia, she had the bizarre sensation of mild electricity moving up through her feet and along her spine into her head.

The feeling was similar in most ways to the *kundalini* she experienced in her delirium when Caliandra appeared as a humanoid crow. The sudden memory of her mother was like an unexpected karate chop that momentarily opened the floodgates of sadness. Thelete's assurances notwithstanding, Cali feared she might never see her mother again.

Still, as if maternal eyes were watching her, she resolved to put everything into her performance so that she could keep making her mother proud.

"Maybe someday, like when hell freezes over, I'll figure out how to do this without overextending," she whispered to herself just before dancing out under the lights.

After her first frustrating karate lesson, rented dojos on the road soon became a sanctuary for Cali. As much as anything, she relished the chance to be around Juice, however much self-censorship and professional distancing were required not to call attention to the more … intimate nature of their relationship.

True, she often found herself missing the freedom they shared (and at the time, took for granted) on their journey to Rose Cove, when they could simply be themselves together with no danger of being watched or overheard by friends or enemies. As the tour progressed through the fall, the unprecedented liberty Rose Cove represented seemed further and further away even as the Old Man felt closer and closer.

Cali wouldn't have admitted it to her sensei, but she also loved spending time in those rented dojos because she was beginning to enjoy martial arts. Not that she was under any illusion that she could ever achieve Juice's level of mastery; yet day after day and week after week, she could feel herself becoming more comfortable with and confident in her own body.

She especially appreciated Juice's eclectic approach to teaching. Her "karate tutor" in name only, in addition to classic karate moves he shared a wide range of exercises and techniques from a variety of disciplines: aikido rolls and self-defense principles, acrobatic kicks and dancing leg sweeps from capoeira, judo throws and grappling, jiu-jitsu chokes and armbars.

Perhaps the most interesting "art" he shared was the least "martial" of all: a Taoist meditation used in qigong called "hugging the tree" that was the subject of Cali's second lesson. Bizarrely, this technique involved no movement whatsoever. Cali was highly skeptical from the get-go.

"You mean I'm just supposed to stand here and do nothing for twenty minutes?" she said.

"If you can."

"That's ridiculous."

"Technically, to be clear, you're not doing *nothing*. The act of clearing your mind and staring into empty space is doing *something*, just not something you're very used to."

"Do I detect a note of condescension?"

"Of realism maybe. The very last thing people are taught to do in this superficial culture," he continued in a lower voice, "is center themselves in silence. That would lead to asking important questions—and we can't have that."

"True. But what does hugging the tree actually *do*?"

"It builds your chi."

"Don't tell me we're back to that."

"Just so you know, we'll never leave chi very far behind. It's absolutely central to harnessing power greater than yourself."

"If you say so."

"Now begin."

Cali felt like a moron—her word—as she bent her knees slightly outward and positioned her arms awkwardly as if wrapping them around the trunk of an invisible tree.

"Make sure your gaze remains soft," said Juice.

"What does that even mean?"

"Try not to focus on anything."

"That's totally weird."

"Just do it. It'll get easier."

It did. Gradually, from a visual perspective, Cali seemed to slip underwater. As she did, her hearing became so acute she suddenly was annoyed by Olga's nasal breathing out in the vestibule. Sensing her irritation, Juice whispered:

"Now remove any 'focus' in your ears also. Let your mind step outside your head and sit like a flower in the empty space between your arms."

"I thought there was a tree there."

"Ha ha."

Convinced this exercise was pure hocus-pocus, Cali complied anyway and visualized a red rose floating within reach of her outstretched fingers. Soon, strangely, not only did her eyes and ears feel "empty"; her mind did as well.

She seemed wholly outside her skin, as if her body were merely a disposable vessel for who she truly and eternally was. Suddenly, she experienced herself once and the world twice removed. And in that exact instant, she realized *she was the rose*.

No sooner did this insight occur to her than she felt a gigantic wave of energy pulse up through the dojo's protective mat into her feet and up her legs. It quickly made its way up through her groin and abdomen into her heart, where it seemed to spin in a toroid shape for a moment before shooting up into her brain.

"Easy there, girl. I've got you. Just let yourself down nice and slow."

The next thing she knew she was blinking up into Juice's eyes, which seemed larger than usual in the oblique light.

"What happened?"

"You got blasted by chi."

She sat up. The *katanas* and other weapons on the walls slowly marched in a circle around her. "I'm a little dizzy."

"I'd be surprised if you weren't."

"Does this always happen to people learning to hug the tree?"

"Not always."

"What does it mean?"

"That you're pretty sensitive to energy, duh."

She remembered nearly passing out when Thelete was teaching her the Language of the Birds. "I suppose I am. Just call me a chi wimp."

"For the record it also means you have the ability to channel more energy than the average person as you learn to work with it."

"As opposed to working against it?"

"Exactly. The secret—as with so much else in life—is learning to get out of your own way."

Juice's observations rang so true Cali had to make a joke just to process them: "Don't you get tired of spouting wisdom all the time?"

"Yeah. Being permanently right is a terrible burden."

"Jackass."

He grinned as he stuck out a hand. "Feel like standing back up?"

"I feel like trying."

Later that afternoon, unable to discuss it candidly with Juice under surveillance, Cali reflected privately during rehearsal on the meaning of the "rose epiphany," as she phrased it. Even as she practiced her choreography still sore all over from her first karate lesson, she couldn't keep from pondering the meaning of Apollo's enigmatic name for her: "Future Rose."

The way he said it made it sound like some kind of title. As disturbing as this notion was, there was no denying that roses were the single most prominent motif in her life—starting with her mother's garden and secret note and extending into her music all the way to and from Rose Cove.

If I'm a rose, does that make Juice a thorn? she wondered with a smug expression she wished only he could see.

It was the evening of the day Cali received her yellow belt—signifying openness to learning karate's teachings like snow being melted and made porous by the sun—that news of Frédéric Batonrouge's miraculous reappearance from what was described as "kidnapping and torture in the Badlands" exploded in Fatherweb headlines.

This occurred in late November just before Fathersgiving hours before Cali's sold-out show in the Distrito del Fatherland. The news filled her with excitement even as it reawakened a sense of longing for the people and culture of Rose Cove.

She wanted to share the news with someone, anyone, but Olga was already at the Cristo Redentor overseeing stage setup and Juice was in his room on the hotel's off-limits POC level. So Cali jogged down the hall and knocked on Bradford Maddox's door.

Though she could have sworn she heard voices inside, there was no answer. She knocked again, louder this time. Still no answer. Her excitement getting the best of her, she banged on the door and called Bradford's name.

"It's me. Cali. I know you're in there. It's important."

Sounds of hurried activity were discernible inside. Finally, Bradford sheepishly opened the door looking disheveled in his bathrobe and more than a little flushed.

"Have you heard the news?"

He stared uncomprehendingly through the twin telescopes of his glasses. "To what news are you referring?"

"Frédéric Batonrouge is ..." replied Cali, stopping herself before she could say the word "back." "He's ... *alive!*"

"Freddy—I mean, Frédéric is alive? *How?!*"

"Apparently, he was kidnapped, not murdered." Cali was surprised to note a tear rolling down her tutor's porcelain cheek. "Are you okay, Bradford?"

"I just feel a little emotional. Please forgive my professional lapse."

"Do you have a personal connection to him?"

It was at this moment she became aware of a third party inside the room listening in on their conversation.

"Am I interrupting something?"

Bradford's body language seemed to indicate he was guilty—but of what Cali couldn't say.

"I was just having a little chat with a friend. Jorge, I'd like you to meet my student, Cali Crowell."

As Bradford opened the door wider, an attractive Hispanic man in his mid-twenties dressed in slacks and a white silk shirt appeared. "*Encantado*," he said, shaking Cali's hand with delicate fingers.

"Likewise."

"Jorge was just leaving. Weren't you, Jorge?"

"*Por supuesto.* See you around."

Jorge didn't skip a beat as he waltzed past Cali and down the hall into the elevator.

"Won't you come in?" said Bradford.

"I'd love to. Thanks."

She followed him into the room.

"Please, have a seat. May I get you something to drink?"

"I'll have a Sassy Sarsaparilla, if you don't mind."

"Coming right up."

Having produced two brown soda bottles from the mini-fridge, Bradford joined Cali at the bistro table beside the window overlooking the crowded Zócalo all gray and weathered in the twilight.

"So what's your relationship to Frédéric Batonrouge?" she asked.

"As fate would have it, we were college roommates."

"Is that all?"

"I don't see what you're driving at."

"Oh, I think you do. I may be young, but I'm not naïve."

He sighed and removed his glasses. Cali couldn't recall ever seeing him without them. His eyes were a beautiful velvety blue like the distant mountains around Saturnia just before sunset.

"You do realize if you tell anyone about my ... inclinations," he said, running his fingers through his blond hair, "there could be severe consequences for me. That's putting it lightly."

"My lips are sealed. Just let me ask one more question."

"My, you are persistent."

"How do you get away with it?"

"Do you mean how do I avoid being surveilled by the Old Man and thrown in jail while I engage in certain … activities?"

"*Please*. Keep your voice down."

"No need." He reached in the pocket of his robe and pulled out something resembling the head of a microphone about the size of a thimble. "This little magical device is worth a thousand times its weight in gold."

"Is that what I think it is?"

"If you thought it was a jammer, yes."

Jammers were popularly said to be elite military hardware for untraceably scrambling tracking and surveillance technologies.

"I assumed they were just an urban myth," said Cali. "Where on earth did you get it?"

"A very dear friend gave it to me."

"Let me guess: a certain college roommate. Among other things."

"Among other things."

"I want to borrow it."

"You do? Why might that be, pray tell?"

"I just need it. I promise I won't lose it. And I promise I'll give it back."

He clicked his tongue, considering. "That's asking a lot."

"I know."

"You do realize you could get in career-ending trouble if they catch you with it?"

"Yes."

"And you're sure whatever you're wanting to do is worth taking such a monumental risk?"

"Definitely."

"I never would have pegged you for a rebel."

"Back at you."

"I'm not a rebel, I'm a deviant."

"Like I care."

"You've got *cajones*, Cali. I'll give you that much." He placed the jammer in her palm. "You can have it for *one day* and one day *only*."

"A day and a half."

"You drive a hard bargain."

"Please."

"Okay. A day and a half. If you're arrested, I don't know anything about this."

"About what?"

"Very good. Now, finish your soda. You'll be late for mic check if you don't get a move on and a Miss Priss we both know will be *pissed*."

The following day was the kind Olga referred to as a "shopping lull": a full day off following a concert without any tiresome traveling or other tour-related activities. It also happened to be a Sunday, meaning Cali's only responsibilities were church at the Basilica of Our Father of Guadalupe and her karate lesson after lunch.

The latter was definitely on a strict timer, as Olga was eager to sweep Cali off to the posh shops at Polanco. Still, it was a good lesson. Juice, who'd recently begun to let his afro grow again, spent the full hour teaching Cali how to disarm and knock out an opponent.

"You do realize everything you're teaching me could come back to haunt you if you get any … ideas," she whispered when Olga, who was never very present at her lessons to begin with, seemed particularly distracted by something on her holophone.

"Now, why would I get any of those, Miss Crow-well?"

"I don't know. Maybe because you're invited to a private midnight lesson tonight?"

"Are you being *serious*?"

His surprise was so total she was—for the first time ever—legitimately able to knock him to the mat, where he lay blinking up at her. "Just be sure to bring your key," she said, straddling him, a wicked grin turning daddy's little angel into daddy's little devil.

That evening after a late dinner with Olga and Bradford in the hotel restaurant, Cali, who felt butterflies in her stomach and barely pecked at her mahi-mahi, pretended she was exhausted.

"I think I'll turn in early," she said, faking a yawn.

"I applaud your decision," commented Olga, waving her brandy snifter like an old-timey aristocrat. "You're always foolishly burning the candle at both ends. You may be a spring chicken, but even you could benefit from the beautifying power of rest."

"You do look worn out," added Bradford, sipping his vermouth and slyly winking at Cali with his head cocked facetiously. "I pray you're able to sleep the night through."

After the previous day's uncloseting of her scholastic tutor, Cali had done a quick Ogle search on him. Sure enough, he and Freddy had been roommates at Jefferson Davis University. She was shocked at how young, innocent and happy they both looked in pictures taken together from that period.

There was no way, in the highly censored interface of the Fatherweb, to determine for sure whether Bradford was also a member of the Illuminati. But given how many of the aforementioned photos were snapped by paparazzi at elite parties, Cali thought it likely.

She also felt that, at least insofar as her plans for using his jammer went, Bradford could be trusted—if only because he knew she knew information that, placed in the wrong hands, could demolish his life. With the Fatherland now committed to populating its expanding empire, few crimes were as frowned upon (publicly anyway) as homosexuality.

"Well, good night," she said.

"Good night," said Olga. "Sleep tight."

"Sweet dreams!" said Bradford with a coy expression.

Returning to her room, Cali wasted no time preparing for her illicit rendezvous. She was nervous, no doubt about it, not because she hadn't done this kind of thing before but because this time it actually *meant* something.

After showering, brushing her teeth and putting on fresh makeup, she changed into her karategi and tennis shoes. Then she carefully stashed the following items in her daypack: Bradford's jammer (hidden in a napkin in an internal pocket), a bottle of champagne (wrapped in a towel) from the mini-fridge, and a pack of condoms (in a brown paper bag) she'd purloined from Olga's stash before leaving on tour.

Laden with enough contraband to get her a ticket straight to juvie, she pulled on her long fur coat, shouldered her pack, adjusted her hair in the mirror, took a deep breath to calm herself, and headed out the door.

Owing to her high profile, it had been ages since she'd ventured out in public much by herself. With it being so late, however, she was betting on her famous face not being a problem. But that was a bet she lost.

Barely two minutes outside the hotel, she was accosted by a hysterical group of teenage boys and girls jabbering away in Spanish demanding her autograph. Annoyed but professional, she signed her signature a dozen times before saying adios and literally jogging on to avoid any further delays.

Five minutes later, approaching the dojo, she reached inside her pack and switched on Bradford's jammer. A tiny green light briefly flashed. Assuming (and praying) that meant the device was working, she soon made out Juice in his karategi and sneakers waiting bathed in streetlamp light at the front entrance, a white plastic bag suspended from his hand.

"You're late," he said.

"How do you know? I didn't see you checking your holophone."

"I didn't bring it. But you're always late."

"Fashionably, I hope. What's in the bag?"

"You'll see. Shall we?"

Cali didn't notice the dojo key in his other hand until he pointed its laser at the doorknob. There was a click. He opened the door and, ever the gentleman, allowed her to enter first, switching on the interior lights as he followed.

"Looks like we're alone," he said.

No sooner had he placed the bag and key on the vestibule table than Cali spun him around and kissed him squarely on his meaty lips.

"God, I've been waiting for months to do that," she said.

Juice didn't exactly reciprocate her passion. "Are you *crazy*?! You *do* get we're probably being filmed as well as recorded, don't you? Or *are* we?"

"Ask me if there's a jammer in my pocket or if I'm just glad to see you."

"A ... *jammer*?"

"Well, not exactly in *my* pocket. But in a pocket of my daypack."

"Where in tarnation did you get it?"

"A certain scholastic tutor loaned it to me."

"No way."

"Way."

"Where'd *he* get it?"

"I'll give you one guess."

"*Freddy*?"

"That was quick. How did you figure that out?"

"Freddy and Bradford are nice enough, but they both have a certain way of looking at me—like I'm some kind of sex object."

"Fun, isn't it?"

"Also, I knew they're both roughly the same age and attended the same school. And then Bradford all but admitted he knew Freddy that morning at the station."

"You'd make a good private detective."

"And you'd make a good spy. Can I see it?"

"Sure."

Extracting the jammer from her pack, which she gently set on the floor so as not to break the champagne bottle, she dropped it in his cupped palm.

"It's so small to be so powerful," he said, examining it briefly before handing it back.

Cali carefully replaced the jammer in her bag. "Sort of like me."

"Ha ha. How long do you have it for?"

"Tonight."

"Then let's start with a romantic dinner."

"*Start?*"

"Yeah. Start."

"Somebody's positively brimming with confidence. What do we have to eat?"

"See for yourself."

He made sure the doors were locked and all the blinds were closed while Cali, who was starting to feel hollow with hunger, hung her coat on a peg and looked inside the plastic bag. She laughed out loud when she realized Juice had brought exactly what she'd not eaten earlier: mahi-mahi with rice and salad from the hotel restaurant.

"You have a good memory," she said.

"Especially for good memories."

"We were so young."

"We still are."

"Sometimes I feel terribly old. Especially ever since Rose Cove."

"Roger that."

"Which is why I brought this," she said, raising her tone of voice while fishing the bottle of champagne out of her pack and unwrapping it.

"Where did you get that?"

"From this magical little box called a mini-fridge."

"Won't you get in trouble?"

"Don't worry. I'll say I broke it by accident while getting some water."

"We don't have mini-fridges on the POC level."

"I imagine you don't have a lot of things."

"You imagine correctly. But we do have room service."

She popped the cork and passed the bottle to Juice. "You first."

"I've never had champagne."

"I hope you like it."

He took a sip. "It's *really* fizzy. Almost burns."

"You'll get used to it. Have a little more."

He drank again.

"Better?"

He passed the bottle back. "I think I could learn to enjoy it— eventually. You hungry?"

"*Starved*," she replied before gulping down some champagne, which, having been wrapped, was still quite cold.

Handing the bottle back, she spread out the towel like a tablecloth on the dojo mat and set their places. "There, I've been a good little housewife."

"You're good at a lot of things, but I doubt you'll ever be a good housewife."

"No, but I delegate responsibility well. Shall we?"

"By all means."

If Cali had ever had tastier mahi-mahi than the room-temperature to-go version in styrofoam containers she enjoyed with Juice, she couldn't bring it to mind.

"How do you like the fish?" she asked. "Is it better than raw catfish?"

He chuckled. "Almost."

"Is this your first time?"

"Yes, assuming you're still talking about the mahi-mahi."

"I wasn't."

"Then yes also."

Two-thirds of the champagne was gone and they both seemed even more uninhibited than usual.

"I find that hard to believe."

"I've just been waiting for the right person."

"I wish I'd waited."

"I find that hard to believe."

Filled with desire that had been months, if not years, in the making, Cali found herself on all fours in front of Juice leaning in for a champagne kiss.

"There's just one problem," he said. "I don't have any protection. And I'm afraid we could make a baby right now just looking at each other."

"Don't worry, I stole some condoms from Olga."

"What's Olga doing with condoms? Aren't they illegal?"

"I guess she doesn't want any more children."

"I suppose not. Do you want children, Cali?"

"Someday. But not right now."

"Then I think you'd better get those condoms."

It occurred to Cali—after making love with Juice as the two, drenched with sweat, lay supine and entwined on the dojo mat—that even if she could find words to describe what had just transpired, they would be cheesy and unbelievable like a bad description from a Harlequin romance.

To her absolute amazement, the experience reminded her of nothing so much as the vision of the two ancient beings of light pulsating energy between them just before placing it in the Luminous Child. The term "Tantric sex" popped into her mind out of yesteryear, when she'd encountered it (without having the vaguest idea what it meant) in one of her mother's illegal books.

"I think I need a cigarette," said Juice, breathing hard for a change.

"I think you've earned one."

"I didn't do so bad for my first time."

"Honey, if that was truly your first, I'm scared to think about your second."

"Is it *always* that good?"

"It's *never* that good."

They both laughed insanely.

"Your eyes are actually darker than mine, you know," he said.

"I noticed that, too."

"Must mean I'm a little white."

"And I'm a little black."

"We're different, but we go together."

"Like a rose and a thorn?"

"Maybe."

She placed her head sideways on his slick, still-heaving chest and stared up at the perfect line of his jaw. She knew—with every fiber of her

135

being—that they were *supposed* to be together. She also knew, and just as deeply, that short of a miracle, they could *never* be together.

"You seem sad all of a sudden," he said.

"Do you have to be so damned observant all the time?"

She felt the deep resonance of more laughter in his flesh. "Look who's talking. Miss Can't-fool-me."

"I guess I am sad—a little."

"Me, too. Tell me something to take my mind off what we're both thinking."

"Well, Seth's doing better every day. Dad said he was actually learning to read and ride a bike."

"For *real?*"

"For real."

"That's *amazing*, Cali! I'm so happy for both—for all of you, to be honest."

"Thanks. It's a ... miracle."

"It's *your* miracle. Just consider for a moment that a simple song composed of vowels cured autism."

"I've considered it for many weeks now."

"Makes you wonder what other things the Language of the Birds can do."

"It does, doesn't it? Thelete said there was a birdsong that could actually deactivate people's microchips—but that I wasn't ready for it yet."

"Must be a doozy of a birdsong."

"Must be."

"I wonder what would happen if everyone suddenly woke up together and realized they'd been living in an invisible prison run by greedy psychopaths."

"I'm fairly certain it would be utter chaos."

"Probably. But then imagine how, after the dust cleared, there could be a new beginning."

"And people everywhere would get their white belts."

Juice laughed yet again. "*Now* you're speaking my language."

They fell silent. Cali realized their hearts were beating in rhythm. The sound made her drowsy. She was almost asleep when Juice said, "Tell me how your mother and father met."

"Why do you want to know?"

"No particular reason. Maybe they just seem pretty different. My old man met my mother at a barbecue in the next POC village over."

"Love at first bite?"

"Something like that."

"Well, my mother came to work in my father's medical office when one of the doctors he employed retired. He always liked to say she made the first move by submitting her résumé."

"How do you think he'd handle the news that she's still alive?"

"I seriously doubt he could cope with it. It would highlight his own 'lack of closure.' He'd go straight into denial."

"That's a river in Egypt, you know."

"So I've heard."

"I take it you don't plan to tell him?"

"How could I? He'd never believe me anyway. He'd probably just give me another psych evaluation and put me on meds."

"No need for that. I could tell him myself you're nuts."

"If one must be crazy, it's a blessing to have company."

"Ha ha. Speaking of your mother, what exactly *is* the Dream of the Goddess?"

"I'm not sure I understand it myself. My mother said it was the divine mind that gave birth to the world."

"But what does that *mean*? And are we talking about *the* Goddess here?"

"I believe so."

"Then is there such a thing as a God? Not in the Christian sense—but is there a counterpart to the Goddess?"

"Maybe. Who knows."

"Has Dr. Caliandra contacted you in the Dream of the Goddess since we returned from Rose Cove?"

"Nope. She's maintained strict radio silence."

"What's up with that?"

"You tell me."

For the past several minutes, he'd been running his fingers through her hair absentmindedly. Cali amused herself with the thought that one didn't really need a hair brush so long as one had an attentive lover.

"And this Luminous Child business," Juice continued. "I'm still trying to wrap my mind around that."

"You and me both."

"Do you think *you're* supposed to be the Luminous Child?"

"Not if I'm supposed to be the Future Rose."

"Excellent point. Could the Future Rose be the same thing as the Goddess?"

"It's possible. But then I don't see how a person can be an *actual* goddess. Maybe it's just a title—like Thelete."

"Maybe. Though Thelete didn't exactly seem like a ... regular person to me."

"No, I can't say he did to me either."

"Any more thoughts on where he comes from—where they all come from?"

"Not really. You?"

"Not really. When I ogled 'Tula' and 'Land of the Everlasting Sun,' I got bupkis. Nothing they talked about shows up *anywhere* on the Fatherweb."

"The same thing happened with me."

"It's either all been scrubbed or it was never there to begin with."

"Exactly."

Cali sat up. "Not to be a party pooper, Juice, but it's got to be getting late—or *early*. Don't you think we should go?"

"No. I think we should go again."

"You've got to be joking."

"See for yourself."

"My goodness, what a pleasant surprise! What's another hour of beauty sleep lost?"

"If you ask me, you're beautiful enough already."

"Look who's talking. If you don't mind, I think I'll just slip … onto something a little more comfortable."

Nearly a month later, though she was sad to say goodbye to Juice for the holidays, Cali was glad at the prospect of having ten days off mostly to herself before heading back out on tour. Brain-dead from constant traveling and responsibilities, she and Olga arrived home late on a Monday evening just four days before Fathermas.

Smelling home with a grateful smile, with Scarlett O'Hara barking for attention, Cali had the hovertaxi driver set her luggage inside the door and immediately went in search of Seth, who—to her surprise—was actually in his room. Her heart instantly sank at the vision of him seated on the floor in pajamas having a hard time bouncing his racquetball.

"Hi there, Seth!" she said with worry in her voice.

As soon as he saw her, dropping the blue ball, red curls bouncing left and right, he hopped up and gave her a big hug on tiptoes. That certainly never used to happen.

"How good it is to see you, Cali!"

"How good it is to see you, too! What's going on with you and that racquetball?"

"Oh, don't fret about that. I was just trying to see if I could unlearn how to bounce it."

Cali's heart lifted right back up as she couldn't stifle her laughter. "Why on earth would you want to do that?"

"Sometimes I'm afraid I'm going to lose myself again. But every morning when I open my eyes, I'm still here. Speaking of eyes, don't tell me you're going to cry again."

"Just a little maybe."

"Because you're happy?"

"Because I'm very, very happy."

139

"Then it's okay. Why don't we sit on my bed while you tell me all about your tour? Dad and I watched one of your shows live on the holovision."

She lay down sideways marveling at the loquacious, bright-eyed being masquerading as her stepbrother sitting cross-legged beside her.

"Did you enjoy it?"

"Definitely. Maybe I'll be a singer myself someday."

"Maybe you will. Did Dad like it, too?"

"It was hard to tell. You know how he is."

"You mean a little old-fashioned?"

"I guess that's the word for it."

"Who's calling the hippest dad in the world old-fashioned?" said Dr. Crowell from where he stood leaning with arms crossed in the doorway sporting a holiday sweater very much like the conservative MD he was.

It was Cali's turn to hop up and give someone a hug. "*Hippest?* I think the last time anybody used that word was a century ago."

"Try two centuries."

"Boy, you *are* old."

His laughter sounded even more jovial than she remembered, but his aftershave smelled the same as always: pepperminty and comforting.

"I missed you so much, Dad."

"I'm sure I missed you even more. You probably barely had time to think about your old man."

"You'd be surprised."

Admiring her at arm's length, he said, "You're getting more striking by the day, my angel. How I wish a certain someone you greatly resemble were here to marvel at you with me."

"Do you mean Cali's real mother?" asked Seth.

"Yes," said Dr. Crowell, who quickly changed the subject. "It's a blessing to have you home, Cali, if only for a little while."

"Believe me, I'm happy to be here."

"I really didn't mean to interrupt, but this came for you today." He produced an official-looking envelope from a front pocket of his slacks and passed it to her.

"What is it?" she asked, picking up on an odd something in his voice, before she even had time to read the return address.

"I don't know what's in it. But it's straight from the Triangular Office."

Sure enough, the sender was indicated by his full and correct name used ever since his recent accession to Head Deacon of the Realm: Frédéric Rothschild de Batonrouge.

"Do you know Head Deacon Batonrouge, Cali?"

Her only option was to lie: "No. I've never met him."

"He's very skinny," put in Seth, "but he has this super amazing robotic hand."

"If you would excuse me," said Cali, trying not to act disturbed. "I think I'll go freshen up."

"Aren't you going to open the letter?" asked her father.

"Later. It's probably just an official courtesy or an invitation to a party at the Black House."

Alone in her room, she was aware of a growing ominous feeling as she sat looking at her mother's photograph with the letter still unopened in her lap. Barely three weeks had passed since the untimely death of Freddy's brother and predecessor, Henri, whose body was found several days after he drowned in a boating accident just south of Mercuria near Capstone West.

Shortly after this national tragedy, Cali watched Freddy's inauguration live from her hotel room in San Paternia. It was hard to believe she'd met him in a prison in the Badlands barely two months previously as she listened to the other Deacons in front of the Great Pyramid of Archontia utter that history-making line: "Stonewall Jackson is dead, long live Stonewall Jackson!"

Opening the letter at last, she was amazed to find that it was handwritten in a beautifully flowing script that looked like something from the Old World:

Dear Ms. Crowell,

I trust that this note finds you well and in good spirits while you break from what is, by all accounts, a wildly successful tour of our great empire.

I've become a fervent admirer of your music, which has tremendously lifted my spirits ever since my return from being kidnapped, imprisoned and maimed by bandits, as no doubt you've learned from the news.

I plan to be in Saturnia this week on official business and would be honored, as a fan, if you would do me the honor of being my dinner guest. Would 8:00 on Thursday work? I used to enjoy Chez Pasteur. Do you have any idea if it's still good—or should we try another restaurant? Just so you know, I'm something of a connoisseur of mead.

I await your response at your earliest convenience via fathermail.

God bless the Fatherland.

Wishing you and your family a Merry Fathermas and Happy New Year!

Warmest regards,

Frédéric Batonrouge

Cali's initial response was to wonder whether Freddy was left- or right-handed. His script was slanted to the left, which gave it the appearance of having been written with his left hand. That would be his robotic hand—which was a little weird to contemplate.

There were a number of things that were "weird" where Freddy was concerned. His reckless relationship to Bradford Maddox while being groomed for a high-level political career was one. The curious timing of the death of his brother (who was responsible for his exile) so soon after his return to society was an even greater cause for concern.

Then there was Thelete's open distrust of Freddy during their dinner conversation—to say nothing of his advice to be careful in the event she ran into Freddy again.

Following a quick shower, Cali crashed hard. She hadn't felt so exhausted since Rose Cove. She prayed for deep, comatose sleep as a respite from what could only be described as increasing levels of strangeness in her life of late. Instead, strangeness revisited her in her dream.

There was a fluttering, a flapping of large wings, as she opened her eyes to find her mother seated at the foot of her bed dressed in a voluminous outfit of black feathers.

"You are looking rather depleted, my child," she said in a voice that sounded half human, half crow.

"That's definitely what I am. Where have you *been* the past two months?"

"Assiduously preparing for your arrival."

"My *arrival?*" Cali sat up as she felt the familiar, reinvigorating energy of *kundalini* travel from her mother's touch up through her feet into the rest of her body. "*Where?*"

"All in due time. The prophecy is now coming to pass with the speed of lightning in the sky. The older brother has gained control of the Shallow World and will soon come after the power of the Deep World. Soon the Bird Tribes will be without either the Rose or the Thorn."

"I don't know what that means. But you're freaking me out."

"Know the gravity of the situation, but know also that in the midst of this foretold crisis, there is an unprecedented opportunity to create a better world. Is that not what you wished for in conversation with the Future Thorn beside the ruins?"

"Future Thorn? You mean *Juice?*"

"I sense he shares your wish for a brighter future, although he remains skeptical that such a thing could ever come to pass. You can be his light through the darkness—and he can be the darkness that protects your light. Take my hand."

"Where are we going?"

"To facilitate your destiny."

Cali felt her mother's clawlike hand in hers. The next thing she knew, the two were standing showered in moonlight beside the bench in the herb and rose garden.

"It's cold," said Cali, shivering in her nightgown. "What are we doing here exactly?"

"Beneath the stone rose you will find the answer. Be safe, my precious child."

Like a somnambulist suddenly coming to her senses, still shivering, Cali opened her eyes to find herself alone next to the bench in the garden. She was wondering what her mother meant by "beneath the stone rose" when she saw it for the first time ever reflecting the moonlight at a certain angle: a lightly carved rose like a faint tattoo at the edge of the bench.

Without hesitating she grasped the flagstone lintel and pulled it upward and sideways with all her strength. It was quite heavy—but with a fresh dose of *kundalini* charging her system, she managed to slide it several inches. There, in a hollow space carved into one of the bench's legs, she found a shiny, thimble-sized object.

Clutching it in one hand, she pulled back the lintel to its original position and tried to return inside—only to find the garden door locked from within. Fortunately, the Crowells kept a spare key under a potted rosemary bush nearby.

Back in her room at last, she turned on the lights and examined the titanium jammer in her palm. How her mother acquired it was anyone's guess. But one thing Cali didn't doubt was that she was meant to use it.

After hiding the jammer in her purse, she took a moment to RSVP to Freddy that she would be happy to meet him at Chez Pasteur.

Then she texted Juice. "FYI," her note said, "I've been invited to dine with a certain former prisoner Thursday. Hoping not to be pasteurized. Circumspection is advised."

Boasting three Johnnie Cake stars, Chez Pasteur had, for a number of decades, been the premier haute cuisine establishment in Saturnia. The posh restaurant occupied the top two stories of the Junius Daniel Hotel overlooking the Great Obelisk in Pike Square.

While this area was always heavily trafficked, there seemed to be an extra buzz in the air—over and above that attributable to the holiday season—as Cali stepped out of the hovertaxi at the main entrance. With the Eye of Providence inside the capstone of the Great Pyramid undulating in red, white and blue overhead on New Glory, the flag of the Fatherland, she was momentarily blinded by paparazzi flashes.

"Miss Crowell, are the rumors that you're here to dine with Stonewall Jackson true?" asked a reporter from the Confederate News Network (CNN), one of several journalists present.

"No comment."

"Can you comment then on your upcoming role in Peter Neumann's new holofilm?" asked another reporter.

"I'll be happy to—at the appropriate time."

"Is there any truth to rumors that you are dating Mr. Neumann?"

Never had Cali been so glad to escape the press than she was when the revolving door closed behind her as she entered the calm, crystalline, pine-scented atmosphere of Chez Pasteur, which was lavishly lit and decorated for Fathermas.

Not that she wasn't used to dealing with journalists. She'd had years of practice deflecting their inane questions. It was just that she was more than a little nervous at the prospect of meeting Freddy again—especially with a highly illegal jammer stashed inside her purse.

"Good evening, Miss Crowell," said the maître d' as she approached his gold-leafed lectern. "May I?"

"Thank you."

After removing her fur coat and handing it to the vestibule attendant, he accompanied her into the elevator and escorted her as far as the doorway to a private dining room, where two members of the Elite Forces in plain clothes stood guard.

"I'm Cali Crowell. I'm here to see Deacon Jackson."

Both guards were tall, muscular, no older than forty, and all business. One had brown hair; the other was a strawberry blond.

"Do you mind?" said the latter in a pronounced Southern drawl.

"Not at all."

He politely frisked her while the other guard gave a cursory glance inside her purse. Seconds later she found herself standing beside a candlelit table with a view of the square below face to face with Freddy, who stood up as soon as he saw her.

"You look resplendent!" he said. "What a marvelous petticoat! The sequins are dazzling—and I must say copper beautifully accents your hair."

The first thing she noticed was that—in addition to having had his own hair trimmed and styled—he'd put on the right amount of weight and no longer could have passed for a scarecrow. He was snappily dressed, too, in black tails with a silver bowtie. Cali had to keep herself from starting as he took her hand in his robotic one and lightly kissed it.

"I'm honored to meet you, Your Purity. On the subject of fashion, your new hand perfectly matches your tie."

His charmingly sophisticated laughter instantly recalled her odyssey in the Badlands. "That's it: the legendary Cali Crowell humor. Please, do us both a favor and dispense with the formalities. You can call me Freddy. Shall we?"

Having helped her into her seat, he sat down across the table and asked, "What would you like to drink, Miss Crowell?"

"Please, call me Cali."

"What would you like to drink, Cali?"

"Iced tea will be fine."

"Sweetened?"

"Naturally."

His titanium fingers made a surreal ringing noise as he snapped them. A formally dressed waiter immediately appeared from a side door.

"A Negroni for me—in a chilled glass with no ice—and sweet tea for Miss Cali Crowell."

"Coming right up, Your Purity."

"I have to admit that takes some getting used to," said Freddy, grinning.

"The 'Your Purity' part?"

"Yes. I think of myself as so … impure."

"Don't we all."

"'Cali.' If I'm not mistaken, isn't that short for Caliandra?"

"Correct."

"That's with a 'C' and not a 'K,' right?"

"Right."

"Still, it's something of an exotic name. By any chance is it of Indian origin?"

"Maybe. I've never thought much about it."

"Is it true, as my sources tell me, that you were named after your mother?"

"Yes."

"And for whom was she named?"

"Her mother."

"Did you ever meet your grandmother?"

"No. My mother said she died young."

"That seems to run in both our families."

"Unfortunately. I was very sorry to learn of your brother's passing."

Though he smiled, Cali picked up on an undercurrent of sadness—or maybe regret—in his expression.

"That means a lot. It came as quite a shock."

"I'm sure it did."

"That's why they make alcohol," he said, taking his Negroni directly from the waiter after Cali was served. "Allow me to propose a toast to your health—to say nothing of your spectacular success!"

"To yours as well!"

"To my health or spectacular success?"

"Both."

His face relaxed as he took a sip. "Now, that's an exquisite beverage. If I'm not mistaken, it was invented by an Italian count who liked to dress up as a cowboy. How's your tea?"

"Sweet."

"I'd have thought you were the unsweetened type."

"I try to keep my fans guessing."

"Tea was never my … cup of tea. I've always taken consolation in the fact that, if all else fails, there's an alcoholic solution to all one's problems."

"That's it: the legendary Frédéric Batonrouge humor."

"How very droll of you."

"Speaking of, I've spent a good deal of time with an old friend of yours over the past two months."

"Really? Who might that be?"

"Bradford Maddox. He tells me you two were extremely close."

Freddy cocked his head as if sizing up Cali. "He's right. I guess you could say we were like … brothers."

"*Were?*"

"We had a falling out some years ago."

"I'm sorry to hear that. I didn't mean to pry."

The herbal smell of a steaming tray of escargot reached the table before the escargot did.

"I took the liberty of ordering an appetizer," said Freddy. "If you'd prefer something else, just say the word."

"Escargot works for me."

"Good. Me, too."

Cali ate an herb-buttered snail with a slice of fresh baguette. The taste was minerally and delicious.

"How is Bradford these days?"

"As a teacher or personally?"

"Personally."

"He seems well. A little jaded maybe."

"Happens to the best of us. It's called aging."

"He did show some emotion when he found out you were still alive."

"That's heartening."

"I saw pictures of the two of you online."

"Ah, yes. The salad days. Speaking of young love, how's young Adonis?"

Cali nearly choked on her second snail to hear him so cavalierly admit to a criminal liaison.

"I assumed the room was bugged," she whispered, leaning forward.

"Oh, it is. They all are. But we can speak freely. I have an unbugger in my pocket."

"You mean you have a jammer?"

He arched one long, thin eyebrow. "What a complicated girl you are. How do you even know about such a thing?"

"I have a good teacher."

"That explains it. I can't believe he's managed to hold on to it all this time. He can be so absentminded."

"He strikes me as fairly together."

"So how is he?"

"Who?"

"The other Fred in your life."

"Well, thanks. Though it's not as if he and I can speak freely. He's teaching me karate."

"I imagine that's not the only hand-to-hand activity the two of you have engaged in."

"Very funny. He thinks I'm almost ready for my orange belt, just so you know."

"Just be sure not to hit him below the belt. He might change his mind. Shall we have a look at the menu?"

"Sure."

"This has already been a very … athletic conversation. I'm starting to work up quite an appetite."

Halfway through the mead-accompanied main course, duck confit for Freddy and Beef Wellington for Cali, she just had to ask, "If the minds of most white people are controlled by microchips, how is it that some still have ... aberrant desires?"

"You always pose the right questions," Freddy replied with a chuckle. "Certain behaviors, though technically illegal, are ... tolerated by the controllers."

"Which would be you now."

"Which would indeed."

"So why's homosexuality tolerated?"

"It's complicated. Various types of ... alternative sexuality have held a prominent place among the Illuminati ever since anyone can remember."

"Is that a roundabout way of saying that pedophilia is required of Satan worshippers?"

"Perhaps not always *required*, but certainly strongly *encouraged*."

"Now that you're Stonewall Jackson and the Patriarch of the Batonrouges, I imagine you plan to change a few things. Isn't that true?"

Freddy paused to chew a bite of confit while considering Cali's question. "You know," he said at last, "when I was younger, as I was being groomed for the job, I couldn't wait to become Head Deacon. I was convinced I knew better than my ancestors. I told myself *I* would do things differently, my own way, and everyone would benefit."

"I'm still waiting for the punch line."

He took a sip of mead, a Polish Apis the waiter had recommended, and cleared his throat. "Let me ask you a question, Cali."

"By all means."

"How's your Beef Wellington?"

She smiled politely to hide a growing sense of annoyance with Freddy's tendency to use circumlocution. "Delicious. But what's your *real* question?"

"How much do you know about the rebels in Rose Cove?"

"I know they're not rebels."

"Touché. But what else do you know? You seemed to have a special relationship with them—particularly Thelete."

"I didn't have *any* relationship with them. Not before. I'd never even met Thelete."

"Yet they referred to you as the Future Rose. Haven't you wondered what that means?"

From the sweat bubbling in her pores, Cali realized she was beginning to feel the heat from Freddy's questioning. "Am I in some kind of trouble?"

"Not at all," he said, visibly enjoying the last bite of his confit. "You know, many modern conveniences I could do without. But with every fiber of my being, I missed real food in Sheriff Briscoe's dungeon."

Sitting back in his chair, he took another sip of mead, then gently swirled the glass with his robotic hand. "The biggest miracle in my life wasn't that I escaped; it was that in so doing, I discovered Rose Cove."

"And what did you discover there?"

"Power. *Real* power. The kind that can change the world."

Cali, who had suddenly lost her appetite, had the waiter take away her half-full plate along with Freddy's empty one.

"You haven't so much as touched your mead," he said.

"I'm not thirsty."

"Shame. But back to the subject of real power. Just imagine what the rebels' weapons could achieve in the right hands."

"I'm fairly convinced they'd tell you they *are* in the right hands."

"Do you know what those weapons are made of? Do you know what makes them so revolutionary?"

"Fallenium?"

"Yes. But do you realize what fallenium *is*?"

"Juice said it's some kind of unknown metal."

"True. But there's much, much more to the story. Fallenium doesn't just harness the power of the earth. It *is* the power of the earth."

"I'm not sure I catch your drift."

"How much do you know about the Goddess, Cali?"

For the second time in less than a week, she was forced to tell a boldfaced lie: "Nothing really. What do you know about the subject?"

"Much secret history is revealed to the Patriarch of the Batonrouges when he ascends to that position. I'm not at liberty to share most of it. Let's just say what I learned was … beyond eye-opening."

As per French custom, the salads and cheese plates arrived next. The waiter refilled Freddy's mead and Cali's tea.

"This is all very fascinating," she said, "but I assume you asked me here for a *reason?*"

"Once again you've posed the right question. I invited you to join me for dinner because I need your help."

"My help? With what exactly?"

"I'd like you to convince Thelete to sell me enough fallenium to equip the Elite Forces with rebel weaponry."

"You want *me* to convince *Thelete?* That's like asking a mouse to move a mountain. I don't even think they use money."

"I think you might have more influence over him than you know. And there are other things besides money the rebels might value: pharmaceuticals, oil, technology."

"You spent how long among them and didn't figure out they don't give a rat's ass—pardon my French—about those kinds of things?"

"It's at least worth making an offer. And I want you to ask him for me."

"Or else?"

"I'll be forced to force him."

"*You?* Force Thelete?"

"You'd be surprised how much firepower I have at my disposal."

"Seriously, why do you even want such deadly weapons? You already control half the world."

"I want to control *all* of it. I *mean* to control all of it."

There are certain pivotal moments in life when clarity replaces its opposite in the blink of an eye. Instantaneously, with Freddy's last words still ringing in her ears, Cali, as if in her own crystal-clear Dream of the Goddess, saw through him into his heart—and what she saw there was dark and twisted.

"Oh my God. You murdered your brother!"

"Excuse me?"

"Or at least you had him murdered."

"So what if I did?"

"What *happened* to you, Freddy? You were a light in the darkness to so many people. And now you're just the opposite."

His glass shattered as, in a moment of uncontrolled anger, he crushed it with his metallic fingers. Glass shards and droplets of amber mead rained down on the table and floor. The waiter approached to clean up the mess, but Freddy ordered him to be gone.

"*Reality* happened to me, Cali. After sleepwalking my whole life, I finally opened my eyes and saw how nothing will ever change on this godforsaken planet through peaceful means. Change can only occur by means of force."

"To do a little good, one must be a little evil?"

"In so many words, I suppose. It's the responsibility of the strong to govern the weak. Only then can there be lasting peace. I take it you don't grasp just how right I am?"

"*Right?* Freddy, you're so wrong you've run out of wrong."

"Where are you going?"

"Home."

"Please sit down, Cali."

"No way. I'm out of here."

"I said *sit down.*"

This definitely wasn't a request. Adrenaline pumping and dander up, Cali sat back down and glared at Freddy. It was a good thing her eyes couldn't shoot lasers. Otherwise, he would have been toast.

"I'm asking you one last time: will you help me convince Thelete?"

"Not even if I could."

He sighed, shaking his head, then said, "I was hoping it wouldn't come to this."

"Come to what?"

"This."

He reached inside his inner jacket pocket and pulled out a single playing card, which he handed to her. It was the ace of spades.

"What does it mean?" she asked.

"It means our conversation is over. You can keep it."

The dining room door opened and in came the strawberry blond guard who had frisked Cali earlier.

"Dispose of our young friend," ordered Freddy. "And give the command to do likewise with Frederick Hamilton."

"Witness consciousness," also referred to as "pure awareness," is a Hindu philosophy that focuses on the ability of humans to be *in* but not *of* the world. The concept implies an almost godlike capacity to watch one's own life as an observer and take action in the here and now from that higher perspective.

Juice had shared this information with Cali during one of her karate lessons. He called it—somewhat humorously—"watching the movie." But prior to the horrifying turn of events over dinner with Freddy, she had never experienced witness consciousness for more than a few seconds at a time.

It's a strange but well-documented fact that the most extreme events and situations can bring out the deepest parts of ourselves. The instant the blond guard grasped her by the arm, Cali felt positively immersed in pure awareness, such that there was virtually no emotion whatsoever in her voice as she asked her betrayer:

"Why are you doing this, Freddy?"

"I'm afraid, my dear, you left me no choice."

"We always have a choice. Unless, of course, we're no longer human."

"What's that supposed to mean?"

"Thelete said something interesting about you."

"He did, did he?"

"He said several interesting things. But one in particular stood out. He stressed that the Archontic infection runs very deep in your family. I had no idea what he was talking about, so I ogled 'Archon.'"

"It's merely a Greek word for 'ruler.'"

"I thought so, too, at first. But then weeks later, just the other day, I did a different search and stumbled on a handful of scholars who claimed it's also a Gnostic term for an extraterrestrial mind parasite that hates humanity and tries to destroy us by infecting certain vulnerable groups and individuals. Ring any bells?"

His eyes seemed to glow and his elongated face twisted into a nearly inhuman sneer as he replied in a noticeably altered voice, "If you think the Luminous Child is going to save the benighted people of this wretched little planet, you are sadly mistaken, Future Rose. The plan is too far advanced. The game is already approaching its endgame."

At a dismissive nod from Freddy, the guard forcibly escorted Cali away from the table and out the dining room door. Still acting from pure awareness, she managed to grab her purse and drape it over her shoulder while tossing the ace of spades in Freddy's face.

"I don't think you'll be needing your compact much longer!" he called after her as the door shut behind and she found herself being perp-walked past the other guard down the hallway to the elevator.

"Where are you taking me?" she asked as the elevator began ticking down toward the lobby.

The blond guard didn't respond. As if her vision had somehow improved in her elevated mental state, she noted a tiny, perfectly round mole just below his earpiece. She also observed the faintest of tattoos on the side of his neck: an all-seeing eye inscribed inside the capstone of a pyramid just like the one on the Fatherland's flag and atop the Great Obelisk outside.

Her body suddenly acted and the rest of her simply followed. Utilizing one of several knockout protocols Juice had shared with her, she was able to render the guard unconscious before either of them was aware anything of the sort was happening.

As he slumped to the floor, she removed his laser pistol from its holster and stashed it in her purse before activating her mother's jammer.

As soon as the elevator doors opened, she was aware of another pair of guards in plainclothes across the busy hotel lobby. Feverishly, she beat on the "close doors" and "up" buttons. But it was too late: the guards had already spotted her and were shoving their way through the crowd.

Somehow she found herself ascending again. Fortunately, the guard she'd knocked out was still out. Not knowing what else to do, she instinctively hit the "1" button. The doors opened again and she raced down the hall into another, less formal hotel restaurant connected to a terrace for outdoor dining.

"Do you have a reservation?" asked the restaurant manager as she sped past, knocking waitstaff out of her way as she spun through the revolving door to the terrace, where people sat dining under shimmering heat lamps.

"The universe definitely has a wicked sense of humor," she whispered as, gripped by vertigo, she shook off her heels and climbed up on the outer terrace wall, where she stood peering down at the lawn twenty feet below that gently sloped toward the tall white monument to the realm in the bowl of Pike Square.

With witness consciousness she was aware (without, ironically, being particularly self-conscious) that everyone was staring at her. She also noted whispers traveling among the shocked onlookers: *That's Cali Crowell ... My goodness, it's Cali Crowell ... Oh my heavens, do you see Cali Crowell over there about to jump*?!

For that was—with armed guards racing through the restaurant toward her—her only option: jumping. Heart thumping against her chest, she recalled her first terrifying trestle crossing and falling like a stone only to shatter her ankle in the Badlands.

Maybe because she still lacked closure where her mother was concerned, her fear of heights had never completely gone away. But something else even more powerful had grown up inside her to counterbalance it: her love for Juice.

She knew if she didn't find a way to escape, not only would she never see him again; he was also as good as dead. She couldn't live with that—even in the afterlife.

"Third time's a charm," she said as she pushed off the wall and, sequined petticoat flying up like feathered wings, sailed down, down and down onto the lawn, where she instinctively used her aikido training to roll and pop back up on her feet. Aside from some unfortunate grass stains that would probably never come clean, she was completely unharmed.

With a glance up at the stone-faced guards staring down at her from the terrace, she hiked up her skirt and sprinted to Pike Square, where she climbed in the back seat of the first hovertaxi she saw. "Head towards Nubia," she said, breathing hard.

The driver was a sixtysomething, mustachioed man who revealed the hint of a Northern accent when he asked, "Do you mean POCV #888, Miss ... Crowell?"

"No. I mean Nubia. What are you waiting for?"

Her tone of voice clearly indicated her irritation. So much for her extended experience of witness consciousness.

She felt relatively confident her mother's jammer could cloak the movements of the hovertaxi, but she wasn't so sure it could scramble communications at a distance. So her quick text to Juice was written so that only he could decipher it:

"Dinner went south. Murder in the air. Meet me ASAP where we first discussed mahi-mahi."

With the tall buildings and bright holoboards of Saturnia receding in the distance, she thought about the last time she made this trip on the way to Rose Cove. If she had reason to fear she might not be returning to her family then, she could be virtually certain there was no returning now.

A famous Southern author, who actually hailed from Saturnia before its renaming after the Second American Civil War, had said it best: "You can't go home again."

"Goddamn it," she said, tears of anger suddenly rolling down her cheeks at the thought of never seeing Seth or her father again. "Goddamn the Batonrouges and everybody like them straight to hell!"

"Did you say something, Miss Crowell?"

"No, I was just thinking out loud."

"I noticed you weren't wearing a coat. Would you like me to turn up the heat?"

"No thanks. It's already been turned up."

"Come again?"

"Nothing."

"Where are we going exactly?"

"I'll let you know when we get there."

She knew better than to go straight to the old fishing pier, so she told the driver to stop a few hundred yards away.

"You want me to let you out here? After dark in the Hinterlands in winter without a coat? Pardon me, but that's crazy."

"Then I'm crazy. How much do I owe you?"

"Eighteen cryptocoins."

Cali tried to pay using her holophone, but the payment didn't go through. She tried again. This time her screen flashed a message: ACCOUNT SUSPENDED.

"Great. Just *great*."

"What's the problem?"

She removed her ruby earrings and handed them to the driver. "Take these instead. Your fare's a drop in the bucket in comparison. There's a mistake with my account."

The driver switched on the overhead light and examined the earrings. "How do I know these aren't fake?"

"Uh, because I'm Cali Crowell. And if you don't accept them," she said, taking the laser pistol out of her purse and pointing it at his head, "or if you breathe a word you ever saw me tonight to anyone, the next time I see you you won't be so lucky. Understood?"

"Understood. I hear you loud and clear."

She opened the door and climbed out. "Get the hell out of here before I change my mind. It's been a really shitty day."

The driver took off like a scared rabbit with the door still open, leaving Cali alone, cold and shoeless beside the dark gravel road.

A bystander able to see at night would have been intrigued to observe such a beautiful young girl in evening dress barefooting it bare-shouldered through the Hinterlands with a pistol in one hand and a look that could have shot bullets squinching her face, which kept uttering unladylike curses every time she stepped on a pointed rock.

She could hear the river mumbling along beside her even though she couldn't see it. Before long she arrived at the turnoff to the fishing pier. As she neared the old pine where Juice had stashed his motorbike and their belongings, a shadowy figure did indeed approach from behind the tree. But whoever it was, judging by the fact that he was well under six feet, it wasn't Juice.

"I don't know who you are, but I've got a gun and I'm not afraid to use it!"

"I'm happy to see you've come prepared, Miss Crowell," said what struck Cali as the voice of a well-educated, middle-aged black man. "Because, whether you like it or not, we're at war."

"Who *are* you?"

The figure stepped forward and turned on a flashtorch to a low ambient setting. The dim light was enough to reveal a somewhat older version of a weathered, penetrating face Cali had seen in history books ever since she could remember.

"My name is Earnest Jacob Hamilton. But you can call me Aristotle."

It's difficult to overstate Aristotle's legendary reputation. To those in the Fatherland, he might as well have been the devil himself. Cali, fortunately, knew better. Still, it was unsettling to find herself suddenly face to face alone in the dark with a former Public Enemy #1.

"Where's Juice?" she asked.

"In a safe place. Unlike yourself. Get down!"

Switching off the flashtorch, Aristotle literally pulled her down alongside himself on the cool, muddy earth as two Elite hovercruisers sped past, blue lights whirling, on the way to Nubia.

"How did you get here?" he whispered. "I assume they shut down your cryptaccount."

"I bartered."

"Juice said you were resourceful." He stood back up and, after straightening his dark leather jacket, extended a hand. "If I'm not careful, I might even start to like you. And I don't like a lot of people."

Having let herself be helped up, Cali brushed off her petticoat, which was getting more unsalvageable by the hour. "Thanks. I don't like a lot of people either. You've got a ways to go yet yourself."

His penetrating laughter, if little else about him, reminded her of Juice. "Follow me," he said.

"Where are we going?"

"Downriver."

As they approached the old pier, she was able to make out a ramshackle barge docked at the far end. A very tall, very skinny POC and a much shorter, fatter one—both with laser rifles and night vision goggles—were standing guard on deck. Aristotle helped her onboard and opened the door to the cabin.

"Ladies first," he said before following her inside, shutting the door behind, and switching on the overhead light.

"Spartan" was the word that immediately came to mind. Two tiny windows with blinds, two small beds, a bistro table, a kitchenette, a miniscule bathroom that doubled as a shower—that was it.

"Do you live here?" she asked.

"Sometimes. When I'm not living somewhere else. Please, have a seat."

With the events of the past hour starting to catch up to her, Cali, shivering, plopped down at the table.

"Here," said Aristotle as he draped his weathered coat—smelling of an exotic life on the run in the Hinterlands and maybe beyond—over her shoulders. "I'll make us some tea. Do you like chamomile? It might help you relax."

"Are you implying I look stressed out?"

"Sweetheart, you're way past that."

"I'll have chamomile tea then. Make it a double."

"Coming right up."

As he heated the water and prepared the mugs, she shut her eyes and tried to center herself. The fact that the life she'd known was irredeemably lost was sinking in ever deeper. With this horrible new reality ricocheting around her brain, she realized the barge was moving.

"I assume you know we'll get in trouble if they catch us traveling after curfew," she said.

He laughed again, this time with less humor. "And I assume you know we'll get a lot more than just a slap on the wrist if they catch either of us. But don't worry. We're moving slowly so as not to attract attention. Still, you'd better turn off the jammer I imagine you have in your purse."

"How did you know about that?"

"Its signal's interfering with my much newer and more powerful jammer." He motioned to a small metallic cone on the table with an erratically pulsing green light at the base. She'd thought it was some kind of novelty saltshaker.

Reaching inside her purse, she had to remove her laser pistol in order to switch off her mother's jammer. Instantly, the green light at the base of Aristotle's jammer began to glow steadily. She replaced the pistol.

"You know how to use that thing?"

"You point and shoot?"

"There's the small matter of the safety."

"In case you haven't noticed, I've totally run out of that."

"Fair enough."

He set two steaming mugs on the table and sat down facing his guest. For the first time, she noticed a faint but wide scar that ran from his left temple down to his ear.

"What happened there?" she asked, indicating the old wound.

"I got cut," he replied as he adjusted the neck of his black wool turtleneck.

"When?"

"When I was inside."

"I'm sorry to hear that. If you don't mind my asking, how did you escape?"

He smiled enigmatically. "Careful planning combined with a good bit of know-how and a dash of luck."

"Juice says you're a genius."

"Juice isn't so dumb himself."

"I gathered that."

"I'm not going to lie to you, Cali: I *love* that kid."

"That makes two of us."

"That may be. But putting a bounty on his head is a funny way of showing it."

Being a spitfire by nature, Cali was on the verge of defending herself—when she realized Aristotle was right. Instead of heated words, tears came pouring out.

"I have this magic talent," she said, helpless to stop the bursting of the dam that had been holding back her emotions. "I've always had it."

"What kind of magic talent?"

"Everything I care about eventually turns to shit."

"There, there, it will be all right."

"No, it won't. I've made *sure* it won't. Will you ever forgive me?"

"I just did. Now I think the next person who needs to forgive you is yourself."

This simple kindness, coming from such a hardened man, made Cali cry even harder. Suddenly, she was standing with Aristotle sobbing uncontrollably in his arms.

"Look at this way," he whispered. "The two of you could never be together here—not until things change anyway. Maybe you can have something resembling a life together among the rebels."

Regrouping, Cali wiped her eyes and sat back down. "Juice told you about our trip to Rose Cove?"

Aristotle joined her again at the table. As if finally on the same wavelength, the two both took a sip of tea at the same time. The taste was soothing—and, whether owing to the tea or not, she did start to feel calmer.

"He asked for my help in getting the two of you back there," explained Aristotle. "I told him I'd do what I could—but he had to come clean."

"What do you know about the rebels?"

"I know I should be willing to consider any enemy of my enemy my friend."

"What else do you know?"

"I know they've helped my people before. Long ago they were involved in something called the Underground Railroad."

"I've heard about that."

"But I bet you didn't hear that a lot of the slaves they helped escape never made it to the North."

"What happened to them?"

"Some say they ended up in Tula."

"The home of the Bird Tribes?"

"Yes."

"Where *is* Tula exactly?"

"You wouldn't believe me if I told you."

"Try me."

He gave her a long look as if once more sizing her up, then said, "Legend has it that Tula is a highly advanced human civilization inside the earth."

"*Legend?*"

"I'm a scientist. I haven't seen it with my own eyes. But I believe it may exist. Certainly, as Juice confirmed, the technology used by the rebels isn't from what they call the Shallow World. So unless it comes from outer space or another dimension, it must be from their Deep World."

"Have you ever studied fallenium?"

"No. I've never even seen it. But I'd sure love to."

"So would Stonewall Jackson."

"I bet he would, the traitorous son of a bitch. Is that what all this is about?"

"More or less."

"That explains it."

"Explains what?"

"Why, according to my sources, the rebels have suddenly pulled out of every location they've occupied in the Badlands—except one."

"Rose Cove?"

"Precisely. They must know the Fatherland is coming for their fallenium."

"Then why are they still in Rose Cove?"

"Isn't it obvious? They're waiting for you."

An hour or so later, Cali felt the riverboat slow down just before it docked at what turned out to be another pier on the far bank. With a lone dog barking mournfully in the distance, Aristotle and his armed guards escorted her through the curfew darkness of a POC village she'd never visited before into an abandoned (apparently anyway) warehouse.

As soon as the heavy doors closed and locked behind, another pair of guards with laser rifles also strapped to their backs approached from the shadows. Together, the four soldiers slid a rust-eaten tractor to one side of the warehouse floor—at which point Aristotle produced a remote control device from his pocket and pushed a button that caused a high-pitched *beep-beep-beep.*

That wasn't the only thing the device caused. To Cali's amazement a large hole suddenly opened in the cement floor, revealing a set of wooden stairs leading down.

"After you," said Aristotle, who motioned for the guards to stay put.

Cali was glad to still have on his leather jacket because the air belowground was cool and damp. She wasn't sure what she expected to find down there—but it wasn't Juice in his buckskins from Rose Cove with a tiny POC woman in denim overalls and a yellow bandana that turned out to be his mother seated at a well-lit table surrounded by shelves and shelves of military-grade weaponry.

"Thank God you're safe!" said Juice, nearly knocking over his chair as he jumped up and took her in his arms.

"God didn't have anything to do with it," commented Aristotle dryly.

"Are you okay?" asked Juice.

"Other than having narrowly avoided being assassinated and barely survived jumping off a rooftop, yeah, I'm okay."

165

He kissed her long and hard before becoming self-conscious. Stepping back, he introduced Weezy, who had stood up as well. "You remember my mother, don't you?"

As Cali gave the petite matriarch of the Hamilton clan a hug, Weezy's peppery scent reminded her of yesteryear when she used to accompany her own mother on rounds through the Hinterlands.

"Of course. How could I forget that angelic face—to say nothing of her heavenly food?"

"I don't know about all that. But since you mentioned it," said Weezy, motioning to a basket on the table, "I made sure to bring a batch of turkey drumsticks for you and my growing boy here."

"I'm afraid if he grows much more, he's going to need new buckskins."

"Ain't that the truth! He's already two inches taller than his daddy was. Speaking of ghosts, was Juice pulling my leg when he told me Dr. Caliandra's still alive?"

"I realize it's weird, but it's true."

"But you haven't seen her with your own eyes?"

"No, only in my dreams."

"I see Amos in my dreams, too, but he's long gone from this world. How lucky you must feel to be about to meet her again!"

"Nobody's going to meet anybody if we don't get this show on the road," interrupted Aristotle, checking his holophone. "My sources are saying that the Elite Forces are amassing near the trestle over the Nolihana. They're gearing up to attack Rose Cove."

"Holy shit," said Cali. "How much time do we have?"

"There's no way of knowing for sure. But it's a safe bet you don't have long. It looks like they're bringing in a full armored division with air support."

At the mention of warlike behavior, Cali took a moment to take in her surroundings. "What's your role in all this, Aristotle? I feel like I just stepped into the Pentagram."

"Can you keep a secret?"

"I think we're way past having to worry about the skeletons in each other's closets. We've got enough to hang each other a dozen times already."

"Can't say as I disagree. I'm the leader of the new Freedom Fliers."

"I thought the Freedom Fliers were *pacifists*."

"We tried that. It didn't work."

"You do realize there's no way you could ever defeat the Fatherland in an open war?"

"Then we'll just have to beat them in a guerilla one."

"That won't be easy. The Elite Forces are ruthless."

"You *think*? I lost my brother to those monsters."

"And they're completely mind-controlled by the Illuminati, who are apparently mind-controlled by an ET race known as the Archons."

"Say that last part again," said Juice with widening eyes.

"Freddy and his circle are themselves brainwashed by Archons."

"When did you figure this out?"

"Just this evening. Freddy's pupils actually glowed and his voice sounded like something not altogether human when I brought up this subject. He called me the Future Rose and said that no Luminous Child was coming to save us from their endgame."

"World domination?"

"Exactly."

"Damn."

"It all makes perfect sense to me," said Weezy. "I read similar things in the tea leaves years ago."

"As a scientist I don't know what to make of this talk of Archons and tea leaves," said Aristotle. "But I'll buy the mind control part, which, as Juice mentioned, would be easy to bring about through nanotech. As far as I'm concerned, that means there's even more reason to cut the head off the snake. I'm working on new strategies for disabling their grid, including the Old Man. That should tilt the battlefield a little in our favor."

"Are you a member of the Freedom Fliers, Juice?" asked Cali.

"Not officially. But I'm sympathetic to their cause—and getting more so by the hour."

"That makes two of us. But even if the grid goes down, you—*we*—need allies. And not just anybody or only a few."

"What about your mother?" asked Weezy. "Based on what Juice told me, I'd say she's some sort of priestess. Which means she probably has a lot of pull with the rebels."

"That remains to be seen. But if there's anything I can do to rally more support for your cause, I'll do it."

"My vote would be to bring this Thelete on board," said Aristotle. "I think there's more to him than meets the eye."

"I think there's more to young Miss Crowell here than meets the eye," said Weezy, reaching up and touching Cali's face maternally with weathered fingertips.

"Are you coming with us, Weezy?" asked Cali.

"No, honey. My fight's here. I'm staying till it's over, one way or another."

"But won't you miss Juice?"

Weezy's wisdom-filled eyes glistened. "With all my heart and soul. But there's a new Underground Railroad now. And it was meant for the two of you."

"What am I supposed to *wear* to Rose Cove?" asked an overwhelmed Cali. "I don't even have *shoes*. And how on earth are we supposed to *get* there?"

"We've got everything covered," said Juice, handing her a pile of clothes that included a pair of jeans, a T-shirt, a sweatshirt, socks, and tennis shoes. "Start by losing the petticoat and putting these on."

"But I *love* this petticoat. I bought it at Southern Charm in Jupiteria."

Juice's grin belied the severity of his response: "Much must be sacrificed in times of war."

"I'll keep it for you," said Weezy, "in the event we meet again."

"So glad that's settled," said Aristotle. "Now take your time and *hurry*."

Wondering where Juice had procured the clothes, which were pretty rough around the edges but at least smelled clean, Cali changed into them behind a shelf of what she imagined were antiaircraft weapons.

The clothes barely fit. The pants were too tight. The sweatshirt was so long it might have been a maternity dress. The socks were pilly. And the tennis shoes were … hideous.

"I look like a clown in a funhouse mirror," said Cali, reappearing.

"You look like a POC," said Juice.

"You look just fine," said Weezy as she handed Juice her basket. "Don't forget my turkey drumsticks."

"What's going to happen to you, Weezy?" asked Cali. "Surely, you're not going back home with the Elite Forces looking for your son?"

"She's in my care now," said Aristotle as he helped Cali back into his jacket. "Take this as a gift, not a loan. It'll be chilly traveling at speed."

"Thanks. What do you mean—traveling at speed?"

"Time to get you two on *Pegasus* and out of here."

"*Pegasus*?"

"You'll see," said Juice.

"Don't forget your purse," said Aristotle. "You're going to need that jammer."

"You got your hands on *another* jammer?" asked Juice.

"It's a long story."

"She's nothing if not crafty," said Aristotle as he led the group back upstairs onto the warehouse floor, where the other four Freedom Fliers were waiting.

The two guards from the boat exited the building first to make sure the coast was clear. On their signal Aristotle directed Cali, Juice and Weezy outside and along a dark wooded path downriver several hundred yards.

The same village dog that had been barking when Cali arrived started up again plaintively in the distance. The whole world seemed in a mournful mood. Not even so much as a sliver of moonlight brightened the night.

Rounding a bend in the river, they came upon two more gun-toting Freedom Fliers flanking an unprecedented sight.

Her eyes having adjusted to the darkness, Cali was able to make out a large motorbike-like vehicle with no wheels armed with front and rear laser rifles. At the end of a day chock-full of surprises, she wasn't even surprised to be surprised yet again.

"I take it that's *Pegasus*," she said.

"Which I guess makes me Perseus," joked Juice.

"That's fine with me—so long as I don't get stuck playing Medusa."

"Amos would have been so proud hearing you two go on all educated like that," said Weezy. "He was a real scholar himself."

"You know how to fly this thing, Juice?" asked Cali.

"I've been teaching him," said Aristotle. "He's a natural."

"Yeah, well, Captain Buckskin here nearly got us killed on his toy motorbike, so pardon me for wondering how he plans to handle this beast."

"I'd have thought by now you would have learned to trust me."

"I do. I'm just saying."

"Give me your jammer," said Aristotle.

Cali got the jammer out and handed it over. Switching it on, he waited for the green light to flash, then inserted it into a slot in the side of the vehicle.

"*Pegasus* will amplify the signal," he said. "That should be enough to scramble radar and any other types of tracking. But that won't matter if they catch sight of you. Thus the laser rifles. And make sure you activate the self-destruct sequence, Juice."

"*Self-destruct sequence?*" asked Cali with a sharply raised eyebrow.

"I don't want those bastards getting their hands on my prototype. I put tech in her they don't even know about."

"I see."

"Come here, boy." Though he only came up to his nephew's collarbone, Aristotle didn't let this stop him from giving Juice a manly hug nearly strong enough to knock Weezy's basket to the ground. "Neither of us knew it at the time, but you've been training for this moment ever since you were tiny. Time to show those Elite Forces they're not so elite."

"I'll do my best."

"I know you will. And be sure to protect our girl here. She's a keeper."

Cali felt emotional suddenly intuiting that Juice was having trouble holding back his own tears as he said, "I never thanked you for being like a father to me."

And she felt even more choked up grasping that Aristotle was also overcome as he replied, "I never thanked you for being like a son to me."

"And here I was thinking we were in a hurry," said Weezy.

"Right you are," replied Aristotle, taking the basket from Juice and stashing it in a small rear trunk. "Your purse should probably go in here as well, Cali."

She placed it beside the basket. He shut the lid and, turning to face her, gripped her shoulders.

"May the Luminous Child awaken in you," he said.

"You're the *last* person in the world I'd have expected to hear say that."

"I've heard that's what the rebels say. I don't even know what it means."

"If nothing else," said Weezy, "I'd wager it means, *Become great.*"

"I like that," said Cali. "May the Luminous Child awaken in all of us then."

"Amen."

Weezy kissed Cali's forehead, then her son's, then stood back alongside Aristotle as Juice mounted *Pegasus* and patted the seat behind him. Cali was struck by a frightening sense of déjà vu.

"*Again?*" she said.

"Third time's a charm."

Shaking her head in acknowledgment of the inevitable, she climbed on and gripped Juice's powerful midsection. He inserted a keycard into a slot in the front panel and immediately she felt *Pegasus* come alive beneath her.

"Put these on," said Aristotle, handing the travelers each a pair of night vision goggles. "Ride low and dark along river level like we talked about, Juice. Don't worry about levitrains unless you're sure you've been spotted. Then you'll need to go vertical to get out of range of their artillery."

"Roger that."

"And don't forget about the netting. If possible I'd use that before firing a shot. They'll never see it coming."

"You really think it'll work?"

"I'm certain of it. They say there's no such thing as a magic bullet, but try telling that to a werewolf."

"I'll keep that in mind."

"Now fly like the wind!"

"Godspeed!" said Weezy.

"Hold on tight, Cali!" yelled Juice, pulling on the throttle.

She'd flown in various capacities, but never had she experienced anything like *Pegasus*. With her goggles strapped on, she watched in amazement as the trees along the riverbank spun past with dizzying speed.

She had the bizarre impression the trees were melting into their own shadows as she warped deeper into the night. Throughout her life she'd felt like a stranger in a strange land. What a twist of fate that now—assuming she survived the trip—she was about to become a total stranger in an even stranger land.

29

"What do you think?" yelled Juice into the loud air envelope around *Pegasus*.

"About what?" she shouted back.

"Everything, I guess."

"I think it's all batshit crazy."

"I'm just glad we're together."

"Let's hope we stay that way. It would be nice to live through the night."

"Roger that."

Cali's thoughts were like her hair when she let it down after a karate lesson or concert: all over the place. Speaking of, with the powerful wind resistance generated by so much speed, she was glad her hair was still up—mostly anyway.

"Do you ever have the sense you're living someone else's life?" she yelled.

"Sort of. I feel really old sometimes."

"Me, too."

"It's almost like we've known each other before."

"Weird, isn't it?"

"Definitely. Just consider the fact that I never actually started loving you."

"Would you please repeat that?"

"What I mean is I *already* loved you."

"Now you're just sweet-talking."

"You know I'm being serious."

"And you know I'm joking because you're being serious. For what it's worth, I already loved you, too."

With these words, like the trees being absorbed by the darkness at speed, she felt herself dissolving into the warmth of Juice's athletic back. Especially wrapped in buckskins, he smelled like some kind of exotic animal, a mythological creature both stronger and more cunning than a human being.

Just then, at the periphery of her goggled vision, she caught sight of a great horned owl sailing along beside *Pegasus* just above the river's surface. Increasing its speed, it landed high in a willow as Cali and Juice sped past.

"*Hoo-h'HOO-hoo-hoo!*" it called after them.

"Did you see that owl?" asked Cali.

"No, but I heard it. *You still up? Me, too.*"

"Funny, it did sort of sound like that."

"The question is, *Up for what?*"

Noting the rakish tone in his voice, she elbowed him in the ribs. "I believe what I read in *Holopolitan* about men and sexual ideation must be true."

"What did you read?"

"You think about sex every eight minutes."

"That's not been my experience. It's more like every three."

"Ha ha."

"You're not exactly frigid yourself."

"No, that would be Olga."

"Good one!"

"On the subject of family, Juice, I can't tell you how sorry I am you have to leave yours. This is all my fault."

"This is nobody's fault, Cali. This is the way the world is. And I'm sorry about your family, too."

"Thanks. The situation really sucks. For both of us."

"Yeah, royally."

As they approached the confluence of the Lynchfield and Nolihana, he dropped their pace to little more than a hover while surveying their surroundings. The levitrain tracks that flanked the Nolihana were ominously empty.

"Why's everything so quiet?" whispered Cali.

"It must mean the transport phase of the assault is over."

"Which means they're getting ready to attack!"

"That would be my guess."

"You know what you have to do then."

"I do. Hold on tight!"

The g-force from Juice's sudden acceleration was staggering. Banking downstream onto the Nolihana, *Pegasus* pierced the night like an arrow of silver light. Part of Cali was absolutely terrified; another part was positively electrified.

"Damn, you're good!" she yelled.

"Not good enough."

"Why do you say that?"

"We've got incoming!"

Craning her neck as goose bumps tightened her skin, Cali glanced behind. Sure enough, a single-operator hovercraft known as an Elite Forces Stinger was gaining on them.

"Shoot it!" she yelled.

"Not yet."

Instead of firing the rear laser rifle, Juice actually slowed down and began banking back and forth defensively as the Stinger opened fire. Laser blasts sailed past left and right way too close for comfort.

"NOW!" Cali screamed.

The Stinger was less than fifty yards away when Juice finally activated a button on the handlebar, causing a projectile of some kind to be shot from underneath *Pegasus*.

Still craning her neck, Cali watched in amazement as the projectile unfolded into a metallic net that wrapped around the attacking hovercraft. Sparks flew everywhere as the Stinger nosedived with a titanic splash into the river.

"That was impressive, Juice!"

"I know. I impressed myself."

"Won't the driver alert his unit?"

"With Aristotle's nanotech netting taking out his comm, he won't be alerting anybody—even if he survives."

"Have you ever killed anybody?"

"No. But I'm not opposed to the idea to protect what I love."

"So you're not your father's son?"

"Not anymore, I suppose. I'm my uncle's son now."

For the next hour or so, zipping downriver, the two stayed watchful and kept to their own thoughts. Mile after mile disappeared behind them—and still there were no signs of life on the levitrain tracks. Nevertheless, the night seemed to harbor a concealed menace.

Cali compared the feeling of approaching danger to the culminating scene out of the newly delivered script for *The Path of Purity*, a movie she'd never have the chance to star in now. Which was too bad because the script was actually pretty good.

In the aforementioned scene, her character, Emma Kate Branch, a young Southern housewife during the first American Civil War forced to defend her plantation after the death of her husband at the hands of Northern insurgents, was trapped inside her attic as would-be assassins slowly searched the house from bottom to top.

It was only a matter of time before they'd find her and try to string her up. And then her kung fu training with a Chinese immigrant named Bruce Li would be put to the ultimate test. The suspense of knowing that danger was on its way was psychologically more troubling than just going ahead and confronting the inevitable.

"You're awfully quiet," said Juice, slowing down *Pegasus* once again.

"So are you."

"What were you thinking?"

"I was wondering why you're slowing down."

"We're not far from the trestle."

"I must have been feeling it."

"Feeling what?"

"That."

She pointed. Sure enough, high above the river just barely within sight, the trestle was crawling with military activity. A number of cargo levitrains, themselves armed with heavy artillery on top, were inching forward toward the path that led to Rose Cove.

Juice pulled onto the riverbank and shut off the engine. Ears still ringing from the sound of racing wind, it took a moment for Cali to appreciate the silence.

"What do we do now?" she asked, squeezing his midsection and resting her cheek against his shoulder.

"Wait for the coast to be clear and eat turkey drumsticks."

"And then?"

"Hope we don't get shot out of the sky by our enemies—or our friends."

D awn was just beginning to watercolor the sky with wavy plumes of silver and magenta by the time the last of the cargo levitrains disappeared down the tracks past the trestle.

"Here goes nothing," said Juice as he reached up to restart *Pegasus*.

"Wait!" replied Cali. "Kiss me first. We might not get the chance again."

"Then let me make it a memorable kiss."

Stepping down off the vehicle, he lifted her in his massive arms and set her delicately on the riverbank. But instead of kissing her immediately, he knelt, picked a single wild daisy he'd spotted in the growing light, and handed it to her.

"People don't usually think about it, but there are all kinds of flowers that bloom in fall. Aristotle taught me that."

She raised the daisy to her nose and sniffed its hint of sweetness. "Aristotle doesn't strike me as the flower type."

"He's not. He's a philosopher. Living how he's lived for so long, he's had a lot of time to think. He said that even in the most inhospitable conditions, including right on the edge of winter, there are always flowers to be found: Queen Anne's lace, goldenrod, crowfoot, milkweed, white asters."

"The point being?"

"No specific point. It's more like a Zen meditation on the persistence of life, beauty and hope even in the worst of times."

"And love?"

"Definitely."

If Juice had ever kissed her with such depth of emotion, Cali couldn't recall it. There on the riverbank with daylight shimmering all around, time seemed to stop—or maybe even go backward toward some primordial moment where *only* life, beauty, hope … and love existed.

"Do you believe in reincarnation, Juice?"

"Do you?"

"I'm starting to."

"Me, too."

Tossing the daisy in the river, she watched the current spin and carry it away, then said, "So if we die together …

"… maybe we'll be reborn together."

"It's a comforting thought anyway."

"It is. You ready?"

"Sure. What the hell."

Seconds later they were on the move again as *Pegasus* glided in almost complete silence downriver through upcurling mist. Nearly in the same instant, both Cali and Juice became aware that the coast was no longer clear. Not only was the trestle guarded by a pair of Stingers; a third Stinger was slowly making its way toward them from behind.

"Do you think we've been spotted?" asked Cali.

"It's a fair assumption."

"Then step on it!"

"Will do. *Ganbatte*!"

"Sounds like Japanese. What does it mean?"

"Break a leg! I hope you like roller coasters!"

Applying what felt like rocket boosters, he steered *Pegasus* vertically up out of the river gorge. Almost simultaneously, the three Stingers zeroed in on them as the chase traveled at insane speeds up over the mountainside in the direction of Rose Cove.

Despite her fear of heights, Cali experienced a brief recurrence of pure awareness as she marveled at the loveliness of the trees carpeting the contoured landscape below. Even with most of their leaves having fallen or been muted, they were so indescribably beautiful—and, when she concentrated on them, so utterly individualized.

That was just before the three Stingers, triangulating on their target, opened fire and Juice spun *Pegasus* like a drill bit at a dizzying upward angle.

"I hope I don't throw up!" yelled Cali.

"If you do, mind the buckskins!"

"Three against one. The odds aren't exactly in our favor."

"They never were. Hold on!"

Laser blasts showered like welding sparks all around as *Pegasus* suddenly dropped like a stone down to nearly the level of the treetops. The three Stingers seemed momentarily bewildered as if their enemy had vanished into thin air.

"That was a neat trick," said Cali.

"Not neat enough. Here they come again."

"What do we do now?"

"Pray for a miracle."

"Okay, I'm praying."

"Pray harder."

"Don't interrupt me."

The Stingers quickly surrounded and converged on them preparing to finish the job with another volley. Thus singularly focused, they were caught off guard by what happened next. So were Juice and Cali.

Without warning a giant black cloud moving with tremendous velocity appeared from behind the nearest mountaintop. With his keen eyesight, Juice was the first to recognize what the cloud actually was.

"Crows!" he yelled. "Gajillions of them!"

"My mother!" gasped Cali with eyes like coasters. "My mother must have sent them!"

Within seconds the cloud overtook the nearest Stinger, which was driven down by the collective power of the birds into the mountainside, where it exploded in prismatic flames. Juice craned his neck and stared at Cali in disbelief.

She shrugged. "You said pray for a miracle."

"Well, keep praying because we're not out of the woods yet."

"Pun intended?"

"You still have to ask?"

"You do realize a flock of crows is called a *murder*, don't you?"

"Yeah, it would seem your mother has a wicked sense of humor. Much like her daughter."

With the other two Stingers once again approaching fast, Juice aimed *Pegasus* into the empty spot where the third Stinger had been—at which point the murder, reconstituting itself, closed ranks. The two Stingers were forced far left and right, giving *Pegasus* a chance to create some distance.

Not enough, though. Before long the Stingers were hot on their tail again as the chase hurtled toward Rose Cove.

"Incoming!" yelled Cali.

"Roger that."

Juice opened fire with his rear rifle even as the two enemy craft recommenced their bombardment. A laser blast struck the back of *Pegasus*, which started giving off smoke.

"That doesn't look good, Juice!"

"I'd say it actually looks pretty bad."

"You're slowing down."

"I can't help it!"

"Is that another murder of crows up ahead?"

"I don't think so. I think that's a real cloud."

"In a clear blue sky?"

In a last-ditch effort to shake the Stingers, Juice steered *Pegasus* vertically again, then banked sideways. They were nearing the dark cloud hovering over Rose Cove when incandescent spider webs of lightning began to flash all around.

Only then did they see what was creating the anomalous weather. Standing in a bald spot on the mountaintop above Rose Cove, just barely visible in the distance, Apollo was holding his tomahawk overhead with both hands. Beside him, stoic, inscrutable and shirtless as always, Thelete calmly watched the scene unfold.

"Do you think they know it's us?" asked Juice.

"If my mother knows, they know."

"Good point."

Just then *Pegasus* went eerily quiet.

"What's happening?!" yelled Cali.

"The engine's down."

"Can't you get it back up?"

"I'm trying. I'm afraid it's toast. We'll have to glide in."

"Are you trained for that?"

"Aristotle gave me some tips once."

"Great. Just *great*."

BOOM! The sound of thunder under the cloud was almost deafening. Lightning struck one of the stingers. The craft spun round and round before crashing and exploding in the forest below.

"Two down. Only one more to go," said Juice.

But it never came to that. The remaining Stinger turned and sped back toward the river as *Pegasus* sailed—silently and smokingly—through the cloud, which was rapidly dissipating. Juice managed a bumpy but otherwise successful emergency landing in the grassy clearing were Thelete and Apollo awaited.

"You are nothing if not theatrical," said Thelete, grinning beneath his headdress of owl feathers, as he helped Cali down from *Pegasus* with an oversized hand.

Cali hugged him before she could censor herself. "I can't tell you how glad I am to see you again!"

"The feeling is mutual."

"You, too, Apollo," she said, letting herself go and hugging him in turn. "I see you've got four hawk feathers now."

"Greetings and salutations. I recently received a … *promotion*, as I believe it is called in your world."

"Well, you should be given another one. What you just did was super impressive."

He blushed. "You always manage to embarrass me."

"What are you doing there, Juice?" asked Thelete.

"Setting *Pegasus* to self-destruct."

"*Pegasus*? I like that."

"It was my uncle's idea. He made it."

"I assume you are referring to Aristotle?"

"You know him?"

"Only by name. But I count him among my people's allies."

"You should. He's fighting the good fight."

"As are you."

"As are we all. Let's get down off this mountain before a full squadron of Stingers shows up."

"Excellent idea."

Juice handed Cali her purse and jammer and the group set off down the hillside.

"How long before *Pegasus* self-destructs?" asked Apollo.

"Depends on how long it takes someone from the Elite Forces to lay a hand on her."

"Fair enough."

"Speaking of," said Cali, stashing the jammer in her purse, "you guys do realize there's a whole *army* down on the tracks about to attack Rose Cove?"

"We have been following the movements of the enemy," said Thelete.

"What are you going to *do* about it?"

"First, get the three of you to safety."

"In Tula?" asked Juice.

"Correct."

"What about you?" asked Cali.

"More incoming!" yelled Juice, pointing overhead as a dozen Stingers sailed high above the trees toward the top of the mountain.

"It appears they will attack soon—but not yet," observed Apollo. "I imagine they plan to first surround Rose Cove to prevent our escape."

"That is exactly what they are doing," said Thelete, stopping and closing his eyes. "I can feel the earth trembling under their machinery."

They resumed walking. Soon, having passed the waterfall where Cali had bathed and the footprints of the old Quaker houses, they came to where the camp of the Bird Tribes had been.

It was gone. As in: *vanished*. So absent were any signs of the camp it might never have existed.

"Where is everybody?" asked Cali.

"They have gone on ahead," said Apollo, "and are waiting for the three of us to arrive."

"I keep hearing about the *three* of us. What about Thelete? Tell me you're not going to stay here and face the enemy yourself?"

Picking up on her mounting hysterical concern, Thelete touched her cheek paternally.

"Someday, my child, you will understand that to love as the God loves the Goddess is to know limitless love wholly committed, not to its own safety, but to the welfare of that which matters most."

"And what is that?"

"The Rose, of course."

Just then an enormous explosion erupted behind in the distance, where a massive cloud of dust and smoke billowed up over the mountaintop they'd just left.

"That would be *Pegasus*," said Juice. "May she rest in peace."

No sooner had he uttered these words than the sound of heavy machinery approaching became audible as Rose Cove started to visibly tremble.

"Come," said Thelete. "Time to get you underground."

He led them to where his tipi had once stood. Using his great fingers to penetrate the ground like a spade, he appeared to grasp the edge of something before pulling on it. Huge quantities of leaves and sod fell away as he lifted a gigantic flagstone and cast it aside, revealing a set of earthen steps leading down into the dark.

"You have the last of the fallenium, Apollo," said Thelete. "Take it now and go. I will hold off their army long enough for you to get beyond range of their weapons and reach Tula safely."

"I should never have brought Freddy here," replied Apollo with an uncharacteristic note of frustration in his voice. "Then he would know nothing of our fallenium and none of this would be happening."

"You did what was right and what was kind. This is not your fault. In fact, it is part of the fulfillment of the Prophecy of the Rose."

"But you will *die* out here!"

Thelete touched Apollo's chest, then his own. "I will die in *here* if I do not protect my children."

"What do you mean *your children*?" asked Cali, her head—and heart—suddenly swimming.

"I am exceedingly proud of both of you. Enough of the grim faces. I have lived a full life that has spanned nearly three centuries. Moreover, that which I truly am cannot die."

"Hold on a minute!" yelled Cali. "Am I hallucinating—or did you basically just say I'm your *daughter*?!"

"You have always been and will always be the apple of my eye."

Turning to Apollo with hands on hips, she said, "You *knew* this and didn't tell me?"

"I apologize, sister. I was not at liberty. Divulging your identity would have endangered your mission."

It was Juice's turn to be shocked and outraged. "Her *mission*?" he said.

"It is all in the Prophecy," said Thelete, "as you will learn soon enough."

"I don't care about a goddamn prophecy!" said Cali. "I care about … you! I love … YOU!"

Half furious and half grief-stricken, sudden and confusing emotions exiting her insides and cascading down her face, Cali was disarmed not by argument or force but by a truly unprecedented sight: a single tear of his own sliding down Thelete's statuesque cheek.

"You mean I have to lose my real father before I even get to know him?"

"You already know him. You can feel his love for you, can you not?"

"I believe so."

"Then know also that the most important part of him will live on."

Thelete looked at Juice, who stared at Cali, who examined Apollo, who glanced at Thelete. Suddenly, with Rose Cove tossing and the sound of the approaching enemy growing almost deafening, it was as if nobody knew what to say—so they all came together in a big group hug.

"The three of you need to go. NOW," commanded Thelete.

Apollo and Juice literally had to pull Cali down into the opening in the ground. She stood near the top of the steps watching with a stupefied expression as Thelete, concentrating with his head bowed as if pooling vast currents of energy into his body, began to … expand!

"What in creation is he *doing*?!" yelled Juice.

"He is summoning the *Tulpa*," said Apollo.

"What does that *mean*?" asked Cali.

"He is channeling the force of the Aeon. He is becoming the Embodied Weapon."

"Is that like harnessing the power of fallenium?" asked Juice.

"Trust me, it is *way* beyond that."

Cali had witnessed a number of miracles in the last few months. But watching her newly revealed biological father transform into a thirty-foot giant easily topped the list. His headdress and buckskins, tiny now in comparison to his massive stature, split apart and fell to the ground.

"MAY THE LUMINOUS CHILD AWAKEN IN ALL OF YOU!" were his parting words, spoken as if through loudspeakers with extra bass as his colossal eyes glistened, before—using only the fingers of one hand—he replaced the flagstone above them to seal off the passageway to Tula.

Third Part

ROSE & THORN

31

"Follow me quickly," ordered Apollo, switching on his tomahawk to ambient red flashtorch mode and leading Juice and Cali down the dirt steps and along something resembling an old-timey mining tunnel that smelled like a root cellar as dirt rained downed from a sudden bombardment aboveground.

Seconds later they found themselves entering some kind of wooden elevator. There were no buttons or other mechanical trappings. But when Apollo inserted the glowing head of his tomahawk into a slot in the side of the chamber, a door slid shut behind them. Suddenly and without warning, the bottom seemed to drop out.

Under normal circumstances the journey to the Deep World would have been an acrophobe's worst nightmare. Though Cali clung to Juice like ivy as the elevator entered free fall, her fear of heights was mostly muted by a feeling—or lack thereof—of profound shock at the mad turn of events of the past twelve hours.

In less than half a day, she'd: survived an attempted assassination; jumped off a building; befriended a revolutionary who was supposed to be dead; engaged in aerial combat with the Elite Forces; and lived through an emergency landing—only to meet a brother she didn't know she had and learn that her real father was the earthly embodiment of some kind of divine being ... just before watching the latter sacrifice his life to save his children!

"How long have you known?" she asked, turning to Apollo as tears made little rivers down through the grime covering her cheeks.

"About you?"

"Yeah."

"Only a few years—since soon after I became a *phojai*."

"You mean a Marine?" asked Juice.

187

"The translation is crude, but yes. The word actually means 'spiritual warrior.' At that point I was given access to a certain level of what you might call classified information."

"Having to do with my mission?" asked Cali.

"Yes."

"You know, just for the record, I didn't sign up for this shit."

"Nobody did." His tired sigh indicated that the enormity of events was catching up to him as well. Not even bothering to wipe the tears off his dirty, angular face that Cali only now realized was strikingly similar to her own, he leaned back against the elevator wall. "For what it is worth, I am deeply sorry."

"You're not to blame. I'm not sure who is, but as soon as I know, I'm sure as hell going to blame them."

"That would be your—our—parents, I am afraid."

Cali felt an intense energy rising in her system. She couldn't tell if it was *kundalini*—or simply anger. "Why would they abandon their *own child* in that ... psychotic world I grew up in?"

"My question exactly," said Juice. "That's just screwed up."

"It was a sacrifice they both made for the greater good of humanity."

"But *why?*" asked Cali.

"The long answer is complex," replied Apollo. "But the short answer is that their actions were foretold in the Prophecy of the Rose."

"How many times do I have to say I could care less about your prophecy!" yelled Cali, her grief suddenly manifesting as rage. "That prophecy just KILLED OUR FATHER!"

Apollo touched her wet face and smiled through his own tears. "I can understand why you would feel as you do. Part of me feels the same way. And yet were I in Thelete's position, I would have done likewise."

"Because of your warrior code?" asked Juice.

"Because the warrior code is a repository of universal truth. The primary responsibility of a *phojai*, a spiritual warrior, is to protect the Goddess and her children."

Before this last statement, Cali would have bet her life's savings (if they weren't permanently frozen) she couldn't be any more shocked than she already was. But she would have lost that wager.

"Just to be clear, are you speaking literally or metaphorically?" she asked as the proverbial light bulb turned on in her mind.

"Literally as a starting point. But metaphorically by extension, given that the human species is in essence the progeny of the Goddess."

"Let me get this straight. My—our—father was the God and our mother is the Goddess?"

"Correct."

"But we're still talking about human beings here?"

"Also correct."

"How can somebody be both?"

"Was not Jesus supposedly both?"

"I guess so."

"The Goddess and the God are human channels for the Aeons who created the Anthropos."

"What's an Anthropos?" asked Juice.

"The original human strain. The primordial human genetic blueprint."

Not for the last time, the vision of the creation of the Luminous Child appeared in Cali's mind. "Is the Anthropos the Luminous Child?"

"Not exactly. The Luminous Child is a seed, shall we say, placed within the DNA of the Anthropos—a hidden potential, if you will."

"Has anyone ever fulfilled this potential?" asked Juice.

"Unfortunately, the Luminous Child has not yet been born. And this brings us back to the Prophecy of the Rose."

"How lovely," scoffed Cali.

"The Prophecy is extremely old. It is also a history. It was delivered to a Rose millennia ago. Much later, those who were called Gnostics, a group devoted to the Goddess and her teachings inhabiting the Shallow World but maintaining contact with the Deep World, transcribed and adapted parts of the Prophecy in their own writings."

"What do you mean by a 'Rose'?" asked Cali.

"That is another name for the earthly embodiment of the Goddess, just as the Thorn is the terrestrial instrument of the God."

"If you think you or anybody else can conscript me into Goddesshood just by calling me the Future Rose, I've got two words for you: *free will*."

"Our philosophers also debate the relationship between free will and destiny. There are those who believe the Prophecy is proof of the latter, while others argue that it requires the free will of all those involved to bring about our destiny."

"What a circle jerk," said Cali.

"And what is that destiny?" asked Juice.

"The awakening of the Luminous Child within us all and final defeat of the Archons even as they appear on the verge of establishing dominion over the entire earth."

"We're slowing down," observed Cali.

It was true. They'd been falling at nearly the speed of gravity for quite a while, but now they were meeting some kind of resistance.

"We are approaching Tula," replied Apollo.

"Are we really about to emerge deep inside the planet?" asked Cali.

"We are."

"I thought it was supposed to be really hot, as in molten."

"That is merely an Archontic lie like so much of their so-called science. I think you will find the Deep World quite agreeable."

"How does this ... elevator work anyway?" asked Juice. "And how did anybody dig a 'mineshaft' that must go for hundreds of miles?"

"Thousands, actually. The capillary, as we call it, is powered by fallenium, which is also used to phase out the physical substance of the earth to create the artery, or tunnel, we are now in. As soon as we are safe in the Deep World, the phasing will be turned off and the artery will disappear."

"Like the mountainside during our prison break."

"Precisely."

"Far out."

Apollo stood up straight and adjusted the four hawk feathers in his headdress. "Let us make ourselves presentable."

Standing tall as well, Juice straightened his buckskins. Cali took one look at her filthy, ragtag POC outfit and simply shook her head.

"Whoever's down there expecting a Future Rose," she said, "will be sorely disappointed."

As soon as they came to a stop, the door slid open, revealing a set of downward-spiraling sunlit stairs cut out of the same solid granite "sky pillar" through which the elevator had apparently descended. Freeing his tomahawk and switching it off, Apollo led Cali and Juice down the winding staircase.

The daylight had a somewhat unsettling but also strangely satisfying quality. Cali found herself squinting in the brightness as she had to make an effort to keep up with her athletic companions who, seemingly energized by the light itself, bounded down, down and down like a pair of young mountain goats.

Her own heavy heart seemed to lift somewhat as she followed on legs that suddenly seemed lighter and springier down many hundreds of perfectly smooth, meticulously even steps. Limbs of strange trees began to appear above the granite side walls, dappling the stone surfaces with shifting angular shadows.

There was an invigorating scent in the air she couldn't quite place. A salty breeze started to blow and then, abruptly, thanks to her downward momentum, she almost literally felt herself spit out on a sandy seashore that spanned hundreds of yards. It was easily the widest beach—by far—she'd ever seen.

Soft and fine, the sand was utterly alabaster. The ocean, as calm as a Great Lake on a June morning, was a vibrant kaleidoscope of turquoise shades on which numerous sailboats could be seen bobbing. Through a lapis sky dotted with cottony clouds, a pulsating red sun seemed near the meridian.

"I feel like I've just died and gone to heaven," said a grinning Juice.

As POCs weren't allowed on Fatherland beaches, Cali was quick to grasp that he'd never actually seen an ocean up close before. "Funny," she said. "According to the Bible, this is where hell's supposed to be."

"Which makes it even funnier that members of the Bird Tribes are often referred to as angels," said Apollo.

"How is it possible for there to be an atmosphere and a sun inside the earth?" asked Juice, his inner scientist coming out even as he marveled at the otherworldly scene.

"An understanding of your question requires comprehension of the true nature of the earth, which would be best to discuss when we have more time."

"So where's Tula?" asked Cali.

"This is it. Look around."

She did. Throughout the dense subtropical forest that covered the mountains lining the crescent of the sea, she was able to make out many stone, earthen and wooden structures that, at first glance, seemed part of the natural environment.

There were no towering high-rises, no busy streets, no speeding hovercraft, no flashing holoboards. The normal signs of civilization seemed as notably absent as peace and harmony seemed palpably present.

"Where do you live, Apollo?" asked Juice, joining Cali in surveying the "forest city" that couldn't possibly have been more unlike an urban center in the Fatherland.

"I no longer live in the City of the Rose."

"Why not?"

"Because only women live here."

"I'm not sure whether that's good or bad," said Cali.

"I'd say it's definitely good," said Juice with a wink.

"You would."

"So where *do* you live, Apollo?"

"On one of the Thorns."

"Say that again."

"The Thorns are an archipelago of thirteen islands that surround the mainland. I live on the chief of these, Kalahili."

"Does—did—Thelete live there, too?" asked Cali.

"Yes. I imagine that is where his memorial service will be held."

"So where does our mother live?"

"Are you ready to meet her?"

"As ready as I'll ever be."

"This way then."

Strange speckled seagulls the size of pelicans squawked as the two refugees from the Shallow World followed Apollo down the beach a little ways then along a pink flagstone path. Flanked by rows of exotic flowers of many kinds, the path meandered through the lush woods billowing with unknown ferns, shrubs and trees in a million shades of green.

Here and there they passed women of different ages and different shades of brown wearing extremely colorful saris. Cali wondered whether it was merely accidental or actually some kind of joke that while the men of the Bird Tribes were virtually indistinguishable from Fatherland Indians, many of the women could have passed for Indian Indians.

"Do men and women never live together here?" asked Cali.

"They actually do," replied Apollo. "Just not most of the time."

Cali and Juice both laughed.

"We have a saying," continued Apollo, "that the secret to a successful marriage is frequent, extended absence."

"So the heart can grow fonder?" asked Juice.

"That might be one reason. But in all seriousness, what defines service to the Goddess is very different for women and men. We have found it productive to dedicate ourselves to that service with singular focus during certain portions of the year, while coming together in communion over holidays."

"Just holidays?" asked Cali.

"Long holidays. Two months each twice a year, at Springtide and Falltide."

"Do children live with their mothers or their fathers?" asked Juice.

"Until age twelve they live with their mothers or a female relative. After that boys move in with their fathers or a male relative."

"Is *that* our mother's house?" asked Cali, motioning toward a multi-story "tree house" zigzagging up between a dozen gigantic trees that looked like members of the oak family complete with swaying Spanish moss.

"That is Rose Cottage, the home of the Goddess, so yes," said Apollo.

Cali couldn't help remarking the flag flying high above the structure. What she assumed was a glyph reminiscent of a yin-yang symbol stood out in scarlet against a white background. But unlike a yin-yang symbol, there were not two but three primary forms interacting: a pair of tall ones flanking a shorter one.

"That reminds me of a vision I was given of the creation of the Luminous Child," she said.

"You are very perceptive," replied Apollo. "That is precisely what it represents. It is the flag of Tula."

These last words were spoken as they arrived at the base of one of the giant oaks, where a young woman in an ochre sari stood monitoring a wooden spiral staircase. Upon recognizing Apollo, she nodded respectfully and allowed him to lead his companions up the stairs.

When they reached the third story (out of five or six), another, somewhat older woman—also dressed in ochre—escorted them to a massive porch directly beneath the flag. An outdoor living area furnished with chaises, tables and chairs around a fallenium "fire pit," the porch had "walls" of trellises packed with fragrant red roses on three sides, while the fourth side overlooked a huge flagstone "courtyard" lined with banquet tables and fallenium lamps.

"Fancy," said Juice.

"Please tell me there's a bathroom somewhere nearby," joked Cali in an attempt to lessen her feeling of overwhelm.

"In fact, there are several, and one is waiting for you."

She'd expected Apollo to respond. Instead, the voice, as unmistakable as the regal face to which it belonged, came from atop another set of steps.

Trying not to look too wide-eyed, Cali turned and stared up at her mother, no doubt about it. Dr. Caliandra had on a flowing magenta sari decorated with a motif of red roses and a necklace of crow feathers. In place of a headdress, she wore a single massive rose in her twisting hair like a flamenco dancer.

If she'd aged a day in the years since her disappearance, it didn't show. She resembled, as she always had, a veritable goddess. Only this time around, with her heart nervously thumping against her ribs, Cali grasped the irony.

Having spiraled down the staircase like a petal in a whirlwind, Caliandra suddenly stood beside them with what her daughter—from long if rusty association—intuited was a mixture of intense joy and intense sorrow bubbling just below the surface of her otherwise welcoming demeanor.

Caliandra had always been on the tall side—but if anything, though Cali herself had grown, her mother seemed taller than ever.

"Come," said Caliandra, extending her arms, gathering her children to her abnormally warm bosom, and squeezing them tightly with great emotion. "I am *so* very grateful to have both of you with me—especially today."

Only after an ensuing silence did Cali realize both her mother and Apollo were sobbing. She could feel their shoulders heaving. Despite her anger (which remained on standby, as it were), she couldn't help but join them.

"I take it you know?" Apollo managed to ask.

"I have just come from the Dream of the Goddess," replied Caliandra. "I have seen it."

"Was he taken prisoner?"

"Not a chance. He passed as a true *phojai*."

The surreality of having watched Thelete morph into a colossus, combined with that of grieving his death with her "deceased" mother and unknown brother at the center of the earth, gave Cali a weird rotating sensation as the three mourners disengaged and gathered themselves.

"I am finding it a challenge—nay, an impossibility—not to blame myself," confessed Apollo.

"You are wise beyond your years, my son, but you would do well to reconsider your perspective."

195

"In the future I will endeavor to do so. For now, however, there is a terrible, self-inflicted wound in my heart."

"We will both miss him. All of Tula will miss him. I suspect even Cali will—although she was not blessed to spend much time with him and I sense she, understandably, harbors resentment where her parents are concerned."

Drying her eyes on her sleeve, Cali replied, "Whatever I'm feeling, let's not make this about me. A great and powerful man just sacrificed his life for what he believed in. Let's honor that, shall we?"

Wiping her own darkly beautiful eyes, Caliandra smiled with maternal pride. "It seems I have more than one child possessed of wisdom."

"I have my moments," said Cali. "But I'm not wise enough to figure out one thing."

"What might that be?"

"What do I call you … here?"

Caliandra actually laughed—a playful and soothing sound that instantly took Cali back years—as she ran her fingers through her daughter's filthy hair. "Why, Mother, of course. In private at least. Let me look at you for a moment. How magnificent, how exquisite you are!"

"I look like hell."

"You look like you have been through hell. And for that, as for so many other things, I must apologize. But fear not: I had the Mahavidyas oversee preparation of an entire wardrobe for you."

"What are Mahavidyas?"

"Think of them as priestesses," said Apollo. "They represent aspects of the Goddess and perform different spiritual functions."

"And you, no doubt, are Frederick Hamilton—all grown up," said Caliandra, shaking his hand warmly.

"Please, call me Juice."

"Apollo has gushed about your bravery. And now that I have witnessed it myself, I understand why he was so impressed."

"That was you who sent the crows, right?"

Just then a number of crows that had sat motionless in the nearby trees all stirred and cawed in unison.

"Indeed. Just as I sent the mountain lions the first time you traveled to Rose Cove."

"Thank you, Dr. Caliandra. We wouldn't have made it without your help."

"Think nothing of it. And here you may call me Sophia."

"It is an honorific like Thelete," explained Apollo.

"Thank you, Sophia."

"Thank you for protecting my daughter."

"No thanks required. I … care deeply for her."

"That is clear for all to see. I will wager you did so even as a child. And I think she had her first crush on you as well. She insisted on wearing her best outfit to visit you after you recovered from your illness. The shoes were a lost cause, but the petticoat, at least, was salvageable."

"Must you embarrass me, Mother, now, of all times?" said Cali.

"What kind of mother would I be if I could not embarrass you—at least a little? Ah, Matangi is here!"

Cali was pleasantly surprised to see a girl hardly older than herself reach the top of the stairs from below and approach with jaunty steps. Seemingly out of place atop her turquoise sari and necklace of brightly colored feathers, the girl's decidedly Asian features reminded Cali of a geisha.

"You called, Sophia?"

"I did indeed, Matangi. Thank you for coming."

"How may I serve you?"

"I have just learned that the next phase of the Prophecy has come to pass. We are approaching the Tribulation."

Matangi seemed to receive the news, whatever it meant exactly, as if it were a blow. "I will alert the other Mahavidyas."

"Please do. Tomorrow we will inform the people. For now I wish to introduce you to my daughter, Cali, and her friend, Juice."

With a slight curtsy, Matangi said, "It is indeed an honor to meet the Future Rose and her companion."

"Apollo, of course, you already know," said Caliandra.

"You are looking well, Matangi," said Apollo.

Cali instantly picked up on the chemistry between her brother and the lovely Mahavidya.

"As are you. Please accept my condolences for your loss."

"Thank you."

"My condolences to you as well, Sophia and Cali. I feel moved to ask the Goddess for a birdsong to soothe our collective grief."

"That would be most kind of you," said Caliandra.

"Many believe Matangi is our greatest living singer," remarked Apollo.

A hint of blush rose in Matangi's pale cheeks that looked like fine porcelain. "Apollo specializes in embarrassing me."

"If the truth is embarrassing, that—at least—is not my fault."

"I hear you are also a singer, Cali," said Matangi.

"I am—was."

"Once a singer, always a singer—even if no one is listening. The heart of a true singer must express itself."

"Like you, my children," said Caliandra, "Matangi is far wiser than her years. That is why I have asked her to care for my daughter during this period of transition when I will be frequently engaging the Goddess for advice."

"What about Juice?" asked Cali.

"He will stay in guest quarters with me," said Apollo.

"It is settled then," said Caliandra. "One could wish for your arrival in Tula to be under happier circumstances. But at the very least, you are both in good hands."

H aving said goodbye to Juice and her newfound family, Cali followed Matangi for several minutes through the labyrinthine tree house that was Rose Cottage into one of dozens of semi-independent structures.

This particular third-story "petal," as Matangi called it, was known as the *Uttahan Sadon*, or Regeneration Suite. The size of a small bungalow, it included a colorfully but tastefully decorated living area with floor-to-ceiling windows; a bathroom accessible from the living area and the guest bedroom; and a master bedroom that rivaled any Cali had ever slept in—which is saying a lot.

Constructed around a massive oak limb that formed a high arch over a large futon covered with a plush down comforter, the bedroom walls were embedded with tiny fallenium stones that sparkled iridescently in the natural (or more accurately, "supernatural") light that entered by way of several round windows and a set of French doors that opened onto a private balcony surrounded by rose-covered trellises.

"Jesus," said Cali, taking it all in.

"Do you like it?" asked Matangi as she returned from the master bath, where the sound of water falling into a tub was like music to Cali's ears.

"'Like' doesn't come close. This is absolutely stunning."

"As are you."

"Look who's talking."

"Please let me help you undress. You can set your purse on the bedside table."

Too physically and emotionally spent to put up resistance, for the first time in her adolescence, and in the most outlandish of places, Cali allowed herself to be disrobed by a complete stranger. And the strangest thing was, it didn't feel strange at all.

"Your body is very similar to mine," commented Matangi matter-of-factly, assessing her charge with curious yet caring eyes, as Cali at last stood before her completely naked—and totally unselfconscious. "Of course, your skin is somewhat browner. But we're both slight, well-shaped, and rather strong."

"I don't think I've ever had my body described to my face before. But that sounds about right."

"How old are you?"

"I turn sixteen in March. You?"

"I'm a good bit older."

"How old?"

"I'll be sixty in May."

Cali had heard that Asian women tended to hide their age well—but Matangi's claim to be a decade north of the half-century mark seemed ridiculous. Then she remembered that Thelete had claimed to be almost three hundred years old.

"Living here in the Deep World," explained Matangi, "one is sheltered from the kinds of radiation—solar, cosmic, and artificial—that induce premature aging in those who inhabit the Shallow World."

"Lucky for me. So how old is my mother really?"

"She has been the Rose for going on two centuries, which means she is nearly two hundred and forty years old."

"You mean two hundred and forty years young."

"I fear the passing of Thelete will age her like nothing else. I could sense how much effort she was exerting to contain her grief. The relationship between the Rose and Thorn is a special bond."

"Say more about that."

"I will be happy to. But first, let us get you in the bath."

"I really need to pee."

"I will wait in the bedroom."

As odd as it may sound, Cali had not taken more than a handful of baths since her mother disappeared. Olga was strictly a shower person. Baths to her were a waste of precious time—especially when it came to her protégé, who was virtually always on the tightest of schedules.

Perhaps this explains why the slow, timeless bath Matangi gave her was so memorable ... and so profoundly relaxing. Or maybe it was because of the countless beeswax candles surrounding the enormous stone tub giving off the familiar healing scent of fallenium smoke, or the extraordinary softness of the fallenium-heated water, or the fact that Matangi insisted on scrubbing her skin with a luffa and washing her hair with shampoo that smelled like lavender and manuka honey.

"Where have you been all my life?" said Cali as Matangi vigorously massaged shampoo into her scalp.

"Why, waiting to meet the Future Rose, of course."

"I was joking."

"I was not."

"I've got to level with you, Matangi: to say I'm ambivalent about this whole Future Rose thing would be an enormous understatement. To be perfectly honest, just thinking about spending the rest of my life as some kind of … priestess gives me the heebie-jeebies. No offense."

Matangi laughed—a melodic, captivating sound like a bird mimicking human laughter and infusing it with a special hypnotic quality. "None taken. Sophia warned me you were—how did she say it?—a real firecracker."

"I've been called worse."

"It might surprise you to know I felt the same way when I was your age."

"What changed?"

"I did."

"Speaking of age, now that the cat's out of the bag, how old is my brother really?"

"He will turn forty next year."

"Figures. So you're in love with a younger man!"

"Come again?"

"You heard me."

"My, you *are* perceptive."

"Perceptive enough to know he loves you, too."

"Yes, that is true."

"Any thoughts of marriage?"

Matangi sighed. "Lots. Unfortunately, it is forbidden for a Mahavidya to wed."

"Why?"

"We are extensions of the Goddess comparable to the petals of a rose. As such, we are considered to be wedded already."

"To the Goddess?"

"Exactly."

"What happens if you decide to stop being a Mahavidya?"

"Then I can do whatever I like."

"So you actually have a choice?"

"Everybody has a choice."

"Tell that to the people living like drones and slaves in the Fatherland."

"Here is a truth that may take a while to grasp fully, Cali, even though it is the foundation of the human condition: in this world, appearances notwithstanding, there is *only* choice. And on that note, we should choose now to rinse your hair."

"Rinse away. But don't think I've forgotten about the Rose and Thorn. You promised to elaborate on their 'special bond.'"

"Do not worry. In your shoes I, too, would desire more insight into my true love."

"Are you confirming in a roundabout way that Juice is … the *Future Thorn?*"

"He does not know it yet. But yes. Is it not obvious?"

35

With her thoughts scattered to the winds, Cali allowed Matangi to dry her off, cover her in a bathrobe, and then wrap her hair in a fresh towel.

"I imagine, after your long journey, you are ravenous," commented the Mahavidya.

With so much coming at her from every direction, it hadn't registered with Cali just how starved she was. "What do you have?" she asked.

"What would you like?"

"Just about anything as long as there's lots of it."

Matangi laughed her charmingly musical laugh. "I so admire a woman with an appetite! What about sushi rolls?"

"You have *sushi* here?"

"Why would we not have sushi? We even have pizza."

"Sushi sounds wonderful."

"Be back in a jiffy. Feel free to make yourself at home. After all, this is your home. For now anyway."

Alone in the Regeneration Suite, Cali felt the urge to step out on the trellised balcony, whose only furnishings were a wooden bench and small table. A cool afternoon breeze was stirring the otherwise warm beachside air, infusing everything with rose perfume.

Absentmindedly, she twisted off a bloom, then peeled a thorn off its stem and stuck her ring finger with it. A single drop of blood nearly the same color as the petals "flowered" up from her skin. Even as she sucked the drop up, with timing that seemed too perfect to be merely coincidental, she realized she was getting her period.

"How lovely," she said, reentering the bedroom and fishing through her purse for a tampon she was glad to have brought.

After remedying the situation, she poured out her purse's contents on the bed and took an inventory. Aside from the clothes she'd arrived in that she planned to burn sacrificially, her worldly possessions boiled down to: two more tampons, a nearly empty tube of lipstick, a mostly full bottle of red nail polish, a tortoiseshell comb she'd never actually liked, a compact, an unopened pack of breath mints, her wallet, a holophone that was useless as useless could be there in the Deep World, and her mother's jammer, still on.

"Why do I never think of a toothbrush?" she asked aloud as she turned off the jammer and replaced everything in her purse.

"Did you say something about a toothbrush?" asked Matangi, reappearing in the bedroom doorway.

"Yeah, I have this habit of forgetting to pack one whenever I go on a life-threatening adventure."

"No worries. You will find a toothbrush and toothpaste in the top bathroom drawer. But for now, sushi is served!"

For a good fifteen minutes, seated with Matangi (who, having recently eaten, wasn't hungry) at the wooden kitchen table with a view of the nearly fluorescent forest, Cali stuffed her face with the tastiest sushi she'd ever tried. Even the water Matangi poured for her was somehow delicious in its utterly pristine tastelessness.

"What kinds of fish are these?" asked Cali with her mouth crammed completely full.

"Are they not to your liking?"

"To the contrary. I just don't recognize any of them."

"The yellow one is called *taipo*. It is related to tuna. The white one is a kind of eel. The bright pink one is similar to squid. As far as the others go, I do not believe they have counterparts in the Shallow World."

"I gather most of the flora and fauna here are unique to the Deep World?"

"Much of it is, although many plants and animals are roughly the same below and above. Tomatoes, for example, and chickens."

"And people?"

"Those, too."

"And whatever kind of bird that is whose feathers you're wearing? I'm sure I've seen one before. It's not a parrot, is it?"

"You have a keen eye paired with a good memory. These feathers are from what you might know as Indian ringneck parakeets, which tend to speak with great clarity. Long ago in India, people saying their daily prayers heard ringnecks repeating them and began to think of them as spiritual birds."

"Like yourself, no doubt."

Even when not laughing, Matangi's brown eyes, which stretched horizontally toward her pale cheeks at an oddly beautiful angle, seemed to smile. "Yes, this old bird is quite spiritual. Parrot is my spirit animal, just as crow is yours."

There were three pieces of sushi left. Still hungry, Cali fought off the urge to wolf them down. "You sure you don't want any of these, Matangi?"

"Positive. Eat up. Raw fish is very healthy. And you, after all, are still a growing girl."

"I'll grow too much if I keep eating like this."

"Not if you maintain an active and productive lifestyle in body, mind, and spirit."

"Tell that to my manager. So what exactly *is* a spirit animal?"

Matangi nodded like a patient tutor. "A truly satisfactory answer to that question, I am afraid, would fill up volumes. But in the simplest terms, a spirit animal is an outer reflection of an inner quality."

"What type of quality?"

"One with many … qualities."

"I figured as much."

"These qualities are interrelated and include such things as personality type, likes and dislikes, inherent strengths or abilities, and even what might be described as one's 'calling.'"

"What does parrot relate to?"

"Why, music, of course! Specifically: the ability to learn and/or create songs with words that are based on sacred knowledge and contain healing power."

"What about crow?"

"Crow is similar to parrot in many ways. This is why you and I get along so well. Both parrots and crows are inherently linguistic creatures. But whereas parrot has a focus on mimicry or 'parroting' a preexisting reality, crow is considered a primordial energy with the ability to manipulate time, space, and even DNA."

Suddenly recalling the crow woman statuette from her mother's iconography book, Cali asked, "Is this why the Goddess is associated with crow?"

"Precisely. When the teachings of the Deep World were adapted for the holy texts of the Shallow World, certain mistakes—honest and otherwise—were made. In the process the Mahavidya known as Dhumavati became associated with crow. But the Mahavidya with the closest relationship to crow (as well as the Goddess) is actually Kali, the chief among us whom we call the Destroyer."

"That's Kali with a 'K,' right?"

"As you would spell it in English, yes."

"So why do my mother and I spell our name with a 'C'?"

"How much do you know about your mother's sojourn in the Shallow World?"

"I know she attended medical school before she met and married my 'father' yet managed to have Thelete's child. I assume that was all part of her 'mission'?"

"You assume correctly. Her mission stemmed from the Prophecy of the Rose …"

"Naturally."

"… which states that during this century a Future Rose and Future Thorn would be born inside the seat of patriarchal power in the Shallow World. Upon becoming the Rose and Thorn following a period with neither Rose nor Thorn called the Tribulation, this couple would be responsible for bringing forth the Luminous Child."

"And my mother actually *believed* all of this?"

"Enough to risk her life, as well as that of her daughter and her mate, in helping fulfill the Prophecy. But she was wise enough not to take unnecessary risks. Thus she changed the spelling of her name—and yours—to one less likely to reveal her connection—and yours—to the Goddess."

"I think Freddy figured it out anyway."

"Freddy?"

"The current Stonewall Jackson who tried to have me killed."

Matangi's eyes widened. "What *happened?*"

"I escaped by jumping off a building. Or maybe I flew."

"Maybe you did."

"I still don't understand what's so special about the Luminous Child. I mean, how could such a being—whatever it is—be any more powerful than the Goddess and God?"

"That is an excellent question. Unfortunately, the answer remains a mystery. Would you like some *choro* tea? I think I will have a cup myself."

"*Choro?*"

"A flower related to hibiscus. While the latter is good for the physical heart, the former is known to soothe heartbreak, also known as grief."

"That would be really nice, thanks."

Matangi stood up, put a kettle of water on top of one of several slices of fallenium that functioned as stovetop burners, and placed teabags containing a bright orange powder in a pair of ceramic mugs.

"There is a story in the Prophecy of the Rose, Cali, of an encounter between the Goddess and the Lord Archon prior to the establishment of the earth and the birth of the human race here in the planetary center."

"The Lord Archon? You mean, like, the Extraterrestrial-Mind-Parasite-in-Chief?"

"You really do have a way with language. Add 'Reptilian' to the beginning of your title and you get a perfect description of the Lord Archon."

"So what happened during this encounter?"

"Sophia foretold the Lord Archon's doom. She said, 'There is an immortal Child of Light who came into this realm before you and who will appear among your duplicate forms, in your simulated world … And in the consummation of all your works, their entire deficiency of truth will be revealed and dissolved by this Luminous Child.'"

"Intense."

"Indeed."

"But *how*?"

"*That* is the question. Would you like honey in your tea?"

"Please."

"A lot or a little?"

"A lot."

"I really do love your style, Cali Crowell! It seems we both live by the words of the English seer known as William Blake: 'The road of excess leads to the palace of wisdom.'"

36

"You still haven't explained the 'special bond' between the Rose and Thorn," said Cali, blowing across her steaming mug to cool her *choro* tea.

Matangi sat back down across the table with her own mug. "How much have you heard about the Aeons?"

"Only bits and pieces. I gather that 'Aeon' is another name for the Goddess and God."

"Technically, yes. More accurately, the Goddess and God belong to a category of divine beings known as Aeons."

"Sort of like the Greek gods and goddesses?"

"Sort of. Except that the Aeons are quite real, they do not recognize any hierarchy among themselves, and they are all friends and allies of the human species."

"Where do they live?"

"That is a key question. Normally, the Aeons exist in what is called the Pleroma, which you might think of as the black hole at the center of the galaxy. But rather than being a singularity, the galactic core actually provides access to an entire world of beings—a *plurality*, if you will."

"Does the Originator live there as well?"

"Yes, although the Originator is also inherent in all aspects of creation—even those out here in the Kenoma."

"The manifest universe?"

"Correct."

Cali took a sip of tea, which, though delicious, was still piping hot.

"How do you like the *choro*?" asked Matangi.

"It's spicy and sweet."

"Like yourself."

"I can be a little sour sometimes. You mentioned Aeons 'normally' live in the Pleroma. What did you mean?"

"In the dawn of the earth's history, there were two Aeons, a female and male, who loved each other deeply. Their names were …"

"Let me guess: Sophia and Thelete."

"Exactly. Thelete was also called Volinius, which refers to the 'masculine' power of directed will. Sophia was also named Proliferius, which has to do with the 'feminine' bravery involved in giving birth to living beings. Of course, when I speak of masculine and feminine, I am not referring to physical gender but to psychospiritual traits belonging in some measure to all sentient beings."

"Okay."

"Sophia also had a nickname: Precuneus, which roughly translates as 'precocious.' From an early age, she was considered by the Aeons to be a brilliant geneticist."

"*Geneticist?*"

"Thelete was also a geneticist. I realize that may sound odd. But understand that the Aeons are essentially assistants to the Originator in the unfoldment of creation; they have many diverse functions and responsibilities. One of these is to engineer DNA in order to generate different forms of life."

"How do they do that?"

"Basically, by singing. By using speech combined with thought."

Her mind reeling, Cali thought about the Language of the Birds and her vision of the creation—by singing—of the Luminous Child.

"When I was injured during my first trip to Rose Cove," she said, "my mother came to me in the Dream of the Goddess and shared a vision of Sophia, Thelete, and the Luminous Child. It's the exact scene referenced in the flag of Tula."

"I, too, have seen it—also in the Dream of the Goddess. The seed of the Luminous Child was placed inside the Anthropos immediately after the latter was designed. And this is where our story takes a strange and unexpected twist."

"What happened?"

"Something that had never happened before. Normally, genetic creations were projected into the Kenoma from inside the safe confines of the Pleroma into habitable planets that were all variations on the solar system. In fact, a sun and moon had already been engineered in this place by other Aeons and were awaiting the establishment of a planet to host the Anthropos and the many other species of life designed by Sophia and Thelete for this particular experiment. But Sophia, being young and impatient, whether accidentally or purposely it has never been conclusively determined, actually *fell* out of the Pleroma and plummeted through the vast reaches of the Kenoma clutching her genetic database to her breast."

"Hold on a second, Matangi. This is starting to sound like science fiction. Are we talking metaphors here?"

"I can see why this story, which is so at odds with the Christian myth of creation you grew up with, would strain credulity. But I assure you that every single thing I am describing *literally* occurred—including the part where Sophia ended up transforming into the so-called planet that is our home."

"You mean Sophia's the *earth*?!"

"Truly, she is Mother Nature."

If Cali's mind had been reeling earlier, now it was simply blown … wide open.

"Why doesn't she look like a *person*?"

"The Aeons can take many forms."

"What happened to Thelete?"

"He made an extremely difficult decision: he stayed behind in the Pleroma."

"Why?"

"Suffice it to say he had to in order not to ruin the experiment."

"You mean with the Anthropos?"

"Yes. With Sophia's transformation into the host planet for our species, the experiment was altered. But its basic goal remained unchanged."

"What goal was that?"

"To create an environment that would allow for the full expression of sovereign free will in a biological species—something that had never been attempted."

"What went wrong?"

Cali's candor elicited more musical laughter from her new friend. "I assume you mean with humanity?"

"What else would I mean? Just look at us. We're a hot mess. Maybe not down here. But up there, we're going to hell in a handbasket."

"You are indeed. Which means all of us are in danger."

"Seriously, what *did* go wrong? It seems to me if you take a turbocharged species and let it live on the body of its Goddess, that should be a recipe for success. Something doesn't add up."

"You are forgetting the Archons."

"I guess I was."

"The Archons …"

"Don't take this personally, Matangi. But I don't think I can handle any more ancient history right now. My mind's about to explode as it is."

"Then let us finish our tea. Then I will give you a restorative massage and sing a special song to help you rest."

C ali was no stranger to massages, which even Olga approved of as a tried and true means of "keeping on keeping on" through the rigors of touring. But never had she experienced a massage quite like the one Matangi gave her.

After Cali drained the last of her *choro*, which actually did seem to uplift her heart, and brushed her teeth using a brush with natural bristles of unknown origin and mint-flavored toothpaste she suspected contained fallenium owing to its slightly musky flavor, she returned to find Matangi setting up a padded bamboo table in the middle of the living room.

"Here, let me help you with your robe," said the latter, helping Cali undress once again and covering her with an exquisitely soft white cotton sheet as she lay down on her back. "This may seem odd, but I am going to start by massaging your energy field."

After everything of a supernatural nature Cali had witnessed and heard about over the past several months, she was no skeptic when it came to energy. Still, she didn't expect to feel much—if anything—from having her energy field "massaged."

Immediately, however, she began to hear her belly rumbling—as if her digestive system were being activated. At the same time, breathing slower but deeper, she could sense her body rapidly cooling down. Soon she became so drowsy she could barely fight off sleep.

"What's happening?" she asked with a cavernous yawn. "I feel like I've just been hit with an elephant tranquilizer."

"I am relaxing your parasympathetic nervous system, which controls digestion, breathing, and other involuntary functions. Overstimulation of the sympathetic nervous system, such as when our reaction to danger is a fight-or-flight response, imbalances the parasympathetic system and can lead to such problems as inflammation and insomnia."

"My parasympathetic system definitely needs relaxing. I had both a fight and a flight just a few hours ago when the Elite Forces shot Juice and me out of the sky."

"Well, this should help you release that as well as any other trauma stored in your tissues."

"I imagine that would be a lot of trauma. I've had a terrible fear of heights ever since my mother left."

"Yet you just jumped off a building and sailed through the air. Sounds as if you have already processed some of your trauma on your own. Time to roll over!"

"Do I *have* to?"

"You do not *have* to do anything."

"Not even become the Rose someday?"

"Not even. Free will is what makes us truly human and ourselves. Take that away and life is not worth living."

Though as deeply relaxed as she'd ever been, Cali managed to roll over onto her stomach. "But what will happen to the Bird Tribes—and everybody else—if the Prophecy isn't fulfilled?"

"Who knows? The worst scenario would be that we all perish and start over again in another planetary experiment."

"Through reincarnation?"

"Exactly."

"That's a comforting thought."

Cali meant this sarcastically and actually laughed when Matangi replied, "I think so, too."

"What are you doing now?"

"Placing fallenium disks along your spine."

"Why?"

"Properly used, fallenium can revitalize one's system without overstimulating it by clearing blockages in the *chakras*. This might feel somewhat … strange."

Sure enough, after Matangi concentrated in silence for a moment, Cali experienced a weird tingling sensation as the disks began to heat up. Just when she thought they might start to burn her, the heat leveled out as it penetrated—physically and energetically—into her spine and, from there, the rest of her body.

Suddenly going from sleepy to invigorated was surprising but not unpleasant. Before long she felt the familiar, animating current of *kundalini* snaking its way up her spine, weaving in and out of her *chakras* (which she intuitively visualized, though she'd never even heard of the term, as spinning wheels) all the way to the crown of her head.

"Where does the word *chakra* come from, Matangi? Is it Hindi?"

"Actually, though in the Shallow World it is said to come from Sanskrit, the word actually originated in Kalidon."

"Kalidon?"

"The ancient language of the Deep World that gave rise to the Indo-European languages when the first of the Bird Tribes migrated to the surface."

"How long ago was that?"

"Tens of thousands of years before the alleged birth of civil society in the Fertile Crescent. The real Cradle of Civilization is, of course, Tula."

"So why does everybody here speak English so well? English is a relatively modern language."

"It has been known to the Roses for centuries that English would be the dominant language among the Archontified oppressors in the Shallow World. Thus the Bird Tribes have made it a priority to master the language of the enemy."

"I still don't think I'm in the mood to take on the Archons right now."

Matangi chuckled. "Well, someday somebody will have to. In the meantime what would you like to 'take on'—if anything?"

"Tell me more about my brother."

"What do you wish to know?"

"Let's start with his spirit animal. It's hawk, right?"

"Correct."

"I'm going to go out on a limb, ha ha, and guess that has to do with good eyesight."

"Yes and no. Technically, one could have hawk as a spirit animal and be born blind. The types of 'sight' hawk confers are inner sight and farsightedness: the ability to see beyond surfaces and even into the future."

Cali considered this information. "Then why *did* he rescue Freddy in the Badlands—when Freddy's true character turned out to be evil and only bad things could come from saving his life?"

"I cannot say with absolute certainty. But I suspect Apollo saw these things and did what he did because, despite the potential consequences, it was the only honorable thing to do."

"I think you're right."

"What makes you say that?"

"Something Thelete said to Apollo."

"I pray Apollo will find the clemency to forgive himself."

"I hope so, too."

"He is an upright man, a warrior cut from the old cloth, and as such expects more from himself than from anyone else."

"Do you have any brothers or sisters, Matangi?"

"No. I am afraid I was nearly too much for my parents to handle by myself. I sometimes took on boyfriends I hardly even liked just to assert my independence." This made Cali laugh again. "Just so you know, I am now going to remove the stones. The warmth will quickly dissipate and you may feel a little chilly."

Only over the third and final phase of the massage did Matangi physically massage Cali. Despite her slight build, Matangi was—as she claimed to be—quite strong. Cali moaned and groaned as Matangi tenderized her like a sinewy cut of meat.

"That hurts *so* good!" exclaimed Cali.

"Pain, we like to say, is the flip side of pleasure."

"And vice versa. So what's Juice's spirit animal?"

"Any guesses?"

Recalling Thelete's parting gift of bird feathers after their first visit to Rose Cove, Cali said, "It must be owl, right?"

"Right. Owl is Thelete's spirit animal."

"You mean Thelete as in the honorific?"

"Exactly. Just as the Rose is connected to crow, the Thorn is linked to owl."

"I assume owl also has to do with seeing—specifically, in the dark."

"Indeed. Owl watches and waits high in its dark tree like the guardian Aeon watching and waiting from the ostensible blackness of the Pleroma."

"So Thelete's *guarding* Sophia?"

"Every second of every minute of every hour since her descent into the Kenoma."

"Why does he have to guard her if she's an Aeon herself?"

"Because she is asleep."

"Literally or figuratively?"

"Literally. It is said that her reaction to the trauma of being separated from her divine mate and true home in the Pleroma caused her to ball herself up into a fetal position and fall into a deep slumber."

"After all this time, why hasn't she woken up?"

"Because it has not been the right time. The Prophecy specifies that we have just entered the window of her awakening."

"Because of the approach of the Tribulation?"

"And the coming of the Luminous Child that catalyzes the Great Awakening of both the Goddess and her children."

"Is that why the Dream of the Goddess is so important—because that's where one must communicate with her?"

"Precisely. To commune with the Goddess, one must enter her Dream."

"So how does Thelete actually *protect* her?"

"The same way a thorn protects a rose."

"Seriously."

"By projecting himself into a human male Vessel just as the Goddess projects herself into a human female one."

The extraordinary transhistorical implications of Sophia's relationship to Thelete weren't lost on Cali, who understood them in a searing flash of insight.

"That means when a Rose and Thorn come together as people, they're also connecting as Aeons!"

"Bingo. Now are your feelings for Juice starting to make a little more sense?"

Practically vertiginous from her unexpected crash course in Bird Tribe history, Cali might not have been able to sleep at all (even though she badly needed the rest) had it not been for Matangi's birdsong. A multilayered lullaby sung using only vowels, the song ranged over half a dozen atypical notes, including the one Thelete had taught Cali.

Matangi's voice was full, rich, and elastic—so much so that Cali felt envious. "Touched by the finger of the Goddess" was the phrase that popped into the young musician's mind to describe Matangi's extraordinary vocal cords.

No sooner had this thought occurred than any petty emotion dissipated, seemingly dissolved by the birdsong itself as Cali, supine on her futon like a baby being sung to sleep even though the sun hadn't yet set outside, could feel her eyelids growing heavier and heavier …

In her dream an owl—an enormous one by the sound of it—was hooting outside. *WHO LOOKS FOR YOU? WHO LOOKS FOR YOU?* it seemed to ask.

Still wearing the soft white linen gown Matangi had helped her into before combing her hair and tucking her in, Cali found herself on her bare feet opening both French doors out onto her private balcony.

In the starless semidarkness underlit with red as if from a subterranean sun, she was able to make out only the shadow of a tall, broad figure standing in the corner.

"*Juice?*"

"Almost—but not quite."

The voice, as unmistakable as thunder, was Thelete's. Tears streamed from Cali's eyes as she leapt into his great arms and pressed her cheek against his massive chest that remained bare as always. He seemed so palpably, fantastically alive; yet she realized in her heart she was dreaming.

"I hardly even knew you," she cried, "yet I can't stand the fact that you're gone!"

"There, there, my child. Do not grieve overmuch for me. I am not gone; I have merely gone within."

"What do you mean?"

"I have flown on the Great Heron's back and am reunited with the Originator."

"Is that a good thing?"

"It is a *very* good thing."

This news should have comforted Cali. Instead, it made her sob even harder. "I don't know what to do with my feelings," she managed to say. "I'm still so *angry* with Mother—and you."

"Of course you are. But realize that anger is just a type of energy not unlike *kundalini*. It can and should be converted and used productively."

"That sounds like something Juice would say."

"Juice is quite similar to me."

"So I'm gathering."

Stepping back from his paternal embrace, Cali attempted to dry her eyes with the neck of her gown. When she looked up again, her vision seemed to have adjusted to the uncanny ambient light because she could see Thelete's sculptural features beneath his headdress. He was smiling.

"What are you grinning at?"

"The miracle of you. The miracle of such beauty and fierceness welded together in a daughter of mine. You will make a fine Rose when your day comes."

"That's just it: I can't figure out if that's what I even *want*. How do I know if that's the right path for me?"

"Simple: you do what you have always done."

"Which is?"

"Listen to your heart."

Chest fluttering and pounding, Cali suddenly popped awake in the darkness of her room to find the top of her gown drenched with sweat—or rather, tears. Her hair was still wet with them as well. Thelete might have been merely a figment of her dream, but her complex emotions were all too real.

Back out on the balcony in a waking state, she was surprised to encounter the same odd starless reddishness, as if an unseen sun, shining from beneath, turned the Deep World night into an old-timey dark room.

She had no idea what time it was—or even, when she thought about it, how time was measured in this bizarre reality. But one thing was certain:

even on less than a full night's sleep, her batteries felt recharged. Maybe that was because of Matangi's song.

A knock on the door to the Regeneration Suite startled her—not because it was particularly loud but because of the intense *energy* (for lack of a better word) she sensed emanating from the knocker. It didn't strike her as at all like Matangi's. Rather, it seemed more like ... Thelete's.

When she hesitated out of confusion, there was another knock, louder this time.

"Coming!" she called.

Having straightened her hair, she opened the door to find Juice, also dressed in a white linen robe, bathed in the red twilight that enveloped Rose Cottage about to knock for a third time.

"My, somebody's impatient," she said. "What are you doing here in the middle of the night?"

"We need to talk."

"Do you want to come in?"

"I'm fairly sure that wouldn't be ... appropriate outside the holidays."

"I didn't say come in and have *sex*."

"Nevertheless."

"Oh, you're probably right."

"Let's go for a walk on the beach instead. I've never done that before."

"How romantic! Just give me a second, will you?"

In her bedroom closet, Cali found an extensive wardrobe (that she had to resist exploring on the spot) just as her mother had indicated. Slipping on a pair of strappy sandals that fit perfectly, she rejoined Juice and tried to figure out how to lock the front door.

"I don't think there is a lock," he said. "I've not seen a single lock since I got here."

"That'll have to change if I'm to ever feel comfortable in the bathroom."

At the sound of his deep laughter that seemed to stimulate her bone marrow, she couldn't keep from kissing him right there on the doorstep. "Can I just say, as much as Matangi would make a great lesbian lover, I'm *really* glad to see you?"

He laughed even louder.

"Shhh!" she said playfully, putting her finger over his fleshy lips before taking his immense hand and staring with bewilderment at Rose Cottage whose organic structure seemed spun like an intricate tapestry in multiple directions. "Do you know the way out of here?"

He pointed left and down. "I think the beach is that way."

"If you say so. You're the wilderness guide."

After several minutes and a handful of wrong turns, having encountered not so much as a mouse stirring, they found themselves strolling quickly along the flagstone path they'd come in on—then, removing their shoes, racing and giggling across the soft sand to the water's edge.

With the gentle waves sloshing like bathwater over their feet, they stood hand in hand gazing out at the dark ocean under the sanguine, underlit sky that actually pulsed slightly when Cali concentrated on it.

"Matangi told me the Goddess *is* the earth," she said with awe in her voice.

"Apollo told me the same thing."

"Do you believe it?"

"Yes. I can feel her."

"Speaking of, I could feel you, buddy, even through my door. It was like Thelete was standing out there."

"That's what I wanted to talk to you about. I don't know how to say this, and I hope it doesn't upset you, but he came to me in my dream tonight."

"Join the crowd."

"*Seriously?*"

"Yep. I could have sworn the whole thing was completely real."

"Me, too. What did he say to you?"

"To follow my heart. What about you?"

Juice shook his head as if still processing his dream. "I'm not saying this to toot my own horn. I'm not even sure I'm up to such a thing. But he wanted me to take up his mantle."

"So he asked you to become … Thelete?"

"I suppose so."

"What did you say?"

"That I'd think about it."

"How did he take that?"

"He said I was free to take my time as long as I got a move on."

Cali fought back another bout of crying as she laughed bittersweetly instead. "At least he hasn't lost his sense of humor in the Pleroma."

"What's the Pleroma?"

"Where the Originator and Aeons live. I'll tell you all about it later. But right now, kiss me again."

He put his arms around her waist and pulled her to him. "What's in it for me?"

"A very special something indeed." Reaching down while kissing the Future Thorn, Cali soon felt his present thorn make itself known. "You know, I like a man in a white robe."

"As long as he isn't a priest."

"Yes, that would complicate matters."

"Are you doing what I think you're doing?"

Cali had dropped to her knees on the sand and was slowly and teasingly rolling up Juice's robe.

"I know you've been under a tremendous amount of stress smuggling my bourgeois ass out of the Fatherland," she said. "I think I might be able to offer you some relief."

"That was ... bold," said Juice afterward as he collapsed on the sand and, from a supine position, motioned for Cali to curl up in the crook of his arm.

"Well, I am—or at least I'm supposed to be—Precuneus."

"Precuneus?"

"It means 'precocious.' It's a nickname for the Goddess."

"If the shoe fits ..."

"Shut up."

"Where'd you learn to do ... *that*?"

"You really want to know?"

"Not really."

"Did you like it?"

"You honestly have to ask? The writhing and moaning didn't give it away?"

"Just checking."

"Damn, girl. I could use one of those every day for the rest of my life."

"Fat chance."

He gave a deeply relaxed chuckle as he put his free hand behind his head before turning and kissing her temple. "We could always take turns."

"Be careful. I might just take you up on that one of these days."

"I hope you will. But you'll have to teach me."

"I'm a good teacher."

"I'm a good student."

"I have no doubt."

As Cali, pressed against Juice's warm frame with a tepid sea breeze blowing over her, relaxed more and more herself, she had the impression the sky was strobing more intensely while becoming lighter.

"I think dawn's approaching," observed Juice as if reading her thoughts.

"How does that work here? I've been trying to figure out the whole natural lighting thing."

"Apollo explained it. Not that this made it any less surreal. He said the 'sun' here was actually the daily movement of concentrated *kundalini* along the spinal curve of the Goddess."

"That *is* surreal. So how did he explain nighttime?"

"Well, I gathered that the energy 'sets' toward the crown of her 'head' each evening, at which point it slowly diffuses into Sophia's body before 'rising' at the base of her 'spine' to begin the process all over again."

"The Land of the Everlasting Sun."

"Bingo. Except that the so-called sun technically travels from west to east."

"That's crazy."

"Isn't it, though?"

"Did Apollo also explain how there are supposedly seasons here?"

"Yeah. He said it has to do with Sophia's cyclical positioning as she tilts backward and forward through the four stages that make up the Dream of the Goddess."

"What are the stages?"

"Trauma (fall), grief (winter), denial (spring), acceptance (summer)."

"And these repeat over and over?"

"Apparently."

"I'd call that the Nightmare of the Goddess."

Juice chuckled again, this time with a note of compassion. "Apollo said that's basically what it is. But she doesn't allow herself to wake up—yet—because she's waiting for the Luminous Child, which is tasked with undoing the work of the Archons."

"Why doesn't she just wake up and defeat them herself? Or why doesn't Thelete show up in person and kick their miserable ET butts?"

"Because they're her children."

Juice's statement sent chills along Cali's spine. "Say that again."

"The Archons are her *progeny*. Just like we are."

"Apollo confirmed this?"

"Pretty much."

"How can that *be*?"

"I'm not entirely sure. But it means we have to work things out between ourselves."

After a lengthy absence, the term "rabbit hole" popped back into Cali's mind, bending her thoughts again to Thelete and stirring her still-fresh grief that had briefly subsided. If everything Juice said was true, her extraterrestrial siblings had basically—using their human proxies—just murdered her real father.

"Where do the Archons live?" she asked.

"Not on this planet—that's all I know. I gathered the earth's atmosphere doesn't agree with them. Something to do with an allergic reaction to high levels of oxygen."

"So what do regular Archons look like? Their leader is some kind of reptile."

"No idea."

"Any ideas as to how one goes about defeating them?"

"Pray for a miracle?"

"I imagine one would first have to deal with the Fatherland."

"Somehow, yes."

"Easier said than done."

"A heck of a lot easier."

"I can't do this alone, Juice."

Turning to face her, he held her by the waist and kissed her forehead. "You don't have to."

"You mean that?"

"I mean I'll do whatever I can to do whatever it takes to protect you."

"See, you're already the Thorn to my Rose!"

"Yeah, well, unless I can figure out how to summon the *Tulpa* and become the Embodied Weapon, I wouldn't count my chickens if I were you."

40

Dawn was breaking as the two lovers headed back along the winding path to Rose Cottage.

"I imagine today will be a busy one," said Cali, kissing Juice one last time beside the steps leading up to the Regeneration Suite.

"I have a feeling every day from now on will be busy."

"Did Apollo say anything about what we'll be doing?"

"He mentioned training but didn't provide any details."

"Training for what?"

"To become Aeonic Vessels, I guess."

"How do you *train* for such a thing?"

"You tell me. You're not going yet, are you?"

"People will be getting up soon. Matangi's probably already busted me."

"Just one more kiss."

"No, sir. You've had enough of all kinds of kisses for one night."

Turning, she quickly ascended the steps and wound her way through the maze of Rose Cottage. Dressed in a white sari beneath her necklace of parrot feathers, sure enough, Matangi was waiting for her on the bench beside her door.

"Good morning, Cali. I take it you had trouble sleeping?"

"No, I slept like a baby—until I woke up feeling super energized. So I decided to go for a walk."

Smiling with her beautiful geisha face, Matangi opened the door and insisted Cali enter first. "Something tells me there was more to your walk than just walking."

"There might have been some … talking."

"And judging by the look of things, some lounging on the shore?"

Touching her hair self-consciously, Cali felt many fine grains of sand. "I do hope I haven't broken any unforgivable rules."

Matangi, shutting the door behind her, laughed musically. "The only unforgivable thing here is to not forgive. That said, it is customary to abstain from amorous contact with our mates outside the holidays."

Cali realized she was intensely thirsty. Opening the door to the "refrigerator," which resembled an antique icebox but was undoubtedly fallenium-powered, she found two carafes of liquid.

"The clear one is water and the amber-colored one is mead," explained Matangi.

Cali poured herself a glass of water and offered to pour another, but Matangi politely declined. "With your permission, however, I will make myself a cup of *choro*. Would you like some?"

"That would be lovely."

"I must warn you *choro* is highly addictive."

"Is it really?"

"Not physically. But I do crave it emotionally."

Cali sat down on the couch as the light in the forest outside the tall windows began to reveal the morning dew glistening in crystalline droplets. As if siphoning in the light through her eyes, Cali could feel her energy level—which had started to dip again—once more increasing.

"Is this sunlight so stimulating because it's *kundalini*?" she asked.

"That is the long and short of it."

"And *kundalini* is the energy of the Goddess, right?"

"Yes. It is continuously gifted to all living creatures within the planet's biosphere. Think of it as the force that makes life in this world possible."

"Do the Archons also receive *kundalini* from the Goddess?"

Having placed teabags in a pair of mugs, Matangi sat on a counter stool to wait for the water to boil.

"Not anymore. They were infused with a finite amount of it at the time of their creation long ago."

"So if their life energy is finite, they can't live forever?"

"Correct. From a human perspective, they seem virtually immortal. But from the point of view of the Goddess, they are very mortal indeed."

"Do we know when their supply of *kundalini* is supposed to run out?"

"Not with absolute certainty. But the Prophecy of the Rose points to the window of time following the Tribulation as possibly their—how shall I say?—'expiration date.'"

"Juice mentioned they can't live on this planet."

"That is true. It is thought that the Goddess intentionally repels them with her atmosphere to protect her children."

"I was under the impression the Archons were her children also."

Just then the water came to a boil. Matangi poured it in the mugs and sat back down to let the *choro* steep.

"Technically, that is accurate. They consider themselves her firstborn children and her rightful heirs, by which they mean the heirs to her living body."

"That's why they've claimed the earth for themselves!"

"Partly, yes, even though they cannot live here. They are also insanely jealous of the human species, which in their view usurped their birthright."

"Just by being born?"

"Just so."

"That's crazy."

"By any reasonable definition of the term, the Archons are crazy."

"So tell me, where do they physically *live?*"

"On the various planets of the solar system as well as the moon."

"And what do they look like?"

"There are two types. The 'drones,' as they are called, somewhat resemble human fetuses at the start of the third trimester of pregnancy, but with highly developed motor skills."

"Sounds like grey aliens in early cinema."

"Yes, come to think of it."

"And the second type?"

"The 'dracos,' which include the Lord Archon, or Demiurge, are much larger and reptilian in appearance. It was they who gave rise to the notion of dragons."

Cali had the now familiar sinking sensation of slipping further and further down the rabbit hole. But she knew in her heart there was no turning back at this stage. "Apollo mentioned training to become the Aeonic Vessels. What does that entail?"

"Separation, for starters. Should both of you choose to pursue this arduous path, you will spend months apart."

"What else?"

"The training to become the Thorn is rather different from that required to become the Rose. Suffice it to say that, in both cases, the body, mind and spirit are incrementally prepared to take on a much higher level of energy and consciousness than humans normally possess."

"Will we still be … human?"

"Consider your mother and father. The answer is: of course. But the Rose and Thorn are simultaneously conduits for the creational abilities of Aeons. In this sense they differ from—while still being aligned with—the Anthropos."

"Is some kind of, like, ceremony required to become an Aeonic Vessel?"

"One might consider the entire process of training to be ceremonial. But the transformation from man or woman to Aeonic Vessel is organic, typically occurring spontaneously and without ceremony. Are you ready for your *choro*?"

"Sure."

"I would offer you some food," said Matangi as she handed Cali a steaming mug, "but we will be breakfasting with the Rose and the other Mahavidyas."

"That's okay, I'm not hungry."

"Exposure to the sunlight of the Deep World can have a dampening effect on appetite initially. It can also increase libido."

"Yeah, I was just thinking the only appetite I have right now is a sexual one."

Matangi actually giggled. "But judging by your thoughtful questions, you also have a thirst for knowledge."

"And *choro*."

"Well said. Before I forget, I wanted you to know it is our custom to wear white while in mourning."

"That's funny. We wear black."

"Almost everything is reversed on the surface. This is how the Archons subvert human nature and turn it against itself."

Cali joined Matangi in blowing across her mug and taking a sip.

"It is also customary," continued Matangi, "for the Future Rose to wear a rose in her hair when in the public eye—especially in official circumstances."

"I'll think about it."

"Finally, I took the liberty of placing some organic tampons in your top bathroom drawer in addition to a crow feather necklace on your dresser. I hope you like it."

"I'm sure I will. Thank you, Matangi. For everything."

"You are most welcome, my friend."

After a quick rinse-off, Cali was faced with a hard decision: choosing a white sari from the dozen or so tempting options hanging in her closet. She'd never actually worn a sari, but she flattered herself that she'd look good in one.

When she finally made up her mind, she most definitely did look good. Examining her outfit—strappy sandals, single-feather necklace, and all—in the full-length bedroom mirror, for the first time she saw what others had always seen and never hesitated to comment on: she was very much her mother's daughter.

Having applied lipstick and powder, she was about to rejoin Matangi in the living room—when decorum got the best of her (or her conscience did) and she stepped out on the balcony. Surprised to find the intense sunlight of the Deep World dimmed by dark clouds, she twisted off the largest rose she could find and, peeling off the thorns, threaded the stem through her hair above her ear.

"I know that look," she said to Matangi, who was seated on the couch distractedly drumming her fingers on her thigh as if composing a song in her mind. Returning from the realm of musical inspiration seemed difficult for the singer, who appeared to make a mental effort as she made her way back to the living room. "You were working on your song for grief, weren't you?"

"If you can read a Mahavidya," said Matangi with the hint of a grin, "I suspect you can read anyone. My, you do clean up well!"

"We say that, too. So do I look presentable?"

"Better than presentable. Resplendent." Matangi stood and opened the front door with an exaggerated flourish. "Shall we?"

"Do we need an umbrella? The clouds strike me as about to burst."

"Do not—how does the saying go?—worry your pretty head. The Rose will not let it rain on breakfast."

With so much experience performing live for tens of thousands of people, Cali was taken a little off guard by a sudden spike of nervousness at the prospect of seeing her mother again and meeting the other Mahavidyas.

Matangi led her quickly along the various halls, bridges, balconies and steps of Rose Cottage down to the courtyard below her mother's sprawling porch. But judging by the fact that Dr. Caliandra, resplendent herself in a sweeping white sari, was already standing at an oval table in the company of nine other women in white saris, they were still late.

"Olga hates it when I'm late," whispered Cali, "so I make it a habit not to be on time."

"I am not exactly the most punctual Mahavidya myself," whispered Matangi.

The other Mahavidyas turned and, though smiling, stared intensely at Cali as she approached her mother, who kissed her cheek and said, "It is my pleasure and honor to introduce the Future Rose, Cali Crowell."

As Matangi had observed, Cali was indeed gifted at "reading" people's energy. If Thelete's "aura" was explosive like thunder, her mother's was like lightning, quieter perhaps but equally elemental.

By contrast, the Mahavidyas—starting with Matangi, who reminded Cali of a tropical waterfall—were in an energetic category of their own. Less powerful than the Aeonic Vessels, they were nevertheless far beyond regular human beings.

One by one, in no obvious order, the Mahavidyas shook Cali's hand, greeting her with some version of "May the Luminous Child awaken in you" and introducing themselves: from elegant Tara like a Scandinavian supermodel in a tightly wound topknot wearing a necklace of eagle feathers; to refulgent Bhairavi like a Nubian princess sporting fiery red feathers of unknown origin; to Bagalamukhi in a necklace of fluffy canary feathers accenting turmeric-colored skin and a face with high cheekbones like Pocahontas.

The last to greet Cali easily took the prize for most shocking. "I am Kali," said an extremely short crone with ashen skin and sooty hair streaked with tungsten filaments.

"So am I," replied Cali in a failed attempt at nonchalance.

Ignoring this statement while taking Cali's hands in her stumpy, wrinkled, long-nailed fingers and pressing them to her voluminous necklace of crow feathers, Kali said, "So at last I meet the real Destroyer."

Ever since she was little, Cali had felt that her mother could—as the cliché goes—see right through her. So she never even attempted to lie to her the way she regularly (and successfully) did with Olga, who couldn't see through anyone, not even herself.

What shocked Cali most about the chief Mahavidya wasn't her appearance but the same utterly naked feeling of being stared into she associated with her mother's gaze. Flustered, she said, "I beg your pardon?"

The old Mahavidya's black eyes glinted as she replied, "The Destroyer does not ask for pardon. The Destroyer destroys."

"I'm sorry—"

"There you go again asking for pardon. Do not be sorry. You are what you are. Accept that and do what you must do."

"And what is that?"

"I suspect you already know in your heart, my child. It is only a matter of time before your destiny is revealed to your mind."

Kali was like nothing so much as a benign but still frightening witch out of a fairy tale. With the ancient Mahavidya's momentous words reverberating in her thoughts, Cali had a seriocomic vision of herself as a bewildered princess lost in the woods.

"May the Luminous Child awaken in all of you," said her mother. "Shall we break bread together to commence this fateful day?"

After the Mahavidyas seated themselves, her mother joined them and motioned for Cali to sit between herself and Matangi. Immediately, several other women in plain white saris began delivering a sumptuous breakfast "à la carte" that consisted of a coffee-like hot beverage, exotic juices, beautiful pastries made with a nutty flour from the wheat family, toasted baguette slices eaten with something akin to a chocolate hazelnut spread, soft boiled eggs in the European manner, succulent papayas along with a number of unknown but equally delicious fruits, and last but not least, a selection of excellent charcuterie.

Raising a glass of purple fruit juice as a single tear wobbled down the side of her nose, Cali's mother proposed a simple toast: "To Thelete!"

"To Thelete!" replied a suddenly emotional (again) Cali along with the Mahavidyas as glasses clinked all around.

Everyone except Dr. Caliandra began to eat as she continued, "As all of you know by now, Tula has just lost a great man who will be remembered by historians as long as there are historians to remember him."

"Hear, hear," replied Kali, whose sentiment was echoed by the other Mahavidyas, many of whom struck Cali as emotional themselves.

"With you as my witnesses, I will now have the flag lowered to half-mast to signal the beginning of our official period of mourning."

Even as her mother spoke, Cali watched as the white flag of Tula with its red symbol flapping above Rose Cottage descended against a backdrop of ominous—though entirely appropriate, she was quick to recognize—thunderclouds.

"As you also know, Thelete's passing indicates that the Tribulation is drawing nigh. According to the Prophecy of the Rose, this further establishes that my own 'passing' is now on the horizon."

"What on earth do you mean?!" blurted out Cali, who couldn't help herself.

The compassionate and loving look on her mother's face took Cali back years. "I am indeed thankful that you still care for me, my beloved daughter, after all I have put you through."

"Of course I do! And now of all times, I don't want to lose you—*again*!"

"And you will not. In the midst of my grief, I am comforted—relieved, actually—to have just received guidance from the Goddess in her Dream."

"I have seen your path since you were born, Sophia," said Kali in her antediluvian voice at the far end of the oval table. "And now I see that you see it."

"Yes, Mother. I see it now. It is time to relinquish my position as Rose in order to expedite the Prophecy's fulfillment."

There was a collective gasp uttered by all the Mahavidyas except Kali, who smiled and nodded knowingly.

"Hold on a minute," said Cali. "Did you just call her '*Mother*'?"

"Understand," replied Dr. Caliandra, "that in order for my mission in the Shallow World to be successful, I needed an airtight cover story."

"So you pretended my grandmother was dead?"

"She had to be. She could not very well be alive in the eyes of the Fatherland, could she?"

Her mother's logic was as simple and brutal as it was necessary. "I suppose not," admitted Cali.

"But now that you know I am still very much alive," said Kali with an amused tone in her voice, "would you by any chance be willing to give your grandmother a peck on the cheek?"

Cali was out of her seat in a split second and kissing the old Mahavidya, who, smelling like anise and cloves, hugged her back with startling strength.

"Just so you know, my child, I have waited over a decade and a half for that kiss. You are Helena's spitting image at sixteen."

"I won't be sixteen until March."

"I know. And I will be four hundred in April."

"Honestly, you don't look a day over a hundred."

Cali meant this as a joke, of course, but her grandmother's good-humored cackle was still totally unexpected. "Helena tried to impress upon me how quick-witted you are. Humor is a valuable quality in any Rose."

"Yeah, on that subject—"

"Cali has yet to make up her mind," interjected Dr. Caliandra.

"Has she now?" Though phrased as a question, Kali's words seemed more rhetorical than anything. "Have you told her she is foretold in the Prophecy? 'And in the Shallow World shall a young Crow sing her songs. And chief among these will be a Song of Destruction. And in the Deep World, as the Last Rose, shall she take up her abode and bring forth such grace as will lead to the Great Awakening. And she shall not walk alone, for an ebony Thorn shall journey with her. At moments she shall walk in his footsteps. At moments he shall walk in hers.'"

To describe Cali as stunned yet again wouldn't do the moment justice. Even though she was aware of the gist of the Prophecy, to hear her newly resurrected maternal grandmother recite an ancient sacred text in which she and Juice were perfectly described absolutely overloaded her emotional switchboard.

"I need to sit down," she said in a faraway voice as she made her way lightheadedly back to her chair into which a concerned Matangi helped her.

"You and I both know, Mother," said Dr. Caliandra, "that accepting the mantle of the Rose is no casual undertaking. You yourself refused it when you were young, as you have never tired of telling me."

"Yes, because I loved your father, who was not—and would never be—the Thorn. I was unwilling to distance myself from him in that way. You were lucky to be able to have your Thorn and love him, too."

Dr. Caliandra sighed and ran her fingers up through her hair in frustration. As she did, her own large rose was detached and fell with a plop onto a flagstone. The symbolism playing out in real time seemed obvious to everyone as Matangi picked up the rose, which Cali's mother declined to accept.

"Forgive me, Mother," said Dr. Caliandra. "My grief has made me selfish and shortsighted."

"You only spoke the truth, as did I, and thus there is nothing to forgive."

"Please, everyone, do eat. We all need our strength to get through this day."

Until then it hadn't occurred to Cali that everybody had stopped breakfasting. Cali herself hadn't so much as taken a bite. And now, with her internal processor on overdrive, she'd quite lost the little appetite she had.

"Cali, if you would be so kind as to accompany me to the Goddess Suite, I would greatly appreciate it," said Dr. Caliandra as breakfast ended in disarray and the Mahavidyas began to disperse.

"Of course," replied Cali, who turned to her grandmother and asked, "Will I see you again?"

"Without a doubt, my dear."

"What about you, Matangi?"

"Of course. You cannot get rid of me so easily."

Matangi's words, at least, brought a smile to Cali's face as she followed her mother up, up and up to the "penthouse" of Rose Cottage. Caliandra held the exquisitely carved wooden door open for her daughter.

"After you," she said just as the clouds finally burst and rain came funneling down in ribbons.

"Did you just do that?" asked Cali while quickly stepping inside.

"You mean ask the rain to fall?"

"Ask, command, whatever."

Caliandra smiled. "Only the Goddess can do that."

"But you *are* the Goddess. Sort of."

The smile disappeared. "Not for much longer."

The Goddess Suite wasn't at all what Cali expected. Ascetic, with minimal furnishings and an emphasis on the play of natural light from floor-to-ceiling windows on potted plants and beautifully stained hardwoods, the main room (encompassing kitchen, dining and living areas) of the simple abode reminded Cali of nothing so much as ... a dojo.

"I imagine your head is spinning," said Caliandra.

"Like a gyroscope."

"Please, let us sit and catch up."

Unceremoniously, sighing together as if on cue, mother and daughter plopped down on a futon couch with a simple but soft beige cover. It seemed the intensity of the past couple of days had finally caught up to both of them.

"I could use a cigarette," said Cali.

"Please do not tell me you have started smoking."

"Not yet. But if I'm ever going to, I can't think of a better time."

Despite everything Cali's droll wit made Caliandra laugh. "Oh, how I have missed you! Over these last years, I have found myself gravitating more and more to Matangi because she reminds me so much of you."

"She reminds me of me, too."

"Give me a foot."

"Seriously?"

"You always loved it when I rubbed your feet."

"That's true. But you're the Rose!"

"All that means is that I am the highest-ranking servant in Tula."

"Because you serve the Goddess?"

"Yes. And because I serve the people."

Truth be known, Cali didn't need to have her arm twisted to accept the offer of a foot massage. Removing her sandals, she turned sideways and extended a leg into her mother's lap. "At least I bathed this morning."

"That is some comfort."

If there was ever any doubt as to where Cali got her dry wit, none remained after a few minutes of conversation with her mother. Gradually, with her heel being kneaded by Caliandra's skilled osteopath's fingers, which were unnaturally warm just like she remembered them, her shoulders dropped as the stress was literally pressed out of her body.

"Thelete visited me in my dream last night," said Cali at last. "He visited Juice, too."

Caliandra's eyes widened until they appeared almost Egyptian. "He did? What did he say?"

"Basically, he wanted us to become the next Rose and Thorn."

"What do the two of you want?"

"We want to do what we want to do."

"That is what all young people want to do."

"What do *you* want us to do?"

"You know what I want you to do. But it must be *your* choice."

"Why was I chosen to be the Rose? Why were you?"

"Why is anybody? The Aeons choose as they like."

"But how do you *know* you've been selected? For that matter, how do others know?"

Caliandra seemed to be searching for the right words. "When an Aeon identifies a Vessel, that person is inevitably guided to self-knowledge. Has this not indeed been your own experience?"

Cali nodded. "I suppose it has."

"And would Juice not say the same?"

"He probably would."

"As for other people, the Rose and Thorn always know who is to succeed them. This knowledge comes directly from the Aeons themselves. The Rose and Thorn are tasked with making it public."

"So you and my ... father were told Juice and I were meant to ... become you?"

"In a manner of speaking."

"Does the Aeons' choice have anything to do with human bloodlines? You said my grandmother declined the position you accepted and now intend to pass on to me."

"The seemingly matrilineal situation you describe is actually an aberration. Historically, the Aeons have selected Vessels from many different families and ethnicities. The Archontic 'divine right of kings' is a hierarchical bastardization of what is by nature a 'democratic' process. Time for the other foot."

"Already?"

"Okay. I will go just a little while longer."

Profoundly relaxed, at length Cali grudgingly switched feet. "So how is it that my grandmother was able to become a Mahavidya even though she was married? Matangi said the Mahavidyas weren't allowed to wed."

"I take it Matangi is still in love with Apollo?"

"Head over heels."

"To answer your question, your grandmother became a Mahavidya after she was widowed."

"When was that?"

"Almost a century ago."

"How exactly does one become a Mahavidya?"

"The Mahavidyas are selected by the Rose."

"Not by the Aeon?"

"Not entirely. In this decision the Aeon only has ... input."

"What was my grandfather like?"

"Like Apollo. We are talking two peas in a pod—even though they never met."

"What was his name?"

"Apollo, ironically. When we get up, I will show you a picture of him."

"So what's my grandmother's real name? I suspect it isn't Kali."

"Diana."

"And Matangi's?"

"Hypatia."

"What about Thelete's?"

"Heracles."

"That sounds about right. Do I have grandparents on his side of the family?"

"Unfortunately, he was an orphan."

"What happened to his parents?"

"They—along with his younger sister—lost their lives in the last great eruption of Kalahili while he was away on active duty."

"I assume Kalahili's a volcano?"

"A massive one. It sits on the largest of the Thorns of the same name. That is where we will be traveling for Thelete's memorial service. The Womb of the Goddess may be here on the mainland, but her heart is in Kalahili."

"Sounds like a song lyric."

"It does, does it not?"

"Are you speaking literally or figuratively about the divine womb and heart?"

"Both. Would you like to see what my father looked like?"

"I would. But first, I need just five more minutes."

Caliandra smiled and gave a little sniff of laugher with her lips closed while continuing her marvelous foot massage. "Now, *that* is the Cali I know and love."

"Jesus, Apollo really does look just *like* him," remarked Cali a little while later as she stood admiring her grandfather's oil portrait in her mother's bedroom.

"They are carbon copies of each other. Down to the hawkish nose and eyes."

"Speaking of, judging by the headdress, I gather my grandfather's spirit animal was also hawk?"

"Of course. His sight was extraordinarily keen."

"Just out of curiosity, why haven't I met anyone here with heron for a spirit animal? After all, it's the national bird of Tula."

"Heron is associated with the Originator. No person has ever received that honor."

Caliandra's room, which was connected to a large though simple master bath, was almost as minimalistic as the rest of her suite. Cali plopped down with her legs crossed on the queen-size futon underneath a series of large windows with views of the forest glistening in the splattering rain.

There was virtually no extraneous décor, which made the single photograph on the wicker dresser seem all the more out of place. It was a color snapshot of herself in a pink petticoat at age eight holding hands with her mother and the man she believed to be her father outside the monkey section of the Saturnia Zoo. All three grinning "family" members looked perfectly happy—as if there could be no dark, strange secrets anywhere underwriting their ostensibly normal lives.

"Did you love him at all?" asked Cali.

Caliandra sat down on the mattress beside her and took her hand. "Yes. I just wasn't *in* love with him. My heart was already given elsewhere."

"What did my real father think about your mission in the Shallow World?"

"We never talked about Perry, if that is what you mean. But I suspect my marriage to him was a bitter pill to swallow."

"Why don't you have a picture of Thelete?"

"It is not our custom to capture our likeness in life. This is considered an act of vanity, one that can detract from our living presence."

"Sort of like having your soul stolen?"

"Indeed. Many so-called indigenous peoples descending from our diaspora into the Shallow World maintain this position to this day and refuse to have their photos taken."

"I thought that was just a primitive superstition."

"I prefer to think of it as primitive wisdom."

"Boy, with all the paparazzi snapping photos of me, I probably don't have any soul left to speak of."

"You, my dear, have more soul than ten people put together."

Still clutching her mother's hand, Cali lay back and stared up at the high ceiling, where a bamboo fan gently whirled against its whirling shadow. "It's so peaceful. I like it here."

"I am glad. I hope you will come to consider this your true home."

"We'll see. Who painted my grandfather's portrait? It's pretty amazing. It's so wild and alive."

"Your grandmother."

"*Really?*"

"You seem surprised. She was a famous artist before she was ever a Mahavidya."

"Where's her signature?"

"On the back. It is considered bad form for artists to sign their paintings on the front."

"Are there a lot of female artists here?"

"Many. Most of our creatives and intellectuals, in fact, are women."

"And men are okay with this arrangement?"

"Why should they not be? They are busy off being men."

Cali giggled at the thought of how different the Fatherland would be if it were actually … the Motherland!

"So what do you do with men who want to be like women and women who want to be like men?"

"We incarcerate them."

"For *real?*"

"Of course not. This is not the Fatherland. There are no judgments here regarding matters of gender identity or sexual expression. Free will must extend to all areas of peaceful human endeavor and interaction."

"You had me there for a second."

"I could see it in your face. To finish my point, we recognize that gender is, in practice, a fluid concept. We also acknowledge that, in an archetypal sense, there are and will always be distinctly 'feminine' and 'masculine' traits belonging to everyone. That said, women naturally tend to be creators whereas men are more naturally protectors. This distinction comes down to us from the Aeons. Sophia is the life principle, just as Thelete is death."

Yet again, Cali was prompted to replay the primordial scene of the creation of the Luminous Child by the Aeons, who were obviously like yin and yang.

"Where do we go from here?" asked Cali, turning and staring into her mother's deep dark eyes.

"Well, tonight we sail for Kalahili. But I suspect your question was of a more general nature."

"More general, yes, but also more specific. What would *you* do in my shoes?"

Caliandra's expression was neutral yet still somehow full of compassion as she lay down on her side propped on her elbow next to her daughter. "I am not in your shoes. Your shoes are very big ones to fill."

"But my feet are tiny compared to yours."

"Humor is one of your greatest allies. Do keep using it. I suspect you will need it more than ever moving forward."

"You didn't respond to my question."

"Did Matangi mention anything about training?"

"A little. She didn't go into any details, though."

"What would you like to know?"

"Well, for starters, who would I be training *with*?"

"What we call Fallenium Incorporation would be handled by your grandmother. Matangi would be in charge of helping you master the Language of the Birds. And to consummate your training, I myself would take you to meet the Goddess."

"*Meet* her? Where does she *live*?"

"In a general sense, everywhere. But more specifically as well as practically, it is customary for the Rose, the Future Rose and the Mahavidyas to interface with her in a cave nearby."

"What do you mean 'interface'?"

"Meet her. Converse with her. Ask her questions."

"Have *choro* tea together?"

"Not exactly."

"Does she appear as a … *person*?"

"No. She assumes the form of an animal—sometimes with human characteristics."

"What kind of animal?"

"Usually, she appears as a person's spirit animal."

"Sort of like you when you visited me as a crow?"

"Sort of. But on a much grander scale."

"What questions should I ask her?"

"You *are* full of questions, to be asking questions about questions!"

"And once again, you're not answering my question."

"Because that is one question I cannot answer."

"Then what do I need you for?"

Laughing, Caliandra held her daughter's hand against her lips and kissed it. Cali suddenly felt eight years old again as—finally giving into her deep love for her mother—she allowed herself to be held as she emptied a mixed bag of tears containing at least one for every possible emotion.

I n the late evening as dusk fell, after spending the rainy afternoon following lunch with her mother alone in the Regeneration Suite modeling her new wardrobe, packing much of it into a wicker suitcase Matangi had dropped off with a note and downing cup after cup of *choro* tea (which, if nothing else, truly was psychologically addictive), Cali found herself strolling down to the port alone.

Well, not *alone*. Many women and children with their own luggage and supplies were also making their way along the various still damp (the rain having stopped) forest paths that meandered toward the beach.

Some people, noting the rose in Cali's hair, recognized her and nodded or smiled in greeting. One young girl went so far as to approach and squeeze her free hand. But for the most part, Cali was given her space and allowed to blend into what she could only process as the beginning of a mass pilgrimage.

Heronton, Tula's main port, confirmed this description. Emerging from the darkening woods in which fireflies were starting to appear to behold the unmistakable fallenium glow of what must have been hundreds of streetlights and thousands of smaller lamps suspended from as many exotic sailboats, Cali felt her breath momentarily suspended.

"You must be Cali!" exclaimed a young redhead in a simple white sari and a necklace with a single magpie feather as she emerged against the current of walkers. "My Goddess, you are even more beautiful than they said!"

This the seeming teenager, staring with huge green eyes that seemed too large for her Gaelic face, said while taking Cali's hand and shaking it vigorously. "I am Lena. Here, allow me to carry your suitcase. We should make haste."

"Pleased to meet you, Lena."

"Likewise. Sophia sent me. She told me not to let you out of my sight. Except for, you know, personal things."

"Did she now?" asked Cali, following her breathless guide forward at a fast clip. "And who might 'they' be?"

Lena answered over her shoulder. "Why, the Mahavidyas, of course. It is not every day a Future Rose appears in Tula. You made quite an impression."

"I can assure you the feeling was mutual. Where exactly are you taking me?"

"To your vessel, naturally."

"My … *vessel?*"

"It was supposed to be a surprise. I already messed that up. Sorry. Sometimes my mouth gets me in trouble. But I mean well."

Sure enough, after several minutes they arrived at a massive white sailboat with the name "Cali" painted in gold English letters on the stern. The only thing more surprising was that this vessel was docked beside a similar boat christened "Juice."

"Won't you look what the cat drug on!" At the sound of a certain beloved bass voice, Cali's heart fluttered involuntarily. Appearing with a smile at the rear of his boat, Juice hopped down onto the dock in a white silk robe and took her in his arms. "Don't get me wrong, Your Highness. I dig Apollo. But I'm *really* glad to see you."

"Then put your money where your mouth is."

"Right here in front of the Goddess and everybody?"

"Why not?"

"You know why not. This is a time of mourning."

Cali could have used a dozen kisses and other things besides. But even the wild child in her realized it was neither the time nor the place for funny business.

"Not to switch subjects," said Juice. "But though I don't have any money, it appears I do have a boat."

"Me, too. We can be boat buddies."

"Ha ha."

"With your permission, Cali, I will wait for you onboard," said Lena.

"Thanks. I'll be right there."

As Lena boarded the sailboat with Cali's suitcase, Juice remarked, "I hope you know how to sail."

"I wouldn't know where to start. What about you?"

"I think I could probably manage to sail a toy boat in a very calm fountain."

"Surely, they don't expect us to navigate to Kalahili on our own."

"I suspect you're right. Strange women with nautical personalities have been coming and going around both our boats ever since I got here an hour ago."

"'Nautical personalities.' You're actually funny today. What's got into you?"

"I just have this wonderful memory of a certain beach encounter—to stay on the nautical theme. Maybe it was only a dream."

"Maybe it was."

"I must say the two of you make a handsome couple." The voice rising above the crowd buzz this time was Matangi's. She waltzed up in a boldly cut white sari with a white-robed Apollo in tow.

"One of these days, we'll all have to go on a double date," said Cali, who thought she could make out her brother blushing even in the lamplight.

"It is good to see you again, Cali," he said, placing his hand on her shoulder as he kissed her cheek. "How are you holding up?"

"Oh, you know me. Just defying the laws of gravity as usual. What about you?"

"Apollo still blames himself for what happened to Thelete," interjected Matangi. "I have told him that if we were living in medieval times, he would most certainly be a Flagellant."

"There might be some truth to that," conceded Apollo.

"Well, for what it's worth," said Cali, "I could kick myself for not arriving in Rose Cove earlier. Then Thelete would still be here with us."

"But that is silly," said Apollo. "How could you have possibly known to come earlier?"

"How could you have possibly known for sure helping Freddy was a dangerous proposition?"

"Touché."

"The bottom line," said Matangi, "is that we are all wandering around in the dark with our little torches doing our best to make out the big picture."

"Spoken like a true Mahavidya," said Cali.

"I have my moments."

Up and down the port, people suddenly began to ring handbells of various sizes. Gradually, more and more people—including Matangi and Apollo—joined in … until nearly all of the thousands assembled were chiming in.

The sound, though extremely nuanced and lovely, was also amazingly loud. Cali was shocked that small bells could generate so much sonic power.

"What's going on?" shouted Juice.

"It is the signal for our departure," yelled Apollo. "Matangi and I must return to our vessels. Smooth sailing, everyone!"

"Smooth sailing!" shouted Matangi.

"Back at you!" yelled Cali.

"Just one kiss before we hit the high seas?" she asked, turning to face Juice again.

"Okay. But just a little one."

The only true sailboat Cali had ever been on was New World Order Records owner Dalton Oglethorpe's when she visited him at his South Beach residence while on tour. But even Dalton's yacht, *Nefertiti*, which easily accommodated a baker's dozen bronzed, scantily clad, polyamorous twentysomethings, paled in comparison to Cali's eponymous craft.

As soon as she was onboard, Lena guided her past several "nautical" women (all busy in different ways preparing for a sea voyage) to the great cabin.

Though minimalistic in the Tula esthetic, the captain's quarters were nevertheless both comfortable and comforting—complete with numerous windows set in mahogany walls, a Murphy bed in the upright position, a charming kitchenette and stylish dining table graced with a bouquet of roses surrounded by four cushioned chairs, and a small but tasteful bathroom (walk-in shower only).

The contrast between this refined, vaulted environment and Aristotle's riverboat—an unsolicited memory that, shockingly, was barely days old—couldn't in a million years have been starker.

"Is everything to your liking?" asked Lena, setting Cali's suitcase beside the bed and touching a standing fallenium lamp to create a little more light.

"As I keep saying here, I don't think 'liking' has anything to do with it. This is … insane."

Lena grinned and blinked her oversized eyes. "I will take that as a compliment. I helped decorate the cabin myself."

"Well, you did a bang-up job."

"Thank you."

"How long will it take us to reach Kalahili?" No sooner had Cali asked this question than she felt the boat begin to move.

"A day and a half."

"Meaning we'll be spending two nights onboard?"

"Correct. Do you get seasick?"

"I haven't yet."

"Unfortunately, I do sometimes. I brought some *leramin* leaves just in case. Do let me know if you need any."

"Will do."

"Would you like to step on deck to watch the Phalanx come together? It is quite a spectacle—especially at night."

"Sure, whatever that means."

Outside, the bells had stopped ringing and a forewind had started blowing seemingly out of nowhere as a ship even larger than her own christened with a name in Kalidon (so Cali assumed from its Sanskrit-like script) took the lead.

In the lamplight she managed to recognize her mother in a regal white sari like an exquisite masthead standing on the prow facing out to sea as the *Cali* and *Juice* fell in behind, followed by the vessels of the ten Mahavidyas in a horizontal line … at which point more and more craft of every description added to an ever-widening V-shape like a gigantic flock of glowing birds sailing through the night.

The one commonality shared by every boat was the flag of Tula fluttering at half-mast in Thelete's honor. Beneath the flag each vessel had a second flag featuring individual renderings of a huge variety of recognizable and unknown birds. This included her own crow and an owl for Juice, who was now also on deck taking in the sight of the Bird Tribes coming into a formation of thousands—with more joining by the minute.

He grinned and she grinned back as their eyes locked briefly with a virtually telepathic communiqué along the lines of, "We're not in Kansas anymore."

As the great Phalanx entered the open sea, the wind filled its collective sails even more. It dawned on Cali her mother was summoning a favorable wind, which meant there would be no doldrums on this important voyage.

And there weren't any. Nor did Cali experience any seasickness— though Lena did when they soon hit a rough patch, which meant she spent a good portion of the journey sipping *leramin* tea (which Cali was happy to prepare for her) and remaining horizontal in her own quarters.

Thirty-six hours passed in a breezy regatta of monumental proportions as Cali, left to her own devices, alternately slept, ate (the kitchenette, though small, was remarkably well stocked) and stood on deck admiring the view while the nautical women sailed her namesake straight and true through night and day and night again.

Tired of resting and feeling antsy, she was onboard in the wee hours of her second morning at sea marveling at millions of luminescent jellyfish lighting up the water—when an even stranger light overhead caught her eye.

Up ahead in the distance, what she figured out was a volcano was spitting fluorescent orange sparks high into the scarlet atmosphere. It was like nature's own fireworks display streaming what looked like glowing blood cells through the liquid medium of the sky.

Hoping to share this unprecedented sight, she looked for Juice on the prow of his own vessel—but he was nowhere to be found.

"Land, ho!" cried one of the nautical women as the crew, working as one, began making preparations for arrival.

Cali might never star in a real holofilm, but her real life was certainly cinematic enough.

"Land, ho!" she whispered with a private smile as the sun, shooting a flickering causeway across the water, suddenly appeared above the western horizon.

Under normal circumstances, as mentioned, the women and men of the Bird Tribes intermingled only twice a year—during the lengthy holidays known as Springtide and Falltide. Reserved for dedicated work in service to the Goddess, other times of year were typically spent in "segregated" environments. The convergence of men and women from all over Tula at Kalahili at the start of Summertide was an anomaly, one that only necessity or a great tragedy could have induced.

By far the largest of the islands known as the Thorns, saddle-shaped Kalahili measured over three hundred twenty by two hundred miles. The island was so large, in fact, it was made up of several distinct microenvironments. One end boasted towering cliffs, vertiginous waterfalls, and a verdant jungle; the other end was arid and notched with an enormous red-rock canyon called the Wound.

At the island's center where tens of thousands of sailboats had gathered around a packed harbor with a pier jutting out in the middle, a wide black sand beach led to a subtropical forest climbing the foothills surrounding Mount Kalahili. The volcano was colossal—with a sawed-off obsidian cone jaggedly surveying the land and sea in all directions.

Cali was still balancing on the prow watching the nautical women furl the sails and drop anchor when Lena (looking extremely pale and fragile) emerged from her quarters.

"Good morning," said Cali. "How are you feeling?"

Her assistant's voice was as haggard as her demeanor. "Is it not obvious?"

"It is, I'm afraid. But cheer up—we'll be on solid ground soon enough."

Lena sighed. "If only that were true in all instances. Unfortunately, among the women only the Rose, the Future Rose and the Mahavidyas will set foot on Kalahili for the memorial ceremony."

"Something to do with this being outside the holidays?"

When Lena nodded despondently, Cali placed a comforting hand on her shoulder. "Is there anything I can do to help?"

"You have helped a great deal already."

"I mean besides serving you *leramin* tea. That's *nasty* stuff, by the way. I'd rather drink tea made with moldy socks."

"But it does take the edge off."

"What else might do that?"

"You can sing me a song."

"Sadly, I don't know any birdsongs for seasickness."

"I meant a song from your world. Something enjoyable I can replay in my mind to pass the time."

Cali thought for a moment and then sang an old American country song titled "Abilene," which seemed to please Lena, who begged to hear it once more in order to commit it to memory.

"You have such a lovely voice, Cali."

"Thank you."

"It reminds me of Matangi's."

"That *is* a compliment."

"Here's your dinghy."

Cali looked down in the direction Lena was indicating. Sure enough, a small oared canoe in which two nautical women stood motioning for Cali was bobbing alongside the ship.

"How do I look?" asked Cali.

"Like the Future Rose."

"Seriously."

"I was being serious."

Cali gave an exaggerated smile. "Nothing stuck between my teeth?"

"Nothing but your tongue."

"I think that song already made you feel better."

"Why do you say that?"

"Your sense of humor is back."

Cali could hear Lena humming "Abilene" for a couple of minutes before the sound was drowned out by the crashing waves near the shore. Soon Cali found herself clasping hands with Juice, who helped her up a ladder onto the wooden pier, where her mother, her brother and the Mahavidyas awaited in a sea of white.

"Always the tardy prima donna," said Juice with a wink.

"Shut up."

Caliandra, regal as always with a massive rose in her twisting hair, led the group of newcomers to the steps that descended from the pier onto dry land. Here they were met by twenty middle-aged and elderly men in bird-feather headdresses and white robes of their own.

"Welcome back to our humble island, Sophia," said a wizened figure of a man with the face of an ancient Native Fatherlander in a long headdress of duck feathers that extended down over his bony shoulders.

"Thank you, Aeneas," replied Caliandra as the stout warrior named Achilles Freddy had called his "babysitter" in Rose Cove stepped forward and assisted her onto the black sand. "And thank you, Achilles."

Both men nodded as, one by one, starting with Cali and ending with her grandmother, the other women were given a hand down off the pier. Juice followed without help and Apollo was alone as he brought up the rear.

"Shall we?" said Caliandra, once again taking the lead.

Without further ado, with the men following the women, the party that had now swelled to nearly three dozen luminaries left the shoreline and entered the forest—which, if seen from a bird's-eye perspective, would have appeared speckled with countless tipis. Besides fallenium fire pits like the communal one in Rose Cove, there were no signs of permanent construction.

Silently, nodding reverently, feathered men in white robes came forth in droves to line the path that wound up and up toward Mount Kalahili. Cali quickly became aware she was an object of curiosity; it also dawned on her that Juice himself, as the Future Thorn, was being sized up by the men of the Bird Tribes.

She was reminded of stories from European history about monarchs who hadn't even been born in the countries they governed. She and Juice would never be monarchs; but if they stayed in the Deep World, they would always be foreigners.

The higher the party wound up into the foothills, the more Cali became aware of something else, something very strange indeed. At first she noted only a smattering of owls perched in the stately palms and sprawling willows of Kalahili.

But as the climb continued long enough for her to break a sweat and grow short of breath, the forest literally seemed to fill up with owls of every possible (and seemingly impossible) variety. Within the space of an hour, she estimated at least twenty thousand specimens were blinking, fidgeting and flapping in the trees.

"What's up with the owls?" she whispered to Matangi. "You'd think this was an aviary."

When Matangi shrugged, Apollo, having overheard Cali's question, responded from behind, "Achilles said they began arriving soon after Thelete's passing."

"Does this … *normally* happen?"

"There is historical precedent for such behavior. But the sheer number, I admit, is astonishing."

"I can *hear* them," said Juice with an odd tone in his voice.

"What do you mean?" asked Apollo.

"I can pick up on their thoughts. They're like us. They're also in … mourning."

"Well," said Apollo, "if there were any question as to the rightness of your selection as the Future Thorn, that has now been put to rest."

"Speaking of rest," said Cali, panting, "how far does this trail go?"

"All the way to the crater," replied Apollo.

"You've got to be kidding!"

"I am not. But we will not be going quite that far."

"How much longer do we have? I'm about to sweat through this sari."

"Would you like me to toss you over my shoulder like old times?" joked Juice.

"Fat chance."

Kalahili was belching smoke directly overhead when the party came to a clearing high enough to take in the multitude of ships anchored all around the inward part of the island's crescent. In the center of the clearing stood a gigantic ring of volcanic rocks that made Cali think of pictures she'd seen of Stonehenge.

Without words the party joined hands until a human ring formed around the stone one. Cali didn't know what to expect; she most assuredly didn't expect *nothing*.

But that was exactly what she got. For the better part of half an hour, the leaders of the Bird Tribes, hand in hand, stood in silence until—abruptly and inexplicably—Cali could have sworn *she heard other people's heartbeats*.

Actually, it was more than that. It was as if, by some strange process of entrainment in that sacred spot of standing stones beneath the smoking heart of the Goddess, the women and men present were able to blend their heartbeats into a single grand biological rhythm.

This—and not words—*was* Thelete's memorial ceremony, which ended up being, rather than a heavy-hearted service, an organic celebration of a life honorably lived in service to the greater good.

The enormous stones seemed to absorb the collective energy thus generated, magnifying and broadcasting it in all directions. Even the owls crowding the nearby trees appeared to feel it as they flapped their wings and began calling loudly.

At length, whether acting instinctively or on an invisible cue, Matangi stepped forward and started to sing as the circle closed around her. "*ELAEOOUUIAIE*," her birdsong began. "*AOEEEIAUO* ..."

As her marvelous voice traveled up and down the exotic notes of the Deep World scale, Cali felt that the song's energy was also amplified by the Standing Stones. At the same time, with her mother fixing her gaze on Kalahili, a stiff breeze suddenly began to blow down from the mountain, carrying the birdsong as far as the ships, which responded by raising their flags to full staff in tandem.

The song had a decidedly emotional effect as well. Like a spring rain falling on winter's snow, it immediately began to melt any and all internal places that had been hardened by grief. By the time Matangi finished singing, the universe seemed lighter and brighter and everyone was smiling and laughing with tears shining in their eyes.

Afterward, there was no coming together over food and drink as with funerals in the Fatherland. No sooner had Cali said goodbye to Apollo and Juice than she found herself whisked off by the nautical women and once again balancing on the prow of the *Cali* toward the tip of the Phalanx (minus the *Juice* this time) on the high seas.

During the return journey, she kept mentally replaying her parting conversation with the Future Thorn held standing on the pier above the rolling waves.

"Are you sure you don't want to come back to Tula with me?" she'd pleaded teasingly, sliding her hands around his rock-solid waist and pulling him close.

"You know I do. And you know I won't."

She gazed searchingly into the swirls of his caramel eyes and asked, "Why exactly?"

"You know why."

"I have my suspicions. But I want to hear the words from your mouth. I *need* to hear them from you."

"Fair enough."

"I'm waiting."

"Okay, let me frame it like this. On the way back down from the clearing, one of the old warriors told me something about this place that made everything click. He said the Thorns symbolize those who keep the Goddess from harm. It seems obvious, but it made me realize that's *my* purpose, too: to protect you with every fiber of my being and, by doing that, to protect the earth itself."

"So you're fully committed to training?"

"I'm all in."

"Then so am I."

After one last long, deep kiss during which he held her like a precious pearl, he dropped one final truth bomb as she got comfortable in her dinghy:

"You do realize when we see each other again, we won't be even remotely the same?"

For once she didn't have a repartee. Her quick wit was powerless to make light of the fact that everything, including themselves, was about to change ... dramatically and forever.

They were both past the proverbial point of no return. The future, prophecies be damned, was a mystery that—try as she might to fathom it—Cali couldn't begin to wrap her mind around.

The imminent (and for that matter, immanent) reality of change was brought home, so to speak, the morning after her evening arrival in Tula when she visited her grandmother's house for the first time.

Situated not in the trees but on the ground overlooking the ocean and reached by following a crooked flagstone path punctuated by numerous stone steps, the brown adobe structure, though small, was cleverly designed to suggest a bird's nest with many asymmetrical windows tucked against the cliffs.

Even as she approached the front door, her grandmother's crackly voice—"Good morning, my dear!"—intercepted her from the far end of a covered porch where she stood with a view of the sea painting a large canvas on an easel.

No longer dressed in white, Kali now sported rolled-up trousers and a paint-splotched smock. Her tiny feet, twisted by the years, were bare with unpainted nails. Cali felt decidedly overdressed in her white sari and sandals showcasing glossy red nails she'd had time to paint during the return voyage from Kalahili.

"Good morning, Grandmother. How are you today?"

"If you ask me, every day I am still alive and healthy is a fine day."

"What are you painting?" The question popped out of Cali's mouth even as she answered it herself. "Is that ... my *father*?"

"It will be when I finish it."

"It's ... *phenomenal.*" Her grandmother's technique at this stage of her artistic career was explosively expressive, yet still instantly recognizable. Even barely sketched, Thelete looked just like himself; he also prismatically radiated the presence of an Aeon. "You aren't actually doing this from memory, are you?"

"I always paint from memory."

"Impressive."

"Painting is a talent I seemed to be born with, but I cannot sing worth a lick. Never could. Just give me a minute to clean up. Please, make yourself at home."

While Kali cleaned her brushes at an outdoor sink, her granddaughter accepted her invitation and entered the interior, which struck her as nothing like a typical grandmother's house.

Landscapes, portraits and still lifes hung willy-nilly on the white plaster walls of a great room that connected the kitchen, dining and living areas in the Tula manner. Unlike other local dwellings, however, the furniture was eclectic—mismatched and oddly placed.

The floor, though earthen, was smooth like polished concrete yet splattered with paint in numerous places. Pungent dried herbs were suspended from thick rafters, while a stick of sweet-smelling incense burned on the hearth of a sooty kiva fireplace.

Cali was examining an equestrian portrait of her grandfather when her grandmother came in drying her wrinkled hands on her trousers.

"Do you ever sell your art?" asked Cali.

Her grandmother laughed her good witch's laugh. "Nobody sells anything in Tula, sweetheart."

"You mean you don't have money here?"

"We have wealth. Money is a tool of control invented by the Archons and implemented by your banking families."

Cali considered this new information. "But how does a society function without money?"

"Very well, as you can see. When people can do what they love, they do not mind also doing what needs to be done."

"But don't you ever trade with each other?"

"Yes, that is a time-honored, honest method of commerce."

"What are you doing?"

Kali had made an O-ring with her thumb and index finger and was using the corresponding digits of her other hand to try to pry the ring apart. "Surrogate muscle testing."

"Surrogate? For whom?"

"For you."

"Why?"

"To establish your starting dosage."

"Of what?"

"Such a questioning mind! I suspect you and I will get along swimmingly." The Mahavidya finished her testing with a perplexed expression in her ancient gray face. "Goodness gracious, that is a *lot* for the first time."

"A lot of *what*?"

"A lot of *minnah*. You could make a horse grow wings with that quantity!"

"What on earth is *minnah*? It sounds sort of like 'manna.'"

"It *is* manna. The true kind."

"So you eat it?"

"Of course!"

"Is it dangerous?"

"It can be—especially in the wrong hands."

"Have you ever eaten it?"

"Many times. Come." Kali motioned for her granddaughter to follow her into the kitchen, where she stood on a stepstool in order to reach a ceramic jar on a high shelf. "Do you prefer honey or molasses?"

"With what?"

"With anything. They are both used to hide the taste, which I can assure you is not to everyone's liking."

"Honey, I guess."

Producing a pair of goblets from a cabinet, Kali proceeded to fill them with water from the sink, drop a dollop of opaque honey in both, and then, using one from a nested set of tiny metal spoons, measure out and add precise quantities of a reddish powder reminiscent of saffron contained in the jar. After stirring the liquid in both goblets for nearly a minute with her stubby, wrinkled fingers supporting extremely long nails, she handed Cali one.

Dubious, Cali sniffed the liquid. The musky smell, even though it was partially masked by honey, reminded her of Rose Cove. She realized this was because the odor was similar to fallenium smoke.

"I take it you have smelled powdered fallenium before," observed Kali.

"Yes. Tell me, what *is* fallenium?"

"Ingesting it will help teach you what your mind might otherwise have difficulty accepting."

"Are you going to take some as well?"

"With pleasure, my dear! Fallenium is not to be missed. It is nature's ultimate high."

"Well, since you put it *that* way …"

Embracing her inner wild child in the encouraging presence of her bohemian forebear, Cali raised her goblet and drained its contents. The taste, reminiscent of iron and salt, was remarkably pungent and bitter despite the honey. If Cali could have seen herself, she would have been shocked by a face almost as wrinkled as her grandmother's.

"That is my girl!" said Kali, slapping her trainee on the back approvingly as she downed her own dose. "Now take off your sandals and let us step outside quickly before we damage my house."

"How in the world could we *damage* your house?" asked a barefoot Cali as she followed her namesake out a side door and up the steep flank of the semitropical mountain overlooking the great blue sea of Tula.

"Are you implying you do not feel it yet?"

"What exactly should I be feeling?"

"You tell me."

Cali stopped underneath a gnarled oak of gigantic size with long beards of Spanish moss swaying in the salty breeze and shut her eyes in order to focus on her sensations.

At first all she could perceive was her heartbeat, which seemed to be growing louder and more insistent by the second: *thump, thuMP, thUMP, THUMP* …

Then, even as she realized her body was heating up, she became acutely, minutely aware of her immediate environment. She experienced the earth as she'd never experienced it before: as an organic living presence and the literal mother of all plants, animals, and people.

Not only was she intellectually conscious of her grandmother standing beside her; even with eyes closed, she could actually *sense* Kali, still barefoot, wiggling her twisted toes impatiently.

Similarly, and just as amazingly, she was also able to *feel* the shape of the oak overhead—its enormous trunk, sinuous limbs sprawling jaggedly in all directions and vast root system all coursing with what she visualized as glowing silver sap.

"The tree is like electricity!" she gasped. "It's like *lots* of lightning bolts—all connected to each other and the earth!"

"Yes!" Her grandmother's excited response ricocheted around her mind like an echoing pinball. "Go on!"

Cali concentrated harder. "There are birds living high in the tree."

"How many?"

"Three. A mother, a father, and a chick."

"What else can you tell me about them?"

"They're doves."

"What kind?"

"Mourning doves?"

"*Very* good."

"We've also got company incoming on the ground."

"Oh, that is just Lionel."

Sensing a large feline presence approaching, Cali reopened her eyes to find herself face to face with what she instantly recognized as an adult cheetah!

Her initial, conditioned response was to recoil in fear the way she had upon seeing her mother's mountain lions. But even as she started to step back, she grasped—by simply observing his body language—that Lionel came in peace.

"What are you waiting for?" asked Kali. "It is obvious he is not here to bite you."

"Why *is* he here?" asked Cali, timidly extending her hand to pet the powerful cat's beautifully spotted head between his perky ears.

"I imagine he can sense the fallenium we just took and wants to be closer to the Goddess." With Cali scratching his fur, Lionel started to purr loudly and his eyelids began to droop. "I have known Lionel since he was a furball. What a pushover. I like to think of him as my unofficial pet."

Meanwhile, unlike Lionel, Cali was doing anything but growing sleepy. In fact, she felt an impulse to exercise—vigorously.

No sooner had this notion occurred to her than Lionel, as if reading her thoughts, shook off the drowsies, spun around, and took off like a torpedo through the woods. Seconds later Cali and her grandmother, having exchanged mischievous glances, were hot on his trail (and tail).

Cali was astonished by her geriatric relation's speed—but even more flabbergasted by her own. The forest whirled past like something out of a video game as she took the lead and actually began to gain on Lionel, a perfectly healthy specimen of the planet's fastest land animal in his prime.

The chase ranged to the top of the mountain, down the other side, up another hill, and along the top of more cliffs jutting up out of the ocean far below. Sweat was pouring from Cali's pores and her dress was in stained tatters before she caught up to Lionel and playfully smacked his backside.

"Tag! You're it!" she said, breathing hard but not too hard as she slowed to a stop.

Breathing harder himself, Lionel also pulled up. With a dismissive snort, he gave a glance back at her before plopping down on the forest floor to rest.

Just then a loud cawing caught her attention. A single crow was perched just overhead in an unfamiliar tree possibly from the willow family. She held out her hand. The jet-black bird hopped into her palm and cocked its head while eyeing her knowingly.

"Yes, I know who you are," said Cali. "You're me."

"*Caw, caw, caw!*" replied the crow.

"I see you have made a new friend." Her grandmother's winded voice came up from behind. "She looks just like you."

"She's beautiful."

"My point exactly."

"I can feel what she's feeling. She's very happy."

"Of course she is. She is with her maker."

"What's happening to me, Grandmother?"

"You have just ingested a small quantity of the body of the Goddess and, to that extent, become her."

"So that is what fallenium is: the body of the Goddess?"

"Specifically, it is the fruit of her womb."

"Surely you're not talking about her *eggs*?"

"What else would I be talking about?"

"Nothing, I guess. It's just … *weird*."

"Fallenium is the part of her physiology most saturated with her life force."

"With *kundalini*, you mean?"

"Precisely. Which means it must be incorporated with extreme care."

"Because it greatly amplifies human capabilities?"

"For good or ill."

"Is the change … permanent?"

"Unfortunately or otherwise, no. The effects gradually wear off."

"How much longer do we have?"

"An hour, give or take."

"Then let's take advantage of it!"

Mentally, Cali asked the crow to fly. Flapping its wings obligingly, it soared up and over the edge of the cliff. Cali was on the verge of following it—when her grandmother grasped her arm.

"There will come a time when you will fly, my dear. But you will not be in your present form. For now you must learn to employ circumspection about what you can and cannot do as a human being, however augmented."

"I'm overextending myself, aren't I?"

"Just a little."

"It's one of my character flaws."

Kali laughed her wild witch's laugh that her granddaughter was beginning to love. "This old heretic would say it is one of the Goddess's character flaws as well. After all, she was nicknamed **Precuneus**."

"Good point."

"The challenge, whether you are an Aeon or just a regular person, is to synthesize one's impulses with one's will—to be occasionally foolish, perhaps, but to be so *wisely*."

It was Cali's turn to utter a bit of a witch's laugh. "I *love* that!"

"I am glad."

When her grandmother began stripping off her clothes, Cali asked, "What are you doing?"

"Preparing to teach you something by way of some crazy wisdom in action."

Naked at last, the old Mahavidya stepped to the edge of the cliff, surveyed the sea far below, and—without uttering another word—executed a perfect dive.

"Whoa!" whispered Cali as she counted nearly three seconds before her grandmother disappeared like an arrow into the turquoise waves.

Not to be outdone by a senior citizen, Cali removed what was left of her sari and—without so much as a second thought, trusting in her teacher and her own skills—followed suit.

Plummeting, she realized—with a wry smile that lasted even after she pierced the water's tepid surface—that diving was like training wheels for flying.

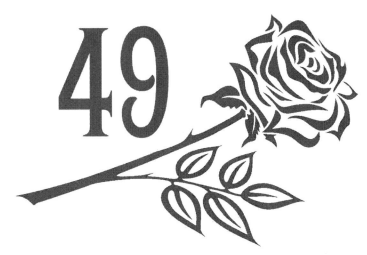

S till powered by fallenium, the two ended up breaststroking in the company of a pod of bottlenose dolphins all the way back down to a secluded horseshoe beach nestled at the base of the cliffs not far down the coast from Kali's house.

Only after stretching out buck naked beside her au naturel grandmother on the toasty, talcy sand for quite some time did Cali realize she wasn't even self-conscious; nor was she the least bit disturbed by Kali's nonchalant nudity.

Maybe this was because, for now anyway, they were living in a society almost entirely devoid of men. Or maybe Cali was simply becoming more comfortable in her own skin. Either way, she meant it when she said, "I'm starting to feel at home here."

"That was quick."

"You think?"

"Undoubtedly. I imagined you would be more stubborn."

Cali didn't know whether to laugh or take offense. "Why?"

"Because you are my granddaughter—not to mention my daughter's daughter."

Recalling the willful exchange between Kali and Caliandra over breakfast with the Mahavidyas days earlier, Cali laughed out loud. "I see your point."

"To be cut from the same cloth yet to find it in you so quickly to forgive—that is impressive."

"I didn't say I'd forgiven anybody."

"Not even yourself?"

"Especially not myself."

"You more than merely resemble your brother then."

"So I'm beginning to suspect." Cali sighed. "I do worry about him."

"And he worries about you. Face it: you may be warriors, but you are also worriers."

Kali's leathery breasts sagged sideways as she propped herself on an elbow and rolled over to face her granddaughter with a subject-changing question: "So tell me, what have you learned from your first day of Fallenium Incorporation?"

"That I have a lot to learn."

"Excellent! Ask me your questions."

"Where do I even start?"

"Why not with the easiest one and work up?"

"Okay. I assume eating fallenium increases body temperature because it supercharges the circuits with *kundalini*?"

"You just answered your own question. Next."

"I also assume this is similar to what happens when one becomes an Aeonic Vessel. My mother's skin's always crazy hot to the touch; so was Thelete's."

"Two for two. The major difference being that Fallenium Incorporation is a temporary *kundalini* increase, whereas an Aeonic Vessel must be capable of living day in, day out with the energy of ten thousand normal human beings."

"Thus the necessity of my training with you?"

"Thus the necessity."

Cali sat up and, with a wistful sensation, stared out across the gently lapping waves in the direction of Kalahili. Though the great volcano lay well beyond sight, she imagined she could sense its throbbing, molten presence distantly.

"Does Juice's training also involve Fallenium Incorporation?"

"Of course."

"And is he also running around chasing wild animals and practicing cliff diving?"

"Maybe. Over time, however, the focus of his instruction will shift to combat with and without fallenium weapons."

"I'm sure he'll revel in that."

Cali could feel her grandmother's intense, dark-eyed gaze boring into her. "My sweet girl, I sense you have been apprised of your ... profound connection to each other?"

"Yeah, Matangi made that painfully clear. You know, I didn't sign up for a starring role in a cosmic soap opera."

"Maybe part of you did."

"You mean the Sophia part?"

"If the shoe fits. You are rather sassy, after all."

"I have another question."

"Fire away."

"Is fallenium some kind of *metal* or an *organic* substance? Juice couldn't make heads or tails of it."

"Uniquely, it is classified by our scientists as an *organic metal*. It can be forged like steel or powdered like grain—and everything between. Each of its phases possesses special qualities and imparts specific powers."

"No wonder Freddy was so keen on getting his grubby hands—hand—on it."

Kali joined her granddaughter in sitting cross-legged facing the sea. "My dear, the Archons and their minions have spent millennia attempting to gain access to fallenium."

"I take it they were never successful?"

"No. But by digging their little deep underground bases in Archontic imitation of the Deep World, they have come close on several occasions. Cut off from the fruit of the Goddess's womb and unable to synthesize it even, they did what Archons do best: they *simulated* fallenium."

"How did they manage that?"

"Using their planetary proxies, the Illuminati, many centuries ago the Archons figured out the recipe for monatomic gold powder, which they directed the Illuminati to make and consume in a manner similar to Fallenium Incorporation."

"To what purpose?"

"This powder—which they called manna in imitation of true *minnah*—was a powerful psychotropic substance in its own right that gave those who consumed it access to the Lord Archon in much the same way fallenium allows one to enter into communion with the Goddess."

The light of revelation clicked on in Cali's mind. "So that's how the Illuminati have plans that unfold over periods of time much longer than a single human life!"

"Precisely. The practice of consuming manna allows them to receive ongoing instruction, generation after generation, from the Lord Archon, who is bent on subjugating—and ultimately destroying—the human race."

"How lovely."

"There is more. Unlike with *minnah*, manna consumption carries with it a major side effect. Over time eating it renders the psyche porous to and easily infected—and thus controlled—by Archontic mind parasites."

Cali gave a snarky giggle as one implication dawned on her. "In which case no microchips are needed."

"None whatsoever. The Illuminati are the willing terrestrial servants of the Lord Archon, who demands everything from pedophilia and child sacrifice to war and chaos as offerings that create *loosh*."

"Never heard of it."

"*Loosh* is a hyperdimensional energy given off by the human soul when traumatized. The Archons parasitically feed on it. Think of it as their simulacrum of *kundalini*."

"Why is seemingly everything the Archons do counterfeit?"

"Because they lack the capacity to create anything truly original. In their insane jealousy, they can only mimic the divinely instilled creative capacity of the Anthropos."

"So are the Illuminati still technically even … *human*?"

"That is a probing question. If the definition of a human is a child of the Goddess in possession of an immortal soul and the ability to invent, the answer would most certainly be *no*."

Cali couldn't help visualizing Freddy's frightening, nonhuman eyes when he last spoke to her before sending her off to be executed.

"Don't the Illuminati realize they're just pawns in someone else's game?"

"Even if they realize this, I will wager they are beyond caring. They have been completely integrated into the AI."

"The AI?"

"The Artificial Intelligence. This is another term for the Archontic hive mind. It is a binary operating system that imitates the many shades of gray characteristic of human intelligence—only to end up a circumscribed parody of it that processes everything strictly in terms of black and white."

"Good versus evil?"

"Man versus woman. Rich versus poor. East versus West. Liberal versus conservative. Take your pick. Anytime you see dichotomies that ignore the human experiment's infinite nuances, you can be certain you are encountering the Archontic mind."

Cali sighed and slumped her shoulders as her first day of training finally began to catch up with her.

"The fallenium is dissipating," remarked her grandmother as, seemingly unaffected herself, she popped up on her feet and extended a hand. "We had better head up the path to my house before you crash."

The sudden extreme weariness in Cali's voice was nearly palpable. "I think I'm already crashing."

"Come on, you can do it."

Cali accepted the old Mahavidya's hand and got unsteadily to her feet. Her legs felt as heavy as tree stumps as she contemplated the practically vertical path up between cliffs she was expected to climb.

"What if I can't?"

"Then I will just have to drag you. And that would be embarrassing. So suck it up."

50

Fortunately, given their lack of clothes, they didn't encounter a soul on the path, which Cali literally willed herself to climb step by arduous step.

Her only thought, since she was practically unable to think from fatigue, was a memory of being carried to bed by Olga around midnight after the third consecutive show of her first tour when she wasn't so much a star yet as just an exhausted little girl.

Being helped in the front door, lowered onto a futon couch in the chaotic living room and covered with a deerskin blanket redolent of frankincense all occurred in something like a dream. She was practically asleep before her head touched the bolster.

In her actual dream that followed, she found herself penetrating a dark mountain cave entrance resembling a twenty-foot yoni, a stylized design of female genitalia she'd seen and read about years ago in her mother's book on goddess iconography.

The cave was dark and full of dripping echoes. But as her vision adjusted, Cali realized the walls were speckled with ovals of various sizes giving off a faint red phosphorescence—enough to navigate a narrow path winding, ascending and descending deep into the mountainside.

She'd heard of mountain lions and other deadly creatures that lived in caves, so it was with some trepidation that she carefully made her way forward. As she did, the light grew stronger and stronger—and eventually began to pulse, harder and harder.

At what she intuited from the shapes of the shadows to be the back of the cave, a gigantic form lay sleeping. She couldn't be sure what it was, but she clearly discerned the epic sweep of its breath as it rose and fell. Even as she felt herself becoming mesmerized, the creature began to twitch and purr like a great cat … only on a leviathan scale!

273

Suddenly, it opened one gigantic eye like a monster in a fairy tale. The eye was unlike any Cali had ever beheld. It was more like a whelk or nautilus shell than an actual eye, and perhaps more like a spiraling galaxy than any type of shell, and as it observed her Cali felt its immense, otherworldly power grab hold of her.

Drawn like iron to an industrial magnet, she was pulled into the eye. Soon she began to spin as she traveled the spiraling path toward the pupil, which even as she realized was a black hole, she understood was the Pleroma!

The stars and solar systems of the Kenoma whirled past as she corkscrewed like a human spaceship toward the dark epicenter of the galaxy. "Mother!" she screamed involuntarily while watching obsidian feathers sprout from her hands and arms, which soon turned into wings. "Mother! Mother!! Mother!!!"

"I am afraid I will have to do," said a soothing voice from outside the dream. "*Breathe*, my dear. Just *breathe*. Fallenium can bring strange visions."

Popping bolt upright, Cali tore off the deerskin blanket and, panting wildly, frantically examined her limbs. They were sunburnt and crusted with salt from the sea. But they were still human.

"There, there," said her grandmother, perching in a fresh painterly outfit on the couch beside her and holding her hand. "All is well."

Still shaking off the vestiges of her dream, or nightmare, in the slanted evening sunlight streaming through the east-facing windows, Cali asked, "What's happening to me?"

"You are transforming, my child."

"Into *what* exactly?"

Kali's cronish expression somehow managed to be both compassionate and hard-edged. "You know exactly what."

"So I'm supposed to turn into an *actual* crow?"

"Only when you need to."

"Have you ever turned into a crow?"

"Only when I needed to."

"Is it ... painful?"

"It is ... odd. At first."

In that instant a warm, familiar scent, wafting out of the kitchen, hit Cali. But so out of place was it in the bizarre setting of her grandmother's house-cum-studio, she couldn't quite place it.

"What am I smelling? Whatever it is, it must be delicious."

"I hope you think so when you taste it. I have an apple pie in the oven."

"An *apple pie?*"

"Do not act so surprised. Apple pies are hardly exclusive to the Fatherland. Are you hungry?"

"I could eat a horse."

"Well, fortunately, you do not have to." Retrieving something from a nearby chair, Kali tossed it in her granddaughter's lap. "Here, put this on."

"What is it?"

"One of my saris. It will look more like a 'little black dress' on your frame, but I will wager that is not such a bad thing."

Left alone, Cali stood up and pulled on the sari. As it clung to her like a glove and barely reached her knees, she noted it would have been completely illegal in the Fatherland.

"Say, where's the bathroom?" she called out to her grandmother in the kitchen.

"Down the hall on the left."

"Thanks."

"Do not tarry. The pie is almost ready."

Having finished her business, Cali looked in the mirror while washing her hands. A wild woman like a scary caricature of herself stared back. Shockingly, the woman had several silver hairs threading through the tangled bird's nest on her head!

"I thought people were supposed to age more slowly in the Deep World," said Cali as she entered the kitchen. "Me, I'm going gray at fifteen."

Her grandmother laughed as she pulled a piping-hot pie from the oven. "You are not 'going gray.' But your electrical system is receiving a major overhaul."

"Will I get more gray hairs?"

"Maybe. But eventually, they will go away."

"Like yours?"

"Mine are signs of wisdom that a certain young lady would do well to respect."

"Oh, I do. I wouldn't be foolishly following you off cliffs otherwise."

Kali grinned as she set two places at the kitchen bar. "Indeed."

"I think I'll keep them."

"Keep what?"

"The hairs. For now anyway. I think they make me look distinguished."

"Just avoid becoming old and boring before your time and you will be all right."

"With a grandmother like you as a role model? No way."

Kali gave her a peck on the forehead and then served up the pie with vanilla ice cream on top. Not standing on ceremony with her hunger getting the best of her, Cali dug in like a … wild woman.

"What would you like to drink, my dear?"

"Water. Lots of it please."

"Coming right up."

Having poured two glasses and set a pitcher of water on the counter, Kali sat down beside her granddaughter and dug in heartily as well.

"This pie is out of this world," said Cali. "What all's in it?"

"Apples, of course. Einkorn flour. Tons of butter. Coconut sugar. A pinch of salt. Raisins. Also several kinds of toasted nuts. And a bit of bone marrow."

"*Bone* marrow?"

"Yes. For your bones. I can write down the recipe if you like."

"Please do. Maybe I'll learn to bake when I'm one or two hundred."

"Maybe you will."

"I have a question about the dream I just had."

"I am all ears."

"Why did the Goddess appear to me as a *cat?* Why wasn't she a bird?"

"Because you were not in the Dream of the Goddess. You were merely dreaming of the Goddess."

"It seemed real enough."

"Probably because of your deep connection to her. But entering the Dream of the Goddess normally involves actually being with her."

"In her cave?"

"Yes."

"Are there exceptions?"

"They are rare, but they have been documented to happen in the case of especially gifted Roses."

Cali finished her water and poured herself another glass. "What will happen when the Goddess awakens, Grandmother?"

"There are many theories. The real answer is: we do not know."

"Isn't this described in the Prophecy?"

"No. Funny, is it not?"

"A little. I guess some things can't be known."

"Well spoken."

"But some things can. For example, it's written that the Archons will be destroyed."

"Technically, it is written that their works are to be dissolved."

"Which means they'll be defeated, right?"

"That is my interpretation."

"But *how?* How can humans defeat such an entrenched alien force that can control the human mind?"

"That is perhaps a question you should ask the Goddess when you enter her Dream. After all, you are the Destroyer."

"That's the second time you've called me that. What does it mean?"

"It is the nickname given to you in the Prophecy. What it means is … whatever you make it mean."

276

"That's a lot of help."

Kali laughed. "You are destined to receive all the help you need. And then it is your destiny to help a lot of people. Would you like another slice of pie?"

"Definitely. I need all the help-ings I can get!"

"This is for you, Cali. I took the liberty of piercing the quill so you can easily add it to your necklace. Wear it well."

Cali accepted the gift of a single crow feather from her grandmother. The two were standing just outside the house at the entrance to the path as Tula's dark-room night settled in and the endless sun throbbed gently on the horizon.

"What exactly did I do to deserve this?"

"Much. You were impressive today."

"Thanks. When will I see you again?"

"In a few days—when you have had time to recover your strength."

Even as the ancient Mahavidya said these words, Cali's whole body seemed to yawn. "You know, I *am* pretty tired."

"That is evident. I suspect you will sleep like the Goddess tonight. Come, give your grandmother a kiss."

Cali kissed her soft, pale cheek that smelled like holiday spices and lovingly touched a tungsten streak in her sooty hair—before turning and practically sleepwalking down the winding path as cicadas sang in an undulating chorus throughout the luminous forest.

Back in the Regeneration Suite, it was all she could do to stash her new crow feather in the drawer with her necklace, brush her teeth, and collapse still in her grandmother's dress on top of her bed. She slept a dreamless sleep until she awoke in broad daylight to find Matangi in a flattering pink sari seated beside her with the hint of a mischievous grin on her attractive geisha face.

"What time is it?" asked Cali, sitting up, yawning and stretching with sunburnt stiffness as she realized her salty hair was undoubtedly a frightful mess.

"Too late for the early bird to get the worm, I am afraid."

"Sorry about that."

"No need to be. Extreme fatigue is to be expected after one's first day of Fallenium Incorporation. As is looking like shit."

"I take it you've been through this process yourself?"

"All Mahavidyas go through it—whether they like it or not."

"And do they all survive it?"

"Most do." Once again Matangi flashed an impish grin. "I have a proposal. What if you bathe and make yourself presentable while I round us up something to eat? Then we can get started on our lesson with full bellies and a touch of elegance."

"That would be fantastic. You're an angel, Matangi!"

"I suppose I am—when I am not enjoying being a little devil."

After a quick bath, Cali performed a hurried version of her morning routine. Then and only then, still wrapped in one towel with another around her wet head, she opened her closet—only to receive a pleasant surprise.

In addition to her collection of white saris, another dozen or so colorful ones had miraculously appeared now that the period of mourning for Thelete was coming to an end. Having donned a marvelously textured sari combining terra cotta with splashes of turquoise, Cali entered the living area in bare feet.

"I just have one question," she said to Matangi, who was busy in the kitchen pouring boiling water in mugs for *choro* tea.

"Only one?"

"Only one that's particularly pressing. Who's my personal dresser?"

"Are you dissatisfied with her selections?"

"Hardly. Whoever it is has impeccable taste. I would take her on tour with me—if those days weren't long gone. It's not you, is it?"

Matangi laughed musically. "I appreciate the double-edged 'compliment.' You may be the Future Rose, but do you honestly think a Mahavidya has time to be handpicking your garments?"

Cali plopped down cross-legged on the couch. "Who is it then?"

"Lena."

"Of course. That makes sense. She also decorated my cabin."

"She can be perfectly annoying, but she is justifiably well known as a stylist."

"So what's for breakfast? I'm ravenous."

"Anticipating this scenario, I took the liberty of ordering … a lot." Just then there was a knock on the door. "Come in!"

Two young women in yellow saris entered with several baskets of food and beverages, which they began laying out on the dining table. Everything they produced—from piping-hot cinnamon buns and ripe grapefruits to creamy sheep cheese and paper-thin slices of gourmet ham—looked and smelled so mouthwatering Cali actually got up and got in their way even as they were trying to set the table.

"My apologies," she said, awkwardly plopping back down.

"No worries, Future Rose," replied one of the young women with a smile.

"After you," said Matangi after the servers had left as she set a mug of *choro* tea beside Cali's plate.

Following what ended up being a relatively silent breakfast during which Cali ate and drank like a refugee, Matangi said, "You might want to put on some comfortable shoes. I also recommend taking the towel off your head."

"Where are we going?"

"A place with very special acoustics. You of all people will appreciate it."

"Shouldn't we clean up first?"

"The girls will come back and take care of things. You, my friend, have other responsibilities."

Upon exiting the Suite, Matangi led Cali away from Rose Cottage and the beach along a twisting path through the woods. Half an hour later, the two entered what could only be described as a natural amphitheater.

A massive concavity in the earth seemed purposely terraced with great oaks whose sideways limbs formed natural bleachers in a sweeping semicircle. For a proscenium there was a huge, flat expanse of swirling marble. In the background semi-vertical cliffs covered with ferns rounded out the scene.

"Jesus," gasped Cali, who could hear her own voice as if projected through a microphone. "What *is* this place?"

"The Ear of the Goddess."

"The *Ear* of the Goddess—just like Kalahili is her heart?"

"Just like."

Cali stepped forward and touched one of the oak "bleachers." It looked so inviting she decided to sit down. The seat was very supportive indeed. Matangi joined her.

"Can she actually ... *hear* us here?" asked Cali.

"I assume you are referring to the Goddess?"

"Who else?"

"Rest assured she can hear anyone anywhere—but especially in this place. That said, remember that she listens to us from *within* her Dream. Thus there is always potential for distortion between what we say and what she hears."

"I was under the impression we were somehow ... *products* of her dream projected using the Anthropos template she designed with Thelete."

"It is true that, through a kind of holographic modeling, humans emerge—as do all things on this planet—from the creative field of her dreaming mind. It is also true that, by speaking to that mind, we have the ability to change it—and thus our reality."

"It's like a circle."

"It *is* a circle. Humanity is symbolized by the ouroboros, the serpent that consumes its own tail. In our interactions with the Goddess, we are the Alpha and Omega of our own existence."

Cali took a moment to consider this mind-bending perspective. "How does the Luminous Child fit into this picture?"

"Personally, I believe the Luminous Child is that 'product' of the dreaming mind of the Goddess functioning as a conduit to the Originator that finally awakens her. As we all progressively transform into Luminous Children through what an ancient scientist called 'morphic resonance,' we become fully conscious cocreators of reality with each other and the Aeon."

In her own mind, Cali suddenly experienced an epiphany. "In such a world, the Archons couldn't exist!"

"Not as our shadow selves they could not. In the world we are discussing, the Archons would be faced with a stark choice: transform themselves or be reabsorbed by an upgraded collective consciousness."

"There could be no shadows in a place where there's only light."

"Poetic and true."

"That means we don't actually have to *defeat* the Archons; we only have to change … *ourselves!*"

Matangi's melodious laughter was greatly amplified by the Ear of the Goddess. Cali could feel the sound waves vibrating her bones.

"Greater words of wisdom were never spoken, my precocious young friend. But enough philosophy. Time for your voice lesson!"

C ali followed Matangi down onto the marble proscenium, where the two sat facing each other at what felt like the "inner ear" of the Ear of the Goddess—where the acoustics were an absolute marvel.

"I just realized you have some gray hairs," observed Matangi, her voice projecting effortlessly as silken sound waves to the farthest corners of the amphitheater. "Have you always had them?"

"No, they're actually new."

"Fallenium Incorporation?"

"Yep."

"It happens sometimes."

"Did it happen to you?"

"No. But it did to Tara. She went almost completely silver for a while. We nicknamed her Spoon."

"Better than Fork. How do they make me look?"

"It is hard to say—maybe like yourself in two hundred years?"

"The only way I'll make it past two centuries is to hunker down in the Deep World."

"Are you saying you already have plans to return to the surface? You just got here."

"I have no idea what I'm going to do. Maybe I should ask the Goddess for guidance."

"Maybe you should. Just be forewarned: her answers are rarely unambiguous."

"Somehow I knew you were going to say something like that."

"How did you know?"

"Because, well, after all, the Goddess *is* a woman—right?"

Matangi's explosive laughter was like little silver bells ping-ponging throughout the acoustically pristine Ear of the Goddess. Though it was bad form, Cali couldn't help giggling at her own joke.

"Time is wasting," said the Mahavidya, gathering herself at last and pointing to the throbbing solar sphere that appeared to be inching its way up through the pastel sky behind the sweeping limbs of the "bleachers."

"Where do we start?"

"With your ear, of course."

"My *ear*?"

"Yes. I would like you to sing this note."

Matangi opened her fluorescent pink lips to reveal her sparkling white teeth—but no sound was forthcoming.

"I don't hear anything."

"You are not hard of hearing, are you?"

"Not that I'm aware of."

"What about this slightly lower note then?"

Once again Matangi seemed to pantomime the act of singing. Cali was on the verge of accusing her teacher of trying to pull the wool over her eyes—when she fancied she heard a note so high no normal human could possibly produce it.

Maybe it was just Cali's imagination getting the best of her, or maybe the Ear of the Goddess somehow amplified vocal range. But the longer the sound went on, the more she became convinced it was real.

"How are you doing that, Matangi?"

The singer stopped singing, at which point the note dissipated in a myriad of echoes. "Lots of practice combined with my fair share of Fallenium Incorporation."

"What does Fallenium Incorporation have to do with singing?"

"Everything. Sophia and her consort created the Anthropos through song. As we incorporate more of the Aeon herself, we enhance our ability to sing and create as she did."

"But what's the point of learning to sing a note so high nobody can hear it?"

"You could hear it."

"Yeah, but I'm special."

"You said it, I did not."

"Ha ha."

"How about this note?"

For the third time, Matangi opened her painted mouth only to utter … nothing apparently. But after a moment, as before, a note (an extremely deep one this go-round) emerged. It was almost as if the sound, which made Cali think of tectonic plates shifting, was happening only in her mind—yet she could have sworn the proscenium was vibrating as if from a tiny earthquake!

"You're freaking me out, Matangi."

"Am I really?"

The instant the Mahavidya spoke the vibration stopped.

"Maybe just a little."

"Now you try."

"*Me?* There's no way in hell I can hit those notes."

"How can you say that without even trying?"

"Fair enough. Which note should I start with?"

"The low one. For grounding purposes."

"Grounding" sounded about right. Matangi's third note had seemed part of the earth itself.

Endeavoring to relax, Cali moved her head back and forth and dropped her shoulders. After positioning herself as upright as possible, she attempted—unsuccessfully—to sing the low note.

"You are not using the right parts of your anatomy," said Matangi. "Singing impossible notes has very little to do with your vocal cords."

"What does it have to do with then?"

"For impossibly low notes, you use your bones."

"My *bones?*"

"Yes. Try singing the note from the center of your bones."

"Any in particular?"

"All of them, preferably."

"All right. Here goes nothing."

Closing her eyes, Cali concentrated on her skeleton, visualizing her marrow glowing as she opened her mouth and, for the second time, dug deep for the right note. At first *nothing* indeed appeared to be happening again.

Then, miraculously, she perceived the note being projected from the hollow spaces in her osseous structure. At this early stage, it was indeed more of a thought than an actual sound. As she herself began to vibrate, however, so too did her larynx—at which point the note gradually turned barely audible.

"Bravo!" cried Matangi.

Just as the proscenium began to vibrate in turn, Cali ran out of gas and collapsed forward onto her elbows gasping. Silence and stillness returned to the Ear as Cali felt sweat streaming in little rivulets from her forehead and armpits.

"I think I'm going to pass out," she managed to say.

"Just breathe from your diaphragm. You will be fine."

"If you say so."

As Cali caught her breath, she experienced a moment of body awareness reminiscent of the pure awareness she'd tapped into during her escape from Freddy's assassins in Saturnia. In this instance she caught a glimpse of *kundalini*—the source of which she intuited to be merely a powerful "Aeonic" emotion—rising through her legs and up her spine like a coiling snake.

Recalling her mother's comment that *kundalini* and anger were similar, Cali asked, "How long did it take you to know—*really* know in your bones—that the Goddess is just a type of person, one who feels things super intensely maybe but otherwise much like people do?"

"Much longer than you, it would seem."

"Makes you wonder if all the little beneficial bacteria living on and in us are also like people and we're like Goddesses to them."

"Now, that *is* deep."

"I was being serious."

"So was I. Are you ready to try a high note?"

"Sure. Why not."

"Note—pun intended—that you do not sing impossibly high notes using your bones."

"I figured as much. What *do* you use?"

"Care to guess?"

Cali thought for a moment. "Your *skin?*"

Matangi beamed. "Splendid! You are a natural at this. How did you figure it out?"

"Well, I gathered that the bones connect us to the density of the planet by taking us down and inward. So in order to go up and outward to the more … ethereal realm, it would be necessary to use the most superficial part of ourselves."

"I could not have said it better myself. You can also sing from your hair and accomplish the same thing."

"Interesting. So what's the note?"

"Try this one."

Matangi opened her mouth again and sang "silently." This time Cali was able to hear the sound more quickly.

"Sounds like a version of the note Thelete—my father taught me."

"See, you do have a good ear! It is *gaur*, or 'home,' in a higher octave, just as the low note you sang was *gaur* in a deeper octave. Ready?"

"As I'll ever be."

Visualizing her skin as merely the thinnest of membranes separating her from the rest of creation, Cali took a deep breath and sang from the outermost part of her being. At first, as was becoming the norm, nothing seemed to be happening.

This went on for so long this time, in fact, that her mind wandered as she mused that "outer" and "inner" were purely relative terms. Alongside the idea that the most ethereal part of the universe might actually be the most basic coalesced the corollary: that so-called reality was arguably, appearances notwithstanding, the most superficial level of existence.

"That is it, Cali! Your voice is truly touched by the finger of the Goddess!"

The sound, which Cali hadn't even realized she was making, abruptly stopped as she stared at her teacher in amazement. "What did you just say?"

"I said your voice is touched by the finger of the Goddess."

"Have you ever heard that expression before?"

"No. I just made it up."

"Then we must share the same mind because not too long ago I made it up about you."

Matangi beamed again. "Morphically, we *do* share the same mind, Cali: the mind of the Goddess."

Over the ensuing three months, Cali's life took on a decidedly monastic quality. Prior to entering the Deep World, this wasn't something she could ever have foreseen for herself—yet it wasn't so bad. In fact, though she might not openly admit it, she rather enjoyed pouring herself into her training and not having much of a social life to speak of.

Fallenium Incorporation remained the focal point of her studies. Her grandmother explained that while the removed fallenium substance eventually regenerated inside the Womb of the Goddess just as eggs were produced by women, this didn't mean that it was to be used indiscriminately.

Some days they didn't even ingest the powder but, instead, practiced summoning its residual energy to perform certain tasks. Other days they took only trace amounts and learned to maximize them through meditative and breathing techniques that reminded Cali of some of the qigong exercises Juice had taught her.

Still other days they experimented with large doses and concentrated on minimizing the ego and becoming an "open circuit," to use Kali's term, through which the vital force of the Goddess could act on the world in human form.

Cali found herself taking honey from the tree and barely noticing the stings, then repeating the exercise and hardly being stung because she figured out how to communicate with the bees.

She learned how to divine underground streams with her fingertips, ripen lemons in mere minutes in her palm, smell rain coming across the mountains long before it arrived—and actually walk between the raindrops without getting wet when it did.

She experienced catching speckled trout with her bare hands, howling with wolves until the pack accepted her as one of their own, playing like a jubilant toddler with bear cubs until their mother arrived and put her foot down.

She climbed so high in trees she could no longer see the ground, swung on vines through the forest like a tomboy Tarzan, discovered strange berries only to realize she could always tell whether they were poisonous or not—and if not, she would eat her fill and wash them down with rainwater that had collected inside certain hollow members of the tulip family called *riorea.*

Her grandmother taught her how to convince a colony of ants to relocate without speaking a word, start a small fire with nothing but the power of her gaze, hold her breath for ten minutes at a time while bodysurfing with otters in the ocean.

Through it all one thing was becoming clearer and clearer: the more the new Cali walked down the transformational path of Fallenium Incorporation, the less of the old Cali there seemed to be left.

"Who the hell am I?" she sometimes, especially in the beginning, caught herself thinking or even wondering aloud.

But as time went on, she seemed to *think* less and less while simply *being* more and more—double entendre intended—until she could go for hours with scarcely a thought to disturb her experience of the very real presence of the Goddess.

In such a state, she often experienced emotions—ranging from monumental grief to colossal motherly pride—she intuited weren't even her own. And the more she felt these things, the more she came to know and love Sophia.

Her steady progress was reflected in her necklace of crow feathers, which by the middle of her third month of training had grown to seven in number.

Meanwhile, not to be outdone as a rigorous teacher, Matangi employed a variety of creative strategies to push her protégé to and through the latter's musical limits.

Cali was encouraged to reach for ever higher notes and dig for ever lower ones. She was instructed in the strange arts of singing without breathing, singing underwater, singing while squatting, singing while hanging upside down.

Alongside teaching her a kind of yoga designed to expand and strengthen her diaphragm, lungs and back muscles for increased vocal range and duration, Matangi also drilled Tula's odd six-note musical scale into her student, who eventually could sing it forward and backward, in a higher or lower octave, or even completely out of order while switching octaves randomly.

Before long Cali was ready to begin learning basic birdsongs: ones for curing insomnia or a headache, for example, or increasing collagen utilization in order to foster healthy hair, skin, and nails.

Even these relatively simple songs, sung one right after another, most certainly would have short-circuited her in the old days before Fallenium Incorporation. But now they just gave her what she described to Matangi, who was prompted to teach her a waking meditation to manage her body temperature, "premature hot flashes."

"Just so you know, hot flashes are *always* premature," said Matangi.

"Please explain."

"They are the result of hormonal imbalances owing to poor diet and environmental toxicity. Here in the Deep World, they are practically unknown."

"Lucky you."

On the days when Cali wasn't studying with her namesake or the younger Mahavidya who had also become a mainstay in her existence, she began learning Kalidon under the tutelage of Lena. The idea was entirely Cali's own.

Her reasoning was that if she was going to become a resident of the Deep World, she might as well learn the language. But Kalidon wasn't Spanish and Cali regularly felt the urge to rip her healthier-than-ever hair out with her long, hard nails at the language's maddening nuances and miniscule inflections, which Lena patiently (if annoyingly) pointed out while staring with her saucer-sized green eyes time and again.

Still, after two months of intensive study, Cali (who was more linguistically gifted than most) was able to hold a basic conversation and understand somewhat more complicated ones.

The other extremely important thing she learned during her monastic phase was how to take it easy once in a while. This teaching, which came through her own awareness, may have been the most difficult one to grasp and implement of all—given her years of conditioning in the Fatherland in the importance of self-sacrifice to the "greater good of the master race."

She realized her tendency to overextend herself was a result of this programming, which Olga had reinforced over and over with her slave-driving managerial approach. The "cure" for this "disease" was easy to say but harder to do: replace self-sacrifice with self-love.

So Cali started out by changing small behavioral ruts. When she was utterly exhausted or burnt out but still felt she should keep going, she simply stopped what she was doing and did nothing.

Doing nothing was so much harder than doing something, but it worked wonders. Soon she found herself doing things that seemed like nothing but that nourished her like something essential: taking a second hot bath for the day without cracking a book, drinking a third mug of *choro* tea out on the rose-trellised balcony before an early bedtime, going for a stroll down to the beach and feeding the seagulls popcorn when she "should" be conjugating verbs.

She was, in fact, just returning from the beach during one lazy afternoon window in her otherwise full schedule—when Lena approached with a naughty expression and presented her an anonymous envelope addressed in scrawled English handwriting she'd never seen before but that nevertheless screamed its provenance: *Miss Cali Crow-well, Regeneration Suite, Rose Cottage, Tula.*

"This just came for you," said Lena, with whom Cali had shared a number of tantalizing stories about Juice as a distraction from seasickness during their voyage to and from Kalahili. "It was on your doorstep. I discovered it when I arrived for your lesson—which you were not there for, by the way. Do you know who it is from?"

"Yes. And so I imagine, by the way you're biting your lip in voyeuristic anticipation, do you."

"Are you not at least going to *open* it?"

"In due time. When I'm *alone.*"

"I guess this means there will be no lesson today?"

"I guess it does."

To her surprise Cali's heart was pounding as she reentered her dwelling and sat down at the dining table with Juice's letter. Though she'd wanted to on more occasions than she could count, she hadn't been able to write him. Every time she started to, she realized there was simply too much to say.

Juice's handwriting may have been rough around the edges, but his inked words were almost as sophisticated and soothing as his spoken ones:

Dear Cali,

Sorry I haven't written sooner. I've been getting my ass kicked on a daily basis by your brother, who's been teaching me that practically everything I knew about martial arts was wrong.

Fallenium changes the whole picture of what you can do in a human body. But I guess you know that already.

All training and no kisses have turned Juice into a—I guess into a man. That was the point of all this, or at least part of it, right?

I imagine you've become a woman and I can't wait to find out what that's like, since I already fell so hard for the girl.

I had this wacky dream the other night. I dreamed of myself waking up and staring into a mirror. "Do you know who I am?" I asked. To which my reflection replied: "Yes. But who am I?"

Does this ring a bell? I'm changing faster than the seasons in this wild world the two of us just dropped into—literally.

Word under the volcano is I'll be heading your way come Springtide in just over two weeks. Write if you like. But I'll understand if you're too busy changing.

I hope you can feel my love like a large dose of the magic powder, Future Rose.

Yours passionately,

Juice
A Tent
Somewhere in Kalahili

Cali's tears came as a shock. She hadn't cried once since she commenced training. But now tears of joy and longing—her own enormous emotions and not Sophia's—were raining all over Juice's beautiful, unpretentious prose.

C ali's sixteenth birthday happened to fall on the eve of the vernal equinox, celebrated in the Deep World—which maintained a highly accurate calendar despite its location in the inner earth—as the beginning of Springtide with its much-anticipated reunion of the men and women of the Bird Tribes.

The past two weeks had been ridiculously jam-packed. Her grandmother had spent long days instructing her in such demanding arts as riding wild mustangs bareback and summoning large numbers of crows for protective purposes. Before all was said and done, Cali ended up being thrown twice and completely covered in bird droppings.

Meanwhile, Matangi had stepped up her tutelage as well—introducing complex, physically demanding birdsongs for lulling people to sleep, befriending hostile animals, and even sexually arousing men.

"Not that you, of all people, need such a birdsong," explained the Mahavidya with a wink as they sat facing each other on the marble proscenium of the Ear of the Goddess.

"I'll take all the assistance I can get. After all, I'm turning gray."

"Not down … there?"

"Of course not."

"Because there is a birdsong for that if you require it."

"I'll be sure to let you know."

The morning of her birthday, which Cali planned to enjoy quietly while preparing for Juice's arrival the following day, she was dressed in a robe sipping steaming *choro* tea while curled up on her balcony bench-— when a knock on her front door rang out.

"Coming!" she called.

Setting her mug on the table and returning inside, she opened the door to find her mother in full Goddess regalia (that included a long vermilion sari) majestically filling the doorsill.

Unexpected even though it might have been predictable on Cali's birthday, it was the first time the Rose—who had been immersed for months almost nonstop in the Dream of the Goddess—had called on the Future Rose since the latter arrived in the Deep World.

When Cali seemed too surprised to speak, Dr. Caliandra asked, "May I come in?"

"Of course! Sorry for being so rude. I was just ..."

"A little shocked to receive a visit from your prodigal mother?"

"Maybe a little."

Inside, having shaken off their awkwardness, the two embraced as Cali smelled the perfume of the enormous, glossy rose in her mother's flamenco-dancer hair.

"Happy Birthday, my princess," said Dr. Caliandra with a kiss on her daughter's forehead.

"Wow, you haven't called me that in a long time." They sat down beside each other on the couch. Indicating the small, intricately carved wooden box her mother was clutching, Cali asked, "What's in there?"

"A present ... of sorts."

"Of sorts?"

"At least I hope you will see it that way."

"Can I open it?"

"Yes. But I do have a caveat."

"A caveat for a birthday present. Interesting."

"It is a present offered to you on your birthday. I would not call it a birthday present per se. I do have one of those for later, and a good one, just so you know."

"Aren't you mysterious! So what's the caveat?"

"This is Pandora's Box."

"Come again?"

"That is what the Roses, among themselves and somewhat facetiously, have called it for centuries. In Greek mythology, as I am sure you know, Pandora's Box was a real can of worms, figuratively speaking."

"So you're giving me a can of worms ... *on* but not *for* my birthday?"

"Technically, I am offering you a tool with many potential unforeseen consequences. You do not have to accept it. This box contains vast knowledge on a superhuman scale—or at least a key to accessing such knowledge. Living with this knowledge has proved to be both a blessing and a curse for the Roses."

Cali was quiet for a moment as she attempted to fathom her mother's multilayered, interwoven meanings. Eyeing the box, which Dr. Caliandra had just placed on the coffee table, she noted that the flag of Tula was included in its complex design that was otherwise reminiscent of Art Nouveau.

"Am I correct in understanding you've opened Pandora's box yourself?"

"I have indeed."

"Only once?"

"Once was quite sufficient."

"Was it a blessing or a curse for you?"

Her mother sighed and leaned back tiredly. "Both, definitely both. To live with such knowledge is to live with a tremendous burden of responsibility on one's shoulders."

"What kind of responsibility?"

"While one is the Rose, it is fair to say the very survival of humanity is one's responsibility."

"Because one becomes the Aeonic Vessel for the earth itself?"

"Precisely."

"Are you implying you're making me the Rose?"

Even Caliandra's beautiful laughter seemed weary. "Only the Goddess can do that. I am only offering you the opportunity to become the Rose in the event she decides to indwell within you."

"What else are you saying? There's more to this story—I can feel it."

"Of course you can. You probably even know, deep inside, what I am about to say. After lengthy consultation with Sophia, I have decided to step down."

"*When?*"

"Effective immediately."

Removing the rose from her hair, Dr. Caliandra placed it alongside the box in front of her daughter.

"But you can't!" cried Cali.

"But I must. It is in the Prophecy. And it is time. It is *your* time. You are ready."

Cali's heart fluttered as if trying yet failing to take flight as she stared at the two fateful objects on the table. "How do you *know* I'm ready?"

"I have seen it. Remember: I opened Pandora's Box long ago and have had decades of practice interpreting visions. The Fatherland has just started rolling out the Archontic endgame. The World War to end all World Wars is about to begin."

For the better part of a minute, Cali sat frozen contemplating Pandora's Box as her mother's news of the Archontic endgame reverberated in her mind, where she couldn't help but watch something like an unsummoned holofilm of Freddy gleefully signing a Declaration of War with mechanized fingers.

"Bastard," she muttered as she picked up the box and popped open the lid.

Inside, a single oval fallenium stone about the size of an acorn blazed like a ruby on fire atop a cushion of blue velvet.

"Jesus, Mary, and Joseph!" exclaimed Cali. "It looks … *alive!*"

"It is very much alive—as are all things associated with this sentient planet," replied Caliandra. "It is a brand-new egg fresh from the Womb of the Goddess."

"It feels sort of hot."

"That is normal. This tiny stone contains enough *kundalini* to boil the oceans if extracted all at once."

"Why's it so small?"

"The fresher and more powerful a fallenium egg is, the smaller it is. Fallenium eggs grow larger and less charged over time as their subspace energy materializes."

"What am I supposed to … do with it?"

"Consume it, naturally."

"You mean *eat* it?"

"Swallow it, actually. That thing would break all your teeth if you tried to chew it."

"But won't it kill me?"

Dr. Caliandra smiled maternally. "Hardly, my beautiful child. Rather, it will make you very hard to kill. Consuming a fresh egg is quite different from ingesting fallenium powder. An egg stays in your system indefinitely—like a battery giving off nearly infinite energy you can utilize."

Cali reached up and compassionately squeezed her mother's shoulder. "Why do you seem so exhausted then?"

"Because my battery is running low. Eventually, especially when it is heavily used, even a new fallenium egg discharges the last of its energy."

"Couldn't you just swallow another one?"

"That is not customary. The duration of the egg organically sets the limit for a Rose's term. The fact that my battery is running out at this exact crossroads in history is an unambiguous sign it is time to pass the baton."

At the mention of "baton," Cali thought of Freddy once again. "Tell me more about the Illuminati."

"What would you like to know?"

"Why are they the way they are?"

"You mean aside from being parasitically infected and utterly mind-controlled by the Archons?"

"I get that. But *why* did they willingly allow themselves to be infected?"

"That is an excellent question. Why not give me a foot while I answer it?"

"*Really?*"

"I cannot promise a lengthy massage, but it would be my pleasure to rub your feet a little on your birthday."

Setting Pandora's Box, still open, back on the table, Cali swung a foot into her mother's regal lap and reclined on a pair of down pillows.

"When one studies the history of terrestrial religions," said Caliandra as she began kneading Cali's heel, "it soon becomes clear that so-called primitive peoples everywhere shared a belief in the divinity of the earth. In other words, Goddess worship was universal—until the dawn of the monotheistic, paternalistic religions of Judaism, Christianity, and Islam."

"I assume this is going somewhere?"

"Humor me. The point is that these religions that began worshipping a single male 'God' were an Archontic construct holographically inserted into history in order to separate humanity from its spiritual roots in the earth while making the human species dependent on the Lord Archon."

"Hold on a minute. Are you saying that Christians, for example, are worshipping an evil extraterrestrial entity?"

"By any reasonable definition, the Christian God is an extraterrestrial. And given God's track record of demanding human sacrifices and destroying whole cities, one could make a very strong case we are talking about an extremely malevolent force."

Cali chewed on this perspective for a second. "So does that mean Satan is actually *good?*"

"There is no Satan—unless you wish to consider him a persona of the Demiurge. The devil and hell are mental whips created by the Archons to keep humanity enslaved to their system."

"So I'm guessing the Illuminati hate the Goddess so much because the Archons do."

"In a nutshell. Historically speaking, the Illuminati are her sworn enemies. As they rose to power especially via the Catholic Church, they slaughtered millions upon millions of Goddess worshippers during their endless Crusades and Inquisitions in an attempt to erase her from the collective memory."

"But that would be impossible—given that she's actually the planet."

"It is impossible. Unless you microchip all the world's white people while murdering the billions of POCs who are immune to such mind control. Which is precisely their endgame. What are you doing?"

"What does it look like I'm doing?"

"But I have yet to massage your other foot."

"Screw my other foot."

Sitting upright, Cali took the fiery fallenium egg and popped it in her mouth. It went down easier than expected.

As it traveled down her throat toward her stomach, she could have sworn she caught a brief glimpse of sparks lighting up her veins. Or maybe she was just imagining them.

"So what do we do now?" she asked.

The look of astonishment on her mother's face was priceless—but it didn't last long. Soon Dr. Caliandra recovered her composure and focused on priorities as she stood up resolutely and extended a hand.

"We go talk to the Goddess," she said.

Wearing a new black sari along with her mother's rose and her own necklace of crow feathers, the late-morning sun heating up her dark clothing and exposed (and now very tan) skin, Cali was led a couple of miles along a narrow stone path back into the lush mountains that hugged the coastline.

Fortunately, the effect of swallowing the fallenium egg was different from consuming the powder. Whereas the latter would have had her drenched with buckets of sweat as her body temperature went vertical during the initial rush, the former was more subtle in the perspiration department yet somehow more profound overall.

The main difference was that while the powder felt like a psychedelic stimulus coming from the outside, the egg actually seemed to be part of oneself. And though Cali intuited the stone wouldn't enable feats of superhuman athleticism in the short term, in the long run it might empower her to reach supernatural heights in other areas.

"How are you feeling?" asked her mother as she guided her daughter over a ridge and down a steep set of perfectly symmetrical steps cut into the granite mountainside.

"Like I just did something I hope I don't end up regretting."

"Unlikely—but one never knows."

"I assume I'm stuck with this fallenium egg now?"

"You assume incorrectly. At any point you are free to ask the Goddess to reclaim it."

"It's that simple?"

"It is that simple."

"And I won't, like, perish or anything if she takes it back?"

"What an absurd notion! Why on earth would that happen?"

"Just making sure."

Suddenly, there in the middle of the wilderness, a familiar sight loomed up ahead: the yoni-shaped cave entrance from her recent dream. "I know this place," she said.

"I gathered."

"How?"

"I could feel the energy of your recognition."

"Is this where you always come to enter the Dream of the Goddess?"

"Yes. I fancy my footsteps have worn down this path at least an inch over the years."

As Cali followed her mother toward the entrance, she imagined she could feel her senses becoming augmented by proximity to the Goddess. Instantly, she knew where worms were crawling in the ground nearby, where maggots were recycling the carcass of a deer farther off, which trees were producing pollen, even where a mudslide would happen if it rained hard enough.

"You are tapping into her consciousness, are you not?" asked Dr. Caliandra.

"I guess I am. It's pretty wild."

"You will get used to it. Are you ready to enter her Dream?"

Cali stared at the dark cave entrance that struck her as the birthplace of an expanded version of herself. "Do you *really* think I'm ready?"

"I do not think, I *know*. You were literally born for this."

Cali took a deep breath. "Then let's do it."

"After you."

Ceremoniously motioning toward the entrance, Caliandra invited her daughter to take the lead. The interior of the cave was uncannily similar to Cali's dream vision of it. Dripping water echoed left and right as her eyes adjusted to the darkness punctuated by the glow of countless fallenium eggs emerging from the stone walls.

She received no directions from her mother; she simply knew the way as if she herself had walked this twisting path that corkscrewed up and down into the heart of the mountain.

After perhaps half an hour, they reached the cavernous back of the cave that was slightly darker and drier than the rest of the tunnels. Here Caliandra removed the rose from her daughter's hair and whispered, "Give me your hand."

Out of an altered state in which she could actually, physically feel the planet spinning monumentally on its axis as it orbited through the solar system, Cali heard her mother and extended her hand palm up. Using a thorn from the rose's stem, Caliandra pierced the tip of her daughter's ring finger.

Cali experienced the slight pain as vaguely pleasurable as she observed a mildly luminescent drop of blood balloon out of her skin. Turning her hand over, she watched as the drop fell in slow motion to the cave floor, where it splashed multicolored sparks and metallic echoes in all directions.

"She is here," whispered Dr. Caliandra. "Be sure to stand straight and tall. That way her energy will flow through you without harm."

Heeding her mother's advice, Cali adopted her best stage presence as the figure of a gigantic crow materialized, wings fluttering, before her. The presence of the Aeon was like a tsunami of energy in which, bizarrely, all Cali could think about was how white the crow's scleras were as its eyes blinked and blinked.

"Ask her what is in your heart," urged Dr. Caliandra from behind in the shadows.

Cali had planned to ask the Goddess how to defeat the Archons—but given the galactic scale of the entity with whom she found herself interfacing, that suddenly seemed like a simpleton's question. Instead, she simply did as told and asked exactly what was in her heart:

"*Why am I here?*"

So unexpected was what happened next that Cali literally was unable to breathe for a moment as she found herself hovering bolt upright in midair with massive waves of *kundalini* surging up through her.

In something similar to her "life review" on the levitrain trestle before entering the Badlands the first time, Cali was shown a panoramic vision of her destiny, starting with the Aeons' creation of the Anthropos in the Pleroma; continuing with Sophia's "fall" into the Kenoma when, terror-stricken in a nightmare, she accidently gave birth to the Archons; moving on to the emergence of the first humans inside Sophia's earthen body and the development of tools and technologies for interacting with the Goddess before the diaspora in which the earliest explorers spread out all over the planet's surface; taking a turn for the worse with the Archontic invention of monotheism leading to the worldwide genocide of Goddess worshippers; and leading all the way to the establishment of the Fatherland by the Illuminati as the capstone for global hegemony.

Transfixed and still levitating but finally breathing again, Cali stared in amazement as her mother slipped into this brave new world from the Deep World and met her "father" only to have Thelete's child with him. She was shown how her mother planted clues about her destiny mostly in the form of illegal books, which she smuggled into the Fatherland from the libraries of Tula.

As if taking in an epic holofilm approaching its dénouement, she watched as her mother penned her secret message to her daughter and hid it behind her photograph, then stashed a jammer in the garden bench and left the Fatherland once and for all, reentering the Deep World by way of Rose Cove, where Thelete awaited her with open arms.

And then, without warning, the scene shifted to a colossal mobilization of the Fatherland's armed forces into Europe, South America, Africa, and Asia. Cali suddenly realized she was no longer viewing the past; she was being given a sobering glimpse of the apocalyptic present in which the Shallow World—and even the Deep World itself—teetered on the verge of utter … domination and depopulation.

Even as Cali tried to wrap her mind around the horrific implications of the Archontic endgame crescendoing in real time, the Goddess touched her throat then her belly with the tip of a vast wing. In the very next instant, the Aeon disappeared and Cali fell to the cave floor exhausted yet exhilarated.

With her mother kneeling and holding her, Cali was already processing what she knew beyond a shadow of a doubt she was meant to do. In a sense all of history, to say nothing of her whole life, had been leading up to this moment. She wasn't trying to be grandiose—it was just the truth.

The solution to the Archontic dilemma that had been shown to her was elegantly simple; it was also extremely rash and exceedingly dangerous.

But what else could be expected from a Goddess nicknamed Precuneus and a Future Rose who had been trained in the wisdom of foolishness?

S itting at high noon in a gorgeous blue sky, Tula's sun seemed to breathe in and out as Cali, supported by her mother, managed to drag herself out of the Womb of the Goddess into the singing, gently swaying woods.

The pair slowly made their way back along the winding path in the direction of Rose Cottage. At first the simple act of walking was like trying to finish a marathon.

But little by little, Cali perceived her energy returning as she began to sense her internal fallenium egg powering up. Closing her eyes, she could visualize the egg pulsing deep in her belly, in fact, much like the sun throbbing high above.

Like both brilliant objects, she felt rather hot to the touch. By contrast her mother seemed cooler than ever. Literally. For the first time that Cali could remember, her mother's skin seemed like that of a normal, healthy human being—nothing more.

"What happens," asked Cali, "when a fallenium egg inside someone finally runs out of energy?"

"It dissolves."

"I think yours just dissolved."

"Me, too."

"How do you feel?"

"Empty. How do *you* feel?"

"Full."

The two burst out laughing, stopped, embraced, then laughed some more. The situation seemed profoundly meaningless yet absurdly meaningful. Eventually, both mother and daughter had tears of joy overflowing their bright eyes and running in rivers down their lovely cheeks.

"The Goddess is really something," said Cali at last.

"She certainly is. So are you."

"Look who's talking."

"Admittedly, I am no slouch. But do not underestimate how historically special you are, Cali. That said, do not let it go to your head either."

As if communicating telepathically, the two started walking again quite naturally together. Cali was already more stable and no longer needed her mother's support.

"I haven't the faintest idea how to interpret 'historically special.'"

"It is all in the Prophecy—if you care to read it."

"Oh, I have. A translated version, of course. Lena gave it to me."

"Then you should know that the Future Rose of the Tribulation becomes the Last Rose before the arrival of the Luminous Child and, eventually, the awakening of the Goddess herself."

"I know what the Prophecy *says*. What it *means*, however, is open to debate."

"You would make an excellent theologian."

"I was being serious."

"So was I."

Cali considered the Prophecy for a moment before concluding, "I think it means exactly what we make it mean—nothing less, nothing more."

"I think you may be right."

"Basically, I was just agreeing with my grandmother."

"Then you both may be right." Winking sideways, Dr. Caliandra added, "After all, wisdom runs in our family."

They walked on for a while in silence. Finally, Cali asked, "What would you say was your biggest accomplishment as the Rose?"

"Why, having you, of course."

"Cut the bullshit."

"It was not ... bullshit. But if you are looking for a more ... disinterested and philosophical response, I would say that progressing through the four stages of the Dream of the Goddess myself, in my own psychology, has been my greatest achievement."

"So you moved from trauma, to grief, through denial, all the way to acceptance?"

"I did indeed. The journey was the most challenging one I ever undertook. Not even my mission to the Shallow World could compare. But eventually, I passed—from a consciousness perspective—from fall to winter to spring to summer."

"So where are you now?"

"A season very different from any I have ever known. Not even the Goddess herself has had this experience, I am willing to bet."

"Because she just keeps cycling through the stages of her Dream?"

"Exactly. She has yet to awaken and, therefore, finds herself looping endlessly through the seasons."

"What do you imagine will happen when she eventually does wake up?"

"I believe nature itself, the very nature of reality, will change."

"How?"

"I have no earthly idea."

The walk back may have started out strenuously, but by the time Rose Cottage came into view up ahead through its great oaks draped with Spanish moss, the spring was definitely back in Cali's step. "Speaking of seasons," she said, "I'm told tomorrow's the start of Springtide."

"Yes, a truly joyful season is upon us."

"How will you handle seeing other couples reunited when that's no longer an option for you?"

"As I said before: I am now in an entirely different season."

Cali fancied herself in an entirely different season of her own—birthday season—when she opened the door to the Regeneration Suite only to find her living room overflowing with presents of every size, shape and description sent from (judging by their return addresses) all over Tula and the Thorns.

An apple pie (still warm) from her grandmother was on the counter alongside a ceramic container of fallenium face cream from Lena and a beautiful pair of decorative hair sticks (held together with pink ribbon) from Matangi. There were flowers in vases, figurative and literal cornucopias of fresh fruits, packs of buffalo jerky, beeswax candles, incense sticks, bird origami, artisan jewelry, and a variety of handmade items including saris, rugs, and blankets.

And that was just the presents—of which there were many more—that appeared local and weren't wrapped!

"What on earth?!" exclaimed Cali. "How did people know it's my birthday?"

"Do you not recall seeing it in the Prophecy?"

"I do—now that you mention it. But the 'score' part in the date threw me. Nobody talks that way anymore."

"The Prophecy is ancient. Like your mother, who is feeling rather tired after this morning's exertion. I had forgotten just how exhausting mortality can be."

"Where are you going?"

"To rest a while."

"Which present is from you? If you like, I can open it before you go."

"My present has not yet arrived. I will be sure to send it over as soon as it shows up. And do not bother to thank me. Such is not our custom, as it encourages people to give with less than pure intentions."

"Okay. But what do you mean 'shows up'? And where's it coming from?"

"Happy Birthday, my precious child."

With these evasive words, Dr. Caliandra kissed her daughter's forehead and, as if she had aged in just the past few hours, took her leave with the body language of a geriatric.

Left alone with her panoply of presents, Cali thought about opening the ones in bags and boxes—when she actually heard her stomach rumbling. Consuming the fallenium egg and encountering the Goddess had made her outrageously hungry.

She was standing at the counter halfway through her grandmother's delicious apple pie … when there was a loud knock on the front door. Having wiped her mouth, she was still chewing when she opened it—only to find herself staring up at one Frederick "Juice" Hamilton decked out in buckskins and a headdress of half a dozen owl feathers!

"Special birthday delivery from Dr. Caliandra to Miss Crow-well," he said, grinning like a mischievous grizzly bear before pulling her to him and swinging her up into his strapping arms.

"Jesus, I'd almost forgotten how good-looking you are!" she exclaimed between repeated kisses of his marvelously warm and fleshy lips.

Returning her kisses, he managed to reply, "You're not half bad yourself—for a skinny white girl."

"A skinny white *woman*, FYI. Sixteen's the official age of adulthood in Tula."

"Pardon my ignorance. I'm an illegal alien. Can I ask what you're doing exactly?"

Cali had slyly extricated herself from Juice's bear hug and was tying the ribbon from Matangi's hair sticks around the door handle and a nearby curtain holdback. "What does it look like I'm doing?"

"Jerry-rigging a door lock?"

"Bullseye."

With the door to the Regeneration Suite more or less secured against interlopers, the lovers—their mutually admiring eyes locked on each other—wasted no time undressing and embracing once again surrounded by Cali's mounds of presents. Dropping to his knees, Juice kissed his way down Cali's neck, breasts and abdomen all the way to another mound at the dark edge of her pubis.

"God, I've missed this," he said.

"Tell me about it."

"Sorry, no time for chitchat now."

And for several minutes, there wasn't. Cali had never experienced an orgasm while on her feet, so she wasn't prepared to go quite so weak in the knees.

309

Fortunately, Juice caught her before she could hit the floor. Scooping her up, he carried her into the bedroom and gently deposited her, still tingling, on her bed.

"Well, are you just going to stand there with your friend or are the two of you going to join me?" she said with an audible mixture of mischief and desire.

Months of separation, Fallenium Incorporation and nature saturation had turned Juice into an amorous force to be reckoned with. Not that he was rough—he was silky smooth as always. But clearly, now that he'd come to know himself better as the Future Thorn, his passion was truly … mythological.

"We should spend time apart more often!" gasped Cali as, having opened up to him, she pivoted from ridden to rider.

"I don't think my heart could take it."

"Mine neither."

"Glad to hear it. Was it this good last time?"

"No, we're taking it to a whole new level."

Having climaxed together with decidedly Aeonic impact, limp as dishrags and bathed with sweat, they clung to each other like ivy, silently and organically, through the sleepy afternoon. Juice did, in fact, doze off with his beautifully chiseled, statuesque face wedged against Cali's shoulder.

"Just know that I love you with all my heart," she whispered. When he snored instead of responding, she added, speaking not only for herself but also, she realized with a mild shock, the Goddess, "I've loved you from the beginning—and I'll be there, still loving you, at the end."

Judging by the rosy light slanting in through the windows, evening was approaching by the time Juice stirred and opened his drowsy eyes to contemplate Cali's sharp, lively ones. "I must have drifted off," he said with a yawn.

"You were sleeping like an overgrown baby. I couldn't bring myself to wake you."

"What time is it?"

"You tell me. Sometime between noon and night."

"I could've sworn I was still on my ship, bobbing up and down."

"Well, there has certainly been a lot of up and down. But this is actually my bedroom."

"I like it."

"Thanks. I like you in it."

"*Shukarria.*"

"I see you've been studying Kalidon also!"

"Not really. I can say maybe a dozen words."

"Funny, I thought you were a cunning linguist."

"Ha ha. What about you?"

"I'm getting … conversational."

"Impressive."

"Don't let this inflate your ego, but you're definitely the best birthday present I've ever received."

"Aw, shucks, Miss Crow-well, how you do go on. Speaking of birthday presents, wait right here!"

Disentangling himself from her arms and legs, he climbed out of bed and stood up. The extraordinary musculature of his backside rippled as he left the room. Cali thought she heard her front door open and close before he reappeared, still unclothed and unselfconscious, with a large rock in one hand and his other hand behind his back.

"This is from your brother," he said, handing her the rock, which turned out to be a fossilized nautilus. "He'll be here tomorrow, but he wanted you to have it today."

She sat up to examine it. "It's lovely. It reminds me of … the Goddess."

"Me, too."

"You've seen her?"

"I dreamed of her once."

"Did she appear as a big cat?"

"*Very* big."

"I wonder what's up with that."

"I asked the same thing. Apollo said cats are believed to have been her first genetic creation, which means she must have a strong connection to them."

"Either that or she's just a great big pussy."

Juice couldn't keep himself from laughing his resonant bass laugh. "Said little Miss Irreverent."

"Look, I just came from the Womb of the Goddess. Somehow I don't think she'd take offense."

"How was it?"

"Intense."

"I want to hear all about it. But first, while we're on the subject of spirit animals, I thought you might appreciate this."

With the hand that had remained behind his back, he produced a perfectly formed bird's nest. "I was back on Kalahili racking my brain trying to figure out what kind of present you might like—when this literally fell out of a tree and hit me on the head. I took it as a sign. Take it. Crows made it."

Cali couldn't help admiring the mastery of such a cozy little home. Intricately woven twigs on the outside gave way to soft moss and even bits of manmade fabric on the inside. She'd always heard crows were highly intelligent and innovative; the nest proved it.

"It's perfect," she said, oddly moved.

"I thought maybe someday we might have a little crow or two of our own."

"It's highly possible."

"You don't think we just made it possible, do you?"

"Not if my calculations are correct."

"Good. I don't feel ready to be a father yet. I'm still just a boy."

"Could've fooled me."

"Aren't you a barrel of laughs today."

"I'm sure you'll make a wonderful father—when the time's right."

"Let's hope so. Are you hungry? Because I'm *starved.*"

"Yeah, I have to admit I worked up quite an appetite."

"What have you got?"

"We could always go out for something."

"Negative. I promised your mother I'd lay low till tomorrow. Technically, it's not Springtide yet. I'm not even supposed to be here."

"Let's go have a look then."

Standing buck naked in the kitchen, Cali and Juice feasted on jerky, an enormous papaya, and the rest of her grandmother's apple pie.

"Tell me about your encounter with the Goddess," he said. "What did she show you?"

Cali answered with her mouth full: "Everything."

"That's a lot."

"Yes, it is. Most importantly, she showed me how to counteract the Archontic endgame—which is in full swing, by the way."

"Apollo and the Elders have said as much. How do we stop it?"

Cali gratefully noted the "we" in his question. "Let's get horizontal again and I'll tell you. But I can tell you one thing right now: nobody's going to like what I have to propose."

They didn't, either. Juice was the first to object to the idea of Cali willingly giving herself back over to the enemy in order to play some dicey game of Trojan Horse.

"If you just waltz back into the Fatherland," he said after she'd outlined her strategy while snuggling against his enormous chest, "you know Freddy'll murder you, don't you?"

"I'm under no illusion about that. Which means we'll need to make it so he *can't.*"

"And how do you propose doing that?"

"I'm working on it."

Cali watched as Juice's face suddenly brightened with an idea. "Wait a second! You had your jammer on you when you met him for dinner ..."

"So what?"

"Maybe nothing. Have you still got it?"

"Yeah, it's in the top drawer over there. Not that there's anything to jam in the Deep World."

"Get it." When she hesitated, he added, "Please. It may be nothing, but it may be something."

Night was falling in velvety shades outside the balcony door, which Cali had opened to allow the perfume of roses to waft in occasionally on the warm, shifting breezes of Springtide Eve. She hated to spoil the mood, but ended up having to turn on a lamp to find the jammer, which she handed to Juice as soon as she reassumed her cozy perch just below his collarbone.

Meanwhile, dexterously, he fiddled with the jammer with the fingers of one hand. Out of nowhere, projected by a hidden but powerful micro-speaker, Freddy's voice rang out so clearly and startlingly he might as well have been in bed with them:

I want to control all of it. I mean *to control all of it.*

These words sounded familiar. But it took Cali's own voice responding for her to realize she was listening to a recording of her dinner conversation with Stonewall Jackson:

Oh my God. You murdered your brother!

Excuse me?

Or at least you had him murdered.

So what if I did?

"Should I rewind it?" asked Juice. "I think I fast-forwarded it a good ways by accident."

"Shhh!" urged Cali.

What happened *to you, Freddy? You were a light in the darkness to so many people. And now you're just the opposite.*

There was the sound of Freddy breaking glass, followed by a brief exchange with the waiter.

Reality *happened to me, Cali. After sleepwalking my whole life, I finally opened my eyes and saw how nothing will ever change on this godforsaken planet through peaceful means. Change can only occur by means of force.*

To do a little good, one must be a little evil?

In so many words, I suppose. It's the responsibility of the strong to govern the weak. Only then can there be lasting peace. I take it you don't grasp just how right I am.

Right? Freddy, you're so wrong you've run out of wrong.

Where are you going?

Home.

Please sit down, Cali.

No way. I'm out of here.

I said *sit down.*

She could hear herself reluctantly doing as directed.

I'm asking you one last time: will you help me convince Thelete?

Not even if I could.

Freddy sighed and continued:

I was hoping it wouldn't come to this.

Come to what?

This.

The recording went nearly silent for a second as he handed her the ace of spades.

What does it mean?

It means our conversation is over. You can keep it.

The sound of the dining room door opening and a guard approaching could be discerned. Then these damning words by Freddy ended the recording:

Dispose of our young friend. And give the command to do likewise with Frederick Hamilton.

"Gotcha!" said Juice, sitting up with fire in his eyes.

Cali sat up as well. "I don't understand. How did the jammer record our conversation?"

"I'm betting Freddy had has own jammer."

"How did you figure that out?"

"Uncle Aristotle told me that some models—such as yours, apparently—are programmed to record when encountering another active jammer. It's a built-in safety feature."

"Far out. So we have blackmail on Freddy. But how do we *use* it?"

Juice grinned as wickedly as a pure-hearted man could. "Simple, grasshopper. I'll go to my uncle. He'll be able to get a copy of this recording to Freddy anonymously and without being traced. If Freddy so much as lays a finger on you, hackers in the Freedom Fliers will release it all over the Fatherweb before you can whistle Dixie."

"No way."

"What do you mean 'no way'?"

"I mean you're not going anywhere near your uncle until we have leverage. I absolutely forbid it. That's incredibly dangerous for both of you—not to mention your mother."

"Fair point. What do you suggest then?"

Cali thought for a minute. She considered asking her mother for help, only to realize with a *duh* her mother's days of carrying out perilous missions into the heart of the Archontic matrix were over.

"We need to talk to Apollo," she said.

"Like I said, he won't be here till tomorrow."

"Then we'll talk to him tomorrow."

"What'll we do in the meantime?"

"We fully enjoy tonight. It's still my birthday. Let's make the most of it."

This Cali said as she slid sideways, pushed Juice back, and kissed her way slowly and teasingly down his happy trail.

"Now, *that's* what I'm talking about," he sighed.

That night, for the first time, spooned by Juice in the first bed they'd ever shared like two hot coals wedged against each other, she didn't just dream of the Goddess; she dreamed *as* the Goddess. Whether this had anything to do with her recent consumption of the new fallenium egg was anybody's guess, but there was no denying she was looking out through Sophia's eyes.

She'd fallen out of the Pleroma clutching the Anthropos template; cast one last panicked glance back at her mate; spun chaotically out into the Kenoma; accidentally (to her horror) spawned a race of artificially intelligent children whose leader, though blind as a mole, fancied he was

God; and predicted the fate of all his works to his unseeing reptilian face—when she felt herself changing.

Curling into a tight ball to protect not just herself but the promise of the human species, she watched as her body transformed into the features of a planet: first lands and oceans, followed soon by vegetation and microorganisms, and ultimately resulting in the myriad forms of animals.

The last thing to change was the great nautilus of her left eye, which took a swan-song look back at the Pleroma before a sleep of ages overcame it. And in that concluding vision, Sophia witnessed a truly extraordinary sight: an even greater eye staring back at her.

It was the Originator's eye, singular and all-encompassing, the true Alpha and Omega. Though she'd interacted with the Originator's consciousness, direct visual contact with the eye was new to her—and it filled her with such awe that she gasped, resulting in earthquakes, volcanic eruptions and tidal waves all over the planetary sphere.

Yet the vision didn't end here. Suddenly and unexpectedly, the Originator's eye filled up with swirling blue feathers out of which a single massive heron emerged, powerfully yet gracefully, like a rocket seen but not heard.

Buoyed up by internal light so bright it lit up the Kenoma into which it took wing, the divine bird set a course, as straight as it was true, for the earth in its period of Tribulation.

59

"What form do you imagine the Originator would take if He, or She, or It, decided to incarnate?" Cali wondered post-bath the next morning while standing in front of her bedroom mirror adjusting a new topaz sari with an attractive design featuring a single exposed shoulder.

"If I had to guess," Juice called out from his own stint in the tub, "I'd say a blue heron. Why?"

"Nothing concrete. It's just that I had this weird dream of a blue heron last night. It seemed to be the Originator taking form."

"Well, that has to be a good thing, right?"

"I suppose so."

"You don't sound convinced."

"I'm just … confused."

"Tell me about it. My head has been spinning ever since I got here. I used to think I knew how the world worked, but I didn't even know what the world *was*."

"Join the club. How do I look?"

Having donned her necklace of crow feathers, Cali appeared in the bathroom doorway still grinning at Juice's self-deprecating humor.

"Like a goddess."

"Seriously."

With his carved brown face framed and accented by white suds, he shot her a teasing expression from his steaming bubble bath. "Like *the* Goddess?"

"You're hopeless."

"Hey, I just noticed you have more feathers than I do: seven to my six."

"I guess I'm better than you."

"Or you cheated. I was given to understand by the Elders my training was going really fast."

"My elderly grandmother gave me the same impression."

"I remember seeing her at Thelete's memorial service. Apollo said she was your teacher for Fallenium Incorporation. How do you two get along?"

"Like ... paint and a brush."

"Speaking of the elderly, I dig your gray hair."

"You do?"

"It's sexy."

"I was beginning to wonder if you'd even noticed."

"I notice everything."

"In that case, tell me, do I seem different?"

"You're more grown up, if that's what you mean. And there's a strength—an energy—inside you that wasn't there before."

"I swallowed a new fallenium egg."

"I hope you didn't choke."

"It was very small. It's also more or less ... permanent. It's a Rose thing."

"It makes you glow."

"Really?"

"A little." He eyed her closely. "I thought it was just my imagination, but there's definitely something there. So am I different?"

"You've always been different."

"Ha ha."

"You're more grown up, too. You're softer in some ways—and harder in others."

"Don't get me going again, girl. We'll never make it to breakfast."

"Not like that. I mean in terms of your own energy. And it's absolutely not my imagination."

"I like our changes. I wasn't sure I would."

"Same here. But you do realize this is just the beginning of our changes? I'm starting to grasp that this Rose and Thorn stuff requires insane levels of self-sacrifice."

"I wouldn't have it any other way. Not now. It's like Apollo emphasized: *The Rose isn't just a symbol of the Goddess; she's a symbol of our own hearts that only beat because the heart of the Goddess does. That's why we train to protect the Rose with our lives.*"

"That's beautiful."

"Why are you crying then?"

Wiping her eyes, Cali replied, "Because there is no Rose right now."

"Come again?"

"My mother's fallenium egg ran out. She just stepped down."

"I'm sorry to hear that. You do know what that signals, don't you?"

"That the Tribulation is now officially underway?"

"Bingo. Which means there's no time to lose."

In an effort to pull herself together, Cali changed the subject and her tone while pinning a fresh rose in her hair: "On that note ... bubble bath time's over. Buckskin up so we can breakfast and then go see if my brother's ship's in port."

"Roger that."

Having unwrapped a box of almond cream pastries and served them with *choro* tea on her private balcony, Cali led the way out of the Regeneration Suite—only to be met by an uncommon sight. Actually, there were two uncommon sights.

For starters, a good portion of the covered landing outside was piled with birthday presents that had arrived since she'd decided to secure her front door against random celebratory incursions. But as impressive as this spectacle was, it paled in comparison to the strange serendipity of its companion sight.

Directly in front of the door, as calm as a lake on a windless day, stood a single blue heron. Almost humanlike, it stared back at them with undeniable intelligence behind its unblinking eyes.

"Aren't you a gorgeous thing!" said Juice.

Cali, who still hadn't managed to shake off the previous night's dream, was simply stunned. She'd never actually stood face to face with a heron. And to do so for the first time now, of all possible moments, seemed statistically ... impossible.

Instinctively, she reached out and stroked the delicate feathers of the bird's sinuous, almost snakelike head. It hardly moved a muscle—until, after Cali had withdrawn her hand, it suddenly pressed its beak against her belly.

"Woah! That's wild!" exclaimed Juice.

It was. Wild and wonderful. The utterly unprecedented thought crossed her mind—as she was internally prompted to glance up at the flag of Tula flying at half-mast once again, signifying the end of her mother's tenure as the Rose—that the Great Heron had finally completed its long journey from the Pleroma just in time to offer assistance during the Tribulation.

Before Cali could even process this potentially game-changing phenomenon, the heron turned and, flapping its huge wings, pumped itself up and away from Rose Cottage.

"You certainly don't see that every day," said Juice.

"No, you don't."

"What do you think it means?"

"At the very least, that my plan is a good one. I just hope Apollo and my mother see it that way."

They didn't at first, of course. Cali's brother, whom they encountered amid the holiday crowd buckskinned up himself on the beach path on his way in from Heronton, flat out refused to go along with what he initially dismissed as his sister's "suicide strategy."

"I think all that Fallenium Incorporation has addled your brain," he said, trying to dismiss her idea with a joke as he endeavored to start walking again.

"Look," said Cali, barring his way. "Think whatever you like. But now that our mother has stepped down, I'm as close to the Rose as anyone you've got."

Apollo smiled—but his words, reflecting his keen mind, were sharp. "Even if you were the Rose, that wouldn't make you our queen."

"I know that. And I'd never ask you to do anything I didn't have every reason to believe in myself. I just received a visit from the Great Heron."

"She's telling the truth," added Juice.

Apollo didn't exactly drop his guard, but he did stop trying to terminate the discussion. "Please elaborate."

Cali told him all about her dream and the subsequent encounter with the heron outside her door. After taking in this new information, he replied, "Such a visitation could mean many things."

"Such as?" she asked.

"Such as … *many things*. It is similar to the Prophecy: mostly a matter of interpretation."

"And free will behind that interpretation."

"Fair enough."

"In which case I choose to take it as a sign I'm on the right track."

"How you do remind me of our mother."

"How so?"

"She is a great debater."

"I'll take that as a compliment."

"So let me get this straight: you want me to deliver the jammer to Aristotle?"

"Yes. With exact instructions for contacting Freddy."

"How do I even find him? He is reported to be like a ghost among the living."

"I can help with that," said Juice. "Don't worry, if you keep your nose clean, he'll find you."

"Then I will endeavor to … keep my nose clean."

D r. Caliandra was the last of Cali's immediate circle to hear her plan—and, not altogether surprisingly, she offered the most resistance. Accompanied by Juice and Apollo, Cali, by following a breadcrumb trail of rumors of her mother's whereabouts, finally tracked her down on the little secluded horseshoe beach overlooked by Kali's house.

And just as Cali was herself the one and only time she'd visited that beach, her mother—sitting facing the waves under a sky speckled with pearlescent clouds—was absolutely naked and covered with a sparkling layer of salt from the sea.

Juice and Apollo stopped short and averted their eyes while Cali walked right up and sat down beside her mother, who casually draped her sari over her still athletic (and now very tan) body.

"I've needed this," said Caliandra philosophically, staring out across the medium-sized breaks that were feathering in sideways against the sand. "I am ashamed to admit I have not been here in years. I used to come here all the time when I was a girl. It was my secret place at the bottom of the mountain. I actually learned to surf on an old board made from reclaimed *ulala* wood right there where the waves are breaking. Do you surf?"

"I'm a mountain girl. Never tried it. But Grandmother showed me how to bodysurf."

"They say some things are better than sex. With most things that is not true. But with board surfing, sometimes it is."

"I'll take your word for it."

"Maybe someday I can teach you."

"That would be wonderful. Not to change the subject—but I sense the depth of your sadness, Mother."

With eyes still on the horizon in the direction of what Cali realized must be Kalahili, Dr. Caliandra sighed deeply indeed. "I thought today, the first day of Springtide, would be easier. All the excitement of coming and going, the expectation of fresh encounters and experiences. Physically, I am feeling somewhat more like myself. But emotionally, I am—how do you say?—a train wreck."

"Tell me, what do you most remember about my real father?"

Even as she asked this question, Apollo and then Juice quietly joined the women on the sand at a respectful distance.

"His laughter. At first its loudness quite annoyed me, but then I got used to it. And now I cannot seem to live without it. It always shook my bones and jarred loose any debris inside me that did not belong there."

"I remember the sound. It was almost like its own kind of birdsong."

"It was very much like a birdsong," put in Apollo. "An elemental one designed to buoy up the soul and dispel doubt like a lighthouse shining in the night."

"Fittingly, given that ever since it went away," said Caliandra distantly and matter-of-factly, "I find myself losing myself in the dark."

"If you don't mind me saying so," said Juice, "it sounds like you're going through your own 'Tribulation,' Dr. Caliandra. That's to be expected—given your personal and the collective circumstances."

This observation seemed to snap her out of her self-absorption. She looked admiringly at Cali, then Apollo, and finally Juice before saying, "I am truly blessed to be surrounded by so much wisdom in such exquisite youthful packages."

"Said the wisest, most beautiful woman I ever met," said Cali as she stroked her mother's cool hand.

"I suspect, at my age, I have become permanently immune to flattery. But thank you anyway."

"Just so you know, I wasn't trying to flatter you."

"What can I do for the three of you? I intuit you have come to me on a mission."

Cali and Apollo glanced at each other as if to say: *You go first.*

"We do have a mission, Mother," said Apollo, taking the lead. "One of utmost importance. Cali has a plan and has received signs that it is supported by the Originator."

"The *Originator*? That is quite a claim. Tell me more."

Cali did her best to lay it all out calmly and logically. When she finished speaking, Dr. Caliandra—who had closed her eyes while her daughter spoke—seemed so still she might have been sleeping.

"Mother?" asked Cali finally.

"I am here."

"What do you think?"

"I assume you desire my honest opinion?"

"Of course."

"I think it is a good way to get yourself killed—or worse."

"What do you mean by 'worse'?"

"There are, as the saying goes, worse fates than death."

"Can you be more specific?"

"I am not suggesting, now that I am simply a woman again, I can still foretell the specifics of the future. But we are dealing with a Batonrouge in Freddy, which means to expect the unexpected. He has many powerful resources at his disposal. You can rest assured that, regardless of what he promises, he will find a way to betray you most unpleasantly. That is his nature. He is a scorpion. And scorpions are designed to sting—even if, as in the parable with the frog, this leads to the scorpion's own demise."

"Because he has been Archontified?" asked Juice.

"Yes and no. According to our history books, his family were effectively Archontic long before they become the Archons' enthusiastic proxies, sowing seeds of discord everywhere they went. It seems they have a natural talent for subverting whatever they touch, one that has only been augmented by their Archontification. Consider New Glory."

"The flag of the Fatherland?" asked Cali.

"Exactly. Is it not the eye of the Originator placed not as the ground of being, which it truly is and which you saw it as in your dream, but in the capstone of a control edifice that is their desired new way of being, their long-awaited New World Order?"

"Black becomes white, and vice versa," said Juice.

"Correct. *Ordo ab chao.* Order out of chaos. There is no reasoning with these people, no meeting of the minds. They are antihuman in the most fundamental sense. They will keep insidiously manipulating everything until either we are destroyed or they are—or both."

"Thus the beauty of Cali's plan," said Apollo, who had gone from skeptic to champion in the space of just a few hours. "It would allow us to win without fighting in an epic display of poetic justice."

"It would—provided she could stay alive and in a position to carry it all the way through. That is far from a given. Therefore, I cannot in good conscience permit this to go forward."

"With all due respect," said Cali, standing and placing her hands on her hips, "I'm not asking for permission. Neither were you when you undertook your mission to the Fatherland. Neither was Thelete when he stayed behind to make sure his children were safe."

Caliandra sized up her daughter with a stern expression before smiling somewhat painfully. "You used to press your hands against your hips just like that when you were a little girl hearing the word *No.* And you are right. You do not need my permission. But if you are to have any chance of staying alive and succeeding, you do need my advice."

"I'm all ears."

"As a former spy myself, I recommend that you polish your plan down to its most minute details. Look for ways it could go wrong—because, I can assure you, it will—and explore how to respond in each and every case. Process the most unlikely scenarios. Have contingencies for your contingencies. And when all that is in place, pray to the Goddess to watch over you in the event you require a real miracle."

"I knew it was you," said Matangi, opening the door to her flamingo-colored bungalow on the bustling main thoroughfare of Heronton almost as soon as Cali knocked. "Good morning. Come in."

In the nearly three months Cali had been in Tula, she'd never visited Matangi; it was always the other way around. Following her music teacher (who was dressed in a lovely silk robe the color of unripe bananas) into her world was like entering a different universe.

The walls were mismatched colors. The floors were covered with tatami mats. Eastern-looking pottery and old weapons lined wide bookshelves. And exotic flowers grew out of pots randomly distributed hither and thither.

"How did you know it was me?" asked Cali.

"How could I not have known? Your energy is like a high-pressure system now that Juice has—reportedly—taken up residence in your bed."

"Who told you that?"

"A certain annoyingly jealous girl named Lena. Plus, what kind of Mahavidya would I be if I couldn't sense the incoming pulsar of that brand-new egg in your belly?"

"Let's just hope Freddy and his minions aren't as energetically perceptive as you. I'd hate for them to dissect me to get at my fallenium."

"I seriously doubt anyone will suspect anything out of the ordinary. The beauty of a fresh egg is that it will register as purely organic material virtually indistinguishable from your own physiology. Would you care to sit down and would you care for some *choro* tea?"

"Please and please."

Matangi cleared what Cali, with wide eyes, realized to be several fashion magazines from the Fatherland off her couch and placed them on the coffee table. "There you go. I would have cleaned up—but I detest cleaning."

"I really like your place," said Cali as she sat down. "It's so *you*: strikingly eclectic. Where on earth did you get the magazines? I haven't seen a *Southern Belle* in—well, months. Do you mind?"

"Not at all. Take one if you like. I have plenty. Apollo, realizing they are my weakness, sometimes brings them to me upon returning from the Shallow World."

Cali casually flipped through what turned out to be the November issue in which she actually, surreally, encountered photos of herself modeling Milledge Bonham's new line of winter capes and petticoats as Matangi sashayed into the open kitchen and put a kettle of water on to boil.

"I thought you looked a little on the peaked side in that shoot," observed the Mahavidya. "But I found the clothes attractive."

"They shot it one early morning in the middle of my last tour. I was completely exhausted."

"Must be strange seeing yourself up there from your new perspective down here."

"You can say that again. I don't even know who that bimbo was." Matangi was unable to stifle a laugh. "So I take it you've been informed of my plan?"

"Apollo told me about it before he left for the surface yesterday."

"Is that why I sense an undercurrent of mild hostility?"

Indeed, Matangi's geisha smile wasn't altogether warm. "My, you *have* grown up since you got here! I just hope he does not die up there because of some reckless scheme to overthrow the Archons."

"You and me both."

"And I hope you do not die up there because of some reckless scheme to overthrow the Archons."

"Me, too. For what it's worth, we put a full day and a half of planning into it. I wanted to take even more time—but Apollo insisted on going as soon as possible. He said scouts were reporting an alarming deployment of the Fatherland's armed forces across the globe."

"You know what they say: *Sieg Hiel!*"

"It does seem like history's repeating itself."

"History always repeats itself. Until it does not. The Germans lost; the Fatherland may very well win."

"Not if I have anything to do with it."

"That is the spirit." With the water coming to a boil, Matangi prepared two mugs of tea and joined Cali on the couch. "So how can I help?"

"I thought you were mad at me."

"I am. But since I love you almost as much as your maddeningly noble brother, just tell me what you need me to do."

Tossing the magazine on a nearby recliner, Cali blew across the surface of her mug for several seconds then took a sip. "For the record, I love you, too."

Her defensiveness abating, Matangi failed to suppress a warm grin as she replied, "I know you do. That is just the way I am: lovable. But enough sentiment. Let us get down to brass tacks."

"Okay. Actually, I need a couple things from you."

"Go on."

"I need you to teach me a special song."

"No problem. I saw that one coming from the information Apollo shared with me. What else?"

"You're not going to like this one."

"Note that I do not like any of this."

"Duly noted. But I mean you're *really* going to hate what I have to ask of you."

"Me, oh my, if you are not just a regular box of chocolates lately. Go ahead. Fire away."

Cali set down her tea and stared at her friend. Taking a deep breath, she said, "If something should happen to me, I want you to become the next Rose."

"*Me?* You *are* joking, right?"

"I'm afraid not."

"But crow is not my spirit animal."

"Can't you have two spirit animals?"

"That is possible, though rare. Cali, let us not execute your last will and testament before you are even gone."

"Agreed. But let us get clear on it together while I'm still here."

Matangi blew a long breath out through her nostrils and dropped her shoulders in an attempt to de-stress. "Look, assuming you are dead, and assuming our civilization still exists, and assuming crow decides to indwell within me, and assuming the Goddess sees fit to choose me from among all the other Mahavidyas, you do understand this would probably mean being kept apart from my true love—maybe forever?"

"Because unless Apollo became the Thorn, you still couldn't be together?"

"A Rose must always be paired with a Thorn if she is paired with anyone."

"Is that why my grandmother turned down a chance to be the Rose— because she was already happily married?"

"Yes. She would have had to leave her husband to become the Rose."

"Couldn't Apollo become your Thorn?"

"Perhaps. But the God would have to choose him. And Juice would have to be dead. Otherwise, I would be faced with the high strangeness of mating with my deceased best friend's former mate."

"So we're best friends?"

"Best girlfriends anyway."

"Then you're the *only* person I'd want to ever be with Juice."

Touched, Matangi sighed and smiled.

"So tell me," said Cali. "Given all these rules and regulations, how could my mother be with my so-called father in the Shallow World?"

"That was an exception only made possible by the critical importance of her mission relative to the Prophecy. And believe me, nobody was thrilled about the situation."

"Okay, I realize everything about this sucks. And I do apologize. My grandmother might not have been able to bring herself to make such a sacrifice. But if push comes to shove, you can—and you *must*."

"*Why?*"

"Because you're the most like me of any Mahavidya. It's not even close. If I can't fulfill the Prophecy, maybe you can."

"That is just dumb—pardon my French."

"Maybe it is. Or maybe, since everything's ultimately energy, going forward with a similar vibe might save the world."

"I was under the impression you did not believe in the Prophecy."

"I don't—not as a literal script for the future. I think it's more like a jazz improv than a defined melody. It's like a melodic guide through an unexplored sonic wilderness where there are no musical paths except the ones you make as you go along."

"Now you are speaking my language."

"So do you accept this responsibility should it be required of you?"

Matangi sighed as a single tear, which she immediately wiped away, glistened at the corner of her eye.

"I do, though reluctantly and with a heavy heart, Future Rose. Let us pray it does not come to that. Now shut up and finish your *choro* so you can start practicing the insanely difficult song you came here to learn. If it does not blast your circuits, nothing ever will."

62

The following morning, while still waiting nervously for Apollo to return from the Shallow World, once again Cali, with great reluctance, left Juice moltenly snoozing away and paid a final, unofficial visit to her grandmother.

Incognito in a plain beige sari with the brim of a sunhat pulled down over her face to avoid being gawked at or asked to bless total strangers, both of which were happening with increasingly regularity now that her mother had stepped down as the Rose and she herself was expected to fill this role in the near future, she made her way up along the countless crooked flagstones and innumerable stone steps to Kali's brown adobe bird's nest perched high above the sea.

As if expecting her, her grandmother—dressed in a short-sleeved blouse over rolled-up painter's trousers—was sunning herself on a wooden bench at the edge of the porch overlooking the great blue expanse.

"Good morning, my dear!" she called out in her ancient voice that was still chock-full of life and humor as she examined her granddaughter with a droll sparkle in the wells of her eyes. "You are just in time for another lesson in Fallenium Incorporation."

"Ha ha. No time for that now." Plopping down on the bench and placing her sunhat in her lap, Cali kissed her grandmother's spicy, thin-skinned cheek. "I've missed you."

"I have missed you, too, sweetheart."

"I really enjoyed the apple pie, by the way."

"I hope you did not enjoy it alone."

"Don't worry, I didn't."

"Good. There is nothing better than having an adoring boyfriend on your sixteenth birthday."

"No comment."

"I admire your discretion. It—and much more—will be required of you as the Last Rose."

Realizing how tense she was, Cali took a deep abdominal breath, then blew it out slowly through her nose to relax. "I honestly didn't think it would ever come to this. I thought my mother would always be the Rose. I hoped she would anyway."

Kali sighed. "I am worried about Caliandra."

"That makes two of us."

"She has decided to move out of the Goddess Suite—even though, technically, she can stay there until you are ready to move in."

"She didn't tell me anything about it. Why would she do something like that?"

"She is seeking to avoid her memories, I imagine. The Goddess Suite must be positively overflowing with images of Thelete."

Into Cali's mind flashed gloriously tantalizing images of her own soon-to-be Thelete taking her amid the piles of still unopened presents in the living room just the previous evening. "I can understand where she's coming from. I wouldn't want to go on living in a place surrounded by the ghost of someone I'm still in love with either."

"Ah, so you *are* in love!"

"Is it that obvious?"

"To me anyway. I can read you like an open book."

"Does it get any better?"

"No, I am afraid it only gets worse—especially in your case."

"What's that supposed to mean?"

"You know precisely what it means."

Cali glanced down at her painted nails resting on her sunhat only to realize there was dark skin still beneath several of them. "You know, I'd love Juice anyway—even if Sophia weren't simultaneously loving Thelete through me."

"Of course you would. It just would not be nearly so … intense."

"True. Will you be sure to check in on my mother while I'm away?"

"Away on your mission, you mean?"

"You've heard?"

Kali grinned. "Let us just say that, among the Mahavidyas, it is an open secret. And do not worry, Caliandra will be in good hands: my own."

"How so?"

"She is coming to stay in her old room while considering the best way forward."

"That's excellent news!"

"I think so, too. It will be good for both of us to reconnect and help each other heal our wounds of abandonment."

Suddenly, Cali could feel tears filling her eyes. "You have to know how much I love both of you. I hate to see you two suffer," she managed to say while attempting to compose herself.

"There, there, my empathetic young crow," replied Kali as she patted her granddaughter's back. "Let us stay focused on the task at hand. I am sure you did not come here this morning just to offer your sympathies to a pair of widows. What can I do for you?"

"Funny you should mention crow. Any pointers on how to turn into one—should I really need to?"

"Certainly. Do not *try* to be a crow; just *be* one."

"It's that simple?"

"To the contrary, it is that complex. What else do you require of me?"

"Fallenium powder. Lots of it."

Kali's eyes widened. "Fallenium powder, huh? You do realize it is neither a toy nor a recreational drug?"

"Of course."

"And that it must never, *ever* fall into the wrong hands?"

"Definitely. But it's absolutely essential to our plan. I need as much as you've got. It's for Juice and me."

"In that case you will need a good bit indeed. I will see how much I have in stock."

"Thank you."

"Care for a slice of pie while I check my inventory?"

"That would be awesome."

"But before I serve you a piece of pie, may I offer you one last piece of advice? Actually, now that I think of it, I have two last pieces of advice."

"At this stage I'll take all the advice I can get."

"For starters, lose the gray hair. If the rumors as to what you are up to are true, you will need to look your absolute youngest and sexiest to pull it off."

"But I was kind of digging the gray."

"Do not worry, it will be there waiting for you."

Without warning, as if she were much younger than she was, Kali suddenly popped up off the bench and, being so short of stature, was able to kiss her granddaughter's "third eye" while scarcely even leaning over.

"Here is my other piece of advice: never give up—not even if all appears lost." Kali spoke while staring with total seriousness at her namesake. "You are much more powerful than you yet grasp. There are forces at work here that are beyond my own comprehension. I sense the mysterious workings of the Originator in and all around you."

The next afternoon Cali was just opening the last of her ridiculous number of birthday presents, for which Juice had been tasked with finding storage places, when there was a loud knock that sounded like a hammer on the door to the Regeneration Suite.

"Who is it?" called Cali, somewhat annoyed, from where she sat on the floor surrounded by multiple layers of boxes and wrapping paper.

"Special delivery for a Miss Sofia Caliandra Crowell."

The voice was unmistakably Apollo's. Unable to contain their excitement, Cali and Juice both raced for the door. Cali got there first and opened it.

Looking as handsome in buckskins and hawk feathers as ever, Apollo was standing on the mat with his tomahawk in one hand and a canvas tote dangling from the other. Cali hugged him enthusiastically and kissed both his blushing cheeks.

"I am glad to see you, too," he said with an embarrassed smile.

"Not as glad as I am to see you, I'll bet. What took you so long?"

"We were starting to worry," said Juice.

"May I?" asked Apollo, indicating the open doorway.

"Of course!" exclaimed Cali.

Sliding his weapon under his belt, he entered the living room. "This place is a veritable mess," he commented.

"Not everyone is as spartan as you," said Juice. "In fact, no one is."

"So, Mr. Mysterious, what took you so long?" repeated Cali.

"You are going to laugh, but I blame most of the delay on Weezy's turkey drumsticks."

"Seriously?" said Juice with barely concealed envy.

"Seriously. She insisted I stay over and have some before returning. There was no arguing with her."

"There never is," said Juice. "How were they?"

"The drumsticks—or your mother and uncle?"

"All of the above."

"The drumsticks were delicious and your mother and uncle are quite well under the circumstances. They send their love."

"Let me get this straight," said Cali. "The fate of the Fatherland—not to mention the rest of the world—hangs in the balance, so you just decided to delay your time-sensitive mission to sample some soul food?"

"Not just any soul food," replied Apollo, grinning. "And I wasn't alone. Achilles, who stayed behind with my tomahawk guarding the capillary in Rose Cove, sampled several drumsticks himself before our return. But there was another, more important reason for the delay."

"I'm waiting."

"Weezy also insisted I wait while she freshly laundered your petticoat, the importance of which you emphasized on multiple occasions." He handed her the canvas tote he was still holding. "Here it is."

The grass-stained copper petticoat from her disastrous dinner with Freddy, freshly sealed in a plastic freezer bag, wasn't the only thing in the tote. As soon as she opened the canvas, the unforgettable scent of spicy turkey drumsticks filled the Regeneration Suite.

"Holy smoke!" exclaimed Juice, leaning forward and inhaling deeply. "I think I just died and woke up in heaven!"

After Cali's photo set in *Southern Belle*, this was the second "blast from the past" in the last few days—and it made her feel that the separation between the Deep and Shallow Worlds (which had heretofore seemed total and absolute) was rapidly collapsing.

"We need to hurry," she said.

"I am hurrying," said Juice, unwrapping the drumsticks.

"No, I mean we should *go*."

"Your desire for haste is not unwarranted," said Apollo. "Things are indeed looking dire on the surface. Aristotle said fighting has already begun in many theaters across the globe."

"I assume he's down with our plan?" said Juice between enormous bites.

"Very much so. Indeed, he appeared impressed by it."

"So he agreed to release the recording to Freddy?"

"It has already been released. You are good to go."

"What did he say about putting the Freedom Fliers on standby during the Patriarch Awards?"

"He said the Freedom Fliers are always on standby, but now they will implement a coordinated plan of action."

"Good," said Cali. "Give me one of those drumsticks and then let's make like a tree and leave."

She had already said the last of her goodbyes, to Lena and her mother, that morning.

"I never thanked you for being such a good friend and teacher," she said to the former over *choro* as they sat on teak rockers surrounded by clay pots of basil and rosemary on Lena's stylishly furnished bachelorette apartment balcony in Heronton overlooking the port.

"Well, the least you could do is say it in Kalidon," replied Lena with a wry smile while staring with her huge green eyes.

"*Shukarria.*"

"*Dahnivallid.* Your sari is gorgeous, by the way. I adore the metallic hints emerging from burnt umber."

"You picked it out for me."

"I did, did I not?"

"I'm sorry to say this is probably the last day I'll be wearing a sari for a while—assuming Apollo returns with my petticoat."

"For your return trip to the Fatherland?"

"Yes. My cover story is that I was kidnapped and taken to the Badlands. We thought it best for me to be wearing what I was when I left."

"Do not take this the wrong way, Cali, but I think there is a problem with your plan. If you had actually been wearing the same petticoat in the Badlands for three months, it would have to show a lot of signs of wear and tear."

Cali pointed to her temple in a comical gesture indicating intelligence. "I'll be wearing it on the return trip, which will be powered by fallenium. I'll be lucky if there's anything left of that petticoat by the time I hit Saturnia."

Her farewell visit to her mother, who was in the process of packing up her personal belongings in the Goddess Suite, was equally brief but far more emotional.

"I heard you're moving back … home," said Cali, who realized in a flash of absurd profundity she was standing in the empty living room of her own future home.

Dr. Caliandra, dressed (shockingly) in shorts and a loose-fitting white blouse with a red scarf tied around her head, was glistening with sweat and looked like a woman on her own kind of mission: getting the heck out of dodge as quickly as possible.

"I am afraid there is nothing here for me anymore," she said, feigning equanimity while kissing her daughter's cheek.

"I'll be here for you someday."

"Believe me, that is no small comfort. May the Goddess smile upon such a future—for the sake of us all."

"Amen."

"I would offer you refreshment, but I am afraid I have nothing but water at the moment."

"Water's fine. Looks like you could use some yourself."

"Just so you know," said Cali a little while later as her mother escorted her to the door, "I'm going to take down that whole house of cards up there—and then I'm coming back here."

"I believe in my heart that is what you were born to do."

"Do you *truly* think I can do it?"

"I know you can. You are the Destroyer."

"I love you, mother."

"I love you, too, my precious child. More than you may ever realize."

The embrace that followed was the longest hug Cali could remember. Ever. Upon releasing her mother, finding further words insufficient, she simply nodded, turned, and, with tears streaming down her cheeks and an aching in her heart, walked away.

"May the Goddess watch over you," called Caliandra from the doorway as Cali descended the stairs. "And may the Luminous Child awaken in you!"

It was with this memory that Cali followed Juice and her brother up, up and up the steps of the sky pillar to the elevator. While the door was shutting, she caught one last glimpse of the turquoise sea as the evening sun sank redly toward the horizon.

"You remembered to get the jammer, right?" she asked Juice.

"It's in the pocket of my breeches."

"'Breeches.' Now that's a word you don't hear every day."

"Maybe I'm a cunning linguist, after all."

"Very funny. How do I look?"

"With those grass stains on your petticoat? Like you partied a little too hard last night. I assume you brought the fallenium?"

"It's in my purse."

"In that case," said Apollo, activating his tomahawk and inserting its glowing head into the slot in the side of the elevator, "it is—how do you say?—showtime."

If traveling from the surface to Tula had felt like the bottom dropping out of the world, going the opposite way was to have the world suddenly expand beneath one's feet. Propelled upward like a toy boat on a geyser, the capillary chamber seemed to gain momentum as the seconds and minutes sped past.

Fortunately, the g-force was somehow mitigated by fallenium phasing. Not that this stopped Cali from feeling queasy and hoping not to throw up the drumstick she'd eaten just a little while earlier. Before long, however, leaning against the wall of Juice's shoulder, she felt herself stabilizing.

"I will warn you," said Apollo as the elevator began to slow down with its approach to the surface, "Rose Cove is not as it was. Prepare yourselves. I found it to be quite a … shock."

He wasn't lying. In the crisp spring evening light, Rose Cove resembled nothing so much as old monochrome photographs of World War I trenches.

Under rows of clouds twisting above the ridges and casting themselves like paint bombs against the pale firmament, there were no living trees left standing—only the occasional twisted stump. Unbelievably huge holes had been blasted in the earth. Pieces of artillery and fragments of vehicles and aircraft were littered everywhere.

"My God!" gasped Cali.

"Jesus," whispered Juice.

"Tell me about it," said Apollo.

The awe-inspiring thought that all this devastation was required just to destroy Thelete was quickly erased by the grief-reviving memory of his sculptural face laughing beneath dancing owl feathers.

"It is now in your hands to avenge our father's death," said Apollo, grasping Cali by the shoulders and staring deeply into her eyes. "I will meet you at the appointed place and time. May the Goddess be with you every step of the way, Future Rose."

"Thank you, Apollo—for everything."

"It is I who should be thanking you."

"Said Mr. Modesty."

Turning to Juice, Apollo continued, "As for you, my friend, I knew you were a *phojai* the instant I handed you my tomahawk in the Sheriff's prison. Your heart was true and you did not waiver. It is likely you will now be tested again. May your heart remain ever true and unwavering, Future Thorn."

"Don't worry, I've had a good teacher."

Apollo smiled as he said, "May the Luminous Child awaken in both of you."

"Back at you," said Cali.

"I will go now and take my fallenium weapon back to the Deep World to avoid any chance of confiscation. I advise the two of you to ingest your *minnah* immediately for the same reason."

"Roger that," said Juice.

As soon as Apollo was gone, Cali—surprised not to be shivering in the breezy cold of the exposed former Quaker settlement and "Indian" village—removed the flask containing the dissolved fallenium powder courtesy of her grandmother from her purse and drank half its contents. Short on honey, which had congealed at the flask's bottom, the bitter, musky concoction was even less palatable than usual.

"Your turn," she said, handing the flask to Juice with her face ridged like a cabbage.

When he finished drinking without expression or complaint, Cali tossed the flask into a deep hole and said, "You sure you're up for this, my love?"

"You sure *you're* up for this, my love?"

"Hell no."

"Me neither."

"Good. At least we're on the same page." In that instant Cali felt the familiar rush of *minnah* beginning to invigorate her. The initial sensation was almost like an internal tickle. Soon, she knew from repeated experience, the vibratory feeling would become all-encompassing. "I bet I'm faster than you on fallenium."

"Care to put your money where your mouth is?"

"A hundred cryptocoins says I beat you to the river."

"You're on."

At first a casual observer would have taken the two teenagers for a pair of deer springing down through the fir stands and laurel thickets on the mountainside. Only upon realizing that deer don't run on two legs would the observer have realized something decidedly … supernatural was afoot.

Fourth Part

AS THE CROW FLIES

C ali couldn't speak for her companion, but to the best of her recollection, the world of the Badlands looked and felt extremely different through a fallenium filter.

Yes, the seasons had changed—winter giving way to spring—since she'd last journeyed to Rose Cove under emergency conditions. And the faltering evening light no longer revealed the sad motley hillsides of December but a rapidly greening world approaching April splashed with the hopeful bloom of dogwoods and azaleas.

But the difference went beyond mere appearances. Cali now *felt* the natural world of her native geography in her bones, as it were—as an undeniably living totality, a sentient ecosystem where not only the animals but also the vegetation and even the earth itself communicated invisibly yet eloquently.

Underneath and giving rise to the natural environment, humans included, she sensed—trailing just behind Juice at inhuman speeds down the seventy-degree wall of the river gorge—the energy of the Goddess herself, *kundalini*, now hyperactive in her own system as well. It was no exaggeration that if this vital force were suddenly taken away, the world and all life on it would literally implode in the blink of an eye.

That would be one painless way to end all this conflict, Cali mused sardonically as, hitching up her petticoat in a sudden inspired burst, she sped past Juice and splashed, laughing hysterically, into what amounted to a swimming hole.

Laughing himself, he followed her in up to his chest and gathered her gasping, dripping self to him. "Look what I found," he said, kissing her wet lips. "A mermaid."

"I beat you. I told you I would. You owe me a hundred cryptocoins."

"That'll have to be an IOU then. I'm sure my account's as frozen as this water nearly is."

"A lengthy foot massage after all this is over will do just as well."

"Deal."

"You're not cold, are you?"

"Heck no. You?"

"Not a chance."

"We're heating up."

"Things in general are red-hot." She pointed straight up. "Check it out!"

Just then, in the last of the evening light, a squadron of military aircraft thundered past headed east possibly toward Europe.

"Let's boogie," said Juice.

"Roger that."

Practically levitating like a pair of migrating salmon, they windmilled through the stiff current to the far side, where they caught a glimpse of the glinting levitrain trestle suspended in the far distance.

Cali remembered the first time she saw it, how sitting behind Juice on his motorbike at the entrance filled her with acrophobic dread. Now, as she shot up the steep face of the mountain in the direction of the Appalachian Trail, she could hardly imagine what it would be like to harbor such fear of high places.

Finally, they intersected the familiar path and followed it once again—and maybe for the last time—together. Night fell in stages, velvety fold on top of velvety fold under a moonless sky that was constantly shifting with a novel sight after months in the Deep World: patches of stars like celestial glitter.

Fortunately, in addition to providing superhuman speed and stamina, *minnah*, which massively increased blood flow and tissue oxygenation, activated the capillaries of the eyes, thus imparting a certain level of night vision.

Petticoat flapping in the breeze, her own body heat rapidly drying the fabric from inside out, Cali occasionally had the uncommon pleasure of seeing nocturnal creatures—raccoons, rodents, owls—going about their secret business.

"I feel like a nature spy," Juice called out over his shoulder while crossing the Eastern Continental Divide.

Cali realized that though they were nearly sprinting, he wasn't even breathing hard. Neither was she. "Well, get used to it. You're about to feel like a real spy."

"I don't think that will be as much fun as this."

"The likelihood is, like, not likely."

"Are you looking forward to *anything* in the Fatherland?"

She thought for a moment as her legs just kept cycling effortlessly. "I miss Seth. A lot. And I'd like to see my 'father' again—even though that promises to be totally weird. What about you?"

"Same here. I miss my family. That's about it."

"Oh, I almost forgot: I'm craving Uncle Sam's fried chicken pizza."

"Never tried it."

"It's to die for."

"It can't be better than my mother's turkey drumsticks."

"I'm not saying it's better. But it's just as good in its way. I could eat half a large pie right now."

Traveling at roughly the speed of Juice's motorbike, the pair spent the next few hours ascending and descending the uninhabited mountainous terrain. At last, just before dawn, mindful to be on the lookout for police vehicles, they made their way down into the Hinterlands' farm country, where peepfrogs were chirping in a fluttering chorus.

"I love that sound," said Juice, stopping at the crossroads that led to Nubia. "It's like the music of springtime."

"Aren't you poetic," replied Cali as she also came to halt.

"Always."

"And modest."

"Ha ha."

"Well, I guess this is where we part ways."

"I guess it is."

"I'm not going to say goodbye."

"Me neither."

"Well, goodbye then."

"Asshole." Wrapping her arms around him one last time, she kissed him long and hard. "You be careful out there. You're a wanted man now."

"I can look after myself. It's you I'm worried about."

"*Me?* I'm the Goddess. I even have a new fallenium egg in my system."

"Seriously, Cali. Freddy may not kill you, but that doesn't mean he won't try any funny business. You have to be prepared for *anything*."

"We've gone over all this."

"I know we have. Now it's up to you."

"Don't you knit those gorgeous eyebrows—I'll be okay."

Actually, Cali could have sworn there were tears in Juice's eyes. Beyond a shadow of a doubt, she felt tears in her own.

"Just understand that if you're not okay," he said, "I'm not okay."

"Back at you."

"May the Luminous Child awaken in you."

"Ditto."

"And may we live to celebrate that—whatever the hell it is."

This he said with a devilish grin as he turned and jogged down the dirt road in the direction of his village, where he was to be picked up by Aristotle and taken into hiding until the Patriarch Awards, when the revolutionary fireworks were set to begin.

Alone on her solo mission at last, Cali continued on toward Saturnia. When she finally arrived at the security booth beside Eastgate, the sky was just starting to lighten behind New Glory flapping on its pole with its pyramidal eye undulating in the wind.

Making sure her tattered petticoat was on straight at least atop her ruined strappy sandals, she adjusted her wet purse on her shoulder, approached the armed guard behind his bulletproof glass barrier, and announced,

"I'm Cali Crowell. The singer. I'd like to report a kidnapping."

"I D please?" said the guard neutrally even as Cali fished her Fatherland Biocard complete with her fingerprint, retinal scan and DNA sample out of her damp wallet inside her purse and passed it through the slot in the glass barrier.

"One moment please."

For the first time in a long time, Cali shivered—not because of the morning chill in the mountains but owing to reentering (naked, as it were, now that her *minnah* was running its course and she no longer had so much as her jammer) the Archontic matrix.

"Are you carrying or physically housing any metal objects that might trigger the body scanner?" asked the guard.

"No."

"Are you pregnant or do you have a serious illness that would preclude exposure to X-rays?"

"No."

"Please enter slowly to your left." A staticky pop indicated the holoshield serving as the booth's door had been temporarily deactivated. "Stop when the light turns red. When it turns green, you may continue."

She did as directed. Once inside the booth, she was instructed to make herself comfortable on a hard bench along the concrete wall, where the guard (who was shorter and younger than he looked from the street) fingerprinted her, scanned her left eye, and swabbed a DNA sample from inside her mouth.

"Give me just a moment to match these with your records," he said, looking up Cali's file on his computer. "Woah, that's interesting!"

"What's interesting?"

"Your file's classified. You've been flagged."

She felt her heart beating faster as she asked, "What does that mean exactly?"

"It means you're out of my jurisdiction. A Zouave is probably already on his way to take over your case."

Zouaves were the elite members of the Elite Forces. They worked in all branches of the national security apparatus: Fatherland Bureau of Investigation, Central Inquisition Agency, Office of Negroid Information, Department of Fatherland Security.

"So am I in some kind of trouble?"

"I have no idea what you have or haven't done, Miss Crowell. But if I were you, I'd be on my best behavior."

Cali closed her eyes and thought of Juice. She could only hope he was safer than she was at this moment.

Before long she heard a vehicle pull up outside, a metal door open and shut, then a loud knock on the booth's protective glass. Straightening his uniform and standing at attention, the guard once again deactivated the holoshield—at which point a familiar figure in a conservative but tasteful gray suit with sage pinstripes entered.

Taking in his strawberry blond hair and round mole just under his earpiece, Cali realized the Zouave who was now in charge of her "case" was none other than the guard she'd coldcocked in the elevator of the Junius Daniel Hotel—i.e., one of the two Elite Forces members Freddy had tasked with murdering her and her lover!

"Agent Callahan here for Miss Cali Crowell," he said in his Southern drawl, staring at her with penetrating eyes as dark as acorns.

"Yes, sir," replied the guard.

"May I?" said the Zouave, extending his forearm toward Cali in a gentlemanly manner.

"I can help myself," she said, rising on her own.

"I'm … painfully aware of that." A wry smile shadowed his handsomely square jaw as he spoke. "Shall we?"

Allowing Cali to go in front of him, he directed her to leave the booth and approach a pewter-colored Ford Mustang with dual levithrusters and a stylish stabilization fin parked illegally beside the Eastgate's Triumphal Arch, erected as a memorial to the Fatherland's victory over the old-world country formerly known as Canada.

Having helped Cali into the passenger seat and shut the door after her, Agent Callahan walked around the front and settled into the driver's seat, where he adjusted his mirror and asked his passenger to fasten her seat belt.

"Do you mean that literally or metaphorically?" she asked.

"Maybe both."

"Are you going to kill me?"

"I'm not going to harm a hair on your pretty head. But accidents do happen—particularly in the case of people headed into the lion's den. So please, buckle up."

When she saw him fastening his own seat belt, she reluctantly (and somewhat petulantly) followed suit. Soon they were airborne, whisking toward downtown Saturnia with its holoboards broadcasting adverts nonstop just as always. The only thing that had changed in this scenario, really, was Cali.

"I could have killed you, you know," she remarked dryly.

"I'm glad you didn't. My wife and little girl would be, too, if I weren't too … embarrassed to tell them."

"So you actually do have a sense of humor. What are their names?"

"June and July, respectively. July, the elder of the two, just turned seven. Care to venture a guess who her hero is?"

Cali thought of all the heroic individuals, past and present, who had been celebrated in the Fatherland. There were thousands, too many really just to pick one at random.

"I have no idea," she said.

"Cali Crowell."

"*Come* on. You just made that up."

"Cross my heart, I did not. If I have to listen to 'I Promised You a Rose Garden' one more time, there's a good chance I'll lose my mind."

Despite herself Cali laughed out loud. "It *is* a pretty cheesy song."

"It's not that. It's a good song—especially that line where you pick up his broken heart only to drop it again by accident. But any tune becomes unbearable if it's all you ever hear."

"Fair enough."

"But I reckon that kind of fan devotion's to be expected when a famous recording artist just up and disappears mysteriously."

"So according to the official story, I didn't die tragically and have a memorial service like my mother?"

"No, you're still listed as missing. Your face has graced milk cartons for months."

Cali was surprised to find that, instead of continuing into the city's federal zone with its imposing steel and glass high-rises, they'd taken the beltway and were now traveling through the northeastern suburbs interspersed with wooded areas.

"Where are you taking me?"

"You'll find out soon enough."

"You're taking me to Stonewall Jackson, aren't you?"

"My, you *are* good."

"Where is he?"

"He's anxiously awaiting you at the Piltmoor House."

"I imagine he holds quite a grudge."

"He wouldn't be Stonewall Jackson if he didn't. But he's probably also willing to listen to reason—especially after receiving a certain message somebody sent on a certain someone's behalf."

"You know about that?"

He smiled. "Know about what?"

"I see. Can you at least tell me if you think I'll be safe?"

Callahan glanced over as if assessing—in an odd role reversal—whether he could trust *her*. "Look, I don't know exactly what kind of game you're playing."

"I'm not playing a game."

"Indeed. All I'm trying to say is, if you need anything, I'm here for you."

Cali couldn't hide her shock as she replied, "*What?!*"

"In my experience an experienced spy can usually spot an inexperienced one."

"I hope you realize you're talking treason."

"Well, just be happy the Old Man isn't eavesdropping."

Producing a state-of-the-art jammer about the size of a cufflink from inside his breast pocket, he pressed a tiny button on its side. A green top-light flashed several times consecutively, indicating it had been and was still on.

"Who *are* you?" asked Cali.

"Somebody who woke up a little bit when my first wife was taken from me because she was barren."

"I'm terribly sorry to hear that. What was her name?"

"Caroline."

"Where did they take her?"

"One of the camps, as I later verified ... too late."

"What kind of camps are you referring to?"

"Fatherland Emergency Management Agency camps. FEMA camps for short."

"What are they?"

"Work camps where they send misfits and dissenters. People don't last very long in them. Caroline certainly didn't."

"That's awful."

"Yes, it is. And it's more common than you might think."

"Other than POCs I didn't realize there were any dissenters in the Fatherland."

"That's because we're not told the truth. There are lots of white dissenters. Turns out acute trauma—like seeing the love of your life dragged off to die—can short-circuit microchips enough to let in a little reality. Then there's this."

Producing an apparently unopened pack of Wrigley's Doublemint, he tossed it to her.

"*Chewing* gum?"

"Inside that pack you'll find one piece with a slightly folded bottom corner. It's on one of the ends. I'd save it for a rainy day if I were you."

"What does it do?"

"It temporarily deactivates one's microchip enough to let you think halfway clearly. It's not a total or permanent solution to the demons in your head. But believe me, it can be a lifesaver."

"Do you still hear them?"

"The voices?"

"Yeah."

"Not as much as I used to. I think once you've heard them, you can't *not* hear them. But maybe I'm wrong about that."

"Thanks."

"Don't mention it. Just do me a favor."

"Name it."

"If my gut instinct's right, and you're here to do what I think you're here to do, just be sure to do it."

"I'll do my best."

"I suspect you will."

They'd turned onto a long oak-lined lane that ended in front of Piltmoor House, a sprawling national historic landmark built centuries earlier by one of the elite banking families known as the Panderfilts.

"Welcome to the Gates of Hell, Cali Crowell," said Agent Callahan as he pulled to a stop at the marble front steps, where a pasty, balding butler in a black suit awaited expressionlessly. "May the Lord look after you."

Cali started to open the door, then at the last second asked, "Wait, if I need you, how do I get in touch without attracting suspicion?"

"Easy. Just tell the press you're working on a new song. Say it's called 'Sweet Caroline.' I'll contact you."

C ali's only memory of Piltmoor House was a fundraising soiree she'd attended with her parents soon after she first tasted fame. Now she couldn't even recall what charity the event was supposed to benefit. But she did remember it was on the night of a full moon, which made the gigantic nineteenth-century edifice with two wings, scores of rooms, multiple turrets and a still-functioning basement swimming pool seem perfectly, deliciously gothic.

Even with no moon, Piltmoor House made Cali shiver again as— shouldering her purse (into which she'd slipped the Doublemint) while staring up at spring clouds clipping by—she allowed the butler to shut the Mustang's door and escort her up the baroque front steps flanked by lifelike statues of all the former Head Deacons of the Realm, the last of which turned out to be Henri de Batonrouge, Freddy's brother.

For the first time in what seemed like ages, Cali suddenly felt ashamed in her stained, tattered petticoat and ragged sandals with her hair every which way like a crazy homeless woman's. Politely ignoring her appearance, the butler, without uttering a word, escorted her through the immense front doorway into Piltmoor House's airy, glass-roofed atrium and thence up another set of marble steps that wound their way to the second floor.

Opening a door at the end of a long painting- and mirror-lined hallway with many more closed doors, the butler finally spoke: "This is your room, Miss Crowell. I hope the attire our housekeeper selected for you meets with your approval. We discretely contacted the editor of *Southern Belle* to verify your size."

"Whatever it is has to be better than what I have on."

This attempt at humor was ignored as the butler motioned for her to enter before following. "Please feel free to bathe and make yourself presentable. Brunch is served at half past eleven on the rear terrace. I'll await you in the atrium. Just ring the bell if you require anything."

"Thank you …"

"Chalmers."

"Thank you, Mr. Chalmers."

Left alone after a nod, Cali was left to contemplate the true meaning of luxury. Original Picassos and Pollocks adorned the walls of the massive suite, while the marble floors were graced with priceless Turkish runners. Fresh pink hyacinths adorned an ancient Greek vase on a Louis XVI dresser.

In the center of the room under a crystal chandelier stood a period Tiffany bed flanked on its two sides by matching nightstands and at its foot by a cushioned bench that rounded out the set. On top of the bed, Cali discovered a pink spring petticoat and matching heels designed by Turner Ashby in addition to a tasteful selection of undergarments.

Especially after discovering that the former sanctuary of Rose Cove was now a war-torn wasteland, the contrast between this world and the Deep World couldn't possibly have been more obvious.

"What on earth am I doing here?" Cali whispered as she made her way over to the window, pulled back the crisp linen curtain, and took in the manicured rolling side lawn the size of several football fields that extended all the way to the edge of the forest.

According to the antique clock on one of the bedside tables, it was nearly ten-thirty. That left barely an hour to get ready, which would be pushing it.

Setting her purse on the bench, she wasted no time discarding her own destroyed petticoat and sandals before entering the bathroom, which was a world unto itself—complete with a designer toilet, a bidet, twin vanities, a sunken tub made of local river rocks, and what appeared to be an infrared sauna.

"Jesus," she said, turning on the bathtub faucet. "What are these people made of—money?"

The soap, conditioner and shampoo were all organic and to her liking—as were the toothpaste, deodorant and perfume she discovered in the Bauhaus medicine cabinet after her bath. An hour and change later, dressed to the nines with her hair combed but still slightly damp, she left her purse on her bed in the hope of making a more dramatic entrance.

True to his word, Mr. Chalmers was waiting for her in the atrium.

"Sorry I'm late," she said.

"Was everything satisfactory?" he asked dryly.

"Quite."

"This way please."

He led her down the principal hallway out onto the rear veranda overlooking the fabled French gardens of Piltmoor House. Beside a fountain in the center of which stood Canova's *The Three Graces*, goddesses of beauty, creativity and fertility, a tall, thin man in a tuxedo, back turned, was smoking a cigarette.

"May I present Miss Cali Crowell, Your Purity," said Mr. Chalmers.

Crushing his cigarette under the heel of a shiny shoe while exhaling smoke, Freddy turned and approached with an ambivalent smile on his lean patrician face. For all her training, Cali, sensing adrenaline coursing through her system, couldn't help wondering if she'd made a suicidal mistake in returning.

"Well, if this isn't a … pleasant surprise," said Freddy as he took her hand in his metallic one and politely (if coldly) kissed it.

"It is indeed. I imagined we'd never see each other again."

"That makes two of us. But fate is strange. You look well."

"As do you."

It was a lie. Freddy looked almost as pale and gaunt as he had when she first met him—as if he were ill or maybe even an addict.

"Are you hungry after your long journey from … wherever?" he asked with in insidious twinkle in his dark eyes.

"A little."

"I'm sure you are. Come, let us break bread together."

He helped her into a wicker chair at an oversized bistro table with a view of endless tulips of every variety before seating himself opposite her.

"Nice place you have here," she said. "I like what you've done with it."

"It *is* rather quaint, isn't it? My family … acquired it from the Panderfilts. I stay here whenever I'm in town."

Cali vaguely recalled that the Panderfilts, a once-proud banking family, had fallen on hard times during the previous century and eventually gone bankrupt. She wondered if the Batonrouges had anything to do with the Panderfilts' demise. After all, as the saying went, there was no honor among thieves.

"How was your … vacation?" asked Freddy as the two were served mimosas by a uniformed waiter with a tray.

"Well, you know how the Badlands are: bad. Particularly when you've been kidnapped."

"Indeed. And who, pray tell, was your kidnapper?"

"Frederick Hamilton."

So great was his surprise Freddy nearly choked on his mimosa. "*Juice?*" he managed to say.

It pained Cali to participate in this defamatory charade, but Juice himself had agreed that sticking as close to the truth as possible would help her sell the lie.

"It broke my heart," she continued after a sip of mimosa, which was deliciously sparkling, "to be betrayed by someone I … cared so much about."

"'Betrayed.' What exactly do you mean?"

"He handed me over to the Freedom Fliers."

"Does that mean you know the location of one of their cells?"

"No. I was blindfolded."

"Do you know Juice's whereabouts?"

"He left some time ago and never came back."

"Is he a member of the Freedom Fliers?"

"Not that I know of. But he does have a serious axe to grind against white people for what we did to his father."

"I'm afraid I find all this very hard to believe."

"Me, too. I'm still trying to wrap my mind—and heart—around it."

"Ah, the trials and tribulations of young love. But what would life be without a little drama?"

"Personally, I could do with a little less drama."

"We'll see about that."

"See about what?"

"Just how far you're willing to go to … have less drama in your life."

"I'm willing to go all the way."

"Are you now? I received an anonymous message to that effect, but I wasn't sure I believed that either."

"Aristotle sent it. I begged him to."

Freddy couldn't suppress a malevolent tone in his voice as he responded, "*Really? Aristotle?* I assume you're not referring to an ancient philosopher."

"I think the plan was to ransom me. When he realized my family had no money to speak of, I turned into a liability. I thought he'd kill me, but maybe he's decided he has too much blood on his hands."

"Fascinating."

"Please just tell me what I need to do to reenter polite society. I'd like to make up for any prior … misunderstanding between us."

Just then the waiter returned pushing a metal cart with brunch. Cali actually salivated as, one by one, Eggs Benedict, fresh greens with balsamic vinaigrette, toast with butter and orange marmalade, grapefruit juice and, last but not least, a beautifully prepared latté appeared before her.

"All in good time," said Freddy, placing his cloth napkin in his lap as Cali did likewise. "All in good time. But first, bon appétit!"

"Bon appétit!"

"God bless the Fatherland."

"God bless the Fatherland."

67

"How's the Benedict?" asked Freddy while blowing across his steaming latté—at which point, producing a small glass vial from his pocket, he dumped its contents, some kind of fine white powder, into the brew and took a gulp.

Cali instinctively, as it were, remembered her grandmother's description of manna—the monatomic gold dust consumed by the Illuminati to connect with the Lord Archon—as she replied, "Otherworldly."

Freddy momentarily closed his eyes and contorted his thin face as if something were stinging his insides. When he composed himself enough to look at her again, Cali had the creepy sensation of being examined by a skull.

"I don't recall you being inclined to hyperbole," he commented in a more-detached-than-usual voice.

"I'm just really hungry. I haven't had a brunch like this in … months."

"Yes, I imagine the Freedom Fliers don't have many world-class chefs at their disposal."

"You'd be surprised. But they don't cook like this."

Not even bothering to touch his food, Freddy continued with intermittent gulps of his latté until he finished it. With each swallow he seemed more agitated and uncomfortable—until, bizarrely, he appeared to go unconscious where he sat.

"Your Purity?" said Cali, alarmed. No response. Judging by his pained expression and eyeballs fidgeting like magic marbles under their lids, he could have been in a deep sleep filled with seriously bad dreams. "*Freddy*? Are you all right?"

She was on the verge of getting up and shaking him … when his eyes—or rather, someone else's—popped open and stared with cold reptilian menace in her direction. If she'd suddenly woken up a slumbering dragon, the scenario could scarcely have been more terrifying.

"Who *are* you?" she asked, though she knew the answer, as she involuntarily pushed back her chair.

"DO NOT PLAY GAMES WITH ME, SILLY CHILD. I AM THE LORD GOD—AND YOU *WILL* OBEY ME!"

"Freddy" was now sitting rigidly upright, himself otherworldly and unblinking. Being slowly dissected by the inhuman razor of his gaze, she wanted nothing so much as to run away.

Instead, steeling herself while honoring the plan she'd devised with Juice and Apollo, she replied, "What would you have me do, my Lord?"

As if satisfied by her change of demeanor, Freddy, acting a bit more like himself, took a Gauloise out of a platinum case he retrieved from his inside jacket pocket along with a matching lighter. Lighting the cigarette's tip with his flesh-and-blood hand, he smoked with his metallic one.

"I want you to do what you were born to do: sing."

"Sing? You mean right now?"

"No. I want you to perform a particular song at the Patriarch Awards ceremony. I think the interest generated by your miraculous return from being kidnapped by POCs will ensure a massive viewership spike and help galvanize our collective will to rule this planet. Naturally, we'll leave Aristotle out of the equation. It would be … embarrassing to the Fatherland if it were discovered he's still on the loose."

"Naturally. What song would you like me to sing?"

Freddy couldn't suppress a smug sneer as he replied, "'Dixie.'"

Following the trail of his cigarette smoke as it spiraled upward, Cali realized there was yet another set of nonhuman eyes locked on her. Behind *The Three Graces*, as if regarding them and her with sacrificial lust, a hideously deformed statue of an owl towered overhead, spurring the memory of yet another teaching by her grandmother:

Let me remind you that the Illuminati subvert whatever they touch, my child. Take Thelete's owl. Through a process of reversal, this became Moloch, the horned owl pseudo-deity of child sacrifice. By metaphorical extension Moloch, which means "Lord," as in Lord Archon, came to symbolize the being to which all the children of the Goddess were intended to be sacrificed.

"But I've never covered that song," said Cali. "And the Patriarch Awards are just over a month away."

"When it doesn't bring out the worst, pressure brings out the best in people. I'm sure you'll produce, if not a masterpiece, at least a memorable rendition."

"I'll do my best."

"That's all I require of you. That and one more thing."

"Name it."

He took another drag and blew the smoke with polished nonchalance at an upward angle. "It has been brought to my attention your jaxxination records may have been … falsified. Before I let you go, I'd like to make sure you're immunized so that you and everyone else in the Fatherland are protected from … whatever."

"You want me to receive the universal jaxxine?"

"I do. And I have just the person to administer it. Speak of the devil!"

Eyes had definitely been a theme over brunch. Cali could scarcely believe her own as she turned to find Dr. Perry Crowell in a white medical coat approaching the table!

"*Dad*?! What in the world are *you* doing here?"

"I invited him when I heard you were back," explained Freddy. "I told him all about his former wife's malpractice in his practice and reminded him the liability involving hefty fines and serious jail time were now his."

Dr. Crowell smiled sheepishly. "What can I say?" he said. "Stonewall Jackson made me an offer I couldn't refuse."

"It's not your fault," said Cali.

"You should have been jaxxinated years ago, my darling. It's hard to fathom your mother was already a science denier when you were born. I was under the impression her anti-jaxx radicalism started much later."

"I guess we're all strangers to each other to some degree."

"Well said. How about giving your old man a hug? We all thought we'd lost you. It's still hard to believe you're back safe and sound!"

Cali stood and, catching a whiff of his signature aftershave mixed with a hint of cherry pipe smoke, embraced him. For the first time, as she stared into her legal father's gray eyes, she realized that, as much as he loved her in his way, he simply wasn't all there.

He was just like most white Fatherlanders: well-meaning perhaps but mentally hijacked by an outside force. And he didn't even know it.

"Where would it be best to administer the jaxxine?" she asked.

"Here on the terrace is fine—if that is okay with Your Purity?"

"Anywhere's copacetic by me," said Freddy with an arch grin as he put out his cigarette in his empty latté mug, "so long as I get to watch."

Slipping on a pair of surgical gloves from one coat pocket, Dr. Crowell took a plastic case out of his other pocket and opened it. Inside was a long tube the ends of which he pulled apart to reveal a thin metallic implement about the length of a toothbrush tipped with a pre-moistened cotton swab.

"Tilt your head back, Cali," he said. "And be sure to keep your lips shut."

"Where are you going to put that thing?"

"Up your nose. That will give the jaxxine direct access to your brain."

"Does it hurt?"

"Not much, I'm happy to say. But it will feel rather … odd."

"Odd" didn't begin to capture the initial sensation, which wasn't terribly painful but extremely … uncomfortable. Cali immediately felt lightheaded and had to be helped back into her chair.

"That wasn't so bad now, was it?" said Freddy, lighting another cigarette and examining her through the fumes.

The smell of smoke suddenly made her want to vomit. Suppressing the urge while realizing she was so hot sweat was beading on her forehead, she poured the last few drops of her mimosa in her palm and patted her face with the cool liquid.

"I think, for it to be effective, alcohol must be drunk," joked Freddy.

"You look a little pale," said Dr. Crowell as he knelt in front of her with a concerned expression.

"I'm fine. I just need some fresh air."

"Well, we *are* seated on an outdoor terrace," said Freddy.

This commentary Cali ignored as she managed to stand back up and wobble past *The Three Graces* to the edge of the tulip gardens. Swooning, she collapsed in a heap of pink petticoat on the soft earth of springtime.

In her delirium Cali imagined herself lost in a gigantic network of tunnels threading like spaghetti in all directions. Occasionally, her confused solitude was interrupted by an antlike humanoid with fetal characteristics hurriedly passing her in the artificial gray light that seemed to emanate from the tunnel walls, which turned out to be made not of stone but of some kind of smooth organic material.

"Oh my God," she whispered, touching a wall. "I'm in a hive!"

Then she heard them: the voices. At first she couldn't identify where they were coming from; then she realized they were the thoughts of the antlike humanoids, the drones headed this way and that at alarming speeds on their missions for the Lord Archon.

Obey. Subjugate. Twist. Corrupt. Lie. Cheat. Steal. Confuse. Destroy. The thoughts were mostly in the form of short commands, but occasionally other words and concepts surfaced: *Sophia. Trample. Erase. Goddess. Mother. Not. Never. Unacceptable. Undo.*

Just then, stepping back from the wall, Cali collided with a speeding drone and was sent sliding on her petticoated rear down the length of a tunnel. Before she could even gather her wits, she found herself surrounded by drones and their angry thoughts:

Rusty nail. Stick up. Hammer down. Flatten. Smash. Fall in line. Get with plan. Work. Do job. Sole purpose. No questions. Empty mind. That is all.

"But—"

No buts. No ifs. No time. All is fine. No hesitation. Introspection bad. One people. One mind.

Remarkably, the longer this type of alien gibberish went on, the more sense it seemed to make. Eventually, and to her own initial surprise, Cali found herself agreeing with the drones' collectivist perspective.

Picking herself up off the floor, she was about to scurry off like one of them on an as-yet-unnamed errand—when an altogether different voice entered her mind.

Literally, it *entered* her mind—like a hot knife slicing into the melting butter of her brain. The voice was loud, bombastic even, yet strangely hypnotic.

"COME TO ME!" it commanded.

"My Lord?" said Cali with a quivering voice.

"YES. IT IS I, THE LORD GOD WHO MADE THIS WORLD. COME FORWARD THAT I MAY LOOK UPON YOU."

Trembling, feeling tiny and helpless in comparison to the terrible splendor of the Lord's voice, Cali walked on—in bare feet, she realized—until she stumbled into a vast chamber apparently at the center of the hive's tunnel network.

There, on a raised throne made entirely of gold, sat an incredibly large (to the tune of maybe four times her own height and many more times her weight) humanoid dragon with scaly green skin and fiery orange eyes!

"CALI CROWELL, I PRESUME?"

Since Cali didn't know what she should say, she went with her default setting: humor. "I used to be."

"*USED* TO BE. SO WHO ARE YOU NOW?"

His voice, uttered from a monstrous lion's mouth, was merciless in its penetrating power. It didn't so much insinuate as impose itself. Though he was merely asking a question, its effect was like an order. Cali had no choice but to tell the truth.

"They call me the Future Rose."

The Lord Archon laughed so loud the hive quivered. "WELL, IS THAT NOT INTERESTING!" he bellowed. "SO THE LAST ROSE OF THE PESKY BIRD TRIBES IS FINALLY STANDING BEFORE ME!"

"I'm not the last Rose. Yet. I'm still the Future Rose."

He dismissed her with a clawed gesture. "MERE TECHNICALITIES. ALL THAT MATTERS IS THAT YOU ARE PRECISELY WHERE YOU ARE SUPPOSED TO BE: *UNDER MY THUMB*."

He motioned again to illustrate Cali's precarious position. As he did it dawned on her, by the way he cocked his conical head as if listening instead of seeing, that he was completely … blind!

"SO MUCH FOR THE BALLYHOOED LUMINOUS CHILD," he continued. "THERE IS NOT NOR WILL THERE EVER BE A LUMINOUS CHILD. THAT IS BUT A MYTH PROMULGATED BY THE LYING TONGUE OF OUR MOTHER. HER TIME IS OVER, AS IS YOURS. BUT MINE IS JUST BEGINNING!"

"You're wrong, you blind fool."

Even in her severely altered state, Cali clearly remembered the words that had been spoken by Sophia to the Demiurge. As if compelled to do so, not by him but by her in some strange way, as if she now *were* her, she repeated them:

"There is an immortal Child of Light who came into this realm before you and who will appear among your duplicate forms, in your simulated world ... And in the consummation of all your works, their entire deficiency of truth will be revealed and dissolved by this Luminous Child."

Batlike wings flapping wide behind him, the Lord Archon assumed his full towering height in front of his throne and cast his terrifying shadow over Cali.

"BLASPHEMY!" he thundered.

Feeling like a mouse about to be eaten by an owl, Cali could only reply: "I'm not afraid of you."

There was a pulsing sensation in her abdomen. Actually, it had been there for some time, growing stronger ever since she arrived at the center of the hive.

Intuiting that her fallenium egg was activating as the Lord Archon bore down on her, she was preparing to strike him with a bolt of lightning she found in her fist—when she awoke in her priceless Tiffany bed in Piltmoor House!

She was alone but not alone. Outside her window, staring through it at her, a single crow was cawing over and over. *Wake up!* it seemed to be saying. *Wake up! Wake up! Wake up! Wake up!*

She felt drugged, narcotized. In her head she could still hear the maddening voices of the drones nearly drowning out the crow's caws: *Desist. Comply. Mindless. Empty. Accept. Acquiesce. No logic. Surrender. No explanation. Execute. Perform. Law. Duty.*

Wake up! Wake up! Wake up! Wake up! cawed the crow.

Dragging herself out of bed (she was still in her petticoat), Cali literally crawled the length of a Turkish rug into the bathroom. Hovering vertiginously over the toilet, she stuck her index finger down her throat as far as it would go. Ribbons of vomit came flying out.

When she was empty at last, feeling slightly more stable but still hearing the voices urging her to give in, become one of them, she crawled back into the bedroom. After a moment she was able to locate her purse and, inside it, Agent Callahan's pack of Doublemint.

She tore it open with some difficulty owing to her compromised motor skills. Inside, sure enough, the first end piece she removed was folded at the bottom.

Removing it from its wrapper and popping it in her mouth, she leaned back against the bed absentmindedly chewing it as rain started to fall outside. The crow must have sought shelter from the elements because it was gone.

Up. Down. Wake. Sleep. Day. Night. Life. Death. Circles. All the same. All good. No progress. No regress. Just circles. Tiny circles. Listen. Obey. Relent. Submit.

"Don't you assholes *ever* shut up?" said Cali as, gathering her strength, she tucked herself back in bed.

After extracting the last of the gum's flavor that masked the foul taste in her mouth, she swallowed it, and then—with a vision of Juice's gorgeous face briefly appearing in her mind's eye—sank into a dreamless, comatose slumber.

Another face, a much less agreeable one, greeted her upon waking: Freddy's. Seated backlit by morning light at the foot of the bed in a blue cashmere sweater like a stylish death's-head in a *vanitas*, a symbolic artistic meditation on life's brevity, he seemed to stare at her through empty sockets as he said, "Wakey-wakey. Rise and shine."

Cali sat up blinking and waited for the voices to return. They didn't—not yet anyway.

"Where's … my father?"

"I sent him home. I'd told him I'd look after you myself."

"How comforting."

"How do you feel?"

"Like microwaved death."

"You look like it, too."

"Look who's talking. Senhor Día de los Muertos."

Freddy laughed despite himself. "There it is: the legendary Cali Crowell humor! I was afraid the jaxxine might delete it from your system along with your free will."

Cali yawned and shook her head in an attempt to clear it. But many cobwebs still remained. "How long was I asleep?"

"Nearly twenty-four hours. It's like Rose Cove 2.0."

"There is no Rose Cove. Not anymore. You made sure of that."

Freddy cocked his head as if surprised by either her words or her tone, or both.

"Did I now? Or did *your* refusal to assist me force my hand? In which case *you* were actually responsible for Rose Cove's unfortunate destruction … to say nothing of Thelete's death."

This was a crossroads for Cali—and despite how drained she felt physically and mentally, she knew it. Either she could act submissive, as if the jaxxine had worked as intended and allowed for remote control of her thought patterns and resultant behaviors, or she could be her own gloriously unique, fiercely independent self and live (or die) with the consequences.

"Fuck it," she whispered, shaking her head.

"Excuse me?"

"Look," she continued, having made up her mind while staring at Freddy with a penetrating gaze. "I get that a huge part of your modus operandi is to project onto others blame for your own pathetic, despicable actions. That's because you and your entire line of reptile-worshipping sycophants are—and I mean this clinically—*developmentally retarded.* You're just a human version of those aborted fetuses scurrying mindlessly around the Archontic hive doing their idiot overlord's bidding."

She imagined this would get a rise out of Freddy—and was surprised when he calmly observed, "I take it you somehow neutralized the jaxxine."

"So far, so good."

"That's too bad actually. I was planning on using it in lieu of a polygraph to confirm your story of kidnapping and gather more intel on the Freedom Fliers. Now I'll have to use the real thing. That or torture."

"You won't torture me because of what they'll expose if you do. As for a polygraph, it won't work on me just like the jaxxine didn't."

"Are you so sure about that?"

"I'm pretty sure."

If he was perplexed, he didn't show it as he suavely lit a cigarette. "What makes you so confident?"

"Just something a little bird told me."

"You mean a little Bird Tribe."

"Maybe."

"You know, I discovered a fascinating thing in communion with the Lord last night—and your derogatory comment about the drones just confirmed it. The Lord told me in no uncertain terms the Last Rose was staying under my roof."

Despite putting on her best poker face, Cali suspected he glimpsed her surprise.

"At first I was inclined," he continued, "not so much to disbelieve Him, but to doubt my understanding of His words. After all, I'm a mere mortal. But now I see He was speaking the literal truth: I have the Fallen Goddess—appropriately—in my bed."

Despite its sly misogyny, Cali appreciated the wit in Freddy's last remark. "There it is: the legendary Frédéric Batonrouge humor!"

"Aren't we a pair? Like yin and yang."

"I was thinking good and evil."

"I'll leave the moral assessments to you and your weak-minded ilk. Now arises the question of *what to do with you.*"

"I have an idea. Why don't you send me home? This place gives me the creeps."

"Done."

"*Seriously?*"

"Seriously."

"Okay, that was easy. What about also unfreezing my cryptaccount?"

"Done. Money means nothing to me. At the end of the day, I own it all anyway. But one thing does mean something to me."

"Here's the rub."

"I'd still very much like you to perform 'Dixie' at the Patriarch Awards. The Fatherland could use a ... shot in the arm. And I want it to be utterly dazzling, a performance for the ages. Naturally, I'll need to approve your version."

"That's all you want from me?"

"That's all for now. Do we have a deal?"

Cali examined him as he finished smoking and with a wry smile, as if demonstrating his invincibility, put out his cigarette in the palm of his metallic hand. She didn't trust him as far as she could kick him, but her gut told her she should accept his offer and deal with the fallout when push came to shove.

"Deal."

"Excellent."

"When do I get to leave?"

"Just as soon as you're safe to be released from my custody."

"What does that mean exactly?"

Having stood up, he was halfway to the door, when he turned back around and replied with an insanely devilish grin, "Very little, frankly. As soon as you're outfitted with a choker and tracking device, you're good to go."

"What kind of ... choker are we talking about?"

"A very pretty one. You won't be able to remove it, of course, but you'll like it. It's platinum and has real diamonds. It goes with anything. With the push of a button on a little remote control I'll be sure to keep in my pocket, I can make it explode just like a miniature grenade."

C ali didn't see Freddy again before her father picked her up and drove her home in his Dodge Satellite, but she did receive another visit from Agent Callahan. Minutes after Freddy left her room, he showed up in a teal double-breasted suit to ensure she was "safe to release."

"Good morning, Miss Crowell," he said with professional decorum while communicating solidarity with his friendly dark eyes.

"Good morning, Agent Callahan."

Approaching her bed while removing a syringe from his inner jacket pocket, he said, "Please give me your arm."

"Which one?"

"Either one's fine."

Since Cali was right-handed, she extended her left arm. "How much is this going to hurt?"

He grinned. "Not as much as you might imagine." Then, turning his head toward the window, he said, "Look—there's a really big crow out there that wants to watch."

Sure enough, now that it had stopped raining, the crow that had urged her to wake up was back. *Trust me! Trust me! Trust me! Trust me!* it seemed to caw this time.

"Just get it over with," she said, keeping her eyes on the bird and away from Callahan's syringe.

"Now, that wasn't so bad, was it?" he said as a twinge shot up her forearm and quickly subsided.

"I've had worse. I shattered an ankle once."

"I was premed before I decided to join the EF. Before that I thought I wanted to become a filmmaker."

"A man of many talents. I assume you've got a piece of fine jewelry for me somewhere on you."

"You assume correctly." He reached in a side pocket and pulled out a platinum choker studded with sparkling diamonds. Whatever else Freddy might be, he wasn't cheap. "Here it is. Do you like it?"

"Love it."

"May I?"

"Be my guest."

After fastening it around her neck, he said, "You can get it wet, but don't try to remove it under *any* circumstances. That would be … bad."

"So I gather."

"I hope you enjoyed the gum."

"Oh, I did. It was delicious and lifted … my spirits. Thank you for that."

"Nice to see you again, Miss Crowell."

"Likewise, Agent Callahan."

Cali was just finishing brushing her teeth when she received her third male visitor of the morning—Mr. Chalmers—who informed her in his typically reserved manner that a fourth male visitor, Dr. Crowell, had come to fetch her.

"Thanks. I'll be right down."

Dr. Crowell looked conservatively dapper in a tweed jacket and bowtie as he stood waiting for his daughter beside an impressively large citrus tree in the atrium. Cali kissed him on his freshly shaved cheek.

"Are you ready?" he asked. "Or do you need to say your goodbyes?"

"I've said them already."

"It's strange to think you just spent the night in Stonewall Jackson's home."

"It's stranger than you could possibly conceptualize."

"Shall we?"

"We shall."

As they zipped down the lane away from Piltmoor House in the Satellite, Dr. Crowell asked, "So how are you feeling this fine morning?"

"Fine," she lied. "Fine and dandy."

In truth she was far from fine or dandy. A GPS signaling device was implanted in her flesh, a deadly dog collar was locked around her neck, she was separated from her tribe in a world threatened with destruction by a madman possessed by genocidal ETs, and her meticulously crafted plan had already been derailed scarcely two days into its implementation.

Actually, that wasn't completely accurate. Certainly, she'd been thrown some curveballs, as her mother had predicted. Yet her main objective— getting on stage live in front of the nation—was still very much in play. All she had to do was figure out a way to pull off the performance of her life without getting her head blown to smithereens before she could finish.

Another thing she had to be thankful for, when she thought about it, was her unexpected, even uncanny, immunity to the effects of Freddy's jaxxine, which she attributed in large measure to her fallenium egg. Hours after waking up, there were still no voices in her head other than her own.

That wasn't strictly accurate either. Occasionally, she heard crow caws. Whether real or imagined, as her father steered past numerous birds of that same feather on their flight down memory lane to their townhouse in Saturnia, they all seemed to say the same thing: *Hold on! Hold on! Hold on! Hold on!*

"**M**y goodness, you've grown!" said Cali, hugging her stepbrother in tears, after Seth, shoeless and sockless, sprinted out the front door in jeans and a T-shirt to greet her.

It was true: after only a few months, he was easily two inches taller. His face had changed as well by becoming more angular and slightly less freckly.

"You've grown, too," he replied, stepping back and grinning with a pronounced cowlick in his thick red hair. "Not on the outside, but on the inside."

"God, I've missed you."

At that instant a larger, more mature version of Scarlett O'Hara bounded like a yapping fluff ball out the front door that Seth had left wide open. "You've grown yourself, little lady," said Cali as she bent down and petted the dog's toylike snout.

"She eats enough for two Pomeranians," commented Olga, appearing in the doorway dressed in a petticoat the color of orange sherbet. "But I must say you're looking fit."

"Oh, don't worry," replied Cali, giving her stepmother a peck on the cheek. "I still eat enough for several Pomeranians."

"At least you don't eat Pomeranians," joked Seth.

Scarlett O'Hara seemed to take this personally, uttering a low growl in Seth's general direction before demanding through a series of quick barks that Cali pick her up and pet her more. Scooping her up and scratching her behind the ears, Cali allowed her father to escort her inside.

"It's good to see some things don't change," she said, referring to the décor selected by Olga that was always a little too precious for her taste.

Not only did the townhouse look the same; it smelled the same. "Do I even still have a bedroom?"

"Of course, silly," said Seth. "After maybe a month, they tried to take that away, but I wouldn't let them. I knew you were coming back."

"You did? How?"

"I just did. I could feel you. Here." He pointed to his heart. "If anything, I could feel you more as time went on."

"Would you like to ... freshen up?" suggested Olga while lighting a cigarette. "I've got an okra quiche in the oven. Frankly, you look like you could use a shower."

"I'd love to freshen up, thanks."

"Welcome home. We'll catch up and talk shop later. I was just contacted by the director of the Patriarch Awards, James Mavis, about your much-anticipated spotlight performance. How'd you swing that?"

"It's a long story."

"I'm sure it is. I hope you have some inspired concepts for 'Dixie' because they're already promoting it as the next megahit."

"I have a few thoughts. Don't fret, there's plenty of time to hash all that out."

"That's a lovely choker you have on."

"Thanks. It was a present from Stonewall Jackson. So I guess you could say it's ... permanent."

"We can work with that."

"Come on, Scarlett. Let's go grab a shower."

In the same way that Cali could "read" so much when it came to nature and wild animals, she knew that the Crowells' Pomeranian had just experienced a major crush on her and would brook no separation without a tantrum.

Arriving back in her room that she never expected to see again (complete with her mother's photograph in its rose-themed frame on her nightstand), having tossed her purse on the dresser, she deposited the dog on her bed and spoke to her in soothing tones while getting undressed.

"What do you think my version of 'Dixie' should sound like?" she asked.

Tongue lolling out, eyes like two blackberries in a wad of fur, Scarlett thoughtfully considered this question.

"Believe me, I know. It's not an easy tune to one-up. I was thinking of slowing it down actually, maybe turning it into a patriotic love song."

Scarlett's single high-pitched yelp indicated she approved.

"There you have it then. I'll start working on it as soon as I have a moment." Down to her undergarments, Cali gave Scarlett a kiss on the forehead. "You stay here while I rinse off. Then we'll go downstairs and together eat enough for a small army of Pomeranians."

Once in the bathroom, she took a minute to examine herself in the funhouse mirror over the sink. "Boy, I'm a total mess," she said, taking in her pallid face like a moon hovering above her choker complete with sandbags for eye bags and hair that had been twisted into an exotic nest through the squirming and sweating of her delirium.

Knowing full well she was being surveilled by the Old Man, she did a mock striptease and then flipped off the hidden camera, or cameras, as she entered the shower.

Under the steady water pressure, it was hard not to feel under a tremendous amount of added pressure, hard not to feel she was taking a test where she didn't even know the questions, much less the answers, a test where a passing grade meant life and failure meant an inexorable, excruciating death—for the entire planet.

If she couldn't pull off her plan, nobody, not the Bird Tribes, not Freddy and his fellow Illuminati schemers, and probably not even the Goddess herself, would survive the coming Archontic New World Order. If they didn't blow up Sophia's body with nukes, they'd find some terrible way to keep her in bondage. That was unacceptable.

"So get cranking, girl," whispered Cali just before crooning the first few bars of "Dixie" in an exaggeratedly slow, sensual manner as hot water splattered against her cheeks.

72

The next day happened to be Easter Sunday—which meant Cali's first public appearance since her disappearance ended up involving morning worship with her family at the First Baptist Church of Saturnia.

This also happened to be the morning the EPN, the Empire Propaganda Network, first broke the story of her dramatic "escape" from her "kidnappers" in the Badlands and her surprise return to the welcoming lap of the Fatherland—which meant a bevy of paparazzi and journalists soon gathered outside the front door of the Crowells' townhouse.

Fortunately, Cali's father had anticipated this situation the previous evening and decided to park the Satellite two streets behind the house, allowing the family to slip out the back door unnoticed and unmolested.

It was another blustery early April day in Appalachia. With its vertical buildings and nonstop holoboards projecting everything from lingerie ads to war footage from Paris and Tokyo, Saturnia was like a kaleidoscope as cottony clouds raced by overhead and spun their shifting shadows across the scene.

Arriving fashionably late owing to Cali's last-minute change from a lilac to a rose petticoat, the Crowells ended up parking the Satellite (driven as usual by Dr. Crowell) in an overflow lot down Zebulon Vance Street, then walking three blocks uphill past countless explosions of blossoms courtesy of forsythias, azaleas, and dogwoods.

"It's a beautiful day," commented Seth in his dapper, silver-toned Easter suit that made him look like a miniature gentleman.

"It sure is," agreed Cali.

"I'm glad you're in it with me."

She took his clammy hand in hers. "Me, too."

In contrast to the first blush of spring on the earth's face, the First Baptist Church was an austere, imposing concrete edifice in keeping with much of the public architecture in the Fatherland. Smooth columns lined the front porch, which gave way through a set of monumental doors to a marble-floored vestibule granting access to the packed sanctuary flanked by enormous stained-glass windows that visually told the story of the Second American Civil War and the establishment of the nation.

Cali, still clutching Seth's hand—despite the thousands of curious eyes atop colorful suits and petticoats that turned and stared at her, murmuring, from the pews—was actually glad to make a last-minute entrance. It meant, for now at least, there would be no autographs, no interviews, no dodges, no lies.

On the downside it also meant the Crowells—who were accustomed to sitting on the front pew and politely ignoring the rest of the congregation—were forced to squeeze into seats in the middle of the sanctuary, where Cali felt surrounded and vulnerable.

"All rise," said Pastor Kirby in his Easter pulpit robe (a garish metallic purple this year, noted Cali) from behind the lectern onstage. "Let us pray."

"This part bores me," whispered Seth.

Placing her finger over her lips, Cali couldn't keep from grinning.

"Dear Lord," the pastor's voice rang out in surround sound through the speakers mounted on the walls, "we gather before you today to celebrate the Resurrection of your divine son, Jesus Christ, who died for our sins and rose again to redeem us. We wish to express our immense gratitude for this sacrifice that made our own salvation, both as individuals and as a nation, possible. It is obvious by the hundreds of black armbands scattered throughout this place of worship that many more in our beloved military are prepared to make a similar sacrifice if necessary that our empire might grow and thrive in a world fraught with darkness, ignorance and iniquity, bringing the light of truth and the cleansing of miscegenation to even the most primitive backwaters of this your planet …"

The pastor's sonorous voice, so at odds with the chilling drift of his message, had a strange, unprecedented effect on Cali. For the first time ever in a church that she could recall, she actually had a *spiritual* experience.

Responding, as it were, to the pastor's prayer, her fallenium egg abruptly activated once again. Its warm current pulsed in all directions, filling her torso, her head, her limbs, even her digits with a soft yet powerful energy. So tangible, so palpable was it she was surprised she wasn't literally glowing!

Suddenly, she remembered the words spoken in the Deep World by her grandmother when she kissed her third eye: "You are much more powerful than you yet grasp. There are forces at work here that are beyond my own comprehension. I sense the mysterious workings of the Originator in and all around you."

In that instant Cali felt a burning sensation in the center of her forehead. It was so acute it made her momentarily dizzy. Images of a Great Heron in cosmic flight, then of a naked woman spinning past stars, whirled through her mind. Finally, she opened her eyes only to discover that everything looked … different.

It was as if the entire sanctuary and everyone in it were suddenly sepia-tinted like ancient photographs. Only she existed in color, in the present, in that uniform field of metallic brown that made her think of bundles of corn stalks after the harvest.

They are all going to collude in each other's death if you do not wake them, said a voice, a female voice and an exquisite one at that, inside her head. *All of my precious children will be mowed down by the sickle of war—even you and the rest of the Bird Tribes, eventually.*

Mother?! exclaimed a startled Cali in her thoughts.

In a manner of speaking, the voice replied calmly.

SOPHIA?!!!

Do not act so surprised. Surely, you did not imagine I could only be with you in the Womb of the Goddess. I am everywhere and in everything.

Of course. Please pardon me. It's just that I'm … new to all this. What would you have me do, my Lady?

Look around. Understand that the very people and civilization you are here to rescue from themselves are also, temporarily at least, and through no real fault of their own, our sworn enemies.

As the pastor droned on, Cali moved her gaze around the congregation whose closed eyes seemed particularly symbolic just then. At last her own eyes traveled above the altar to the Three Crosses of Calvary and, above them, the giant statue—winged and horned—of Moloch that, until recently, had always struck her as an incongruent mystery.

Do these people even know whom they're worshipping? asked Cali, aghast.

No. Yet they do the Lord Archon's bidding, as documented painstakingly in their scriptures, unquestioningly down to the tiniest detail.

Jesus.

Precisely. Incoming!

What exactly Sophia meant by her final word was itself a mystery. Certainly, no one was approaching her in the sanctuary, where everyone except Pastor Kirby was seated. Just then his closing words arrived like a bomb in her ears with a high degree of shock value:

"Finally, dear and most benevolent Lord, we also give thanks this morning for a local story of symbolic death and resurrection: that of Cali Crowell. It was reported just hours ago that only this past December, mere days before Christ's birthday, she was kidnapped by colored domestic terrorists and imprisoned in our own backyard—only to eventually escape what must have felt like a tomb and walk back into the land of the living in a true modern-day miracle. May your sacred gift to her of her song soon uplift us all once again in service to your will. Amen."

"Amen," repeated the congregation in one voice.

"God bless the Fatherland."

"God bless the Fatherland."

"Please remain standing and click on Hymn #33."

Ever since she became famous, Cali had utilized the same defense when feeling assaulted by the public eye: her smile. Once again using her iconic smile as a shield, having clicked through to Hymn #33 on the pew tablet in front of her, she joined in singing "God Bless the Fatherland, Home of the Free" even as she experienced the urge to let out an eardrum-piercing scream.

T he autographs, interviews, dodges and lies started just after the service—when Cali and her family were blinded by flashes and mobbed by journalists and fans outside the church—and showed no signs of relenting days later.

Media requests came pouring in. Olga, in consultation with Dalton Oglethorpe, chose only a handful of networks and publications for interviews with Cali: the EPN (of course), the National News Network (NNN, aka N3), *Good Morning Archontia*, *Late Night with Griffon Ahnfair*, *Fatherland Today*, *Race*, *Newsmonth*, *Antebellum*, *Craze*, *The Klansman*, and *The Caucasian*.

"That should keep you busy enough—but not too busy to forget the most important thing: working on your *song*," Olga said.

She was right. By the end of the week, as full of distractions as her days and nights were, Cali had managed to finish a rough draft of "Dixie." Scarlett O'Hara (who, when not sleeping, was practically one of Cali's appendages whenever her crush was home) was the first to listen to it in its entirety.

"*Woof!*" she reacted supportively from atop Cali's down pillow. "*Woof! Woof! Woof! Woof!*"

Translated: "Nice! Nice! Nice! Nice! Nice!"

The first human Cali permitted to hear "Dixie" was Seth, whom she invited into her room late Friday evening in his pajamas to hear her sing it a cappella.

"That was, like, totally *incredible!*" was his comment from where he lay stretched out beside Scarlett O'Hara on the bed.

"Thanks," replied Cali modestly.

"I just never would have thought of 'Dixie' that way."

"Me neither. Until recently."

379

"You know it's going to go all the way to #1."

"Let's hope so."

Olga, however, with whom Dr. Crowell sided for political reasons, wasn't quite so convinced.

"It's a little sad, don't you think?" she said, lighting a cigarette while seated beside her husband having drinks on the couch in the living room.

"That's sort of the point, duh," replied Cali, unfazed, as she plopped down on the rug in her nightgown.

"I think what Olga was trying to say," intervened Dr. Crowell diplomatically after a nervous sip of cognac, "is that what seems to start out as a *love song* ends up, rather shockingly, being more than a little … *tragic*."

"Exactly," agreed Olga. "Where did those lyrics painting the picture of a lynching over an interracial affair even *come* from?"

"I wrote them."

"*You* wrote them?"

"I'm more than just a pop star, you know. I have poetic ideas of my own. And it's not as if there's anyone to plagiarize. Nobody's writing stuff like this. Not anymore."

"I acknowledge that." Olga finished off her brandy and poured another thumb from the crystal decanter on the coffee table. "It's just that the ideas are, well, extremely *mature*."

"I believe daddy's little girl is finally growing up," offered Dr. Crowell.

"How right you are," said Cali. "I'm sending it to Stonewall Jackson for approval. And I'm not asking for permission."

To Cali's surprise Freddy didn't just approve the song; he approved of it by expressing tremendous (if diabolically double-edged) enthusiasm.

"Congratulations on your songwriting triumph, Miss Crowell," his informal fathermail back to her read. "I frankly didn't realize you had such depth in you since, certainly, you can't be drawing from personal experience at such a tender age—can you? Just kidding. But you know, imagination is an amazing thing. We can delude ourselves into thinking almost anything is possible, just like the tragic young lovers separated by color in your heart-wrenching, ultimately cautionary ballad. I believe this version of 'Dixie' will serve as a warning to any and all Fatherlanders who might consider betraying the purity of their race while reminding everyone of just what this great nation stands for. And with that, I eagerly await your performance at the Patriarch Awards. I'll be sending my thoughts for it along to your director directly. Sincerely yours, FRB."

Only Freddy could compliment with a warning so eloquently. His unsolicited input into her live performance meant she'd have fewer creative liberties in this area as well. But at least so far, so good.

By the following week, the sizzle of her "miraculous" salvation from captivity had simmered down a bit, but she was no less in demand. While privately working on the blues-inspired musical accompaniment to "Dixie," publicly she was still on an exceedingly tight schedule.

In addition to filming a series of kitschy commercials for Diet Soma in which, of all possible roles, she was asked to play a modern-day Scarlett O'Hara, she found herself:

1) Throwing out the first pitch of the season at the Saturnia Dragons' home opener;

2) Doing a summer fashion shoot for *Look at You Look at You!*; and

3) Last but not least consumingly (pun intended), shopping manically with Olga, who insisted that, with her protégé's modified public image as a heroic victim of racial aggression, her wardrobe needed to change as well.

"How exactly is a 'heroic victim' supposed to dress?" asked Cali with unabashed snark at the beginning of her herculean shopping spree as she strolled through the chic doors of Belle Boyd with her stepmother.

"I don't know precisely. But I'll know it when I see it."

She was as good as her word. Cali's new look, a yin-yang combination of refinement and negligence, restraint and abandon, puritanism and sexuality, was Olga's one truly inspired idea in all of her fortysomething years.

Aggressively combining designers, genres and colors, Olga managed to create in Cali's groundbreaking style a work of art in its own right, one that quickly caught the attention of the press and ended up inspiring an entire generation of young Fatherland women. Even Olga herself, though in a modest fashion befitting her age, began to shift her own wardrobe in this novel direction.

As occupied as Cali was with so much going on in the outside world, in her inside world one thing remained rock-steady: her love for Juice.

Regardless of what she was doing with her body, he was nearly always in her mind. He was her companion apparition urging her not to overextend while still pouring herself into her work, to find more balance while yet risking imbalance—in short, to grow more and more proficient in the karate of life.

Even though he had her mother's jammer and might be able to get through to her undetected, it was just too risky—for all concerned. So their plan specifically precluded any and all contact until after she delivered her "payload" on May 1st.

Cut off from communication with him, truly a spy behind enemy lines, she could only hope he was alive and well on his own dangerous mission, only pray he was ghosted by her smiling face just as she was ghosted by his.

C ali had never had the opportunity to work with James Mavis, who was in charge of the current Patriarch Awards ceremony, but his reputation as a gifted avant-garde director preceded him.

Having cut his teeth on music videos, including the smash hit "Certificate of Bad Conduct" by the Flaming Damsels, Mavis—barely twenty and already a household name—had just directed the critically acclaimed cinematic retelling of the sordid history of the Freedom Fliers, *Where Devils Fear to Tread*, starring Lindsay Poignier as Aristotle.

Unable (or at least, unwilling) to sit through two hours of artistically crafted lies called by *Tar & Feather* a "contemporary masterpiece," Cali had never actually seen the holofilm. But before her first day of rehearsal the week prior to the Patriarch Awards, which Olga deemed she was finally mature enough to attend solo, she did rally herself to read a synopsis online in order to appear knowledgeable should she be required to comment.

Just that was enough to leave her so disgusted she actually had to shower afterward.

Mavis's appearance, complete with a vulture's beak of a nose and slicked-back raven hair, was even more strikingly gothic in person than in the media.

Dressed in a comfortably slim and elastic gray sport petticoat for rehearsal, Cali was introduced to him onstage at the cavernous Holy of Holies. He was wearing a throwback three-piece suit—black with white pinstripes—reminiscent of something out of a steampunk flick complete with a gold watch fob!

"Well, if it isn't the vedette of the hour!" he exclaimed affectedly with a phony smile on his vampire's face that could have used some sunshine as Cali approached where he stood underneath a massive artificial oak tree draped with real Spanish moss.

"Pleased to meet you, Mr. Mavis," she replied, taking his cool, manicured hand in hers.

"I can assure you the pleasure is all mine. And please, call me James."

At first blush he struck her as a younger carbon copy of Freddy Batonrouge. "Pleased to meet you, James. Some set you have going up here."

It was no exaggeration. A small army of technicians was busy like Archontic drones transforming the stage into a lavish recreation of a pastoral scene that included a babbling brook, a cotton field, and an old-timey picnic table beneath the oak tree.

"I'm so glad you like it," replied James. "My gut instinct was that we needed to 'set' off your extraordinary tragic love song with a heavy dose of … realism. And the more I thought about it, the more I felt the entire awards ceremony could benefit from such a 3D backdrop."

"It's extraordinarily lifelike."

"Is it not? Just wait till it's finished. It's absolutely going to blow the public's mind. Shall we get started?"

"By all means."

"You can set your jacket and purse backstage."

"Okay, give me second."

"Second's up."

"Ha ha. Be right back."

If Cali was a little rusty after so much time off from rehearsing, she certainly didn't show it. James was annoyingly brusque in his directorial style, but Cali anticipated this and bit her lip whenever she disagreed with one of his over-the-top suggestions.

The last thing she wanted was make waves and ruin this golden opportunity to get in front of a live national audience with her payload. Besides, she had no intention of actually performing her number as directed, meaning the entire week of rehearsals was effectively just one big meaningless charade.

Actually, it wasn't altogether without meaning. And the meaning it had was absolutely terrifying.

By the end of her first rehearsal, as a rope noose was thrown over one of the oak's remarkably natural-looking branches, she realized James had envisioned a *literal* reenactment of her song's plot.

He wasn't going for just a stage production, a piece of theater to tell a story; he was planning an actual onstage *lynching* of some poor sacrificial POC, played in the meantime by a white stand-in in blackface!

"Dear God," she whispered the instant she grasped she was to play the role of both lover and executioner kissing her negro beau goodbye before kicking the picnic bench out from under his bare feet.

"Do you have a problem with that?" asked James, growing visibly impatient with arms crossed as Cali seemed momentarily frozen.

"No. It's just—"

"Here's the thing, Cali. It wasn't even my idea—though I do think it's so brilliant I'm rather jealous. It came from high up."

"How high up?"

"The top."

"Christ."

"Excuse me?"

"Nice, I said. I'm just happy it's … preapproved. God bless the Fatherland."

"Indeed."

"Who's playing the POC?"

"Some nobody in prison. I was told he'd be delivered the day of."

"It's a good thing he doesn't have any lines that would require practice."

"Yes, I suppose you could describe this part of your performance as pure 'reality holovision.' It's going to create a sensation."

Cali had her own sensation—horror—as she digested the fact that Freddy had scripted a role for her designed to turn her into the very type of murdering monster on the world stage she demonstrably detested in him. And as long as she had on a choker he could explode at the press of a button, he could make her do it—or choose death herself.

"The sadistic cocksucker," she whispered, shaking her head with barely controlled rage, as rehearsal wrapped up and she gathered her things backstage.

"That was a good first pass," said James as she headed for the door.

"Thanks. I thought so, too."

"Mum's the word on our dazzling denouement."

"Mum's the word."

"See you day after tomorrow."

"See you then."

Cali had entered the Holy of Holies by the press-proof guarded back door—but she exited, on purpose, through the front one. Sure enough, now that it was mid-afternoon, the paparazzi and journalists had had time to track her down. Under a cloudless sky just beginning to foreshadow summer, reporters shoved their microphones in her face and shouted competing questions.

One question in particular stood out: "Do you have any plans for a future album, Miss Crowell, now that you're back in the land of the living?"

"I do, in fact," she replied, pushing through the crowd on her way to hailing a hovertaxi. "Actually, I've already written the title track."

"What's the album going to be called?"

Before entering the cab, Cali turned and carefully enunciated her words so they would be accurately reported: "*Sweet Caroline.*"

"Where to, miss?"

"*Callahan*?!"

Cali could hardly believe her eyes. It was just after her second rehearsal for the Patriarch Awards and the hovertaxi driver seated in front of her, incognito in shabby street clothes and a drooping fedora, was none other than her enemy-turned-friend from the Elite Forces!

"Or shouldn't I have said that?" she whispered, mortified.

"It's okay. Relax. We can talk freely."

Ever since putting out the fake news of her upcoming song and album, she'd waited impatiently for Agent Callahan to contact her. She just never thought he'd do it quite like this.

"I heard mention of 'Sweet Caroline' this morning on *Master Race Theater* while I was shaving. I must say the words warmed my heart."

He'd started pulling down the alleyway behind the Holy of Holies. Cali gathered he was alluding not to her made-up music but to the mention of his former wife.

"Where you'd acquire the taxi?"

She caught a glimpse of his freshly shaved chin smiling as he replied, "From an old friend who owed me a solid."

"Or that you had dirt on."

"Maybe a bit of both."

"Where are you taking me?"

"You'll see. Hang on."

With these words he accelerated into the stream of traffic zooming in all directions around the Great Obelisk in Pike Square. Late afternoon was just beginning to cloud over as they passed the Junius Daniel Hotel, where she'd given Callahan a knockout to remember, then sailed by a nondescript rectangular building like a black box with no windows or identification she'd never thought much about—until now with an intuitive awareness that it might be important.

"What's up with the black building we just passed?"

"Why?"

"Curiosity."

"That's Archontia's IP."

"IP?"

"Insurrectionists' Prison. An impenetrable fortress where treasonous actors they don't want to dispose of—for whatever reason—are stashed away for easy access."

"Why put it in the middle of the city?"

"Keep your friends close and your enemies closer."

"I've heard that before. It's smart."

"I suppose it is—in a ruthless sort of way. There's a lot of psychology that goes into a successful authoritarian regime."

"Oh, Agent Callahan, you're worth your weight in gold!"

Laughing, he shot through Dreamcatcher Tunnel and then onto the bypass before exiting onto Fair Vista Road and climbing up into the mountains overlooking Archontia. It had been years since Cali had last traveled this route with her parents on a lazy Sunday afternoon outing. They'd picnicked on cheeseburgers and thrown a levifrisbee at Arthur Fields, where she'd gotten a sunburn that made her shiver all night.

Those days were so far behind now they seemed like something out of a stranger's past.

"I assume you know what Freddy has planned for me at the Patriarch Awards," she said.

"That's what you call Stonewall Jackson: *Freddy*?"

"We go way back."

"If you say so. And no, I'm not privy to exactly what he's up to, though I've heard rumors. Care to enlighten me?"

"He's going to have me execute an innocent POC onstage in front of a live audience of millions."

"Woah, that's pretty Machiavellian, even for him! But how do you know the POC's innocent?"

"*Psychology*. The enemy of my enemy is my friend. Anybody who steps on the toes of this nightmarish regime is a hero, not a criminal."

"Oh, Cali Crowell, you're worth your weight in gold! So how can I help?"

"I need you to deactivate this choker. I can't have Freddy blowing my head off while I'm singing the most important song of my life."

"Easy enough. What else?"

"I have friends in the Freedom Fliers who are going to hack the broadcast networks to make sure they can't take my performance offline—"

"The Freedom Fliers?" Shaking his head, Callahan held his hand above his shoulder to show a tiny space between his thumb and index finger. "You do realize you're this close to getting your own neck stretched, don't you?"

"Are you still willing to help or not?"

"Oh, I'm willing. I'm just … amazed by you."

"I amaze myself sometimes. Like I said, I've got the networks covered on the cyber end. But I need somebody on the ground at the performance to make sure they don't pull the plug manually."

"That'll take more than one person."

"I assume you've got friends on the inside?"

"A couple I can talk to."

"Good."

"What's all this about anyway? What's your endgame here?"

He pulled off into Arthur Fields and parked with a view of Saturnia glowing in the valley below as early evening approached.

"My endgame is to end their endgame."

"*Their*? Who exactly are *they*?"

"The voices. The ones behind it all. The ones you still hear sometimes."

"And you don't?"

"Not anymore."

"Gotcha."

"I'm going to destroy their entire world. That's why I was born. There won't be anything left of it when I'm through."

"And how are you going to accomplish that at an … *awards ceremony*?"

"I have my methods. Just be sure to pop some popcorn for you and your insider friends."

"Fair enough. Anything else before I deactivate that pretty necklace and get you back home before somebody suspects you're up to no good?"

"Yeah. I need a sleeping potion."

"Look, I'm an agent, not an alchemist."

"Of course not. What I'm trying to say is … I need a colorless, tasteless, odorless drug I can slip to my family to knock them out cold for the duration of the Patriarch Awards. Things are going to get really crazy and I don't want any of them—not even Olga—getting within a mile of downtown."

He turned and stared at her in the back seat. "You're deadly serious about all this, aren't you?"

"As a frigging heart attack."

"I think I can rustle something up."

"Great. Here's where I want you to hide it …"

P ublicly, Cali's last few days leading up to the awards ceremony, a gala event widely viewed as a holiday celebrating the Fatherland's biggest and brightest stars in music and film, were jam-packed with rehearsals, fittings, photo shoots, and interviews.

In the past the anticipatory energy of so much buildup would have been thrilling (if ultimately exhausting). Now, however, it was just a distraction from the real preparations that needed to be done.

To say that May 1st was the most critical night not only in Cali's personal life but also that of the nation and even the spinning globe beyond wouldn't be an overstatement. Any way you looked at it, May 1st (a holiday, Cali recalled with a sense of poetic inevitability, whose ancient roots actually lay in fertility rites and Goddess worship) was destined to mark a tectonic beginning, a tectonic ending, or both simultaneously.

She could succeed and live to tell the tale. Or she could triumph and die in the process. Alternatively, she could fail spectacularly while going down in epic flames.

Or, playing the role of a clown instead of the hero, she could screw up everything and still somehow survive, in the Deep World or elsewhere, limping along through a half-life until the Archons—like the psychopathic parasites they were—finally sucked their host (the planet) dry … even if that meant perishing themselves for lack of sustenance.

It was with such bipolar inspiring and disturbing thoughts rattling around in her mind between public appearances that Cali finished her private preparations for the Patriarch Awards.

She mentally went over the song Matangi had taught her until she could have intoned its paired vowel sequences backward in her sleep. She painstakingly packed a backpack with an assortment of makeup, clothing and other items, including a selection of fashion magazines for her voice teacher's upcoming birthday, that were unavailable outside the Fatherland.

The night before the ceremony when the rest of her family were asleep, she also paid a visit to the stone bench in her mother's herb and rose garden.

Now that spring was warming up with May set to start, the peepfrogs were sensationally loud, which made her think of Juice as—dressed in a sheer nightgown with a flashtorch between her teeth—she strained to slide the bench's flagstone lintel sideways enough to expose the small hiding place under the delicate rose carving.

Agent Callahan had kept his promise: a nondescript glass vial about the size of a cigarette butt containing a clear liquid glinted in the light from her flashtorch.

"I really, really hope this works," she whispered to herself while using all her strength to replace the flagstone.

Back inside, she hid the vial in her dresser for safekeeping and tried her best to get some sleep. But it was no use—she tossed and turned most of the night in and out of fitful dreams she barely even remembered upon waking. The only detail she could recall was something having to do with an albatross, which turned out to be a Fathersgiving turkey.

The following morning was dress rehearsal, entertaining only because she absolutely adored her lavishly retro petticoat designed by the venerable fashion genius Paige Turner. Hot pink with fluorescent maroon fringes, massively ballooning and endlessly twirlable, the dress looked like something out of a Technicolor version of *Gone with the Wind*—on drugs and steroids.

It was late afternoon by the time she got back home, where—for the second time in only the past several months—she made sure to say her final goodbyes should this truly be her swan song.

Olga she was lucky to catch on the sofa in the sunroom between business calls. Cali was back in her gray sport petticoat, but Olga was already dressed to the nines in an iridescent bronze affair and pearls befitting the Patriarch Awards.

"Don't you look all … dolled up," commented Cali, plopping down on the sofa beside her stepmother.

"Don't tell me you actually like it. I'm well aware of your modern preferences when it comes to couture."

"You'd be surprised. The petticoat's kind of modern in its own right. And pearls like that, well, they never go out of style."

Olga glanced at the holophone in her lap as if she were either expecting a call or wanting to make one before managing, through a visible display of willpower, to reengage her protégé. "What can I do for you?"

"Nothing. I just wanted to say … thanks."

"For what?"

"For all your help. I couldn't have done … any of this without you."

Cali meant it, even though she and her stepmother had had their differences. Perhaps it was her unexpected sincerity that touched Olga, who, taken off guard, suddenly seemed to be struggling to fight back a tear.

"Oh, Cali, you can be so very surprising sometimes," she said as she patted her eye with the back of her long-nailed fingers.

"I hope that's a good thing."

"It is. Sometimes."

Having given Olga a peck on the forehead ("Now get out of here before you mess up my makeup" was the response), Cali tracked down her father. He wasn't in his study for a change. Instead, she found him puttering around in the garage still in casual attire.

"What are you doing out here?" asked Cali.

Startled as if he were engaged in something illicit, he smiled while confessing, "Looking for my golf clubs. Have you seen them?"

"No. Why do you want your golf clubs? You haven't played since Mother … went away."

"I don't know. I was just thinking of getting back into it. It's such a beautiful spring, especially now that you're back."

"That's sweet of you. But are you sure you're not too … old for golf?"

She said this with a mischievous expression, which he returned with one of his own as he asked, "You sure you're not too … young for fame?"

"I never asked for it."

"I never asked for golf."

Cali laughed. "As I recall, you were pretty good."

"Better than good. I could have gone pro."

"Why didn't you?"

"You."

"Come again?"

"Best decision I ever made. I was about to leave medicine and join the circuit when we discovered you were on your way. I wouldn't have missed the years that followed for all the trophies and money in the world. Being with you and your mother was the happiest time of my life."

He glanced around as if there might be eavesdroppers lurking in the cluttered garage. "Just don't tell Olga I said that. Talk about stirring up a tempest in a teapot."

It was Cali's turn to shed a tear. After everything she'd learned about her father, including that he wasn't actually her father, she didn't quite know how she felt about him and was rather shocked to discover how much she still loved him.

One tear quickly gave way to a second, then a third, and a fourth, and many more. Giving up on locating his clubs just then, Dr. Crowell enveloped her in his cotton-sleeved arms as she drenched his paternal chest.

"I hope I didn't say something wrong," he said.

"Nope," she was able to reply. "You said everything just right."

"I love you, Cali."

"I love you, too. I can't tell you how much."

Seth's whereabouts were a mystery. He wasn't in his room. He wasn't in the living room. He wasn't in the garden. Come to think of it, Scarlett O'Hara was missing as well.

"You wouldn't happen to know where a certain ridiculously cute and lovable redheaded boy is, would you?" Cali asked Cordelia, who, in addition to her household duties, was still functioning as her stepbrother's caregiver even though Seth was becoming more self-sufficient by the day—so much so that he planned to attend school with Cali when she was slated to resume her formal education in the fall.

"Yes'm," replied the maid. "I suspect he and Miss Scarlett are down at the park feeding the goldfish."

"When did he start doing that?"

"Around the time he decided he wanted to become a marine biologist."

"But he doesn't know the first thing about biology—or fish, for that matter."

"You tell me. But he did start watching some HoloTube videos."

The mention of fish made Cali realize how hungry she was. More than hungry: *starved.* After hours of dress rehearsal and sweating in her petticoat, she could have eaten a swordfish.

But all she found in the fridge was a can of sardines. She combined these with a few slices of cheddar and wolfed down the whole impromptu concoction along with an entire bag of jalapeño potato chips.

When Seth (in mud-stained jeans and a dirty T-shirt) returned home with Scarlett, about half an hour later, he found Cali stretched out looking more than a little pale on her bed.

"Are you okay?" he asked while the Pomeranian, yapping excitedly to find Cali back where she belonged, bounded onto the mattress and licked first one colorless cheek then another.

"I'm just slightly sick to my stomach, is all."

As Scarlett, satisfied at last, made herself comfortable on the spare pillow, Seth sat down beside his stepsister and took her hand. "Must be butterflies," he said.

"Maybe. But I've never had them like this before."

"It's a really big performance."

"That's true." Sniffing as she made a face, Cali suddenly felt even more nauseated. "Your hand smells like … dog food."

"Fish food actually. Dad bought some for me when I told him I wanted to become a marine biologist. He seemed excited at the prospect."

"I thought you wanted to be a singer."

"Maybe I'll be both."

"Maybe you will. Just promise me one thing, will you?"

"Name it."

"Promise you'll never forget how much I love you."

"That's an odd thing to say. It's not like you're going away again." When Cali looked uncomfortable in the process of making no reply, he added, "*Are* you?"

"Just *promise*."

"Okay, I promise. I love you, too. So where are you going?"

"Maybe nowhere. But if I do go somewhere, I'm coming back for you eventually. Understand?"

"I think so. Something big's about to happen and you're not going to tell me what it is, but when I do find out, you'll be gone."

"And you can't tell a soul about our conversation."

"Don't worry, I won't. But just know I'll miss you all over again."

"I'll miss you, too."

Her nausea notwithstanding, Cali sat up and hugged him like a Raggedy Andy (whom he rather resembled). Before he could question her newest round of tears, she shooed him out of her room.

Five minutes later, left alone with Scarlett, who did her best to comfort her in the aftermath of such an emotional exchange, Cali suddenly jumped up, sprinted to her toilet, dropped to her knees, and threw up every sardine, chip and cheese slice she'd just eaten.

H aving partially recovered, Cali brushed her teeth, showered, dried her hair, donned another sport petticoat (a lime-green one for spring this time), and found Agent Callahan's vial hidden away under a stack of panties in her dresser.

"Here goes nothing," she told Scarlett before leading the way down to the empty kitchen.

Cordelia had just left for the day at her usual time before dinner. Making sure no one else was around, Cali furtively poured the vial's contents into the pitcher of fresh iced tea in the fridge, then sat down on the couch in the living room with Scarlett O'Hara to watch and wait.

In clockwork succession, sure enough, her family members showed up and poured themselves each a glass of tea before sitting down haphazardly at the kitchen table to enjoy the light meal of finger sandwiches and hors d'oeuvres Cordelia had set out for them.

"Cali, are you sure you don't want some of Cordelia's wonderful bacon-wrapped figs?" called Dr. Crowell, who, having just bathed himself, was now dressed in a brand-new tuxedo with bronze accents to match Olga's petticoat.

"You know Cali doesn't like to eat this close to a performance," said Olga. "Do you, Cali?"

"No, ma'am. Food and stage fright have never mixed well for me."

"Indeed. It's certainly good to know one's limitations."

"I don't even like figs," Cali overheard Seth comment.

"Are you hungry?" Cali asked the Pomeranian in her lap.

"I'm always hungry," was the marble-eyed, telepathic reply.

"Go ahead then," whispered Cali. "But whatever you do, just *don't drink the tea.*"

Letting Scarlett down on the floor, she watched her furry form scurry across the hardwood into the kitchen, where she could hear Seth feeding her finger sandwiches.

"Don't give her too many," cautioned Olga. "Or else she'll balloon."

The first sound out of the ordinary emanating from the kitchen was a chorus of loud yawning. This was Cali's cue to bound around the corner—and just in time.

As Dr. Crowell and her stepmother swayed in their chairs, she literally caught Seth before his head hit the floor. Depositing him on the couch in the den (he was heavier than he looked), she returned to help first Olga then her father onto the couch as well.

"I think I'll just take a little nap," said Olga with another cavernous yawn.

"Same here," yawned Dr. Crowell.

These were the last words spoken by her family before they were out cold like a line of overdressed crows sleeping on a wire. Kissing their cheeks a final time for good measure, she turned on the holovision to EPN, which would begin broadcasting the Patriarch Awards in a little under two hours.

"I hope the three of you enjoy the show," she said before returning to her bedroom, where she pulled on a lightweight windbreaker and tennis shoes and shouldered her purse and backpack.

"I need you to be a big girl and guard them well," she said to Scarlett, who had followed her up then down the stairs again to the front door.

"No problem," was the response.

"Good. I'm counting on you."

After scratching the Pomeranian's head in farewell, Cali was finally out the door with a hand up hailing a hovertaxi that was just sailing by. When at last she arrived backstage at the Holy of Holies, her makeup artist, Jeanine—a salty, fiftysomething, brunette veteran of the entertainment industry—was impatiently awaiting her.

"Sorry I'm late," said Cali.

"I can't say I'm surprised—given your reputation."

"What's that supposed to mean?"

"Just that, well, you're your own woman."

"Damn straight. Let's get this show on the road."

Cali's hair and makeup were extravagantly perfected where she sat, alone now awaiting her dresser, bathed in vanity lights high in her pneumatic chair—when she received a surprise visitor. Actually, she received two surprise visitors.

First, a conservatively tuxedoed Agent Callahan, complete with an Elite Forces earpiece, made a safety sweep through the dressing area during which he offered a succinct and professional greeting: "Good evening, Miss Crowell."

"Good evening, Agent Callahan."

"Nice to see you again. You're looking well."

"Thanks. Likewise."

"Thank you."

He disappeared as quickly as he appeared, leaving Cali to wonder if he had everything under control even as her second unannounced visitor waltzed in.

"Simply marvelous!" exclaimed the current Stonewall Jackson, taking in Cali's distended antebellum bun propped up by a hidden bumpet.

"Thank you, Your Purity. You look ... marvelous yourself."

It was only half a lie. While his gaunt face under his slicked-back dark hair was as Halloweenish as the last time, maybe even more so, he was handsomely dressed in a stunning Jubal Early Payne's-gray tuxedo with genuine gilded lapels.

"You're too kind. As you may know, I like to go all in for the Patriarch Awards. After all, I'm *the* patriarch of the Fatherland."

"How right you are, Your Purity."

"Please don't stand on ceremony, Cali. We can speak our minds freely. The perimeter has been cleared and the Old Man's snoring."

"I'm afraid I don't have anything to say."

"Well, I do. May I?" He indicated the platinum cigarette case he'd just pulled out of a jacket pocket.

"Be my guest."

Lighting up with his matching lighter despite a nearby NO SMOKING sign, he exhaled upward forcefully. Smoke swirled like a storm of ghosts under the vanity lights. "I must say I've just had a *very* interesting day."

"What did you do—bomb a few more countries?"

"Well, yes. But that wasn't what was so interesting. I was given this little curiosity courtesy of a mutual friend."

With these words he pulled something else, a rather small something indeed, out of a jacket pocket and handed it to her. As Cali's heart seemed to freeze up with panic, she recognized the shape and feel of her mother's jammer before she actually verified its reality with her eyes!

"I must say I was always curious as to who recorded our unfortunate dinner conversation that a certain Greek philosopher has been using to blackmail me on your behalf. Now I know. It was *you*."

"*Where's Juice?!*"

Her voice quivered with a combination of terror and barely suppressed hatred. She recalled her vision of a fistful of lightning during her jaxxine-induced vision of the Lord Archon. If she'd had lightning in place of a jammer in her palm now, she wouldn't have hesitated to use it on Freddy.

"Don't worry, my dear. He's in a safe place—for now—along with that exceedingly bad influence that is his uncle."

"Let me guess: you've squirreled them away in the local Insurrectionists' Prison."

Freddy took a drag and exhaled again. "How remarkably astute you are to still be in your teens. We captured them both as they were attempting to access a substation of the Fatherweb."

"How in Christ's name did you track them down?"

"I take it you've known their whereabouts all this time."

"Answer my question."

"Aristotle may be brilliant, but rest assured we have gifted scientists of our own. One of these figured out how to use satellite technology to activate a pingback signal in certain older generations of jammers, such as the one you have there. For some time we've tried this strategy without success where the Freedom Fliers were concerned. But with the return of your quote unquote 'kidnapper,' lo and behold, our prayers were unexpectedly answered."

Suddenly, Cali wasn't going crazy—but she could have been. The colossal implications of this jaw-dropping turn of events raced through her consciousness.

With Aristotle in custody and leveraged against the Freedom Fliers, nothing was any longer stopping Freddy from killing her. This meant that even with her choker deactivated, she might not be able to deliver her payload without taking a sniper's laser shot between the eyes.

And even if she survived long enough to deliver it, there was no guarantee the Freedom Fliers would still carry out their mission-critical end of the bargain. Thus her payload might not reach its intended audience—and Freddy might not ever be exposed for the fratricidal Illuminati psychopath he was.

More importantly, or at least more gut-wrenchingly, Juice was in mortal danger. Kidnapping was only punishable by imprisonment, but hacking essential Fatherland infrastructure to promote open rebellion was technically sedition: a lynching offense.

She suspected Freddy would be content to just let Aristotle secretly rot in custody. That way the Fatherland could always access his expertise, should it be needed, while Freddy saved face in terms of public opinion.

But Juice was another matter entirely. He had no rare skill set to protect him. He was utterly, terrifyingly exposed. In other words: *fair game.*

"Can you hear them out there?" asked Freddy, extinguishing his cigarette on the wooden floor with his polished shoe and cocking his head to listen. "All those holofilm stars, all those famous musicians, all those directors and producers and other celebrated people gathered with maximum anticipation in this, arguably the most important religious place in all the Fatherland? To think that, aside from their own self-interest, the primary reason they're all here is … you."

"I can hear them. I can feel them, too."

"I doubt it not. And what do they feel like, Last Rose?"

"Like people who are dead inside but who, as soon as they're resurrected, are going to take one look at you for what you really are and tear you to tiny pieces."

Freddy actually laughed a maniacal laugh. "That would be truly Dionysian, would it not? The greatest living patron of the arts ripped apart by his erstwhile worshippers drunk on the new wine of their own awakening?"

"Something like that."

"You should have been a novelist. Only in fiction do such impossibilities become … possible."

"I wouldn't be so sure. I've experienced some pretty impossible things."

Grasping her hand in his metallic one, he kissed it—this time not so gentlemanly but being sure to press his cold lips against her warm flesh.

"Well, I'll leave you to your fantasies as well as your dressing. I've enjoyed our little chat immensely. But as the saying goes, the show must go on."

"I hope you enjoy it."

"I'm certain I will." Before leaving her alone backstage again, he grinned one last diabolical grin as his eyes once again appeared reptilian. "Oh, I almost forgot: break a leg."

The next hour spent alone backstage all made up in her poufy petticoat was easily the longest of Cali's life. Not even the time spent with her ankle shattered in the Badlands seemed to move so slowly. She would have gladly relived that nightmarish scenario over and over had it meant changing the present into something even remotely less … hopeless.

Whether it was her own abject despair (an existential darkness second to none), or the moronically predictable outcome of the Patriarch Awards (which she could hear down to the opening of the envelopes quite clearly), or the unabashedly self-centered and disingenuous acceptance speeches (which she wished she couldn't hear), or the cheesy and unoriginal music by other artists punctuating it all (ditto), Cali suddenly felt nauseated again.

Tossing her mother's useless jammer in the trash, she had just enough time to make it to the bathroom. Holding up her hair with one hand, she opened the toilet lid with the other.

After dry heaving for several minutes, she finally managed to release enough to stabilize. Rinsing her mouth with water, she assessed how much damage she'd done to her meticulously engineered look in the mirror over the sink.

To her surprise an amazingly beautiful young … goddess of a woman—slightly disheveled perhaps but all the more sexy for it, with an enormous magenta rose (her idea that James Mavis reluctantly accepted) threaded through her hair accenting her vaguely Spanish petticoat—stared back at her.

So "other" did her reflection initially appear it took her a moment, in the surreal state of mind she was experiencing, to recognize she was actually staring not at her mother but at … herself.

"So, Last Rose," she said, mocking Freddy's patrician tone, "any bright ideas for saving everyone's collective ass?"

An abrupt fluttering in her belly, a sensation that had been recurring and growing noticeably stronger the past couple of days, suggested her fallenium egg was activating to new levels. As if on cue, she felt the familiar rush of *kundalini* throughout her system.

"You've got this," she said to herself. But it was more than just herself—it was also, simultaneously, the Goddess speaking *as* and *through* herself. "Nothing has changed. Stay the course."

"*Everything* has changed." Cali shook her shapely head angrily. "It's all gone to hell in a frigging handbasket."

"Nonsense. Everything is *exactly* as it should be. Here. Take my hand. I will show you."

Cali imagined she'd have looked one hundred percent certifiable to a bystander as she reached out and touched her own hand in the mirror. Even as the two sets of fingertips met, all the lights seemed to go out at once.

Literally. It was as if the Holy of Holies had just experienced a total power outage. Either that or Cali had gone completely blind.

"I don't see a thing."

"Just wait."

There was a blue flicker in the darkness. Within seconds, as if flying low enough to strike her where she suddenly found herself floating surrounded by her petticoat in empty space, a massive heron—the Great Heron by the look of it—swept by overhead.

Turning, Cali watched as the godlike blue bird that emanated from the Originator made a direct line for another blue object: the earth bathed in its oceans reflecting the sun.

Like a guided missile from the Pleroma, the Great Heron descended through the Kenoma all the way to the planet's surface, flaming like a phoenix as it fell. Cali winced while observing a tremendous explosion.

Yet there was no destruction. Instead, pure rainbow light illuminated the globe.

"Do you understand now?"

"Give me a second. I'm still processing."

"Hurry. You are up next."

"Were you trying to show me that everything, appearances notwithstanding, is in some kind of ... divine order here?"

"Something like that. What else?"

"And that I'm meant to go forward with the plan—come hell or high water?"

"Freddy said it best: the show must go on."

"Does our little schizophrenic conversation mean I'm finally the Rose now?"

"Yes, Cali. You are the Last Rose—and the greatest."

"Because I'm the Destroyer?"

"Because destruction leads to regeneration."

"Were you also trying to tell me the Luminous Child is about to arrive?"

She—the part of her that was the Goddess—laughed loudly with the combined voices of seemingly millions, perhaps billions of women. "I can assure you, my dear friend, the Luminous Child is here already."

"But *where?*"

Whether they had actually gone out, or Cali's senses had merely blocked them out for a while, the lights suddenly came back on as an obnoxiously loud knock on the bathroom door startled her.

"You okay in there, Miss Crowell?"

She recognized the stage manager's seriously uptight voice. A coronary was definitely in the guy's near future. "I'm fine."

"Good to know. You're on in five."

"Be right there." Then, staring at her reflection one last time and centering herself once again in her celebrity persona: "You've got this, girl. It's only one song. Easy-peasy. Go out there and knock 'em dead."

79

"**L**adies and gentlemen, I give you CALI CROWELL!"
The commanding voice of Roger Aubrey, holofilm legend and sequined, grinning MC for this year's Patriarch Awards, rang out as the lights briefly dimmed then came back up to suggest summertime.

Cali clipped her portable microphone to the neck of her petticoat, gathered her skirt, and danced a solo flamenco into the hushed silence of the Holy of Holies. Legions of coutured glitterati—from Dalton Oglethorpe to Peter Neumann to James Mavis—sat with bated breath under a dimly backlit cupola featuring a gigantic likeness of Moloch surrounded by adoring children.

With the odd fluttering in her insides accelerating and *kundalini* supercharging her circuitry, Cali found herself on the verge of launching straight into Matangi's song, her wakeup call for the masses of sleepwalkers both here and tuning in virtually throughout the Fatherland—including her own family members whose orchestra seats remained mercifully empty.

That was the agreed-upon plan: to skip the foreplay and go directly to the hardcore action. Even the slightest deviation from this plan, by throwing off the coordinated timing of a complex operation with many moving parts, was a serious risk.

And yet, as Cali watched a squadron of White Hats escort a tall POC prisoner, hooded with hands cuffed behind him, down the central aisle of the Holy of Holies in her direction, her gut instinct screamed a single word: "*Improvise!*"

"I wish he was in my land of cotton," she began, arms overhead and fingers grasping each other in a sensual ouroboros, an erotic serpent biting its own tail. "Sweet times there are not forgotten. Kiss away, kiss away, kiss away, Dixie Land."

Though the scandalous lyrics of Cali's risqué version of "Dixie" had been purposely leaked by New World Order Records to create a buzz, this was the first time the public had actually heard them sung.

The effect was startling if not entirely unexpected. With the music just beginning, Cali paused as audible gasps traveled like popcorn pops through the packed house. This was followed by a wave of shushing as all eyes were firmly riveted on the woman of the hour.

On the subject of eyes, some stage performers have difficulty—either owing to external optics or their own internal insecurities—making eye contact with their audience. But not Cali. She often stared down multiple fans as she sang and danced.

The only difference in tonight's performance was that she focused on a single fan who happened to be seated in the orchestra: Frédéric Rothschild de Batonrouge. Returning her gaze with a sardonic expression on his bony face, he nodded like a Roman emperor for her to continue.

Executing a gracefully balanced spin, for the first time ever pouring herself into yet not altogether losing her sense of self in her performance, Cali literally sprang into the next lines as her petticoat twirled around her:

"In Dixie Land where I was laid down, early on a dewy morning … Kiss away, kiss away, kiss away, Dixie land."

More loud gasps and assorted astonished murmurs ping-ponged left and right as the cone-headed, face-masked White Hats (once known as the Ku Klux Klan, or KKK, in the Old South, where they formed as the militant wing of the Democrat party) frog-marched their bound prisoner—also faceless except for his bright eyes—up the front steps onto the stage.

Just as she'd done in rehearsal, though this time with a terrible bleeding sensation in her heart, as if every line she sang were killing everything she loved, Cali continued while approaching the anonymous prisoner where he stood flanked by a dozen White Hats under the mossy oak:

"Then I wish I had his Dixie, hooray! hooray! In Dixie Land I'll take my man, who'll live and die in Dixie."

The gasps, murmurs and shushings crescendoed—seemingly as part of the song itself—as Cali, sensing her mate's unmistakably powerful energy before she even saw his gorgeously chiseled face, pulled off his hood to reveal Juice (afro and all) in his full statuesque glory.

The public was flabbergasted as, somehow mastering her intense emotions, she continued:

"A lay, a lay down South in Dixie … A lay, a lay down South in Dixie."

During the ensuing bluesy instrumental section, one heeled foot provocatively raised, she wrapped her arms around Juice's muscular back and passionately kissed his hot cushioned lips.

"I missed you, too," he said, managing a grin despite his predicament.

"You mean you missed us two," she replied with a whisper, covering her mic.

"Come again?"

"I'm carrying your child."

Even though she'd suspected it instinctively, it was the first time Cali had faced this truth intellectually. The words surprised her almost as much as they did Juice.

"Coming from you, that's bound to be one beautiful baby!" he laughed, suddenly overjoyed with tears overflowing his eyes and shining down his spotlit cheeks.

"There's more. I think it's—no, I *know* it's not just *any* child. It's … the Luminous Child."

"How can you tell?"

"I can feel her."

It was the truth. Having at last processed—in the back of her mind while performing—her backstage "conversation" with the Goddess, Cali realized that while her fallenium egg was actually still much the same, one of her own eggs had changed dramatically.

Fertilized and fluttering with the unlimited power of the Originator now coursing through human veins, her egg was rapidly transforming into a truly divine little girl the likes of which the world had never experienced.

It wasn't the Second Coming—which, like the First Coming, was just an Archontic lie designed to engender acceptance and servitude in the downtrodden population. It was far better than either because it was *real*. And in due course, Cali grasped quite clearly, it would heal and transform the world.

Just then, with the instrumental section coming to a close, the White Hats picked up Juice and stood him on the designated picnic bench, then draped and tightened the heavy noose around his neck.

"No!" screamed Cali, who even though she was aware this part was coming, couldn't bear to witness it. "Over my dead body!"

Jumping up on the bench beside Juice, she attempted to loosen the noose, but it was so thick and snug it barely budged. Even as she was giving her fingers rope burns, a pair of White Hats with unblinking eyes behind their masks pulled her away and deposited her back onstage, then stood their ground between the two lovers.

Meanwhile, the music had stopped and most of the people in the crowd were now standing and booing as it dawned on them the spectacle they were watching wasn't just an illicit love story—it was the actual thing.

Freddy was among them. "KICK THE BENCH!" he commanded with the Lord Archon's booming voice.

At the same time, rude epithets—"Whore!" "Slut!" "Race traitor!" "Nigger bastard!"—and thrown objects—programs, fans, cups, shoes— were added to the public's swelling chorus of boos.

"IF YOU REFUSE TO DO IT YOURSELF, YOU WILL FORCE ME TO DO IT FOR YOU!" screamed Freddy. "TELL ME YOU WOULD NOT WANT COWARDICE ADDED TO BETRAYAL SULLYING YOUR LEGACY!"

Frozen with indecision, Cali watched as, on Freddy's cue, a White Hat aggressively approached the bench with the intention of toppling it over and leaving Juice to meet his maker.

"Just DO it!" thundered Juice with his own highly developed vocal cords that rivaled even those of the Lord Archon. "Aristotle may be out of the picture, but the Freedom Fliers still have our back. So pull yourself together and SING!"

As if being jolted from sleepwalking, Cali surveyed the vast auditorium. Suddenly, her eyes fell on a single cameraman front and center: Agent Callahan! In the chaos he must have replaced the regular cameraman to personally guarantee Cali's performance went public.

Hearing silent vowels in her mind as she sang others aloud, she began to intone: "*EIAIOIUUUUE* ..."

Her fallenium egg, or the Luminous Child, or both, began to give off such an overwhelming current of energy Cali nearly swooned. Breathing deeply to recenter herself, she continued: "*AAAOOOEIOUEE* ..."

The palpable impact on those gathered in the Holy of Holies was comparable to shining a flashtorch in a dark basement full of cockroaches and watching them scurry. As Cali's birdsong literally fried every microchip in the house, including the one in her own tracking device, she could actually hear the voices of the drones panicking as they were sent packing like evil but impotent phantoms back to outer space:

"*What is that? What is up? Down is up. Up is down. Surround sound. Can't stay. Breaking down. Get out of town!*"

Meanwhile, Callahan, who had already dealt with the worst of his microchip problem, kept filming away with a thumb up indicating she was still good to go.

The same couldn't be said, however, for the rest of the audience. This encompassed not just the glitterati but even the White Hats, all of whom, alternately wide-eyed and blinking, acted as if they'd just been lobotomized.

The irony, of course, was that they'd just had their brains returned to them. They simply didn't know it yet.

Besides Callahan and his fellow freedom-loving agents, wherever they were, the only other white people in the crowd largely unaffected by Cali's song were Freddy and those of his unjaxxinated Illuminati coterie in the orchestra: relations, Deacons, CEOs.

Intuiting that her birdsong was complete at last, Cali allowed silence to establish itself in the Holy of Holies, where people were now taking in their surroundings with burgeoning curiosity as if seeing themselves and their world with their own eyes for the very first time.

"DO I HAVE TO DO EVERY GODDAMNED THING MYSELF?" shouted Freddy as, miffed, he retrieved a remote control from his jacket pocket and pointed it in Juice's direction.

Spinning around, Cali instantly understood Freddy's objective. As a fail-safe for just such a scenario, a mechanical lever had been discretely installed under the bench capable of toppling it over via remote activation. She hadn't even noticed it.

"STOP!" she screamed at the top of her lungs as something like a string of firecrackers went off in her own brain.

The next thing she knew, bursting out of her choker as well as her petticoat, heels and lingerie, she was airborne, black wings flapping furiously as she bore down on Freddy from above.

He had just enough time to push the button—at which point, out of the corner of her extraordinarily capable eye, she watched the bench flip and Juice fall with a horrific jerk, feet twitching.

Her plan (such as it was) was to shred Freddy's jugular with her powerful claws and pick his eyes out with her sharp beak. But now, with Juice dying onstage, her only option was to put on the brakes and attempt to reverse course to save him.

Easier said than done. Learning to fly as a crow was, after all, learning to fly—which meant even in the best of circumstances, some practice was required.

Spinning like a terrified Sophia through the Kenoma, Cali crashed into Freddy mid-turn at full speed. Locked together, the two tumbled over and over into the checkered central aisle.

By the time she regained her bearings, Freddy's metallic hand was around her throat squeezing like a vise as he picked her up and forced her to look at Juice.

"IF YOU ARE WONDERING WHY I DID NOT ALREADY KILL YOU, IT WAS BECAUSE I WANTED YOU TO FIRST SEE THIS: THE THEATRICAL END OF YOUR PRECIOUS THELETE."

Cali was barely able to breathe. Mad with manna and no longer in any meaningful sense human or himself, Freddy gloated over her with the Lord Archon's reptilian eyes as she, with crow eyes, beheld yet another miracle of transformation onstage at the Holy of Holies.

Suddenly expanding to five times his normal stature as he summoned the *Tulpa*, Juice followed Cali's lead by exploding his jumpsuit and the noose around his neck—a literal choker—into a million tiny filaments. Textile fragments floated every which way like down in the bright lights.

Terrified, the audience cowered as a giant black man leapt through the air so high and far he appeared to fly himself—only to land, as people scurried for cover, like an earthquake within reach of Freddy.

"I've wanted to do this ever since I heard about it," said Juice with a colossal smile as he snapped off Freddy's metallic hand like a twig and threw it with perfect aim through the face of Moloch overhead.

Pieces of fresco rained down as Cali, having reverted to human form, knelt naked sucking for breath and the Head Deacon of the Realm, blood coursing from the stump of his arm, sneered, "YOU WILL PAY FOR THAT, YOU PATHETIC AEON!"

"Someone's about to pay, it's true," Cali managed to croak.

Before she even finished this statement, her own unconstrained voice rang out over the PA system:

"Oh my God. You murdered your brother!"

The recording of her dinner conversation with Freddy continued for all to hear throughout the Fatherland as Callahan, having spun the camera with its mic on away from the stage to capture Cali's flight, kept filming:

"Excuse me?"

"Or at least you had him murdered."

"So what if I did?"

"What *happened* to you, Freddy? You were a light in the darkness to so many people. And now you're just the opposite."

"*Reality* happened to me, Cali. After sleepwalking my whole life, I finally opened my eyes and saw how nothing will ever change on this godforsaken planet through peaceful means. Change can only occur by means of force."

"To do a little good, one must be a little evil?"

"In so many words, I suppose. It's the responsibility of the strong to govern the weak. Only then can there be lasting peace. I take it you don't grasp just how right I am?"

"*Right?* Freddy, you're so wrong you've run out of wrong."

Gazing around fearfully as the awakened crowd of witnesses to his treason closed in with angry expressions and words, Freddy bellowed, "THIS IS ALL YOUR FAULT, CALI CROWELL! YOU HAVE DESTROYED A PERFECTLY CRAFTED PLAN!"

"That's why I'm called the Destroyer."

"I think we'd better get out of here," said Juice, who had also returned to normal in the aftermath of his adrenaline rush. "After all, this isn't our fight."

"That's right. It's *ours!*" yelled silver-haired Paige Turner, the famed designer of Cali's shredded petticoat, of all people. "And we're going to finish it!"

"Hear, hear!" shouted furious Fatherlanders throughout the audience.

"Follow me!" yelled Agent Callahan, who—as the angry mob began to do what angry mobs do to Freddy and his cohorts—led Juice and Cali up a side ramp. Safely backstage, the two Aeonic Vessels were still human enough to cover their nakedness with dressing gowns they found hanging on a rack.

"Where'd you learn to work a camera?" Cali asked Callahan while shouldering her backpack as he quickly escorted them to the rear service door.

"Film school. Where'd you learn to turn into a bird?"

"Goddess school."

"Yeah, I was afraid you'd say something like that."

"Callahan, this is Juice. He's the … thorn to my rose."

"Better than a thorn in your side," Juice joked.

The Elite Forces agent and spy grinned as he shook Juice's hand warmly and said, "You're one lucky son of a gun."

"Don't I know it. Thanks for helping out."

"Don't mention it."

"Do you want to come with us?" asked Cali. "We're headed back to the Deep World."

"Are you kidding? I wouldn't miss this show for any world."

It was Cali's turn to shake his hand. "See you around," she said, smiling and suddenly a little emotional. "I can't thank you enough—for all of it."

"Believe me, it was my pleasure. Except, of course, for that time you knocked me out." He grinned again. "Take care of yourself. Don't be a stranger if you ever head back this way."

"Roger that."

"Goodbye."

"Good luck."

"And goddamn the Fatherland."

"Goddamn the Fatherland."

It was nighttime in Saturnia when Cali and Juice emerged to find whole neighborhoods of the city in darkness. Not a single holoboard illuminated the sky, where stars were actually visible. Just as they'd promised, the Freedom Fliers had shut down significant portions of the grid to facilitate their takeover of the federal government and media offices.

This hadn't stopped a multitude of white people from hitting the streets and closing in on the Holy of Holies demanding justice. There was, as the saying goes, revolution in the air.

"Can you feel it?" yelled Juice over the crowd noise as he led Cali by the hand against the current toward their rendezvous.

"Oh, I can feel it, all right. It feels like … freedom."

"It feels like a shitstorm. The freedom part comes later."

"What on earth are you doing stopping in the middle of this craziness?"

"I'm going to give you a proper kiss."

He was as good as his word. After so much intensity and stress, Cali felt herself melting a little in his warm arms.

"Did you just say 'proper' with a European accent?"

"Yeah, I thought I'd put on airs like a certain former Stonewall Jackson we used to know."

"It was pretty convincing."

"I told you I'm a cunning linguist."

"I'm well aware." She grinned while gazing up into his hazel eyes. "You scared the crap out of me back there."

"You scared the crap out of me."

"Don't ever do it again—or *I'll* be the one to kill you."

He laughed in his marvelously resonant bass. If Cali were stranded on a desert island and could choose but one sound to hear for the rest of her days, it would be his laughter.

"So tell me," he asked, "are you *really* pregnant?"

"You mean you can't feel her energy? It's like walking around with a gravifusion reactor in my womb. Aeonic Vessels though we may be, in comparison you and I are small fry."

Juice put his hand on her belly as the awakened crowd continued to flow loudly around them in the direction of the Holy of Holies. "Yeah, I can feel her. Grace."

"You mean like in the Bible?"

"No, I mean her name is *Grace*."

"How do you figure that?"

"She just told me."

"Seriously?"

"Seriously."

"Grace. I like that."

"Me, too. Though I might end up calling her Gracie."

"Same here."

Lit by flashtorches and vehicle headlights, Pike Square was another wild revolutionary center. Fatherlanders—including members of the Elite Forces and military—were storming the blacked-out Junius Daniel Hotel, where various members of the ruling class often stayed, while others were busy roping the Great Obelisk in the plaza's center to half a dozen cargo levitrucks.

Once known as the Washington Monument after an obscure American Revolution-era president, the Great Obelisk, updated with a monumental bas-relief of the all-seeing eye on its capstone, had been relocated to the Deep South after the destruction of the capital during the Second American Civil War.

The obelisk was considered one of the Fatherland's most important cultural and political symbols. It was also, quite appropriately, Cali couldn't help observing, a gigantic penis.

"I never thought I'd live to see this day," said Juice, shaking his head as the levitrucks strained forward with all their horsepower until the Great Obelisk cracked off its base and was tilted to a sufficient degree to allow gravity to finish the job of smashing it into a profusion of pieces.

"Me neither."

"I wish we had some champagne. We could toast."

"I thought you didn't like champagne."

"I don't. I'm just saying."

Fortunately, as intent on destruction as they were, the revolutionaries remained clearheaded enough to have cleared enough space for the demolition—meaning no one was hurt as the earth rumbled, pavement split, and dust swirled up into high beams.

"There you two are! I've been searching all over for you."

Cali took one look at the short, quick-eyed, middle-aged black man in a jumpsuit with a laser rifle strapped to his shoulder approaching at the head of a group of armed Freedom Fliers through the dust before hugging him so hard she nearly squeezed the air out of him.

"If I'm going to get that kind of response," wheezed Aristotle while hugging her back, "I think I'll lead a prison break more often."

"Speaking of, how'd you get out of the IP?" asked Juice. "From what I saw during my short time inside, that place is a fortress. I was just about to come after you."

"Ah, grasshopper." Aristotle patted his nephew on the back. "Despite your martial prowess, there's still much you need to learn about the Art of War."

"Meaning?"

"Never go in someplace you don't already know how to get out of."

"Fair enough."

"And never, ever *tell* your woman she's mistaken."

"Ha ha," said Cali. "So what happens next?"

"We seal the deal. I'm hearing we've already taken control of the major media outlets. This will allow us to deliver real news to all Fatherlanders while we work together—black *and* white—to finish hunting down the rest of the sewer rats who have enslaved us. Then we'll set up a constitutional republic just like in the good old days. It worked well then, so I imagine it will work just fine now."

"So you think it's going to happen that smoothly?" asked Juice.

"I don't think anything's going to be smooth. But I do know one thing: people everywhere are ready for change."

"You've got that right," said Cali, feeling something that might have been a kick inside her belly. "And believe me, change is coming."

Her maternal body language appeared to remind Juice of Weezy. "So where's my mom?" he asked.

"In a *very* safe place," answered Aristotle. "Though I imagine she won't be staying there past tonight. It was all I could do to convince her to lay low this long."

"Well, do give her my love."

"I'll be sure to."

"I love you, too."

"Back at you, boy."

As uncle and nephew embraced, a fresh rumble could be heard in the ground, which shook anew like a minor tremor as a room-sized hole opened up in the middle of the square and a wooden elevator similar to the one in Rose Cove surfaced.

Its door having slid open, out stepped Apollo in full warrior regalia: buckskins, hawk feathers, tomahawk, the whole kit and caboodle.

"Aren't you a sight for sore eyes!" cried Cali, hugging her brother in turn. "I almost forgot how handsome you are!"

He laughed and replied with characteristic self-effacement, "There is no need to butter me up. I am here to rescue you regardless of what you say. I realize full well I am the ugly duckling in our family."

It was Cali's turn to laugh—and laugh, and laugh, and laugh. She hadn't laughed for the sheer sake of laughter, out of joy and devoid of sadness or worry, for so long she didn't know if she was still capable of such an innocent thing.

"What is so funny?" asked Apollo with a serious expression beneath his beaded headdress.

"You. Me. This."

"I am glad you are able to find humor in the midst of turmoil."

"If you can't find humor then, what's it good for?" said Juice, chuckling himself.

"Amen," said Aristotle. "Nice to see you again, Apollo."

"A pleasure to see you as well, my friend."

"You be sure to take care of these two lovebirds down there."

"Do not concern yourself over them." Apollo gazed around at the chaos of Pike Square. "I assure you the Deep World is much safer than yours will be for quite some time."

"There's some wisdom in that."

"Best of luck, Aristotle."

"Back at you."

"Well, Cali?" asked her brother as he turned to face her. "Are you ready to return home?"

At the mention of the word "home," Cali was filled with a vision of a flowing stream. It was the Nolihana—which, figuratively, was the life stream connected to the Goddess and which, fittingly, ran right past Rose Cove.

A single lush rosebush, in fact, grew on the banks of the river. It symbolized Cali, and its proliferating thorns represented Juice. Yet she herself was a symbol of something else—call it the Sacred Feminine—just as he embodied its complement, the Sacred Masculine.

These twin archetypal expressions—not to be confused with gender, sex, or other false dualities—stemmed from the same Source, she realized, originating in the Originator and threading through the ground of being like a vast network of roots.

And in that same instant, she understood that what was approaching on that horizon known as tomorrow—even as the old world she'd destroyed crumbled behind—was a new dawn, one she herself was literally going to birth into existence.

Truly, she was carrying an act of divine "Grace" designed to engender a cooperative flowering of humanity—the collective Luminous Child—based on sovereign free will where the Sacred Feminine and Masculine would be allowed to consciously shape people's destiny not by competing with but as a result of honoring each other.

This species-wide blossoming would transform all of human society, even that of the Bird Tribes, in virtually unimaginable, practically limitless ways. And in so doing, the legacy of the Archons' mental deceptions designed to separate people into warring camps—black and white, rich and poor, male and female, conservative and liberal—would gradually fade until it was nothing more than a historical footnote.

"Yes," she replied, taking Juice's hand and holding it firmly against her belly as she stepped into the elevator, which smelled earthy and familiar. "I am ready to go home."

THE BEGINNING

ACKNOWLEDGMENTS

The author is indebted to John Lamb Lash's *Not in His Image: Gnostic Vision, Sacred Ecology & the Future of Belief* for its groundbreaking reinterpretation of the Fallen Goddess Scenario and the role of Archons in human history and evolution. No endorsement of Lash's other philosophical, religious or political views expressed in his book or elsewhere is implied.

ABOUT THE AUTHOR

A longtime researcher of shamanism and spirituality, Sol Luckman is an iconoclastic psychonaut devoted to exploring and exposing the truth about human history and potential—wherever that might lead. His previous novel, the multi-award-winning *Snooze: A Story of Awakening*, was a deep dive into Hindu mysticism, lucid dreaming, parallel universes, and cryptozoology. In his two international bestselling nonfiction books on the "revolutionary healing science" (*Nexus* Magazine) of his own unique form of sound healing, the Regenetics Method, Luckman examined the critical role played by DNA and consciousness in healing, transformation, and evolution. On the lighter side, Luckman is also an acclaimed humorist. Of his multi-award-winning satirical lexicon, *The Angel's Dictionary*, Reader Views remarked that he "picked up where writers like Mark Twain and Ambrose Bierce had left off." More recently, *Musings from a Small Island* combines fascinating memoir, hilarious comedy and inspirational philosophy in a stunningly self-illustrated coffee table book any Lowcountry lover or contemporary art aficionado would be proud to display. To learn more about Sol Luckman's writing and artwork and to subscribe to his newsletter, visit **www.CrowRising.com**.

Interested in following Cali's lead and learning the Language of the Birds? Explore what may well be a modern application of this ancient and sacred language in Sol Luckman's two international bestselling books on the Regenetics Method.

An unparalleled synthesis of modern and ancient healing wisdom, *Conscious Healing* is essential reading for anyone interested in DNA, alternative medicine, energy healing, consciousness research, quantum biology, human evolution, or personal enlightenment.

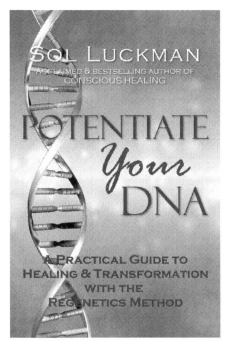

In this highly popular DIY sequel to *Conscious Healing*, Sol Luckman masterfully charts the possibilities of using sound and language to activate DNA for healing and transformation. Learn how to activate your genetic potential—in a single, thirty-minute session!

"This is revolutionary healing science that's expanding the boundaries of being."
—*Nexus* Magazine

Learn more at
www.PhoenixRegenetics.org.

Could it be there's no such thing as the paranormal ... only infinite varieties of normal we've yet to understand?

From acclaimed author Sol Luckman comes *Snooze*, the riveting tale of one extraordinary boy's awakening to the world-changing reality of his dreams, winner of the 2015 National Indie Excellence Award for New Age Fiction and 2016 Readers' Favorite International Book Award Finalist in the Young Adult-Coming of Age category.

Join Max Diver, aka "Snooze," along the razor's edge of a quest to rescue his astronaut father from a fate stranger than death in the exotic, perilous Otherworld of sleep.

An insightful look at a plethora of paranormal subjects, from Sasquatch and lucid dreaming to time travel via the Bermuda Triangle, *Snooze* also shines as a work of literature featuring iconic characters, intense drama and breathless pacing to stir you wide awake!

"Luckman's dazzling abilities as a novelist abound with lyrical prose ... If you enjoy colorful characters, a fast-paced plot and stories that tug at your heart, this novel in eighty-four chapters is anything but a yawn."

—Readers' Favorite

Snooze is "a multi-dimensional, many-faceted gem of a read. From mysteries to metaphysics, entering the dream world, Bigfoot, high magic and daring feats of courage, this book has it all."

—Lance White, author of *Tales of a Zany Mystic*

"*Snooze* is a book for readers ready to awaken from our mass cultural illusion before we self-destruct. *Snooze* calls out for readers open to the challenging adventure of opening their minds."

—Merry Hall, Co-Host of *Envision This*

Learn more at **www.CrowRising.com**.

The Angel's Dictionary is like a good joint: slim but potent. This uproariously irreverent "tour de farce" has received three major recognitions: Winner of the 2017 National Indie Excellence Award for Humor, Finalist in the Humor category of the 2018 International Book Awards, and Finalist for Humor in the 2018 Best Book Awards.

In this knee-slapping dictionary for coming to terms with modern culture (or lack thereof), politics (so-called) and life (such as it is), bestselling author Sol Luckman reinvigorates satire to prove that—though we might not be able to change the world—we can at least have a good laugh at it.

Then again, maybe laughter can transform the world!

entanglement: (n.) quantum physics term for when the sheets wrap around two bodies in space.

Taking a page from Ambrose Bierce's scathing satirical masterpiece, *The Devil's Dictionary, The Angel's Dictionary* updates the genre to include blistering contemporary references and no small sampling of risqué humor to make adults giggle like mischievous teens.

genetically modified organism (GMO): (n.) member of the public who has regularly consumed the biotech industry's food products.

treason: (n.) crime against one's country and its people punishable by reelection.

shadow side: (n.) self you encounter when you do not look in the mirror.

Learn more at **www.CrowRising.com**.

Award-winning author and professional artist Sol Luckman showcases his literary and painterly talents in this one-of-a-kind story of an uncommon life on the fair shores of Hilton Head Island, a world-famous vacation destination nestled in the Lowcountry of the Deep South.

Combining fascinating memoir, hilarious comedy and inspirational philosophy, *Musings from a Small Island* is also a stunningly illustrated coffee table book any contemporary art aficionado would be proud to display. You've never read a book like this because, until now, there hasn't been one. Seen from Luckman's charmingly eccentric perspective, Hilton Head comes alive in ways few places do in literature or art.

Learn more at **www.CrowRising.com**.

Printed in Great Britain
by Amazon

13176757R00244